All it takes, is all you got. Never quit. Never surrender.

To the legion of Extinction Cycle readers, this book is for you. Thank you so much for following Team Ghost and all of the Extinction Cycle characters over the years. This series would not be what it is without the support of the fans, and I am eternally grateful for each and every one of you.

— Nicholas Sansbury Smith

$$— 1 —$$

Azrael walked quietly on taloned feet, surveying the corpses littering the streets of Outpost Tulsa. The stench of death and rot carried on the crisp evening air. His men, Scions and humans both, reveled in that smell of victory, but he could not.

To him, one defeated outpost was not a real victory any more than a single step was a marathon.

His conquest was only just beginning.

One of his Scions, a creature named Jonah, bowed low in front of him.

"Prophet, we have him," he growled, his voice scraping up from his gullet.

Jonah was one of the oldest of the Scions from the first batch of successful experiments. He had loyally served since his transformation from a weak human into the demigod he was today.

"Take me to him," Azrael said with a snarl.

"Yes, Prophet."

Jonah turned on his heels. He walked with the gait of a human, but his physique bore the fruits of over a decade of scientific research. Yellowed, needle-sharp teeth jutted from behind his sucker lips, and slitted nostrils were carved into his face where his nose once was. Golden eyes like a bird of prey scanned the road for any threats. Scything claws hooked from the ends of his fingers, filed down enough so he could use a rifle.

His body was much like Azrael's. Only Azrael, the Prophet, was larger, the bones in his shoulders pushing against his flesh like an ancient knight's armor, ominously protruding under the long black cloak he wore.

Underneath that cloak, body armor pressed tight against his flesh. He was strong, but he did not like to take unnecessary risks. A well-aimed bullet could still kill him.

Jonah stopped to sniff the air, then continued down another street.

Darkness had settled over the fallen outpost, but Azrael and his Scions didn't need lights like humans. Those poor primitive great apes had weak eyesight, unlike the vision Azrael had bestowed on himself and his most ardent followers through genetic engineering. They could see as easily in the dark as they could in the middle of the day.

Black smoke drifted from craters in the asphalt, swirling on the cold wind. Charcoaled vehicles lined the streets between war-torn buildings and piles of scree. The glow of dwindling fires flickered over pale-fleshed Variants feeding on their human trophies.

"Our Thralls will eat well tonight," Jonah said. A twisted grin formed over his beastly face. "The heretics are no match for the New Gods."

"That's because they chose the wrong path," Azrael said, his clawed fingers curling into a quaking fist. "They misplaced their faith. They have wasted so many lives that could have been used to serve us."

These heretics had been deceived by the false promises of a government that had betrayed them, mindlessly following sacrilegious leaders like President Jan Ringgold.

She told the nonbelievers that there was hope for humanity and promised victory. But the only hope for humanity was by joining the New Gods.

Slurping sounds filled the air as a pair of scrawny Thrall Variants dug into two dead soldiers near a machine gun nest. One of the monsters lifted its head, ropey entrails hanging from between its teeth.

The beasts were single-minded predators, but even they could be trained. If only the Allied States could be bent to his will as easily.

Sporadic gunshots echoed in the distance. The howls of hunting Thralls rose like the calls of demonic spirits. A human scream rang out and faded.

Each time the Prophet heard those terrorized screams of fear and pain, he felt a twinge of revulsion.

"I wish it did not have to be this way," Azrael said.

"I know it pains you, Prophet."

"They could be Scions of the New Gods. Just like you. Instead of death, I could give them new life."

"Someday, they will understand what your promise brings them."

Azrael held the keys to unrivalled technology and an army unlike anything the world had seen. And these so-called Allied States citizens could choose to follow him, never living a day in fear for the rest of their lives.

If only they would listen.

Jonah pointed a crooked claw at a large church between two tall office buildings. "The commander is in there."

Half of the steeple was gone, and one of the pinnacles was nothing but a pile of blackened rubble. The jagged remains of colorful stained-glass sparkled in the firelight.

Azrael walked through the shattered wooden doors

into the dark recesses of the former place of worship. Past the broken pews and a handful of corpses, a group of six Scions holding saw-toothed cutlasses gathered around the nave with five prisoners strung up by ropes against the wall at the back of the church.

Jonah bowed, pausing in the aisle, and Azrael continued to the nave. Spent brass bullet casings littered the floor, some lying in puddles of blood. He stepped around the toppled altar to get closer to the prisoners.

A pane of moonlight bled in through the broken stained-glass windows above the humans hanging from the beams across the ceiling.

The golden eyes of Scions followed Azrael as he studied the prisoners. He could smell their festering wounds and their fear.

The first was a man in a military uniform, stubble lining his scarred face. Next to him was a woman, also in a combat uniform. A long gash leaked blood across her cheek. She moaned, her head rolling on her shoulders, barely on the edge of consciousness.

At the end of the line was a second man in a combat uniform. The insignia on his shoulder signified he was a colonel. His head was shaved clean, and from where he was strung up, he alone looked at Azrael in defiance. Tears in his jacket showed where a Variant had clawed at his chest.

This is the outpost commander, Azrael thought.

"The fuck you looking at?" the man grumbled.

One of the Scions moved toward the colonel with his blade. "You insolent heretic."

Azrael held up a hand, and the Scion let out a growl. But the faithful servant lowered his weapon and retreated.

"You were in charge of this outpost," Azrael said.

The commander's eyes narrowed. "I still am."

Azrael shook his head. "A good leader knows when to admit defeat."

"We will win. Maybe not today, but we will destroy you and your disgusting mutants."

With a snort, Azrael took a deep breath, smelling the pheromones leaching off the weak man. He had seen humans act courageous like this before, even in the face of certain death. It was admirable, but ultimately foolish.

"You have already lost," Azrael said.

"Fuck... you..." said the woman with the gash on her face. "You are—"

Before she could finish, Azrael spun away from the commander and slashed her neck, claws tracing her flesh. Blood gurgled out of the wound, and her head fell to the side.

Azrael turned back to the commander and licked the blood off his claws.

The old military man's eyes glistened from the pain of seeing her killed. His bottom lip trembled, even though he tried to clench his jaw.

Azrael wiped his claws clean across the commander's coat, spreading the soldier's blood. "Tell me where President Jan Ringgold is."

"I have no idea."

Azrael wrapped a clawed hand around the commander's neck. "I think you do."

"Even if I did, I wouldn't tell you."

"I want to end this war. I want President Ringgold's surrender. And if she does the right thing, I will allow everyone who is willing to join the army of the New Gods. You too can become a Scion."

"We would rather die than become freaks."

"Freaks?" Azrael tightened his grasp around the commander's neck. To his credit, he didn't so much as flinch. "This is what your military set out to create when they first made VX-99. I perfected it. My people implemented it. We're stronger than you. Smarter. Better in every way. *This* is evolution."

"You're a science experiment gone wrong. Nothing more."

A red-hot heat washed through Azrael. He wanted to tear into the commander, stab his claws right into his meaty gut. He sensed his Scions watching, waiting to see how he would react to the insult.

Azrael exhaled, letting the anger go. His ego was not important. He had to control himself if he wanted to know where the new Central Command was located.

"Tell me where Ringgold is and I will spare you all," Azrael hissed.

"I told you. I don't know."

Azrael stared at the commander. He noticed the small pulsing red vessels in the man's sclera and the way the pitiful human's nostrils flared slightly, twitching with each labored breath.

This man *was* terrified.

Judging by the way his pupils dilated and how he bit back his tongue, he was lying, too. Azrael could sense it just as easy as a wolf detected frightened prey.

But there was another thing he knew. Something he did not need his senses to tell him. This commander would endure untold amounts of physical pain and still he would not give up the president.

Azrael grinned, lips snarling back to reveal his fangs.

He took his claws from the commander's neck. The commander was so insolent he even sighed in relief.

His mistake.

Azrael swiftly slashed at the commander's stomach, tearing open four gashes. Blood drooled from the wounds. The man let out a long groan, sweat rolling down his pallid face.

"I... won't... tell... you," he said.

"I know," Azrael said. "That was for my own satisfaction, but I'm afraid it wasn't satisfying enough."

He heard the snarls of the six Scions waiting around the human prisoners.

"Feed, but leave the commander for me," Azrael said.

Jaws snapping, the Scions lunged forward and tore into the other human prisoners as the commander watched. The sounds of ripping tendons and snapping bones echoed through the church. Organs slurped and smacked against the stone floor, the sounds masked by agonized screams.

The commander's lips quivered. He no longer forced a veneer of courage. A dark stain spread down his pants as he pissed himself.

"You can stop this," Azrael leaned in close, whispering into his ear. "All you have to do is tell me what I want to hear."

"I... I... I..."

"Talk."

More tearing flesh. Blood spilled on the floor, and the stench of voided bowels filled the air.

"I..." the commander's face was still pale, shock hijacking his brain. "Puerto Rico... I think... they're setting up another..." Then his mouth shut, and he locked eyes with Azrael. "That's all I know... all I heard... please stop this!"

"Of course."

Azrael traced his claws over the man's chin, leaving crimson trails. Then he snapped forward and bit hard into the man's neck, chewing into the flesh and gristle.

With the back of his clawed hand, Azrael wiped the blood from his lips, watching his Scions feed on what was left of the prisoners. If the government of the Allied States was retreating all the way to Puerto Rico, then victory was even closer than he had anticipated.

He looked at the dead body of the commander. A waste of a brave man who could have served the New Gods.

At least it would not be a wasted meal. He gave in to the animal instincts ingrained in his genetically engineered body and fed.

***

A cool salty breeze snaked through Galveston. Only a few days had passed since they had held a funeral to honor oil tycoon and rancher S.M. Fischer. Fischer was just another life tragically lost in a war that Captain Reed Beckham had thought was over.

Before this new conflict had erupted, government estimates had reported there were only scattered pockets of Variants left after the Great War of Extinction, most of them living in the abandoned cities.

Beckham had believed them, and he regretted that now more than ever.

Humanity was paying a devastating price for that mistaken belief as outposts and bases fell in droves. Now, while Vice President Dan Lemke was establishing a Central Command for the Allied States government on Puerto Rico, the remnants of the Allied States' civilians and armed forces had retreated to the American Southeast.

General Souza and his LNO Lieutenant Festa had temporarily returned from Puerto Rico to the continental Allied States. With their help, President Ringgold had set up the United States Special Operations Command in Galveston to run special ops missions.

Galveston was one of a handful of bases still standing, especially thanks to General Cornelius who had fortified the island. The city now served as a temporary home for Beckham and his wife, Dr. Kate Lovato, along with their son Javier. Likewise, Master Sergeant Parker Horn and his girls, Jenny and Tasha had relocated here with their dogs, Spark and Ginger.

The kids loved the beaches and the sun, but Beckham knew this idyllic lifestyle would not last long. Soon the Variants and collaborators would advance on this base, too.

But when the enemy arrived, the outpost would be ready.

He stood at the front of a parking lot beside his best friend and brother-in-arms, Horn, who wore a tank top showing off the tattoos adorning his muscular arms. They watched over the training of over a hundred volunteers who had stepped up to defend the walls. Most of the recruits looked beleaguered, covered in sweat. Some could barely stand.

They suffered from exhaustion and hunger, but Beckham knew those conditions would be no better now than when they had to face the Variants in the field. These greenhorns needed to learn the value of perseverance.

"Just one more drill, you maggots!" Horn shouted.

Beckham gave him a look.

"What?" Horn asked. "I always wanted to say that."

"Take it down a notch, man… Jesus."

Sergeant First Class Jeni Rico jogged over. "Yeah, Big Horn," she grunted. "Half of these people are malnourished. Cut 'em some slack."

Horn shrugged. "Being soft gets people killed." He cupped his hands around his mouth and shouted, "Line up, everyone!"

A few groans came from the recruits and volunteers, but one of the new soldiers stepped up, ready to go. Timothy Temper wore a stern look, much like his dad Jake had once donned in the line of duty. The kid was looking more like a man every day.

Timothy motioned for some of the straggling recruits to get into line.

"Almost done, then we get some chow," he said encouragingly.

"Chow for those that put in the effort," Horn said.

Rico shot him a glare.

"Just kidding!" Horn called out.

Every time Beckham saw Timothy, he felt guilty about what had happened at Outpost Portland, not only to Jake, but also to Timothy in the fallout of the outpost's destruction. But he couldn't change the past. All he could do was push forward, just like Timothy was doing.

"The Variants don't care if you're tired or hungry or how old or young you are," Timothy said. "They are the predators and you are the prey until you decide to change that."

A few of the weary recruits straightened.

"He's good," Horn said quietly.

"He's been out there," Beckham said. "He knows what it's like firsthand."

"He's lucky, but he's also got skill, unlike most of these people." Rico sighed. "We got our work cut out for ourselves, my friends."

Horn clapped his hands together. "Get moving, and you will all be soldiers in no time!" He looked at Rico for approval. "That better?"

She smirked and led the recruits with Timothy toward a maze of abandoned buildings that simulated the wastelands and what they would face.

Gunshots rang out at a separate part of the drilling field. It didn't make Beckham happy to be using precious ammo, but these people needed to learn how to shoot or they would waste even more in battle.

Rico signaled for her team to move to an obstacle course. Beckham watched Timothy deftly scale a rope net, then army crawl under a series of low-hanging barbed wire strands. The young man cleared the obstacles and vanished into the old buildings.

"Best soldier of the bunch," Horn said. He rubbed the stubble on his chin. "Maybe someday he'll even find a place on Team Ghost."

The last thing Beckham wanted to imagine was the young man spending even more time out in the field on exceedingly dangerous missions. But there might not be any other option with the way the war was going.

A C-130 flew overhead, engines roaring over the parking lot. It dipped beyond the buildings to land on the makeshift runway along Seawall Boulevard.

"More refugees?" Horn asked, using a hand to shield his eyes from the late afternoon sun.

"I didn't think we had any more coming today."

The drills continued in the distance, but Beckham turned to look at a Jeep that squealed to a stop beside them. A man with a black mustache hopped out.

"Captain Beckham," he said.

Beckham recognized him. It was Sergeant Ken Sharp, a soldier who had helped protect S.M. Fischer's ranch, before joining up with Cornelius.

"General Cornelius sent me," Sharp said, out of breath. "He's requesting you in the CIC now."

"Is there a problem?" Beckham asked. He guessed it had something to do with the plane.

"It's better if I let Cornelius and Ringgold explain. We don't have much time."

Beckham turned to Horn. "Big Horn, you finish training. I'll meet up with you and Rico later. And for God's sake, before we do, take a shower."

Horn lifted his arm and sniffed under his pit. Then shrugged.

Beckham got into the idling Jeep, and they took off for the old Harbor House Hotel along the docks of the northwestern side of the island. Cornelius had turned the building into his command information center (CIC).

Sergeant Sharp jumped out first, followed by Beckham. They entered the hotel lobby where officers milled around desks filled with computers, radios, and mounted recon images from drones and scouts.

"This way, Captain," Sharp said.

He took Beckham into a wide room with a large rectangular table lined by dozens of chairs. Maps of the United States, Texas, and other regions where the Allied States still had outposts were posted on the walls, along with various screens showing live feeds from those outposts.

Seated around the table were familiar faces like General Cornelius with his white mustache, President Ringgold, as well as General Souza and his LNO, Lieutenant Festa. A few of their support staff, including Chief of Staff James Soprano, were also at the table.

Those that Beckham did not recognize wore military uniforms with the red and white flag of Canada emblazoned on their shoulders.

"Captain Beckham, thank you for joining us with such short notice," General Cornelius said. "Our brothers from the north have arrived bearing gifts. This is Colonel Maurice Stilwell from the Canadian Armed Forces."

A man in his early sixties with black thick-rimmed glasses and a square face stood and shook hands with Beckham.

"Pleased to meet you, Captain," Stilwell said. "Your reputation precedes you."

Stilwell introduced the rest of his officers and the political dignitaries who had joined them.

"Please, everyone, take a seat," Ringgold said. Beckham found one next to General Cornelius. "We've got much to discuss. First matter of business, Colonel Stilwell brought the seismic detection system equipment that Ghost retrieved from California."

Beckham's heart lifted at that. The technology that Team Ghost had fought so hard to recover had finally made it into the Allied States. Deploying the devices would help them detect incoming Variant forces and defend against them before they tunneled under outpost or base walls.

"How's Team Ghost?" Beckham asked.

"I've heard they're doing well," Stilwell said.

"They're still stationed at Banff," Ringgold said. "Since

we've lost all our bases up north, we're keeping them in Canada."

"That way we have someone who can respond to threats quicker in those regions," Souza explained.

"In exchange, we've brought some reinforcements," Stilwell said. "Most importantly, we have engineers to help install the SDS equipment you requested."

"We'll be sending half the engineers and SDS equipment to Outpost Houston," Ringgold said. "Houston was nearly destroyed from their last attack, and they've consolidated into an area roughly ten percent the size of the initial outpost. They'll need everything we can send them. The other half will stay in Galveston."

She gestured to the soldiers. "Captain Beckham, you, Master Sergeant Horn, and Sergeant Rico will help set up the defenses around Houston. We want to keep what little is left of the outpost. It's our first line of defense against attacks headed to Galveston."

"We also brought two platoons of soldiers who are willing and ready to assist in the fight against the Variants and Chimeras," Stilwell added. "We can assign them to your defenses or scouting parties as necessary."

Beckham tried to hide his disappointment. Two platoons would be nothing against the coming storm.

"The Mexican President also vowed to commit forces," Souza said. "In total, we're looking at coordinating the deployment of two-thousand additional men and women to assist the Allied States."

Beckham liked the sound of that better, and he saw the worry in Ringgold's features seemed to fade for a moment, too.

"We're grateful for Canada and the Mexican Federation's assistance. It's good to know that the Allied

States is no longer in this fight alone," she said. "With our joint forces and the tireless efforts from our scientific community, I am confident this is the turning point in this war."

The conversation continued for nearly an hour as they discussed the logistics of the incoming reinforcements. When the meeting finished, the group began to disperse, but Ringgold stopped Beckham before he could leave.

"Reed, I know you only just got to the island, but you and Horn will need to start preparing immediately to escort the Canadians to Houston with the SDS equipment," she said. "Now that we have it, I don't want to spend another day without being tapped into the Variant network, either. Kate and her team will go with you."

"When do we leave?" Beckham asked.

"In two hours."

Doctor Kate Lovato picked up a box of laboratory supplies from the warehouse floor and carried it to the back of a waiting transport truck parked next to an Interim Armored Vehicle (IAV) Stryker. Her lab assistants, Ron and Leslie, situated the box among the other crates and supplies in the back of the truck destined for Outpost Houston.

Beckham, Horn, and Sergeant First Class Jeni Rico from Team Ghost were helping load equipment. Even Javier and the girls lugged smaller pieces of lab equipment into the truck, eager to spend as much time with their parents as they could before they left.

Sammy Tibalt, their resident computer engineer, picked up a small crate with a groan and waddled toward the truck, a grimace on her face.

"Sammy!" Kate scolded her. "Let me take that."

She took the crate.

"I'm fine," Sammy said.

There was a slight bulge under her shirt where bandages protected the entry and exit wounds of the bullet that had cut through her abdomen. Sammy had been lucky it had not hit anything vital, but she seemed to press that luck every day, trying to overextend herself.

She sighed. "I hate being useless."

"You're anything but useless," Kate said. "It'll be better if you're well-rested anyway for when we get to

Houston. We need you."

"Now you're just trying to prop up my ego."

"Is it working?"

Sammy gave her a knowing grin.

A group of six Canadian engineers joined them, carrying metal containers with the SDS equipment.

"That's it, huh?" Beckham asked, hopping down, followed by Horn.

"I think so," Kate said.

Javier stood near the back of the truck with them. "Are you sure I can't come too?"

"It's safer here," Kate said.

Javier met her gaze. "But I can fight."

"You can do your part by looking out for Galveston," Beckham said. "Watch out for Tasha and Jenny."

Javier frowned.

"That's right," Tasha said, playing along. "Someone's got to protect us."

"You've already got Timothy," Javier said.

Tasha blushed, and Jenny let out a soft laugh.

"Don't you get any ideas now that I'm leaving," Horn said with a slight scowl. "I'm telling Connor to keep an eye on you."

Connor was the Secret Service agent who had watched the kids back in Long Island. With Ringgold's blessing, he was once again looking out for them while Kate, Beckham, and Horn went out into the field.

"Truth is, Timothy isn't staying behind anyway," Tasha said. "He told me he's headed to Houston."

Horn looked at Beckham. "He's going with us?"

Beckham nodded. "Timothy and Sergeant Ruckley are being sent with a platoon of new recruits to help defend Houston."

NICHOLAS SANSBURY SMITH & ANTHONY J. MELCHIORRI

"He hasn't even finished training," Tasha said.

"I know, but we're so short on men and women, and he's one of the best." Beckham said. "Truth be told, Ruckley also asked for him. She likes Timothy as much as we do."

Tasha looked at her dad. "Can you look out for Timothy? Make sure he's safe?"

"Of course," Horn said.

"Captain, we better get moving," a soldier called from the cab of the transport truck.

Beckham gave him a nod, then bent to one knee and pulled Javier in tight for a hug. "Listen to Connor and be good, okay?"

"I will," Javier said.

Kate took her turn with Javier, squeezing him tightly. Saying goodbye to her young son never got any easier, no matter how many times she had to do it.

"I love you," she said, brushing back some of his hair. "Don't you ever forget that."

"I love you too, Mom."

"Soon this will all be over, and we won't have to go anywhere without each other again."

The soldier in the cab of the truck leaned out the open window again. "Captain, sorry to interrupt, but we're losing daylight."

Kate gave Javier one last hug, and Horn returned from saying goodbye to his girls. Rico was already in the back of the Stryker staring off into space, indicating to Kate she was probably thinking about Fitz.

"I'm sure Fitz is fine," Kate said.

"Yeah, for sure."

She didn't sound convinced.

The diesel engine chugged to life. Kate, Horn, and

Beckham waved to the kids from out of the open back hatch until the warehouse was out of sight.

Beckham closed the hatch, and a few minutes later, the Stryker joined a convoy of other transport trucks and Humvees at the outer gates for the bridge leading to the mainland. Soldiers atop the wall opened the sliding metal gate, and once again, the convoy was off, driving into the wastelands.

They passed by abandoned homes lining a marina. Boats rotted in their slips, many half-sunk. Paint on the houses flaked away like the dead skin off a corpse.

As they left the coast behind, sunlight waned over the Texas horizon, falling in orange hues through the slightly open hatch on the roof and the hatch over the driver. They drove through the outer suburbs of Houston, which looked no better than the neighborhoods closer to Galveston. Charred houses were nearly buried from where they had fallen into sinkholes formed by Variant tunnels.

Kate squeezed Beckham's hand at the shriek of a Variant.

The convoy suddenly slowed to a halt.

"Why are we stopping?" Ron asked.

"Got a roadblock," the driver said. "Bunch of abandoned cars."

Leslie cowered next to Sammy and Ron looked at Beckham.

"Captain, we can't stay here," Ron said.

"I know." Beckham pushed open one of the slotted panels for a look. "Horn, get topside."

"You got it," Horn said, pushing out the roof hatch with his M-249.

"Hunker down and stay inside," Beckham said,

turning back to Kate and the others.

"Shit, we got contacts at our three!" the driver suddenly shouted.

Kate peered around the driver to see a glimpse out the front hatch. She saw the shadows of skeletal creatures running at their Stryker. The chatter of Horn's M-249 came to life above, resonating inside the Stryker.

Beckham spoke to the driver and Kate tried to listen. Judging by his cursing, they were in deep trouble.

"We got to clear the path," he said.

"Can't we just ram whatever's blocking the road?" Ron asked.

"There are too many cars ahead," Beckham said. "But we got guys from the transport truck working on clearing it." He went to the rear hatch. "Rico, on me. Rest of you stay inside, no matter what happens."

He gave Rico a nod. Then they jumped outside. Gunfire cracked immediately from both sides of the Stryker, joining with the chainsaw bark of the M249 topside.

Screams rang out, some of panic, others yelling orders, and then a cry of pain. Not Beckham, or Rico, from what Kate could tell.

"Contacts on our six!" someone shouted.

Something slammed the back of the hatch, and Leslie screeched. Ron pulled her close, and Sammy sat trembling.

"It's okay," Kate said. "We're going to—"

Small arms fire drowned out her voice.

"Timothy!" came a scream.

That was Beckham.

More gunfire cracked, followed by a chorus of Variant shrieks and howls.

"Roadblocks are clear!" the driver yelled.

The back hatch opened, and Beckham hopped inside with Rico, their ACUs painted with blood. Horn dropped down from the top hatch.

"Go, go, go!" Beckham shouted.

The convoy rolled forward, chugging along once again.

"Is Timothy okay?" Kate asked.

"Yeah, he's the reason we're moving again," Beckham said. "Took a big risk, but it paid off."

He let out a sigh and rested his back against the bulkhead.

The scientists from Kate's team simply stared.

The rest of the ride fell into solemn silence. Kate kept expecting another roadblock or for screeching Variants to descend on them, but the ride was smooth. When they finally made it to the outskirts of Outpost Houston, the sky was turning purple and the first few bright stars were beginning to show in the descending darkness.

"We're here," the driver said.

Beckham nodded. "SDS crew, with me and Horn. Everyone else is moving out to the tunnels."

Horn stood, stretching his arms, then patted his belly. "Wonder if they prepared that good old Texas barbecue for us? I'm hungry as hell."

Beckham tossed him an energy bar. "There. That's dinner."

A Ford pickup pulled up toward them. Kate shielded her eyes from the beams until the truck killed its lights. Six soldiers sat in the pickup's bed.

"That must be the welcoming party," Horn said.

Beckham led the group out of the Stryker, and a man stepped out of the pickup to greet them. He was tall and muscular. His sleeves were rolled up to reveal arms rippling with what looked to be burn scars. When he approached, Kate saw that half of his face shone like it was plastic from more burns.

"I'm Commander Leo Jacobs," the man said. He stretched a hand out to Beckham.

"Captain Reed Beckham."

"I know who you are. Practically a celebrity." Jacobs nodded toward a group of men that had jumped off the bed of his pickup. "We don't have much left of the city, but I take pride in what little we've managed to cling to. My boys will get you and your team oriented with the base so you can set up that SDS equipment and consult with our defensive operations."

"Yes, sir," Beckham said.

The six soldiers split up to help the Canadian engineers offload the SDS equipment into the pickup.

"You better go with them," Jacobs said to Beckham.

"Yes, sir." Beckham turned to Kate. "I love you. Be safe."

"You, too," she said.

Beckham, Horn, and Rico took off in the pickup with the engineering team, disappearing into the base.

"You must be Dr. Lovato." Jacobs extended a hand to Kate. "Thanks for coming."

"Thanks for hosting us," she said, shaking his hand.

He climbed into the Stryker. Kate and her team jumped into the back again. This time, six of the commander's armed guards joined them.

Once again, they passed through a steel-paneled gate, this time taking them outside the protection of the walls. A single hospital was to their right surrounded by crumbling apartment buildings. Unlike the apartment buildings, the hospital looked mostly intact.

The soldiers hopped out of the truck first, forming a perimeter.

"All clear!" one said.

The group exited the Stryker with their computers in tow.

"Alpha Security, Jacobs here," the commander said. "Light the place up."

A buzz like a gigantic hive of bees coming to life grew from the hospital. Lights flickered on inside the cracked windows, glowing as the last remnants of daylight faded from the Texas sky.

"The last time the Variants hit us, they tunneled into this hospital's parking garage," Jacobs said.

As they walked up the sidewalk toward the hospital, Kate noticed dozens of soldiers posted in windows, silhouetted against the light. Jacobs led them down stairs in the hospital's lobby to a cavernous underground parking garage with an entrance ramp sealed by rubble.

Banks of lights illuminated the space, and twenty soldiers surrounded the far side. There, a handful of spotlights shone into a sight that had become all too familiar. Pulsating red vines roped out of a tunnel, spreading from the dark soil and over the concrete. Kate's stomach lurched. It wasn't just the sight of the webbing network, but the overwhelming odor of death that came with it.

"This is the tunnel the beasts used when they nearly destroyed us," Jacobs said. "We've got generators down here to keep the lights on and power your equipment. We also requisitioned a clinical laboratory upstairs you can use if needed."

"Excellent, thank you," Kate said. She wasn't used to

military commanders anticipating all her scientific needs like this.

"I'm heading back to base. If you need anything—more men, more computers, more generators—don't hesitate to let me know."

"Thank you very much, Commander," Kate said.

The commander retreated, leaving behind the soldiers who had carried down the scientific equipment. Kate immediately began directing her team to set up near the tunnel. It took them a half-an-hour to prepare.

"All the software is ready," Sammy reported, sitting at her station.

"I've got the microarrays prepped," Leslie reported.

"Initiate the computer connections," Kate said.

Sammy nodded, fingers typing on her keyboard as Leslie inserted the connector.

"I've established an active connection," Sammy said. "We just need you to plug in."

This was the part Kate hated. They had discovered computer communications alone with the Variant network were inadequate to sabotage the messages being sent between enemy forces. Like the difference between a computerized operator on the telephone and an actual human customer service representative, the creatures on the other end of the webbing preferred to talk with "biological" voices.

In other words, they could tell when Kate's team was using solely the computer, which would blow their cover.

"This one's for you." Ron held a piece of webbing in one hand and motioned for Kate to take a seat with the other.

She did as instructed, trying to keep calm and preparing for the voices transmitting over the networks.

Hundreds of them, some calling out in horror, others giving orders. Filtering through them was how they had learned the master of the New Gods they were seeking was actually called 'the Prophet', something she had discovered during the last time she connected.

Ron placed the webbing on the back of her neck, and she felt the familiar, sickening warmth of the tendril.

She clenched her jaw, nerves tingling. Soon her mind would be swimming in the crazed voices of monsters across the country.

And she would be the lone person infiltrating their ranks.

"Ready," she said. "Connect me."

***

Ringgold heard gunshots and screams, the cries of her people rising in the night. Galveston was losing to a fresh siege of Variants, and her people were dying.

Soldiers. Civilians. Women. Children.

She wanted to fight, but she had no weapon, nothing but her hands.

Two gunshots popped in the hallway outside her room. Voices called out, then a scream of pain and the crunching of bones and teeth tearing flesh.

"No," she muttered. "God, no."

Ringgold froze.

A long, deep scratch came on the door. Blood pooled underneath it, soiling the carpet.

She scrambled backward into the corner of the room, cowering.

The Variant outside slammed the door hard, nearly breaking one of the hinges.

She pressed her hands over her ears to block out the screams of people being torn apart. The banging on her door grew into a violent cacophony, broken only by a loud voice.

"Madam President, please open the door."

She jolted awake, sweating where she lay in bed panting.

Get ahold of yourself, Jan.

It was just a dream. Just a nightmare.

But the truth was reality was just as much of a nightmare.

"Madam President," the voice at the door said, followed by another knock.

"One moment," she replied.

Ringgold splashed water on her face in the Galveston hotel room, exhausted as usual. The tasks of organizing the streams of refugees, reinforcing surviving outposts, and strategizing military actions were like throwing a jigsaw into the air and trying to put all the pieces together before they hit the ground.

The burden of all the lives lost, all the people without homes, the prisoners taken by the Variants who might still be alive out there crashed over her like a violent avalanche.

She drank a glass of water and opened the door to find it was Chief of Staff James Soprano waiting outside.

"Madam President, I'm sorry to bother you, but your call with the vice president is in a few minutes." He held out a coffee. "I thought you might need this."

Ringgold took the cup, savoring the aroma. "James, you're a lifesaver. Thank you."

"My pleasure," Soprano said. Then he shot her a concerned look. "Are you okay?"

"Just trying to catch some shuteye." Ringgold stepped out of her room, quick to change the subject. "Any word from Outpost Houston?"

"Yes, we just received a message from Commander Jacobs. The science team initiated their connection with the Variant network and are currently monitoring all communications."

"And Captain Beckham?"

"He's consulting with the Canadian engineering team and Commander Jacobs on how best to reinforce Outpost Houston's defenses. They have also set up the first SDS sensors around the outpost's walls."

"Very good," Ringgold said.

The hotel corridors took them through the second floor that Ringgold had turned into her latest version of the fabled West Wing. As they walked, she tried to count the times she had relocated the country's capitol. No other president in history had moved it as many times as she had.

She and her administration had constantly been trying to stay one step ahead of the New Gods.

This time, she vowed, her administration would not be running anywhere. The truth was, they hardly had anywhere left to run.

While Lemke was setting up a new, safer Central Command in Puerto Rico, she wanted to stay with her people for as long as possible.

Soprano led them down to the first floor to the conference room where she had met with Beckham and Kate several hours ago. General Souza and Lieutenant Festa were already there, ready for their first in-person meeting since arriving from Puerto Rico.

General Cornelius sat across from them at the

otherwise empty table, his face buried in a briefing.

They all stood when Ringgold entered, and she nodded a greeting at them before taking a seat at the head of the table. Soprano placed a conference phone between the four leaders and dialed into an encrypted line.

"Lemke here," a voice crackled over the speaker.

"This is Jan," Ringgold said. "How are things?"

"President Ringgold, good to hear your voice. Things are moving along here. The port was a mess when we arrived, but we've cleaned things up enough to dock a few of the fleet's ships. We're transporting supplies to and from the island by tender for those ships that can't dock."

"Any reports of hostiles?" General Souza asked.

"Only a few Variants," Lemke said. "Nothing's changed dramatically since you and Festa returned to the States. We've taken precautions against the seaborne variety as well, but we haven't faced anything that can't be dealt with easily."

"What we have seen in PR aligns with our intel," Festa said. "It seems the New Gods activity is strictly in the Allied States for now."

"What about human survivors?" Ringgold asked.

"There weren't any in San Juan," Souza replied.

"But there could be pockets of survivors we haven't encountered yet deeper in the island," Lemke said. "We've sent out a few scouts to check likely locations."

"I see." Even more pressing was a question that had pained Ringgold ever since she had left the First Fleet. "Have you found any collaborator infiltrators in the fleet?"

"No, Madam President. Thanks to General Souza's help, we've secured the entire fleet, and I'm confident we're free from any collaborator moles."

Ringgold wanted to breathe a sigh of relief, but she knew not to be too optimistic. "Stay vigilant. We cannot take anything for granted anymore."

"Rest assured, I haven't taken our search for traitors lightly. How are things in the States?"

"We're down to twenty-three outposts as of today, almost all located within the American southeast."

The line went quiet.

"Dan, are you still there?" she asked.

"I am… it's just… my God, only twenty-three?"

"Yes, but I do have some good news," Ringgold said. "Canada and Mexico are committing their first two-thousand troops to the cause. That puts us at nearly nine-thousand men and women fighting against the evil plaguing our country."

"I'm confident we'll retake the States," Cornelius said. "We just have to keep working together."

"You're right, but in the meantime, I'm afraid we have a refugee crisis. Lieutenant Festa has been coordinating our evacuation operations, so I'll let him continue."

Festa took a deep breath, his chest rising. "As more outposts fall, we're approaching the limit on how many refugees we can fit safely in our surviving bases. Everywhere from Outpost Pensacola to Houston are bursting at the seams with incoming refugees. Unfortunately, it's not just a space issue, but also one of resources."

"Organizing resupply lines is becoming almost unmanageable," Souza said. "We're having trouble both securing them and rerouting them as each outpost falls."

"Not only that, but every time we try to relocate people, we're expending fuel, ammunition to secure them, and vehicles that would be useful on the frontlines," Festa said. "Simply put, trying to evacuate people and find them new places that are safe is becoming a losing proposition."

"That's why I need you to ensure Puerto Rico is a safe haven," Ringgold said. "Not just for command, but also for the people of the Allied States. My hope is that we can start sending refugees down there. That way, people will not have to keep moving from outpost to outpost."

"I can start reallocating a few of my private military's planes to help with the evacuation, but we're going to need a place to land," Cornelius said.

"Understood," Lemke said. "How many people are you looking at relocating down here?"

"We have at least forty-thousand people that we're trying to find a secure location for in the immediate future, but if we fail to take back the states…" Festa let his words trail off.

"We won't fail," Ringgold said.

"Ma'am, I hate to say it, but we're losing the war. We need to consider the possibility of losing the country," Souza said. "We may need to evacuate every soul."

The entire room was silent.

"We're not retreating yet," Ringgold said. "There's plenty of fight left in us."

"Indeed." Cornelius stood. "Don't forget where you are, General Souza. Texans don't know how to retreat."

— 3 —

Master Sergeant Joe "Fitz" Fitzpatrick crouched between two pine trees outside the town of Banff, Canada. He was cold, tired, and he missed Rico more than ever before.

His emotions were getting the best of him today, and his prosthetic blades didn't help. Each step, he slipped in the white fluff. He felt like he was shoveling a pile of snow with the blades. Because of the effort it took to walk, the shirts and pants under his outerwear were soaked in sweat despite the cold.

Even the oldest member of their team, Corporal Bobby Ace, seemed to be moving faster.

Sergeant Yas Dohi was ahead of both of them. All three men used night vision goggles and walked with their rifles at the ready. The delicate swirl of falling snow in the green hue gave the cold night a sense of quiet serenity. That peacefulness belied the reason for Team Ghost's mission tonight. They were tracking one of the deadliest Variants of the north. A giant beast that the Canadians called a bear had been spotted lurking outside Banff.

When the scouts who spotted the creature had lost track of it in the mountains just southwest of the Fairmont hotel serving as Banff's command center, General Kamer recruited Team Ghost to do what they did best: track down a monster. About ten yards south and parallel to their position was a four-person squad of Canadian special forces nicknamed Team Spearhead. Fitz was glad to have them along. They had joined primarily for support and education, staying within a dozen yards in case Ghost needed backup.

Fitz sucked in a deep breath. His ribs still ached from the injuries he had sustained in Seattle, but his muscles had recovered some. A little rest and medical attention had gone a long way for him and Ace.

But memories of the deranged Doctor Lloyd brutalizing them haunted him every time he closed his eyes. As tortured as he was by those memories, he could not help worrying about Rico. How was she doing in Texas? And when would he get to see her again? Team Ghost felt emptier without her by his side.

He shook those thoughts away.

Now he needed to focus.

Fitz flipped up his night vision goggles and peered into his scope, surveying the spindly trees ahead. "Contacts?"

"Negative," Dohi whispered.

Sergeant Lucas Neilson shook his head as he led his squad closer to Ghost. "Damn thing disappeared."

Fitz gave Dohi the signal to advance. They followed the massive footprints left behind in the snow from the huge bear.

As much as he disliked being cooped up in the stuffy hotel, he didn't like leaving their prisoner, the Chimera named Corrin, back in his makeshift prison cell alone. After all they had gone through, Fitz preferred that he or someone on his team kept watch over him at all times.

Dohi held up his fist, and Fitz paused, bringing up his rifle once more.

"I see another set of tracks," Dohi said. "Must be two of them."

"You're sure?" Fitz asked. The thought of another

massive beast made him pause.

"Yeah," Dohi said. "In fact, there might be more than two. But the falling snow isn't helping. It's covering their trail, making it difficult to tell."

Fitz hesitated for a few seconds. The threat to their teams just increased two-fold, but it also put the base at risk. He radioed the new information to the lead of Spearhead and then motioned to keep moving.

Dohi stalked the trail between the trees. A freezing wind howled overhead, shaking loose snow from the branches. The resulting rattle sounded like bones knocking together.

The further they delved into the woods, the more Fitz felt like he could feel the eyes of predators watching them. The tracks they followed were not fresh. They led down from the mountain, into a valley, heading northwest toward the Bow River. Dohi had estimated the beasts had been through likely a few hours ago, and they had a long way to go before they caught up to them. Still Fitz could not shake the feeling of anticipation coursing through him. At each turn, he expected to hear an ear-shattering roar as one or both of the monsters charged.

The Canadians had told Fitz that the bears usually ran straight at Banff. They were attracted by the sights and sounds of human activity, all too eager to feast when the opportunity presented itself.

Yet for some reason, the original bear they were tracking had turned away from the sounds of snowmobile and truck engines near the base. And to make matters stranger, the second beast seemed to be headed in the same direction away from Banff.

Fitz had long since learned that whenever Variants acted outside their normal behaviors, they had to be extraordinarily cautious. Usually that meant there was something more nefarious going on, generally involving collaborators or the New Gods. Either way, Ghost needed to find the bears to find out what was happening.

Dohi knelt next to one of the footprints large enough to fit a human skull.

As the Navajo tracker followed the rapidly disappearing tracks, Fitz and Ace scanned their surroundings. Dohi picked up his pace, skirting quicker between the trees as they climbed an incline. The light snowfall had almost buried the tracks.

After another twenty minutes of desperately following the dwindling footsteps, Dohi finally stopped. Fitz watched him search the snow before standing and letting out a defeated sigh.

"We've lost the footprints," Dohi said.

"I say we keep going," Ace growled. "Got to be another way to find them."

The Canadian special forces trudged through the snow toward Ghost.

Neilson paused next to Fitz, his three team members standing behind him. "We should call this off and head back. It's going to be like trying to find a snowball in an avalanche now."

"No," Dohi said, scanning the trees. "Footprints are the easiest way to follow the beasts, but they aren't the only way. I can find their trail again."

Neilson looked at Fitz as if he wasn't sure.

"If he says he can find them, he can find them," Fitz said. "You want to turn around, go ahead. But we're not going back until we find those bears. Rather we find them, than they find us."

Neilson shrugged, and for a second, Fitz thought the

Canadians would start back to Banff.

"Well, we aren't leaving a bunch of Americans out in the Canadian wilderness," Neilson said. "If you stay, we stay."

A large, gruff Canadian named Corporal Sherman stepped up. He had a thick black beard poking out of his parka that bobbed as he talked.

"If your man can actually find these monsters, then all the drinks you want are on me when we get back," Sherman said.

"Sounds like a deal," Ace said. "You heard him, Dohi. Work your magic."

"It isn't magic," Dohi said. "And if you all are coming with, I need you to be quieter than the dead."

"Consider me dead," a skinny man with bright green eyes named Corporal Daugherty said.

The third team member, a woman with raven-black hair named Private Lauren Toussaint nodded.

The Canadians fell in line with the Americans. Fitz signaled for Ace and Sherman to take rearguard. Neilson, Daugherty, and Toussaint watched their flanks as Dohi led the group through the snow.

He did so with deft surety, seemingly following invisible clues. Fitz watched the man trace his gloved finger over a tree, then pause as if he was sniffing the air like a hunting wolf.

In reality, he knew that Dohi was not preternaturally gifted. He had just honed a set of skills that others neglected. The tracker stopped and pinched a single white piece of fur between his fingers, then changed direction.

More and more frequently, Dohi stopped to take in their surroundings. The more they slowed, the more Fitz worried they had indeed lost the trail. Maybe his confident assurance to Neilson had been foolish. Maybe the tracker had finally met his match thanks to Mother Nature.

Then Dohi held up a fist.

The team froze.

Dohi looked back at Fitz, signaling to his eyes, then flashed two fingers.

Two contacts.

He gestured for Dohi to lead them on the invisible path he had uncovered.

They traveled only a few hundred yards to the edge of the forest. There the snow-covered trees gave way to a steep drop-off over a frozen stream. The ice was punctuated by jagged rocks. Between the rocks, Fitz finally saw their targets.

Just as Dohi had estimated, two massive Variants with shaggy white fur were walking on all fours across the frozen water. Judging by their slow gaits, they did not know they were being followed.

Fitz lined up his rifle, tracking their movements. He was still too far to ensure a clean kill shot, especially with the cover of the trees below.

Before Fitz could give the order to advance, Dohi put a hand on his shoulder. Then the tracker pointed to another clearing between the trees.

Fitz's stomach sunk, fear creeping through his insides. They had anticipated running into the two bears.

But those giant beasts were nothing compared to the sight before them.

Neilson audibly gasped.

Fitz peered through his rifle scope, counting each of the bears in the clearing.

Six of them. Six abominations the size of the fabled

Yeti with all the strength and power of a tank. They snarled at each other with long fangs protruding from their humanoid faces. Their white fur was long and clumped-together with dirt. Dried blood stained their chests from past kills.

One bear posed a threat to an entire team, but this many, especially if they were working as a pack was dangerous as hell. The thought sent a chill through Fitz colder than the freezing snow.

The last time he recalled Variants working in an organized fashion, far more dangerous and evil forces had been behind them.

"What do we do now?" Ace said, sounding uncertain.

Dohi directed his goggles at Fitz for orders.

"We keep our distance, stay out of sight," Fitz whispered. "We have to figure out what they're up to."

"Bears aren't smart enough to mount a coordinated attack or anything," Neilson said. "They are mostly just mindless beasts."

"Don't look like mindless beasts to me," Ace said.

Dohi snorted out a puff of misty air. "It's not the bears I'm worried about. It's whoever or whatever has brought all of them here."

***

"Bet you thought you could get rid of me, huh, Temper?" said Sergeant Candace Ruckley.

"Nah, after everything I've seen you go through, I know better than that," Timothy said. "And honestly, I appreciate you letting me join your team. I know I didn't exactly follow your orders in the field."

"Yeah, but you learned how to handle yourself and

kept my ass alive." She gave him a playful punch to the arm. "I'm glad you're here."

"Thanks."

Sitting in the back of a moving Humvee, he checked over his M4A1 rifle and pulled on its sling to ensure everything was secure. Tonight was his first official mission as an enlisted soldier in the Allied States Army. Training in Galveston had only lasted a few days, but Beckham and Horn had agreed the experience he had in the field was even better preparation.

They are short on soldiers, he thought.

Most everyone was dead or injured like Ruckley.

She rubbed her healing arm. Her standard issue ACU-jacket covered the bandages wrapped around the stitches tracing up her biceps.

"How's that feeling?" Timothy asked.

"Fine," she said. "Infection is gone."

Timothy wondered if she should even be on a mission out here. If the outpost doctors weren't already stretched so thin, worried about patients in worse shape than her, they might've even forced her to stay behind. But Timothy had learned that Ruckley, like him, wasn't the type of soldier who sat on the sidelines. She had sweet-talked her way straight out of the hospital and while she couldn't carry an M4, she still gripped an M9.

"Closing in on our target, Sarge," said Corporal Boyd. The middle-aged man with sharp features drove the Humvee with his eyes glued to the road. He had served in the defensive forces of Outpost Chattanooga before the Tennessee town had been overwhelmed by Variant forces.

"Locked and loaded, and ready to go," Corporal Mark Wong said. The Asian-American man was a Houston native who had volunteered to join the scouting mission given his knowledge of the area.

"Good," Ruckley said. "This should be routine. We go in quiet for recon."

"What are we looking for?" Boyd asked. "Couple of gators? Bunch of empty houses?"

"Hopefully more of the latter and none of the former," Ruckley said. "The SDS equipment Captain Beckham and those engineers set up haven't detected any Variants tunneling, but Northside units reported straggler Variant activity just outside the I-610 loop."

"That's a little too close to the outpost for my comfort," Wong said.

"Then hopefully all we see are gators," Ruckley said. "Maybe we can make some good gator fritters if someone's got a decent recipe."

Timothy looked at Wong.

Wong laughed. "What, Temper, you think just because I'm from the south I eat gator? How about you, Boyd?"

"Only time I touched it was when I was in New Orleans," Boyd said, downshifting as they pulled off the empty highway and into a neighborhood. "Kinda tasted like chicken."

"Really?" Timothy asked.

"Well, like really fatty chicken. Not my favorite, but not bad."

Boyd turned the Humvee down a suburban street lined with dark houses, drawing closer to their target. All the yards were covered in wild flowers and tall grass.

"Almost there," he reported.

"Just remember, the beasts out here might be nothing but normal, dumb Variants, but when they're hungry, they're desperate, and we're the snacks," Ruckley said.

Wong leaned forward in his seat and clapped Boyd on the shoulder. "Some of us are more than just snacks."

"Not going to let a Variant get close to me," Boyd said, slowing the Humvee as they entered a neighborhood. "You know how fast you need to be to outrun a hungry Variant?"

Wong rolled his eyes.

"How about you, Private Temper?" Boyd asked.

"Don't have any idea. I shoot them."

Boyd laughed. "Good answer. But the *real* answer is you don't have to be fast. You just have to run faster than your buddy. And I happen to know Wong is slow as shit."

The Humvee slowed in front of a house with broken windows.

"All right, boys, get your shit together, because it's serious from here on out," Ruckley said. "Remember, recon only. Got it?"

"Yes, Sarge," Timothy said.

Boyd and Wong each nodded.

The humor they used to mask the fear and tension disappeared.

Ruckley opened her door first and slipped out into the night. Boyd and Wong went next, followed by Timothy. Each flipped down their night-vision goggles.

The humid night air brought with it a cool breeze. Not nearly as cold as it had been in the northeast, but Timothy still shivered. He tried to pretend it was just due to the wind, but he knew better.

Ruckley signaled for Wong to take point, and Boyd fell in on rearguard. They carried their weapons at the ready as they walked down the middle of the street. Much of the road was covered in mud, splashing under their boots.

Vegetation grew along the exteriors of the abandoned houses with mold and mildew creeping up the sides. The sight was a reminder that Houston had been built on swamps and marshland, and nature was quick to reclaim civilization.

Wong paused at a T-intersection. He gestured for them to take a left down a street where half the houses were nothing but blackened beams and a few lone walls. Trees sprouted from what had once been living rooms, showing this fire had been years ago, likely during the first war.

Wind rustled over the structures and rippled the blades of overgrown grass.

Timothy kept his rifle pressed tightly against his shoulder. While the other soldiers wanted to avoid the beasts, he wanted to find and kill them. The more dead Variants, the faster the war would be over, and then maybe he could have a life, maybe even with Tasha.

He thought of her as he walked, recalling the moments they had managed to steal away together on Galveston. Soon he would be back to the island, and with Horn gone, he didn't have to worry about her dad breathing down their necks every second.

The team continued through the street, prowling through the darkness. They found no animal carcasses or misshapen footprints in the mud or grass, nothing that would indicate any monsters had been here recently.

Wong took them down another boulevard into the second neighborhood they were assigned to clear. The once-picturesque street was lined with the arching branches of southern live oak trees.

A light tapping noise made Timothy halt.

Wong continued forward but Ruckley stopped.

"What?" she asked.

He listened but heard nothing.

Maybe he was just being paranoid.

Then he heard the tapping again.

He held up a fist.

Wong and Boyd stopped and crouched.

Timothy pointed to his ears, then started a hand signal when a shape burst from the grass, exploding toward them.

All four of them spun, but not fast enough.

Before Timothy could fully understand what had happened, Boyd was down on his back. On top of him was a skinny Variant with gray flesh and dilated vessels pulsating over its muscles.

Boyd swung his wrist up to block a snapping bite from the Variant, then let out a cry of pain as it ripped into his flesh.

Timothy rushed forward, letting his rifle fall on its sling. He could not risk taking a shot, and instead he took out his knife and threw his shoulder into the creature's exposed ribs. It reared up, and he jabbed the knife deep into its guts.

The beast let out a pained squeal as Timothy dug the blade deeper, warm blood spilling over his hand. With a kick, he shoved the Variant off Boyd. It scrambled back on all fours, facing Timothy, grotesque face drawn in an aggressive snarl.

Timothy put himself between Boyd and the starving abomination. A suppressed shot burst through its forehead a moment later. Two more shots tore into its chest, and the monster crumpled.

Ruckley stepped beside Timothy, aiming her M9 down the street.

"Thanks, Temper," Boyd said. He winced, holding his bleeding wrist.

"Quiet," Ruckley said. "Might be more."

Wong swiveled on his heels, rifle roving over the empty lawns. No other creatures howled or pounced from the tall grass. Timothy knelt next to the fallen monster to check out something around its neck. He reached down to find a black collar like the one the collaborators had used on their Thralls in Maine. Boyd and Wong appeared confused, but Ruckley knew exactly what the collar represented.

Somewhere to their south, they heard more rustling grass and another growl.

"Quick!" Ruckley whispered. "Get to cover!"

Wong helped Boyd up, and they sprinted the opposite direction, running straight for a house toward the end of the street. Timothy was the last one inside, his boots splashing over soggy, mildew-covered carpet. He followed the team upstairs where they spread out inside a bedroom with broken windows.

They each took a spot along the wall and Timothy snuck a glance out the window while Wong helped Boyd clean and bandage the bleeding wound from the Variant bite. The scent would draw the beasts if they didn't hurry.

"Command, Recon Sigma One," Ruckley whispered over the radio. "We have multiple contacts, standby for location."

"Copy, Recon Sigma," replied the operator. "What's your location?"

Ruckley looked at Wong.

"Riverbend North, Nail's Creek," the Houston native whispered.

Ruckley relayed the answer.

Outside, the sound of gruff voices grew closer, along with another howl. Timothy went still, and Ruckley turned off the radio, silently observing the unfolding scene.

Another Variant ran to the dead one. It paused at the corpse, sniffing at the dead monster, then looked back over its shoulder, teeth bared. Cranking back its head, it let out a short howl.

Timothy expected to see collaborators emerge from the grass with a remote control like Nick and Pete had possessed at Mount Katahdin. Sure enough, three humanoid shapes walked out carrying rifles.

But these weren't men.

The hybrid beasts had scything claws protruding from the ends of their fingers, and their faces were flat and scarred with golden eyes.

They were Chimeras.

Deadlier than normal Variants and collaborators. These were the infamous Scions of the New Gods, the ultimate combination of manmade science and Mother Nature's evolution.

And now they were just outside Houston.

— 4 —

Beckham finally had a chance to grab some shuteye in the Outpost Houston apartment he and Kate were given when frantic knocking jolted him awake. A glance out the window showed it was still dark. Maybe three or four in the morning, if he had to guess.

Kate turned over in bed, planting her feet on the floor. "Wonder who it's for this time."

Together they wandered toward the front door and opened it. Outside was a big red-haired man with a shit-eating grin.

"Morning, boss," Big Horn said with a yawn. "You'll never guess what the cat dragged into Houston."

"Guess it's for me," Beckham said. "You can go back to sleep, Kate. You need it."

"I'm already awake. Might as well go to work."

She disappeared back into the bedroom to change.

"What's going on?" Beckham asked Horn.

"We found some enemy scouts."

All the exhaustion and stupor of being woken up in the middle of the dark early morning hours disappeared in a blast of adrenaline. It took only a couple minutes for Beckham to slip on his ACUs, grab his rifle, and say goodbye to Kate. He followed Horn down the stairs from the apartment to the street where three Humvees waited.

Beckham hopped into the back of the lead vehicle with Horn, and they took off.

"Where are these scouts?" Beckham asked.

"I'll let her explain," Horn said, nodding to a soldier in the front seat.

Rico turned to look at him, a shock of pink hair poking out from below her helmet. "Good to see you, Captain. I've been up all night helping with security detail."

Then she pointed at the driver, a man with sandy blond hair.

"This is Corporal Max Lindquist. He'll be on Team Reaper for the rest of the morning. We've been organizing tonight's scouting and security ops. Recon Sigma ran across some starving Variants about twenty minutes ago."

"You got us up for that?" Horn asked. "Can't they handle some—"

"There are Chimeras in the area, too," Rico said.

Beckham cursed under his breath. He had thought they might have a few more days to prepare the outpost for a potential attack. But hearing the beasts had come all the way down here to Houston dashed those hopes.

"Ruckley's team tracked them to an encampment," Rico said.

"So we're rolling in and carpet bombing them, right?" Horn asked. He rubbed his big hands together. "That's worth getting up before the ass crack of dawn."

"No, command wants one of them alive," Rico said.

"Jesus, command's never going to learn," Horn said.

Rico ignored him. "Since we have so much experience in the field, Jacobs wanted you to lead tonight's snatch-and-grab."

"You got a map of the area?"

Rico passed one back to Beckham. She leaned over her seat, circling the neighborhood where Ruckley had last reported their location and the Chimera encampment.

"Tell Ruckley to maintain her position," Beckham said. "The four of us in this Humvee are Reaper. Humvee two, Bravo. Three, Charlie." He laid out on the map where he wanted each Humvee to park and how they would approach the encampment to give each team clear firing lanes while surrounding the Chimeras.

Rico relayed it over the radio.

After another fifteen minutes of driving they pulled off the highway and wound through roads littered with abandoned cars. The other two Humvees peeled off down separate roads. They killed their headlights, and Lindquist pulled down his night vision goggles, slowing so the engine noise didn't give away their position.

When they finally parked behind a two-story house for cover, Beckham got out first, stepping out onto the pavement with his prosthetic blade. He dropped low immediately, signaling for Horn to take rearguard. Rico and Lindquist took the flanks, and together they prowled through the overgrown grass like sharks after prey.

They followed a creek, staying close to the grass for cover. According to the map, the waterway would take them straight to the camp.

If they had timed everything right, they would converge there the same time Bravo and Charlie did. Then with the help of Recon Sigma, they would ambush the Variants and Chimeras.

As they approached the target, Beckham paused. A park with a rusted playground and several picnic shelters protruded from the unkempt weeds. At one of those shelters, he noticed three Chimeras talking and sharing food.

Even from his vantage behind a thicket of trees and bushes, Beckham could hear the tearing of flesh and meat. He counted another four Variants circling eagerly around the Chimeras, waiting for a morsel.

Where were their lookouts? He didn't see any scouts or guards.

The Chimeras were smarter than this.

Rico knelt beside him, with Horn and Lindquist watching their backs. Across the park, in another backyard lined with trees, Beckham noticed four infrared tags in his NVGs. That was Bravo. To the east, he could see the IR tags glowing from Recon Sigma's NVGs from their position near an abandoned RV.

He didn't know which one, but one of those tags represented Timothy. He knew the young man would be fighting Variants again, but the thought of him facing even the deadlier Chimeras filled Beckham with dread.

Toward the west, he studied the lines of trees next to a pond. That was where Charlie was supposed to be. But no IR tags glowed.

Maybe the team was just slower or ran into some unexpected obstacles. But the fact that a Chimera and two Variants were missing, too, was not a good sign.

Beckham considered breaking radio silence to get a sitrep, but making any noise now, so close to the enemy, could ruin their cover.

Each second without seeing Charlie passed as its own agonizing eternity. The other team had to be out there. No one had called for assistance or reported any issues. He hadn't heard any gunshots either.

Another two minutes passed.

Horn suddenly pointed as two Chimeras appeared from between a couple houses. Each lugged a body over their shoulders. A pack of Variants followed on all fours, snapping and snarling at each other. Then came a second pair of the hybrid soldiers with two more human prisoners.

Beckham took his binoculars from his tac vest and pulled them up to his eyes, zooming in for a better look, confirming his worst fears.

"Son of a bitch, that's Charlie team," he said quietly.

The Chimeras carrying the dead soldiers dumped them on the ground and the Variants dove in for the feed. The two surviving Charlie soldiers squirmed to get away. One thrashed himself free from the grip of a Chimera, only to have his throat slashed.

The Thrall Variants surrounding the shelter dove into the fresh corpses, teeth and claws ripping into the dying soldier.

"We have to do something," Rico said.

The Chimeras tied up the last surviving soldier to a post of the shelter.

Horn wedged up next to Beckham with his M249 SAW, ready to let some lead fly. "Let me at 'em, boss."

One Chimera stuck its nose into the air, freezing, bloody entrails still dripping from its mouth. It sniffed, then signaled to the other monsters. The starving Thralls even stopped feeding for a moment.

Beckham knew this was their only chance to save the final survivor of team Charlie and capture a Chimera, but it would put them all at risk. A long moment passed, the tension nearly palpable as his team looked at him for orders. He squeezed the call button on his radio. "All teams, go!"

Horn practically jumped up to fire, tracer rounds splitting the darkness. The beasts scattered in all directions.

Reaper pushed forward through the tall grass, disappearing into the foliage. Beckham looked for the telltale shifting of blades that would show where the other Variants were. He listened for the clicking joints or growls.

A deep boom shook the ground, halting Beckham. Horn stopped firing for a beat.

"That came from Bravo's position," he said.

Gunshots barked from across the park, followed by the pained howl of a Variant. Beckham pushed through the grass, his vision blocked by the foliage. He took the team closer to the creek that they had initially followed.

That was when he felt it. A slight tug on his prosthetic like he'd run into a fishing line, providing just a modicum of resistance. Then he heard a whir, like a spring releasing.

"Get down!" he roared.

Beckham dropped to the ground, Rico diving next to him. Horn threw himself down onto the edge of the stream.

Lindquist was too slow.

A bounding mine launched from where it had been planted, spraying shrapnel in a wide disc about five feet off the ground. The shrapnel cut into Lindquist's arms and chest, tearing into his neck. He didn't have time to scream before his body hit the ground.

Almost as soon as the mine exploded, Beckham heard a roar to his left and rolled just in time to bring his rifle up. A Variant burst from the grass, claws extended, sucker lips popping. A trigger pull peppered the beast with three rounds.

Gunshots exploded around the park along with the roars of other Variants. Horn pulled on Lindquist, trying to drag him to safety, but the man was dead, his head practically severed from his neck.

"Leave him," Beckham said.

"Chimeras are moving!" Ruckley's voice burst over the radio. "They're splitting up!"

Beckham's heart raced. This wasn't just a chance for the Chimeras to feed. It was a damned trap. Things were quickly falling apart, and he couldn't help but think of Timothy. He couldn't let the young man die out here.

Other voices over the radio cried for help, reporting more men down as the Variants tore into the teams. Gunshots were interspersed with the boom of anti-personnel landmines.

Beckham recalled Outpost Turkey Creek and all those other frontier outposts that had secured their lands against Variant attacks using mines. Now those weapons were being used against them.

"Reaper, Recon Sigma One here!" Ruckley said. "Variants headed your way!"

Beckham stood, trying to watch for monsters and mines all at once.

"Horn, Rico, on me!" he yelled.

They advanced into the darkness, following the creek. Another two Variants exploded from the grass around them. Rico shot one, and the second slammed against Horn. The big man clenched his fingers around the Variant's neck as the beast snapped at him.

He let out a roar, cranking back the creature's neck, followed by a resounding crack. The creature went limp in his grip, and he dropped it to the ground.

Rifle up, Beckham went into the clearing where the picnic shelters were. Toward their south, two Chimeras engaged in a gun battle with Bravo. Recon Sigma had descended from the RV and were at the edge of the park. He spotted Timothy next to Ruckley, both still alive and unhurt.

Thank God, Beckham thought.

Beckham spotted two Chimeras sprinting northward, straight toward his position. The ghastly soldiers saw him, too, and brought up their rifles, firing. He threw himself to the side as bullets stitched the ground, kicking up a spray of mud.

Another roar sounded behind them as Variants pounced at Rico and Horn again.

Beckham kept his focus on the Chimeras. He centered his sights on the first Chimera and pulled the trigger. Rounds punched into the half-man's chest, blood spraying out the exit wounds.

The second beast leapt over the new corpse, firing wildly mid-jump. Beckham had to duck, pressing himself into the side of the creek as the Chimera retreated northward on the other side of the creek.

"Chimeras down!" a voice from Bravo reported. "Engaging Variants now!"

That left this single running Chimera alive.

"I'm going after him!" Beckham shouted as Horn and Rico battled a pair of Variants.

He ran as hard as he could, his prosthetic threatening to slip on the muddy shore. The Chimera turned back only to let off another series of wild shots.

Beckham pushed harder, accelerating, but the creature was far faster. He stopped and aimed his rifle, aiming for a leg.

The shot hit the back of its knee, sending the half-man tumbling.

Beckham kept his rifle up as he approached. The Chimera tried to drag itself away.

Pulling out his combat knife, Beckham ran toward the injured monster. The mutant creature turned and sliced with clawed hands as he approached but he managed to drive the blade hard into his shoulder.

The Chimera roared and slammed its skull into Beckham's nose, knocking off his night vision optics.

Dazed, he fell back, warm blood oozing out of his nostrils. He tried to scramble away to give himself some room to recover.

Footsteps sounded, followed by snarling and a crack.

Vision blurred, Beckham pulled out his pistol and swung it toward the noise, ready to pull the trigger and kill the Chimera.

"Boss!" Horn yelled. "Don't shoot!"

The stars cleared and Beckham saw his friend in the moonlight, wrestling the Chimera on the ground. Rico joined them to help secure the creature. Timothy ran over a minute later, and relief swelled through Beckham when he saw the young man.

"Area is clear," Timothy said, panting.

Beckham put a hand on his nose. "Damn, that hurt."

"At least it's not broken." Horn chuckled. "Kate wouldn't be happy about that."

A little laughter was a good thing, but it didn't last. They had lost a lot of good soldiers tonight and were returning home with fewer men and women to defend what was left of the Allied States.

***

Azrael marched down the long corridor of the Citadel, the command center of the Land of the New Gods. Red tendrils of webbing covered the glass walls like oversized spiderwebs. Scions walked up and down the hall, and a few Variants crawled between them, some traversing the walls or ceilings, using the webbing as handholds.

Across the webbing, cocoons writhed, filled with prey the Variants or his Scions had brought back to feed the organic communication network.

Azrael took his time admiring the ecosystem on his way to the throne room. Two Scions bowed, then stepped aside so he could enter what had once been a lecture hall.

In his past life, he had attended a multitude of scientific presentations here. This had been a place of technological progress. A place where the greatest minds in the world had gathered to exchange ideas and build a brighter future for humanity.

The atmosphere had changed significantly.

Long ropes of webbing hung off the ceiling beams nearly three stories high. Two gigantic masterminds sat on either side of the stage at the back of the hall, their massive pink bodies appeared like brains that escaped from enormous skulls.

Tendrils stretched from their folds and into the network surrounding the throne room. All along the walls, Scions stood guard. Each with the face and gray flesh of a Variant, but the burning intelligence of human beings behind their golden, reptilian eyes.

Azrael ascended the steps to the stage, adjusted his black cloak, and took his seat at a throne made from the red vines of the organic webbing. Within the throne, a few humans were cocooned and imprisoned in the crimson tendrils, their low moans muffled by vines snaking through their mouths. Those insolent animals were now batteries for his network.

It was all a fitting reminder that he alone was the greatest achievement of nature and science, a being who would literally and figuratively sit atop all these mortals. He created and altered life. Death was just one of his instruments.

Yes, this place had once been a place of learning, the pinnacle of humanity's innovation.

The labs within this facility had housed the development of some of humanity's greatest achievements—and weapons.

Now he had created the greatest one. It was only right that this place served as the capitol to the New Gods.

He curled his clawed fingers around the armrest of his throne and surveyed the room. All the chairs that had once been lined in neat rows were covered by vines. The loud, gasping breathing of the masterminds filled the place, and their rotten stench swirled amid the odor of the vines.

A skinny silhouette appeared at the entrance to the throne room. One of the human faithful.

"Enter," Azrael said.

Murphy, an old doctor wearing a white coat walked forward with a slight hunch. His fingers were crooked and knotted in arthritis, but still he dropped to one knee when he reached the throne. "Prophet, I'm sorry to disturb you, but I have news about the Northeast Operation."

Azrael grunted in disgust at the memory of what had happened. The Northeast Operation was supposed to have ended the war by launching the nuke from Mount

Katahdin. But the former leader of the infamous Team Ghost and some other heinous traitors had managed to destroy the base and sabotage the weapon.

"Speak," said Azrael.

"Our Scion scouts discovered a survivor at Mount Katahdin after the heretics sabotaged the base. He was barely alive when the airlift brought him here, but I managed to save him."

"Save him?"

"Yes," Murphy said, his eyes finally rising to meet Azrael's. "And I made him better. Really, I had no choice. His human body was too damaged."

"Did you give him my latest version of VX-102?"

"Yes, Prophet."

"Good. I want to see how well the new formula reacts to the human genome."

Murphy nodded and backed up slowly, never rising above his hunching bow until he had left the throne room.

While Azrael was pleased with the old man's work, there was another who was responsible for this failure in the Northeast Operation whose work he had been less fond of.

"Bring me the general," Azrael rumbled, his words echoing in the vast chamber.

The masterminds both quivered, their fingers twitching and curling, sending signals through the communication network.

Minutes later the general squeezed through the main entrance, bowing like the old man had. His cloak flowed behind him, and he kept his crocodile-snout aimed toward the ground. The bulging muscles along his arms rippled against his flesh, and his massive claws scraped the floor with every step.

"Prophet…" the Alpha Variant said, his voice coming out in a choking rasp.

He was a prime specimen of unrestrained evolution and adaptation, thanks to the impact of VX-99 on his body. His physique was that of a powerful predator, and his aggression on the battlefield had no match. But he was also a glaring example of why Azrael had worked so hard to better blend human intelligence with the body-altering epigenetic changes in the original bioweapons that had warped humanity.

This creature had too many faults. He could barely choke out his own words, and now Azrael feared the general's mind wasn't as developed and intelligent as he'd once thought.

Azrael had trusted this beast with a mission that he realized now was only truly suited for one of the New Gods. One of his creations. Azrael stood from his throne and stepped down the short stairs from the stage to the floor where the general knelt.

"You," Azrael said, drawing closer.

The general, still towering above Azrael even as he knelt, flinched. "It was—"

"You ran like a scared rat," Azrael interrupted, keeping his voice calm. "You should have stayed and fought to the death like a wolf."

The general kept his head bowed. "I'm sorry—"

Azrael snapped his fingers, summoning red tendrils along the floor that rose like cobras. The vines snapped around the general's wrists and legs. They pulled him into the air until he was suspended three meters off the ground.

"The Allied States should already be ashes and

President Ringgold should be dead," Azrael said. He let out a snort. "For nearly a decade, I've been patient, living in the shadows while creating this new world and now I have to wait longer..." He looked at one of the masterminds controlling the tendrils. "Tighter."

The webbing pulled harder on the general, and the monstrous variant groaned, his bones snapping, popping out of their joints.

"You failed, despite all evidence that you should have succeeded," Azrael said. "You defied every probability analysis I ran. It's as though you intended to lose. You sicken me."

Azrael looked at the other mastermind and made a simple waving gesture with his claws.

Red tendrils wormed into the general's mouth and nostril, squirming through his body like parasitic worms. His agonized scream was muffled by the vines stretching down his throat.

Azrael snapped his claws again, and the vines retracted suddenly, letting the general's joints pop back into place. The monster fell to the ground, landing with a sickening smack, then slowly pushed himself back up to one knee, his huge chest heaving.

Blood dribbled out his nostrils.

Azrael approached him, then put his claws under the general's long chin, lifting his face to catch his gaze.

"You will not fail me again, will you?"

"No, Prophet, I will... die before... I fail you again." Each word came out forced, rasping.

Azrael gestured to the two masterminds at either corner of the throne room. "We have detected human interference within our network. They are trying to sabotage our communications."

"Let me find them," the general choked out. "Let me prove myself…"

Azrael retreated to his throne.

"Yes, find these humans, and bring me Captain Reed Beckham," he said. "Or next time I will pull off your limbs myself and feed you to the Thralls."

— 5 —

The light snowfall came down more steadily over the wilderness outside Banff. Cold wind cut into Dohi's parka, finding every entryway to scrape over his flesh. His fingers were beginning to numb, and every breath of air seemed to freeze the inside of his lungs.

He wouldn't let Mother Nature convince him to turn back though.

With the rest of Teams Ghost and Spearhead on his tail, he had only one singular thought: Follow the bears.

They had to figure out why they were organizing, especially if someone was using them for an impending attack on the Canadian base.

Dohi and the others were perched at the rim of the ravine, watching the bears follow a frozen stream nearly twenty meters below to the west. The beasts were heading directly northwest toward the Bow River.

"Where the hell are they going?" Toussaint asked.

"No idea," Fitz whispered back. "That's why we need to follow them."

"I've been in this area long enough to tell you when a blizzard's coming," Daugherty said. "Even the best tracker can't follow his prey when he's frozen solid and buried under a ten-foot snow drift."

"As much as I like solving mysteries, I like staying alive and killing bears more," Sherman said. "Let's just kill these ugly assholes and be done with it."

Dohi lifted his binos and stared as far down the ravine as he could see, trying to find some clue as to where the monsters were headed.

"Dohi, what do you think?" Fitz asked.

Neilson was right, and as much as he hated to admit it, sometimes there was no advantage to being stubborn.

"The weather's going to make it impossible to follow them," Dohi said. "There's no point in going on."

"If we're calling off the pursuit, I'd rather take these beasts down tonight so they're not tomorrow's problem," Neilson said.

"Exactly," Sherman said. "We didn't follow these guys all the way here for nothing. Let's make this count."

Fitz nodded. "You've got a point, but damn, I really want to know what they're doing."

"Weather is shit, boss," Ace said. "We've got the jump on them now. Better than them ambushing our guys later."

"True, but..."

"He's right," Dohi said. "We really should take them down now, while we can."

The bears were still marching in a line at the bottom of the ravine against the unrelenting snowfall.

"Okay, let's do this quick, but safe, and then get our asses back to base," Fitz ordered. "Ghost will run along the ravine to get ahead of the pack. Spearhead, you stay at their rear in case they turn tail. Radio silence from here on out until I give the go ahead."

Dohi took off between the trees, taking the Delta Force operators slightly away from the ridge to stay out of the bears' sight.

Once he judged they had run far enough ahead, he held up his fist. He, Fitz, and Ace then dropped low and crawled back to the edge of the ravine.

Sure enough the bears lumbered along next to the frozen stream, nearly one-hundred yards away. Dohi peered down the lip of the ravine to see the IR tags from Spearhead's night-vision goggles as they too watched from their vantage points nearly fifty feet up from the bears. Spearhead was about twenty yards to the rear of the monsters.

Their positions would not get much better than this. The giant creatures had nowhere to hide along the stream except for a few lone trees and large rocks. But even that shelter was too meager for the hulking monsters.

Dohi raised his rifle and sighted up the first monster. Ace and Fitz mirrored his movements, each picking their targets. Everyone had already palmed in their magazines with armor-piercing rounds. It was their best and only shot of tearing through the thick hides of the beasts.

"Execute," Fitz whispered over the radio.

Dohi squeezed his trigger. Rounds lanced into the chest of the lead bear, punching into its flesh. The creature staggered.

Other suppressed shots echoed from up and down the ravine as the operators joined in the fusillade, painting their targets with the AP rounds.

The bear Dohi had shot stumbled forward when more shots stabbed into its flank. But the big beasts were like walking battleships, huge muscled limbs covered in dense fur. They weren't so easily dispatched. The monster let out a vicious roar that rivaled the bark of gunfire, and its eyes found Dohi.

It charged, opening a mouth full of curved fangs.

Three more bullets crashed through its mouth and forehead, breaking through bone and puncturing one of its eyes. The monster tripped and slid through the snow, pushing up a mound, steam rising from the fresh holes in its still body.

Fitz and Ace worked to take down another, and the Canadians began mopping up the monsters at the rear of the pack with headshots.

Dohi found his next target and unleashed a few controlled bursts into the monster's side to get it to turn, then he sighted the head and fired.

The massive beast galloped on all fours straight for its attackers.

Dohi managed to take down the creature, and it slid across the ice. Another bear leapt over its dead brethren, then scrambled up the side of the ravine. Packed snow gave way under its claws, and it slid back to the rocky bank of the creek.

He fired again and again as the monster tried to barrel up the side of the ravine. A well-aimed round buried into an eye socket, and the creature collapsed, slipping back down over the ice, leaving a trail of crimson.

The last two made it further up, their claws finding purchase in the rock and ice, pulling themselves ever higher and closer to Team Ghosts and Spearhead.

They were nearly on Spearhead, just a few feet from the lip of the ravine. In seconds, they would be within striking distance. Spearhead fired desperately at them, but the thick hide of the beasts slowed the damage being done to them. Desperation and rage fueled them.

Dohi adjusted his aim, sighting up one of the monsters with blood dripping down its side. He fired at the skull and took off the jaw in the blast of rounds. It fell backward, crashing into the last creature.

The two beasts tumbled back toward the floor of the

ravine, cracking against rock on the way down.

A final gunshot echoed and faded away. Dohi listened for the sounds of other howling Variants in the distance, waiting to see if something else would attack in response to the commotion.

He heard nothing except for the quiet of the falling snow.

"Clear," Neilson reported.

"Clear," Fitz said. He waited a beat, then added, "Let's head back."

The accelerating snowfall was beginning to bury the dead bears by the time Ghost caught back up to Spearhead.

"We aren't going to make it back up the way we came," Neilson said.

Daugherty nodded. "Hiking straight uphill in a snowstorm like this is suicide."

"What do you propose?" Fitz asked.

"We can head north until we hit Bow River, then follow it back to base. It'll be a hell of a lot easier than trying to climb straight up the mountain, and it'll save us time."

"Sounds good to me," Fitz said.

They began their trek back toward Banff. Dohi checked his watch under his thick sleeve. By the time they made it back to base, it would be morning.

They marched as fast as they could through the increasingly deep snow. Dohi's muscles burned with the effort to push through it. Neilson had been right. If they had continued following the bears, they would've been stranded in the arctic conditions.

For another hour they pushed through the ice and snow.

"Not too much longer," Neilson said.

"Thank, God," Ace said. "I got to take a shit."

Dohi noticed something different about the path ahead. He held up a fist and the team paused. Then he ducked down into a hunch and pushed through the snow about twenty yards through the trees toward the south.

Ghost and Spearhead were not the only ones who had planned on following the river.

In front of him, long swathes of snow had been pushed aside as if a group of people had come marching through. Given the intensity of the snowfall, it hadn't been long since these people had passed.

Dohi hurried back to join Ghost and Spearhead, lungs burning from the frigid air.

"What's up?" Fitz asked.

"Looks like someone was here." Dohi panted. "Maybe… maybe a group of ten people or so. Are there other patrols out here?"

Neilson shook his head. "Let me find out." He called command on his radio. "Command, Spearhead One. Are there other patrols in our vicinity?"

"Negative, Spearhead One. All other units were recalled about an hour ago."

Dohi directed his NVGs at Fitz. Someone else was out here, and judging by the direction, they too were headed straight for Banff.

"Command, be advised, we found tracks," Neilson said. "And they're headed your way."

***

"You're too exhausted," Leslie said. "Time to let someone else take over communicating with the network."

Kate groaned. She had only managed a few hours of sleep. When Beckham had been called to the field, she knew she had missed her chance at rest. Instead, she had gone directly back to the tunnel entrance in the Houston hospital just outside the outpost gates.

Her staff was here now too, and Leslie had taken the chair, ready to connect. Ron reluctantly held a writhing tendril of webbing at the back of her neck while Sammy watched.

A team of soldiers stood guard over the research site, several of them watching.

"You don't have to do this," Kate said. "I'm fine, really."

"You can't be the only one," Leslie said. "Someone else needs to learn how to communicate with the network like you do."

Kate wasn't sure what the long-term ramifications of connecting to the network like this were, but inwardly, she was glad Leslie had offered to help. All she knew was that each time she did, electricity seemed to pour through the vines of tissue and into her. From her basic studies, the tendrils acted like electrodes against the skin, reading signals passed between her nerves and sending electric signals back into her tissue as feedback.

"When I've learned, we can teach Ron, too," Leslie said. "That way we all share the burden."

Ron looked to the side as if he wasn't sure about that.

"It's okay," Leslie said with a smile.

Kate couldn't help feeling protective over the slightly younger lab tech.

"When you're ready," Sammy said, "I can initiate the connection."

"Let's do it," Leslie said.

Sammy pressed a button on her keyboard, and the tendril went wild, adhering to the back of Leslie's neck. Leslie's eyes closed, and her face set in a grimace.

"Is she okay?" Kate asked.

Sammy nodded. "This is exactly what happens to you each time we—"

Voices echoed down into the parking garage, and a few of the soldiers standing on guard perked, shouldering their rifles.

Kate walked over to one of the guards. "What's going on?"

One of the soldiers on guard put his radio to his ear. "Sounds like Captain Beckham and the scout teams are back. They took some casualties."

"Is Reed okay? Did they say Captain Beckham was hurt?"

"I, uh, don't—"

Kate looked back to Sammy and Ron. "Take care of Leslie."

"Wait, Doctor Lovato!" the soldier said running after her.

Kate took the stairs two at a time with the guard following. She didn't stop until she got to the hospital. Combat medics ran down the hall with soldiers on stretchers. Voices called out orders and requests for help.

Ruckley and Timothy were the first familiar faces she saw. They were helping another soldier whose wrist was covered in bandages. A fourth soldier Kate didn't recognize was with them.

Timothy caught her eyes as he helped his teammate

into a chair where medics began examining his wounds.

"Beckham's all right," Timothy called to her. "Horn, too. They're just behind us."

Kate didn't breathe a sigh of relief until she saw Beckham, Horn, and Rico enter a few seconds later with a prisoner. An entire phalanx of soldiers surrounded them, and she quickly saw why.

The prisoner wasn't a collaborator—it was a Chimera.

Beckham limped away from the group when he saw Kate. He was covered in grime, smelling of sweat and blood, but she didn't care. They met in a long embrace.

Horn joined them, wiping his face with the back of his big hand.

"How bad is it?" Kate asked.

"Six of ours dead, and three injured," Beckham said.

"How?" Kate asked.

"They set a trap," Beckham said, shaking his head.

"I don't understand," Kate said. "We haven't intercepted any messages that they were planning an attack on Houston."

"That's why we brought him here."

Kate watched as the soldiers led the creature into a room and shut the door.

"Rico, call Jacobs and tell him we've got the prisoner secure," Beckham said. "I want to have a talk with the bastard while we wait to see what Jacobs wants to do with him."

"I was hoping you'd let me be part of this 'talk'," Rico said, eyes narrowed.

"Me, too," Horn said. His barreled chest expanded as he took in a deep breath. "A talk he won't forget."

"Go tell Jacobs we've got him first," Beckham said.

Rico left, and Beckham started toward the room where

they had the beast secured.

"Wait," Kate said. "I want to watch."

"It's not safe, Kate," Horn said.

"I need to know more about these creatures," Kate said. "Besides, there's just one of him and plenty of us."

Beckham and Horn exchanged a glance.

"Fine," Beckham said.

They went into the room where three soldiers had bound the beast to a chair.

The Chimera glared at them with his golden eyes, blood dribbling from the corner of his mouth. His muscles tensed across his scarred body. Flat slitted nostrils flared with each breath. The sour lemon scent of a Variant drifted off his sweaty flesh.

Kate had to remind herself that this twisted body contained the brain of an intelligent being.

"We're going to ask you a few questions, and you're going to answer," Beckham said. "Nod if you understand."

Surprisingly, the beast did just that.

"What in the hell were you doing outside Houston?" Beckham asked.

The Chimera said nothing, pressing his thin wormy lips tightly closed.

"Hey, asshole, do you not understand English now?" Horn said.

He reached into his vest and pulled out brass knuckles that he slipped over his fist.

"Know what these are?" Horn asked. "I pulled 'em off a collaborator. They'll make your ugly face even uglier."

"Why were you outside Houston?" Beckham entreated.

The Chimera said nothing.

Beckham nodded at Horn, and the big man let loose a haymaker of a punch that would have laid any normal man flat on his back. It connected with a sickening crunch that made Kate flinch, and she had to look away momentarily.

When she faced the Chimera again, she saw him staring defiantly back up at Horn and Beckham. Blood gushed from the split above his eye.

He hissed at them. "Why would I tell you anything?"

"Depends on how much pain you can endure," Horn said, shaking out his fist. "Because that was just a warning shot."

Beckham tried another question. "How many other groups are out there?"

Again, the Chimera didn't answer, and again Horn whacked the creature in the face.

Kate cringed at the crack.

The interrogation continued, but no matter how they tried to convince the half-man, half-monster to talk, he said nothing. The guards in the room watched with their rifles cradled.

A knock on the door sounded, breaking Kate from her trance watching the beast, and she opened it. Commander Jacobs and Rico stepped inside with another four men.

"I'll take it from here," Jacobs said. He nodded at his men.

The soldiers started untying the ropes on the Chimera and placed heavy steel shackles over his limbs to prevent their prisoner from running. They prodded the Chimera to stand and forced him to shuffle toward the lobby door.

Kate wasn't sure what the commander planned to do with the Chimera, but she doubted he would have any better luck.

"Wait a second, sir," Kate said. "I have another way we can get some information from him."

Jacobs ordered his men taking the Chimera outside to pause. "What's that, Doctor Lovato?"

"He might not be willing to talk, but that won't stop any analyses I can run on his tissue."

The Chimera glared at her with golden, inquisitive eyes.

She decided to step into the hall to tell Jacobs her plan.

"Sedate him and let me take a few biopsies," Kate continued. "I can analyze his blood and other tissues to figure out how beasts like this came into existence."

Jacobs looked back at the door, then shrugged. "Make this quick."

Kate retreated to the lab that Jacobs had set up for them on the second floor of the hospital and returned with a handful of plastic vials and needles. The creature was already out from the sedatives when she returned, but she still approached his scarred body cautiously.

"Be ready for anything," Beckham said to the soldiers standing guard.

Six of the men surrounded the metal table, checking the straps around the creature's legs and arms.

Beckham and Horn flanked Kate as she slowly walked up to him with her biopsy needles. She had a mask on now, but she could still smell the awful scent. After she prepared the first needle, Horn cut off the Chimera's coat and shirt, revealing his twisted body. She was amazed and sickened at the amount of work it must have taken to design such an abomination.

Part of her couldn't help but feel pity for this thing.

She wondered if it was more man than monster. But that was a question for another time.

When she found a good spot on the arm, she jabbed a biopsy needle into the flesh. Piece by piece, she took more tissue samples, depositing them into the plastic vials. Then she used another needle and tube for a blood sample. Finding an accessible vein was no problem with the beast's vessels pushing up against his gray flesh.

"That's it," she said when she finished the blood sample.

"Good job," Beckham said.

"Gross shit," Horn muttered.

She took the samples back to the laboratory. They were just small hunks of flesh and muscle and blood, but it helped inspire newfound confidence. Not only were they now capable of tapping into the New Gods' communications through the organic network, but she had the first usable samples of Chimera flesh.

With these, she could unlock the secrets to the origins of these monsters. Maybe those revelations would even lead them to the Prophet she kept hearing about on the network.

Either way, Kate was certain the small plastic vials with bits of gore she held now would only improve the Allied States' chance of finally turning this war around before it was too late.

"If it's not already too late," she whispered.

— 6 —

Early morning light permeated the dense cloud cover, giving the world a slightly gray glow. Cold still seeped through Fitz's body. He fought the fatigue in his muscles and the biting cold. Thoughts of Rico helped him carry on.

Hopefully Ghost would be sent south soon, and he could finally see her again.

At least the snowfall had temporarily abated. The brightening sun helped him see the tracks of whoever had been following the river before them.

Dohi examined the trail while Fitz surveyed the snow between the trees. It looked as if a couple platoons had marched through here. By the looks of the prints, they were human.

"Jesus," Ace said. "Who the hell are these guys?"

"How many do you think we're dealing with?" Fitz asked.

"Thirty, maybe more," Dohi replied coldly.

They followed the tangled tracks to a clearing in the forest that led to a frozen lake already covered in snow. Once again Dohi was on point, but the footprints were deep enough to lead the way.

Ace and Fitz followed close behind Dohi with Spearhead on the rearguard. They crossed so many intertwining trails that he figured they would have run into them by dumb luck, even if they hadn't found the first set.

Fitz motioned to Dohi to pick up the pace as they continued through the forest, following all the winding paths, until they reached the edge of a frozen lake. Mountains loomed beyond the lake, with pine trees covered in white, looking as if they were giant stalagmites.

The trail they had been following continued over the snow-covered ice and straight toward the opposite side of the lake nearly a half-mile away. Fitz and his team remained in the shadows of the trees as they surveyed their quarry. He lifted his binos to where Dohi pointed.

"My God," Fitz whispered. "Looks like we found where those bears were going."

While most of the contacts were sheltered in the forest, he estimated at least sixty or seventy that he could see, all wearing white coats or camouflage and carrying weapons. They were too far for him to tell if they were Chimeras or collaborators.

Between those soldiers, he saw another two dozen bears. They wore giant black collars, visible against their white fur. Not unlike the ones Fitz had heard the Thrall Variants had worn outside Outpost Portland.

"They've come for Corrin, haven't they?" Neilson asked.

"Hell if we know," Ace said. "Maybe they're just pissed after Seattle."

Toussaint eyed them suspiciously. "Did they follow you from there?"

"We flew," Ace said. "How would they follow us?"

"I'm sure they have their ways," Daugherty said.

"Or maybe this is the beginning of the invasion in the North," Dohi said. "We warned the general about this."

"Doesn't matter why they're here," Fitz said. "Neilson, we should call it in."

"I count twenty-five bears," Dohi said. "Maybe seventy soldiers, but it looks like there are far more in the woods. It's too hard to see from this far."

"These assholes came in right during the storm, right when we pulled our scouts back," Daugherty said.

Sherman leaned over to Neilson and Fitz, then pointed to a spot just north of the enemy. Groups of soldiers looked to be checking over their weapons. Others were lining up as if getting ready to march.

A pit formed in his stomach. These people looked like they were preparing to move, and he feared he knew where they were headed.

Neilson finished reporting the enemy count that Dohi had provided.

"Spearhead One, can you repeat?" replied comms officer back at HQ.

"Command, this is Ghost One. Hostiles are preparing to move. I repeat, preparing to move. You've got to prepare the defenses. Tell General Kamer immediately."

"Roger that, Ghost One."

"Let's pick some of 'em off," Sherman said. "We took out the bears. We can thin this herd, too."

"Son, you're getting ahead of yourself," Ace said. "We killed *six* bears. There's damn near an extra twenty of those beasts over there, plus however many other assholes waiting in the woods."

"Want me to get closer for better numbers?" Dohi asked.

"No," Fitz said. "We stay here for a minute. I need to think."

The most direct path to get a better view was across

the open expanse of the lake. Otherwise they would have to circle around, which Fitz estimated would take the better part of an hour or more to do without being seen.

By then the enemy might already have started their attack. Fitz would rather be helping Banff survive than be stuck out here, half-buried in snow.

"We're better off going back to base," Fitz said. "They're going to need all the help they can get."

Somewhere across the lake, the roar of a bear shook over the ice. It was answered by several more of the bloodthirsty beasts.

Maybe it was already too late.

"Dohi, lead us back to base," Fitz said.

They began the trek southeast, jogging through the snow. They didn't have time to cover their tracks with how quickly the snow was falling. Fitz merely hoped they made it to base before the enemy did.

His breath plumed out in an icy mist as he ran.

Every step strained his already agonized muscles. They had been tracking through the woods all night, and now even the adrenaline of seeing the enemy could not assuage the exhaustion seeping through his injured body, conspiring to slow their retreat.

A gunshot suddenly cracked into the night, the sound ricocheting between the trees.

Fitz dropped low instinctively, his rifle rising immediately. The others sheltered behind the trees. More shots exploded from somewhere to their east, bullets punching into the wood. Bark sprayed over Fitz.

"Agh!" Sherman cried. He fell backward into the snow. Neilson began to crawl to him but more bullets tore into their position. Sherman jerked from the impacts, and the snow around him began to turn red.

Fitz swung his rifle around toward the gunfire. Between the shadows of the snow-covered trees, he saw two men or Chimeras—he couldn't be sure. All he knew was they had his team pinned down.

"Dohi, cover me!" Fitz commanded.

Dohi put down a blanket of suppressing fire and Fitz hobbled to a better position, a few yards out from his team. He had a clear line of sight now into the flanks of his enemy. Both were still focused on the Canadians.

Fitz opened fire. The first soldier went down with a yelp of pain. The second started to turn, but Fitz caught him too. Blood sprayed from the man as bullets riddled his side and neck. His head flipped backward as he fell into the snow, and for the first time, Fitz saw the face of the scouts who had caught up to them.

His targets were monsters, but they weren't Chimeras. They were men. Collaborators.

More gunfire rang out, somewhere just south of them. Fitz adjusted his aim and fired. Bullets pounded against the tree trunks where he spotted three more collaborators. They wore dingy gray and white clothes, a patchwork of military-issue uniforms and old fatigues that looked as though they had grabbed them from an apocalyptic thrift shop.

One of them went down, but the other two ducked behind cover.

Fitz couldn't get a clean shot.

"Ace, flank them!" he called out over the comm.

Ace acknowledged the command with a curt affirmative.

Fitz trained his rifle on the three collaborators and squeezed his trigger, letting out a long burst. That gave Ace just enough time to rush to a new position between the trees. He opened fire and caught all three collaborators unaware.

They crumpled into the snow, steam rising off their still forms.

"Clear!" Dohi yelled.

"Clear!" Neilson replied.

They had killed the last of the collaborator scouts, but the short battle felt nothing like a victory. Toussaint and Neilson knelt next to Sherman, checking his pulse as if by some miracle he might still be alive. The vacant stare told Fitz that Sherman was gone.

Neilson started to lift Sherman with Toussaint's help when a chorus of distant howls erupted into the night. There was no time to move the man.

"Run!" Fitz yelled.

***

The odor of death still lingered in Timothy's nostrils from the brief battle in the Houston suburbs. Late-morning sunlight bathed the neighborhood. He had thought that after killing those Chimera scouts, his time outside the gates of Outpost Houston was done for the day. But he was wrong.

Once again, he found himself in the neighborhood where the battle had taken place with Ruckley, Wong, and Boyd.

This time, they were not alone in the ruined neighborhood. Four other teams of soldiers swept the fields and parks nearby for more landmines. They might be able to risk the additional abandoned explosives, but the team wasn't here just to look for them. Their secondary mission was to search for more intel, anything that the dead Chimeras might've left behind.

Most of the men had bitched about coming back out here, but Timothy thought about what would happen when the outpost was safe again and expanded back into the rest of Houston. Maybe it was too soon, but he imagined a future where he and Tasha grew up down here and raised a family. How horrific would it be if one of their children wandered into this park, looking for a place to play without knowing what terrible traps were waiting just beneath the soil?

Wong swept a metal detector to locate any more planted mines. Timothy, Ruckley, and Boyd covered him while he searched in silence. They hadn't slept much. Everyone was on edge because of the attack and the potential for more mines.

It didn't take long for the metal detector to beep.

Timothy froze, holding his breath.

Wong bent down and picked up a spent shell casing, then flipped it to Boyd. The larger man stuffed it into a bag.

"So many false positives," Timothy said. "This is going to take forever."

"Better it takes forever now than the split second when one of these explodes again on a patrol, or a kid," Boyd said. "If those Variants come back, I'd rather face 'em knowing we found all these things instead of trying to tiptoe around, hoping we don't explode."

A shout echoed across the park from near a rusted playground.

"Mine!" a soldier called, marking his position with a small plastic flag.

An explosive ordnance disposal (EOD) team rushed over from their position and began the delicate process of setting up a controlled explosive to detonate the mine. After they ensured everyone nearby was far enough away, the EOD team detonated the mine with a resonating thud, dirt and grass chunks puffing into the air.

Wong continued waving the detector over the grass. Timothy followed cautiously, stopping when his boots slurped over a mound of what he thought was mud. He looked down to find a sticky hunk of Variant flesh.

Slowly he roved his rifle over the empty houses and tall grass around the perimeter of the park. A few birds called out, their morning songs ringing in the stillness of the early morning.

The humidity began to climb with the temperature as the sun crawled into the sky. The resulting swampy smells made breathing a nasty chore.

Over and over, the team found spent bullet casings and other pieces of metal detritus that had ended up buried here. When the detector beeped again for after what felt like the thousandth time, Timothy clenched up, bored but still on guard.

Wong handed Boyd the detector and knelt for a better look.

"Shit, I think it's a mine." He stood and pointed at the spot.

The EOD team took control of the area and sent Timothy, Ruckley, Boyd, and Wong back a safe distance. Outside the park, groups of soldiers stood guard, watching for any threats.

"What the hell were those things doing here last night?" Timothy muttered.

"Scouting our defenses probably," Ruckley said.

"Or maybe on their way back from doing that," Wong said.

"You think they were already watching Houston?" Timothy asked. "Do they know what we're doing in Galveston?"

"Relax," Ruckley said. She patted him on the back. "Captain Beckham will figure out what they're planning."

The EOD team backed away from the mine that Wong had found, clearing a wide enough space to detonate it safely.

One of the men shouted, "Fire in the hole!"

Another loud bang tossed a cloud of dirt into the air. The smell of hot metal drifted from the blast site.

"Clear," said the same soldier.

"You heard him," Ruckley said. "Get to work."

Wong picked up the metal detector again and started surveying the area where they had left off. The work was slow-going and tedious, and Timothy almost resented the effort. He would rather be out on patrol, searching for new signs of Chimeras or collaborators.

Ruckley was right. There would be more.

"Something else is bothering me," Timothy said. "Why would they send Chimeras? Why not just a group of collaborators?"

"I think you and I both know why," she answered.

"They're closing in for the final blow."

Ruckley confirmed the guess with a nod. The New Gods were constantly ahead of them.

The metal detector went off again, and Timothy halted.

"What is this?" Wong asked. He handed the detector off to Boyd again, before dropping to a crouch.

Timothy looked over his shoulder at a metal cylinder nestled in the grass.

"Looks like a smoke grenade," Boyd said.

"That ain't a smoke grenade," Ruckley said.

Timothy noticed their position was ten yards from the picnic shelter where they had first seen the Chimera scouts camped out.

Boyd called over the EOD team.

One of the techs squinted at it, stroking his graying beard.

"Know what it is?" Wong asked.

The man stared, then gestured for everyone to move back. "I think it's some sort of gas grenade."

"So what?" Boyd asked. "Tear gas isn't the worst thing in the world."

"We don't know what's in that grenade," Ruckley said. "Could be tear gas, but we've never seen these monsters use nonlethal weapons. For all we know it could be some kind of chemical agent they planned to lob into base."

Timothy shuddered. "After what we saw in Mount Katahdin, I'd bet you're right."

Ruckley squinted at the canister. "Maybe it contains a bioweapon. An engineered disease. God only knows."

"Now I hope it's just tear gas," Wong said. "You guys are freaking me out."

"Whatever it is, if the New Gods sent Chimeras to deliver them, it's got to be bad," Timothy said.

Boyd whistled. "Real fucking bad."

"Get it secured," Ruckley ordered. "We need to get this back to the science team."

By the time Teams Ghost and Spearhead returned to base, Banff was already in a state of chaos. Late morning light bled through the dense cloud cover over the Fairmont Banff Springs hotel.

Dohi ran toward the first steel-panel gate outside the hotel. Razor wire spanned the walls, interspersed by wooden guard towers where snipers and machine gunners lay in wait. Guns pointed at them from the men along the walls.

"Spearhead and Ghost, requesting entry!" Neilson shouted into the radio.

The gate blocking the road to the hotel began to shift, snow shedding from the groaning metal. The teams ran inside, and the soldiers manning the gate quickly replaced it, shouting orders to take firing positions along the wall.

Inside the base, soldiers were already preparing snowmobiles and large transport trucks for what appeared to be a potential evacuation.

A man shoved through the heavy snow toward them. Dohi recognized him as Sergeant Prince, the man who had first welcomed him and Team Ghost to Banff.

"Neilson, get up on those walls!" Prince shouted. "Ghost, we need you inside!"

Dohi ran with Prince, Fitz, and Ace past the hotel toward a warehouse-like garage. Inside it, civilians were being loaded up into a bus and a pair of trucks as officers directed soldiers into snowplows.

"Are we fighting or retreating?" Fitz shouted over the din.

"Both," Prince said. "Kamer will explain."

They went to a dark corner of the garage past stacks of crates and supplies that hadn't yet made it on the trucks. Kamer stood next to a group of four officers and a few soldiers, hidden from the civilians, but several children had come over to look at their prisoner.

Corrin was on the ground, limbs bound by chains, body trembling. Blood wept from wounds across his flesh. Kamer continued barking orders.

"What the hell did you do to our prisoner?" Ace asked, interrupting him.

"What you failed to do," Kamer said, turning slightly. "But this asshole is full of lies."

Corrin spat a glob of blood on the concrete. When the red saliva hit, one of his fanged teeth fell out. "I told you. I hate the New Gods as much as you do. They gave me this body. They threatened my family…"

"Bullshit," Kamer said. "Your friends came for you."

"We don't know that," Fitz said. "He's worth more to us alive than dead, General."

"I disagree," Kamer said, pulling out his sidearm.

Ace's cheeks flushed scarlet as he stepped protectively between Kamer and Corrin. "I, for one believe him, and I'm not going to let you kill him."

"You believe this monster?" Kamer flitted the barrel of his pistol toward Corrin. "This freak of nature?"

"I do," Ace said. "He could've given us up in Seattle. Probably would've been rewarded for it. Instead, he got us out of that hellhole."

"He brought this attack on us!"

"Sir, we need to move the civilians," an officer said. "The enemy is getting too close."

"Fine," Kamer said. "Tell the drivers to go out the back."

The pop of small arms fire echoed outside the garage. Dohi instinctively lifted his rifle, waiting for more. Distant shouting and a few voices crackled over the radios of the officers, but the gunfire waned.

"He might have more intel we can use," Dohi said. "For that matter, we might be able to use him as a spy."

"He probably *is* a damn spy!" Kamer yelled. "You spent a little time guarding this *thing*, and he's already corrupted your minds."

"I could help you fight…" Corrin said, glaring up at Kamer.

"Right…" Kamer snorted. "If this beast didn't draw the enemy here, then who did?"

Dohi tried to come up with an answer, but the truth was, he didn't know.

"The only logical answer is Corrin," Kamer said.

The rattle of gunfire sounded again, this time longer. Cries came from the buses already packed full of civilians, and the people still waiting to board dropped low, covering their heads or huddling with loved ones.

"With respect, sir, right now, it doesn't matter," Fitz said. "What matters is we fight back."

"That's exactly what we're doing out there," Kamer said. "Fighting, and *dying*, all because this piece of shit brought the enemy to our doorstop."

A loud boom echoed outside. This time when the gunfire started, it didn't stop. Frightened screams rang out, followed by the shouts of soldiers directing people into the transport vehicles. At the back of the garage, a single big door opened, and the first bus rumbled to life.

One of the officers held his radio to his ear. "General, they're at the gates!"

"Sergeant Prince, evacuate all of the civilians now!" Kamer shouted.

At the beginning of the war, Dohi would've thought the order was foolish. That sending their civilians fleeing just as an attack set in was too rash, too reactive. However, he had seen what the collaborators and Variants did to all those left behind when they conquered a base.

The snowplows and buses revved their engines, leaving the back of the garage one at a time.

Kamer lowered his pistol and shook his head at Corrin. "You've doomed us."

Ace backed away, and Dohi stepped up to Fitz.

"Go with the evacuees," Kamer said. "There are a couple of trucks waiting outside behind the garage. I promised your president I'd get you back to the Allied States, and I intend to do just that."

Shouting sounded outside, but a blast silenced the voices. A current of loud booms rumbled the ground, the unmistakable sound of grenades.

One of the comms officers turned toward Kamer and Ghost. "They've breached the gates!"

"Prioritize defense of the convoys," Kamer said. "And get the hell out of here. Ghost, take that animal with you if you want it so bad."

The bark of gunfire sounded somewhere just outside the garage. Dohi shouldered his rifle. He started to back up with the team toward the exit as the roar of a bear sounded outside.

A dent the size of a tire appeared in the two metal

doors. Then claws ripped through. The beast on the other side pried the massive garage doors apart until a monstrous face appeared.

The white fur around its yellow eyes was covered in blood, and it snarled, baring fangs each the size of a long knife. It let out a roar that hurt Dohi's ears, but he held his stance, firing a burst of armor-piercing rounds into its nose, eyes, and skull.

The monster slumped to the floor, halfway through the gap in the doors. Four collaborators climbed over it, firing wildly into the room.

Kamer ducked, but one of his officers was too slow. Rounds riddled his body and sent him sprawling over the floor.

"Free me," Corrin growled. "I'll help!"

Ace and Fitz exchanged a glance, and Fitz nodded.

"What? Hell no!" said the Canadian soldier guarding Corrin. "We can't trust—"

A bullet punched through his throat and he slumped over, gripping his neck.

More collaborators climbed over the dead bear. Ace sent a torrent of fire their way while Dohi moved toward Corrin.

"Cover me!" he shouted.

Another collaborator with an M249 made it into the garage, the heavy gunfire echoing in the enclosed space.

"Don't make me regret this," Dohi said to Corrin. He picked up the keys and unlocked the chains.

"I won't forget what you've done," replied the Chimera.

For a moment, Dohi feared there was a terrible threat veiled behind those words. Bullets slammed into crates around him, not giving him a chance to think.

The last of the vehicles screeched out of the back of the garage.

"Cover them!" Fitz yelled.

Kamer and his soldiers fired from behind leftover crates to give the civilians a chance to escape.

"I'm out," Ace said.

Dohi tossed him a magazine, then covered him, firing at the collaborators who had stormed the garage. Corrin hunched down next to Dohi, watching with his golden eyes like a predator waiting to make a move.

Behind the collaborators came another shape. This one a hulking figure wearing a frayed cloak. It kept to the shadows, but Dohi didn't need to see the face or features to know it was an Alpha.

"General," Corrin said, his voice dripping with fear.

Not just any Alpha, Dohi realized. This was the brute that had nearly killed Beckham, Horn, and Rico at Mount Katahdin.

Dohi switched on his tac light and directed it at the monster. The beam hit it in the face, and Dohi pulled the trigger as the creature opened its crocodile-like maw to let out a shriek. The beast was so fast only one of the three bullets thunked into its meaty flesh.

The bolt of Dohi's rifle locked back a moment later. He was completely out of ammunition.

A torrent of fire forced Dohi back down, bullets punching into the crates and walls. He pulled out his M9 and looked over his shoulder to see Kamer had fallen. Corrin rushed toward where the Canadian general had fallen.

"No! Corrin!" Ace yelled.

Corrin grabbed the limp general, dragging him out of view. Dohi had to turn back and fire on two collaborators charging his position. The Variant general was out of sight, flanking to pick them off one at a time.

Everything had turned to shit in a matter of seconds. Dohi had made a mistake letting Corrin out of his locks, and the Alpha was preparing to tear them all apart with the collaborator soldiers.

Time seemed to slow as rounds slammed into the crate and whizzed past Dohi.

Turning, he saw Corrin standing now with fresh blood on his chest. No doubt the blood of Kamer. The Chimera raised the rifle and aimed right at Dohi. He had known for a long time he would die in battle, but not because of a stupid mistake like this.

He watched the muzzle flare and bullets lance overhead. But none of them pounded his body. He glanced around the crate to see two collaborators thump against the ground.

A roar sounded from the Variant general. He exploded through a wall of crates and pounded into Corrin, knocking the Chimera to the ground.

Dohi looked over to see Kamer was sprawled out behind the busted crates where Corrin had dragged him to safety. Ace ran to him and lifted the general into a fireman's carry, running toward the back of the garage.

"Come on!" Ace yelled to Dohi.

Dohi watched Corrin struggling against the larger Alpha.

Damn it, he thought.

He couldn't leave Corrin to die like this. He aimed his pistol, waiting for a shot. More collaborators stormed in the garage.

Pulling the trigger, Dohi put a round in the general. The giant beast reared back, and he put another two into the chest. Corrin pushed himself up and ran over to Dohi as the Alpha limped away in retreat.

Together, the Chimera and Dohi ran to catch up with the rest of the team outside the garage.

Behind them, the glow of bright orange spheres of fire lit up the sky.

The hotel was burning.

The snow was coming down heavily again, nearly blotting out their vision despite the light seeping through the gray clouds. Behind the screen of snow, he saw two big trucks with snowplows fixed to the front idling at an open gate.

Thank you, Father Sky, Dohi thought. The cover the snow provided might be what saved them today.

Dohi swung his rifle up at shapes approaching from behind the trucks. But they weren't hulking bears nor did they wear the ragged white and gray clothing of the collaborators.

It was Neilson and the rest of Spearhead with Sergeant Prince.

"Get in!" Neilson said, motioning to the closest truck.

They all piled into the back, hunching down against the freezing metal. Ace lowered Kamer gently onto the truck bed. The man was unconscious, but alive.

Dohi looked out the back of the vehicle at a monstrous shape silhouetted against the fires. *The general.*

The monstrous Variant stood his ground, watching as the truck took off.

"What the hell was that thing?" Neilson asked.

"An Alpha," Fitz said.

"The general," Corrin said. "Leader of the New God armies."

The group fell into silence as the truck raced away for

safety far from the base.

Toussaint broke the quiet. "Is this what it's like?"

"What?" Ace asked.

"The attacks, the monsters, out of nowhere?"

Fitz nodded. "Almost always, there's little warning."

"And most of the time, it's a slaughter," Ace added.

"Good God," Toussaint said.

"I'm sorry," Prince said. "We had no idea."

"No more," Neilson said. "We're in this fight now."

"Where are we headed?" Fitz asked.

"Calgary," Prince said. "We'll regroup there."

Dohi took in a deep breath. He couldn't help but feel Ace was right, and they were heading from one slaughter to another.

***

Beckham knocked on the door to the laboratory. Through a window, he saw Kate working in an isolated chamber. She wore a blue CBRN suit. Yellow biohazard signs hung on the wall near the chamber and above a decon anteroom leading into it.

Kate could not hear him through the double sets of windows, but her assistant Ron was working in the less-restricted BSL-2 portion and noticed him standing there. Ron nodded at Beckham, then went to an intercom connected to the interior of the isolated chamber. Kate turned and waved a gloved hand. She went through the decon process, then carefully removed her suit before finally exiting and meeting him outside the lab.

"Sorry, I know I'm late," Kate said. "I got wrapped up with work."

"Don't worry about it." Beckham held up a paper bag. "I brought lunch."

"Great. I'm starving. Truth be told, I need some time away from the lab."

They left the hospital and met four soldiers outside who had escorted Beckham there. Together they walked under the afternoon sun back toward the outpost gate.

"You know the hospital is only a five-minute walk from the gate," Kate said. "I can make it there in broad daylight, especially with the men Commander Jacobs assigned to protect me."

"I feel better walking you in myself."

Kate wrapped her arm through his. "And that's why I love you."

Once inside the outpost, Beckham led them to the nearest park. Trees dotted the wide, rolling lawns around a long reflection pool leading to a lake. Ducks and geese squawked as they milled about the water, their calls mixing in with the chatter of all the refugees who had recently arrived at Houston.

Dozens of tents had been installed around the park to house the newcomers. The soldiers following Kate and Beckham watched them with suspicion.

"So many people." Kate's gaze followed a pair of young boys kicking a soccer ball back and forth. "And so many families."

Beckham thought of Javier in Galveston with the girls, hoping they were doing okay.

"Maybe we can try and call Connor tonight," Beckham said as they walked. "I'm sure he's doing a good job taking care of them, but it would be good to check in."

"I'd really like that." Kate motioned toward a circle of benches under a roof of curving southern live oak tree branches near the reflection pool. "How about we sit down over there?"

Beckham dropped into one of the benches, then spread the bag's contents between them. Their escort of soldiers fanned out, eying the refugees.

"PB&Js, apples, and a couple of waters," Kate said. "Don't tell me you made it all yourself."

Beckham grinned. "As a matter of fact, I did. Hope it's up to your standards."

She took the first bite of her sandwich, then looked out over the reflection pool. "We started the analyses on that grenade Timothy's team recovered."

"Oh?"

Kate nodded, swallowing her food. "It appears to be a modified tear gas grenade."

"Really? I thought it was some—"

"That's not all," she interrupted. "There wasn't tear gas inside. I've already confirmed it has bacterial components, but we haven't identified what that bacteria is yet."

"Good God." Beckham found his appetite was gone.

"I'll know more soon."

Beckham forced a bite down. "Any other news from the tunnels?"

"We've been monitoring all the channels, but we're no closer to finding out where the Prophet is."

"No indication of any upcoming attacks?"

"Nothing yet."

Beckham suddenly went still. Kate's eyes flitted to the ground, like she was recalling something horrid. He placed his hand on hers.

"Are you all right?" he asked.

"Yeah…"

"You can tell me. It's okay."

"That network… every time I connect, I hear the voices of all the people attached to the webbing. I can hear the monsters communicating with each other, talking about killing people, ripping them apart. And there's nothing I can do to save them."

"Everything we're doing is to save them." Beckham squeezed her hand. He was glad Leslie had been trained on connecting to the network too. He could see his wife desperately needed a break from the immense mental toil that integrating with the network must cost her.

"Even if we eventually succeed, how many will die?"

"We'll do our best to save everyone we can," Beckham said.

"I know," Kate said. "It starts here in this outpost. At least with you and Commander Jacobs on the job, the people here will be safe."

"I'm not so sure." Beckham picked up his apple but stopped shy of eating it. "The first wave of new reinforcements from Canada and Mexico have helped shore a few holes in our defenses. But some of the soldiers they've sent are more inexperienced than the greenhorns who trained with Timothy."

"Then you don't think we'll be safe?"

She too had stopped eating and instead stared out at the reflection pool. A few children were chasing ducks with their parents watching.

"It's not safe anywhere." Beckham saw a couple of families in nearby tents looking over at him. They were too far to hear him, but he spoke in a quieter voice all the same. "The gas grenade you analyzed has me worried the enemy will try something different."

"You're right," she said, starting to stand. "Maybe

taking the time for lunch was a mistake. I need to focus on finding out what kind of bacteria was in that grenade."

"You still need to eat." Beckham looked up at her until she slowly sat back down.

Again, he looked around, making sure no one was listening in.

"I've been working with command to prepare rapid evacuation procedures for all the civilians at the first sign of danger," Beckham said.

"You want to abandon Houston?"

"We have to consider a backup plan in case the reinforcements and defenses don't hold." Beckham's fingers tightened around his water bottle. "I hate to admit it, but after the news we got about Banff, we can't be caught with our pants down like they were. They barely got civilians out in time. And many didn't make it." Beckham looked his wife in the eyes. "If the enemy does come, I want you to be on the first truck out of here."

"I'm not leaving without you."

"You'll have to," Beckham said. "You're the brains of the science operation." He leaned closer. "Most importantly, you're Javier's mother. No matter what happens, he can't lose both of us."

"Don't talk like that. He's not going to lose either of us."

"Kate, we have to be realistic. We have to consider everything."

"Of course we do, but we're not in Canada. We have an advantage they don't have. We're listening to the collaborator network. We'll know before the monsters attack."

Beckham started to nod, but realization stabbed through him of something he had missed. "Kate, you and your team never intercepted anything about the scouts around Houston, right?"

She shook her head.

"And this new grenade weapon—nothing about it?" he asked.

"No, unfortunately."

"And Banff?"

"No, but…" Kate trailed off. "That's all the way north. Maybe they didn't communicate about the attack on our network."

"Are you sure? Back in New York, you were able to intercept intel on attacks across the country. Why would that have changed now?"

Kate arched a brow. "Maybe we're doing something wrong. Our communication efforts might not work as well as I thought—or we're cut off from part of their network here in Houston."

Two of the refugee children playing soccer looked at them, pointing at their food. They started to approach Beckham and Kate, but one of the soldiers stepped to block them.

"It's okay," Kate said. The boys were skinny and dirty. She waved them over and gave them the apples she and Beckham had neglected.

The boys ran away with the fruit, smiles spreading across their faces.

"You and Jacobs are working on a Plan B then," Kate said. "If the communication intercepts aren't working as well anymore, maybe it's time the science team makes a Plan B of our own."

— 8 —

President Ringgold walked down the sidewalk next to General Cornelius and Colonel Stilwell. The president's Secret Service agents shadowed them.

They passed by the Galveston boardwalk. It stretched off the shore outside the fences and barricades lining the eastern side of the island. Once a popular tourist attraction filled with carnival rides, games, and restaurants, it had long since fallen into neglect. The Ferris wheel hung at a precarious angle, rusted and bent.

Ringgold couldn't help but see the symbolism there, comparing it to civilization. But unlike that wheel, civilization still had a chance.

"Today is going to be a good day," she said.

"I have every confidence that you are right, Madam President," Cornelius said before looking toward Stilwell. "The reinforcements from our friends in the north and south will change this war."

Stilwell gave a soft harrumph.

They continued walking side-by-side toward the makeshift airfield that had once been Seawall Boulevard to meet their new comrades. Men and women in uniform hurried between buildings and large olive-green canvas tents. Some wore the standard-issue ACUs of the Allied States; others had black uniforms with the Orca patch characteristic of Cornelius' private army.

Ringgold twisted her wrist to see her watch. "The

planes are a little late, aren't they?"

Stilwell shrugged. "I haven't heard anything about delays."

"Hopefully, no news is good news," Cornelius said.

The sun was beginning to set, disappearing beyond the neighborhoods to the west.

The distant roar of plane engines sounded to their north. Ringgold turned around and looked toward the fluffy clouds glowing orange in the last pangs of daylight. Silhouetted against them, she saw the outline of three C-130s descending toward Galveston. They flew past the city, curving in formation to make their final approach from the south.

"Just three?" Cornelius asked, looking toward Stilwell. "That can't be more than a few hundred troops."

"I thought you said all the troops were coming in tonight," Ringgold said. "Is there another scheduled flight we don't know about?"

"I told you everything I know," Stilwell said.

Ringgold scanned the sky, looking for more planes. "You don't think something happened to the rest of the planes, do you?"

"We would've heard something on the radio," Cornelius said. "A mayday, at the very least."

Ringgold picked up her pace, her heart thudding faster.

"They must still be on their way," Stilwell said. "Maybe they just staggered their arrivals."

"That makes sense," Cornelius said. "They would want to throw off any enemy scouts."

Ringgold would have to take their word for it.

The growl of the first C-130's engines roared as the craft made its final approach. Its wheels touched down with a heavy jolt at the southern end of the airstrip.

Ringgold, Cornelius, and Stilwell made it to the guard station at the northern end of the strip. They waited under a wide canvas tent, with its sides rolled up, so they could watch the plane taxi toward their position.

Crew chiefs and soldiers waited around them, ready to tend to the plane and welcome the reinforcements to Galveston. The aircraft marshaller signaled for the plane to stop near the tent. Before anyone stepped off, a group of Marines boarded to ensure the aircraft's passenger manifest was in order and to perform routine security checks.

The other two planes started their final approach afterward. As the engines wound down on the first plane, one of the lieutenants in charge of the welcoming operations signaled to Ringgold that the coast was clear.

Her Secret Service agents flocked around her, Stilwell, and Cornelius.

As her footsteps clicked across the asphalt, the rear ramp of the plane lowered. Ringgold greeted the soldiers as they streamed off the craft. They looked exhausted. That much was expected. But she also saw them hanging their heads low, their shoulders slumped.

Ringgold caught one of the soldier's eyes. He was a young man, maybe eighteen or nineteen. He stiffened when their gazes crossed, and he readjusted the strap of the rifle over his back.

That fraction of a second when their eyes met was more than enough for Ringgold to see something was wrong.

They look defeated, she thought.

Ringgold searched the crowd for someone who could tell her what was going on. She spotted five men following the troops off. The epaulets on their shoulders and their stiff stances clearly told her they were in charge. She made a beeline for the officers with Cornelius and Stilwell on her tail.

One of the officers turned toward her, stepping away from the group. His head was shaved bald under his green cap, and deep bags hung under sharp blue eyes lined with wrinkles.

"President Ringgold," he said, taking a step toward her. "General Andrew Vance."

Ringgold shook his hand in a tight grip. "General Vance, welcome to the Allied States. We'll see that your men are taken care of. This is General Cornelius. He's in charge of the base here at Galveston. And I presume you already know Colonel Stilwell."

"I trust he's been serving you well," Vance said.

"He has," Ringgold said.

The other two C-130s had landed and were now taxiing toward them, preparing to unload.

"We were preparing for all six planes this morning," she said. "When can we expect the arrival of the other three?"

Vance gestured toward the soldiers and Secret Service agents shadowing them as they walked back toward the tent. "I'd suggest we discuss this in a quieter, perhaps more private environment."

The trip back to their CIC would be at least a twenty-minute drive and Ringgold didn't want to wait any longer than she had to. She pointed at a nearby coffeehouse that had since been requisitioned as an office for some of the air traffic personnel.

When they entered, the Secret Service agents swept the room, ushering away the two officers working at computers on the desks. Cornelius drew the blinds, shutting out the last fingers of light from the sunset, and the room went dark until Ringgold flipped a switch.

Vance looked toward the four other Canadian officers. "I think it would be best if we keep this a closed meeting."

Ringgold nodded to her secret service agents to wait outside with the other officers and soldiers.

"Madam President, I get the sense you don't like to beat around the bush," Vance started as they took seats around a small table, finally alone.

"I don't," Ringgold said. "Especially because we have no time for it."

Vance steepled his fingers together. He looked as if he was searching for words. "There isn't going to be another three planes."

"Not tonight?" Cornelius asked.

"Not ever," Vance said.

"Sir, I was told—" Stilwell began.

"Madam President, we had every intention to deliver our troops as promised, but after the attack on Banff, I'm afraid we realized that was no longer tenable," Vance said. "We need every man and woman we can spare to defend our own country."

Cornelius started to turn red. "We've been over this. Trying to survive this onslaught by hiding behind walls isn't working."

"The only way we're defeating these monsters is with a concerted offensive strike," Ringgold said.

"Our Prime Minister and Armed Forces Council disagree," Vance said.

Ringgold clenched her jaw, trying to withhold the heat rising through her core. "You've been hit by one attack, and your entire country cowers."

"All due respect, you brought these beasts on us," Vance said. "Now you want us to abandon our homeland to help you fight them."

Ringgold took a breath. As angry as she was, he was right. The Variants were a product of the United States government.

"I understand you've been hit hard," she said. "We've endured battle after battle, and we've learned more in these past weeks about the enemy that will help us defeat them. But we can only do that by striking our enemy down together, not by hiding behind walls."

Cornelius nodded. "The president is absolutely right. You have to tell your Council and the PM that they need to send the reinforcements they promised. Mexico is fulfilling their oath. Why can't Canada?"

"I'm sorry," Vance said. "We've sent what we can spare. If you want me and my people to pack up and go home, we will. You saw their faces. They don't want to defend some foreign land while their wives and husbands and children and parents are back up north, unsure if they're going to make it another day."

"I don't believe this," Ringgold said.

"I really am sorry, but this is out of my hands," Vance said. "Remember, you don't fight with the army you want. You fight with the one you have. That's what we're doing—and that's what you'll have to do as well."

Ringgold fumed at the last-minute change, but she understood Canada's perspective. She should have seen this coming. "Cornelius, if we identify a target, does this change our tentative plans to destroy the Prophet?"

"It does," he said. "We'll have to consult with General Souza again, but by my rough estimates, any concerted attack, regardless of the Prophet's location, will require at least another five-hundred troops to make up for what the Canadians aren't sending."

He shot Vance a look filled with daggers.

Ringgold knew that five-hundred troops could make or break their eventual assault. They needed the total number of armed forces properly trained and equipped for an all-out offensive. But she still regretted the solution that came to mind, hoping she would not come to regret it.

"General, you've been working closely with Captain Beckham to train our newest recruits," Ringgold said. "How soon before you believe they'll be prepared for an offensive strike?"

Cornelius was a staunch, confident man, but even he squirmed. "A few of their units have already seen action when we sent them to help reinforce Outpost Houston. They'll be the best equipped in any offensive maneuvers. I can reassign them immediately and focus their training on offensive instead of defensive tactics."

"Do it," Ringgold said. "We might not have long. The final battle is coming, and we need every able-bodied person left to fight it."

***

Azrael savored the smell of blood and antiseptic chemicals. This lab had kicked off his empire, from a single follower to an army on the verge of a decisive victory. Past rows of laboratory equipment was a space that Azrael had personally helped design.

The room used to be a special sterile environment suited for animal experiments.

Now it had been adapted for humans.

It was here, in this very room, where he had created VX-102 and started his initial human trials.

The formerly white walls were covered in a wallpaper of red tendrils from his organic communication network, another testament to the technological achievements he had accomplished with the help of his scientist cohort. Most of them had seen early on the success of VX-102, and they had chosen to elevate themselves to the status of Scions, like himself. He welcomed them into his fold.

Others who were not as mentally fit maintained their frail human bodies. The delicate, skinny fingers of humans were an abhorrent necessity to work with sensitive laboratory equipment, like some of the microscopes and analytical chemistry instrumentation that had been designed for their unevolved bodies.

Fortunately, the Scions' clawed fingers were much better at other tasks. Especially the ones that Azrael cherished, like the one he was about to help with now.

Sporadic screams of horror and pained groans echoed from the test specimens behind the various partitions, all isolated by plastic curtains. The buzz of surgical saws cutting through bone and the slurp of organs sliding from bodies into metal pans was music to Azrael's ears.

He peeled back a plastic blood-spattered curtain to reveal his faithful old doctor, Murphy, working over a humanoid body.

The wrinkled old man held surgical tools and prepared to replace some of the patient's organs with transplants from a dead Variant.

"Is this him?" Azrael asked.

"Yes, this is the one we recovered from Katahdin," Murphy replied. "The latest version of VX-102 has worked extraordinarily fast in him. I believe that with these final surgeries, he'll be complete."

"And his brain?"

"Fully intact, Prophet," the doctor said. "When he isn't passed out from the pain, he can talk coherently. He's very, very angry about something, although it usually doesn't take long for the pain to make him pass out again during my operations."

Azrael traced his own clawed fingers over the long claws jutting from the patient's fingers. "These transplants from Variant donors are truly improving the development of the Scions."

"Yes, you made a wise decision adopting this practice," Murphy said. "Not only do our patients immediately get the benefit of some of the physical attributes of the Scion, but the resulting inflammation and irritation from the surgeries help to activate the body's healing response. All the resulting signaling cascades accelerate the VX-102 activity and enhance the epigenetic changes."

Azrael narrowed his eyes and used a claw to pull down the doctor's mask to reveal the man's lips. The doctor trembled.

"You do not need to explain the science to me," Azrael said. "I invented it. I know precisely what it does."

The man bowed. "Yes, of course, Prophet. How foolish of me to assume otherwise."

"How long until he's complete?"

"He will need at least three more days, and more for recovery."

"You have two," Azrael said. "He will recover just fine."

The Prophet left Murphy's operating area and moved

into another nearby OR.

There a single woman was strung up, red vines squirming into her nostrils, ear canals, and throat. She let out a whimper when she saw him.

"Please... help," she managed to choke out.

"I am about to," Azrael said. "You have been chosen."

He glanced at a surgical tray beside where the woman was suspended. Everything had already been prepped by his assistants as instructed. The only thing he needed was the donor Variant organs, which were waiting on ice inside a cooler near the surgical tray.

"Chosen..." she said, coughing. "Chosen for—"

Azrael didn't give her a chance to finish her words. He swiped at her abdomen with his claw. *This* was something human fingers definitely could not do. He relished the woman's scream. Her face went white, and she squirmed a few moments before she passed out.

That was quicker than he would have liked. He began the tedious process of placing hemostats over severed vessels so she wouldn't bleed to death. His preparations and the red tendrils roping through her body would keep her alive as he cut out a few of her organs to replace with the donor Variant organs his people had harvested.

After an hour of work, the curtains to his surgical room were peeled back.

"Prophet," a rasping voice came. "You told me to meet you here, yes?"

Azrael didn't have to turn his attention away from his patient to know who it was. He had told the monster to meet him here while he worked. "Yes, Elijah. I have a task for you."

"I stand ready, master."

"The general has failed me in Canada," Azrael said,

trying hard not to crush the woman's intestines in anger as he extracted them. He finished pulling out a rope, snapped it in half, and flung it onto a metal pan. "Team Ghost escaped."

"Shall I pursue them?" Elijah asked.

"No."

Azrael licked the blood off his claws and turned to Elijah. The Scion was larger than most with bulging muscles pressing against the fabric of his dark clothes. He wore a ragged cape, and in one set of claws, he carried the front half of a human skull that he had fashioned into a mask.

He was one of Azrael's first creations, a faithful servant, and had chosen the name Elijah after his rebirth.

Azrael picked up a small electric device from his surgical tray. "Do you know what this is?"

Elijah shook his head.

"It's a GPS chip." Azrael held the dime-sized device between his claws, rotating it to reflect the light. "The flexible microelectric arrays hanging off it harvest energy from the body to power it. This device helps me keep track of the faithful."

He went back to the human woman. After cutting into her bicep, he sutured the device to the inside of her flesh and connected the array to her muscle.

"I have allies tracking our quarry up north, thanks to a device like this in one of our escaped Scions," Azrael said. "So you will understand now why I'm less concerned about where these people go. We will always find them, so long as they have the tracked Scion with them."

"Then what do you need from me?"

"I have different plans for you," Azrael said. He finished suturing the woman's bicep and turned toward her guts again. All this surgery was making him hungry, and he caught himself salivating.

"I live to serve," Elijah said.

"You live *because* you serve."

The woman started to wake, her eyelids fluttering. She groaned, blood dribbling down her open abdomen.

"Wha… wha…" she started to murmur.

She twisted her head enough against the tendrils holding her in place to see her stomach. Her mouth opened, and she let out a muffled scream.

This time, the pain wasn't enough to make her pass out.

"You are almost there," Azrael said. He placed a claw on her lips, and she writhed. "Patience."

She thrashed against the vines holding her into place, moving enough that Azrael couldn't continue the surgery.

No matter. It was time for him to eat anyway.

He picked up the length of intestine he had removed from her.

"Do you recognize this?" he held it up so she could see.

Her eyes bulged.

He took a bite of it, letting blood trickle over his chin. "You are delicious."

She finally fainted again, and he finished his meal, throwing a scrap to Elijah. The Scion hungrily stuffed it into his mouth.

"I'm growing tired of these heretics," Azrael said. "It takes too long to turn a person like her into a magnificent Scion like you."

"Yes, yes," Elijah said.

"Unfortunately, we have not located the humans who have infiltrated our network. They have built too many safeguards for our faithful to get past. I've been told it could take weeks to locate the humans. I fear that if we wait too long, they will regroup. And we have heard rumors that they have sought the assistance of other nations."

"They will fail, master, we will stop them."

"Indeed we will." Azrael began suturing the woman's abdomen together again. "I want the rest of the Allied States crushed before we have to deal with too many other nations of heretics."

Azrael looped in the last suture and turned toward Elijah.

"What do you propose, Prophet?" Elijah asked.

"We have the advantage," Azrael said. "The humans don't know we're aware of their activities infiltrating our communication network. It's time that we use this against them. Instead of laboring to root out the heretics, we will bring them to us."

"And then we will defeat them."

Azrael turned and traced a claw along the neck of the patient, watching her sutured-covered chest rise and fall as she breathed slowly. "Then you will get your chance to bring in Team Ghost, Beckham, and all the rest of these traitorous bastards."

"How, Prophet?"

"It's easy. Just tell them exactly what they want to hear."

— 9 —

Strapped to a chair in the parking garage outside a Variant tunnel, Kate's head filled with a thousand pained voices crying out to be free. Men, women, children, all prisoners of the Variants, imprisoned in the webbing network. She wished she could send them some words of reassurance.

But a single moment of weakness would ruin all her efforts.

If she so much as sent them a single message, the masterminds would know she was a spy in their midst. She had to drown out their screams of agony and pleas for help.

The only way to help these people was to zero-in on what really mattered.

Finding the Prophet. Finding where the New Gods were. And sabotage any incoming attacks.

She had already missed the attack on Banff and the monsters' communications regarding the scouts outside Houston.

The longer she remained hooked up to the network filtering through the messages, the more her head throbbed. Cold sweat dripped over her flesh, and she trembled as she listened to the terrified voices of people hooked up to the vines around the country, their bodies wasting away to feed the spreading network.

"Help!"

"Mom? Mom, where are you?"

"I can't... breathe... I can't..."

The voices overwhelmed her. She could hardly stand it.

Feed me. Feed. Food.

Kill it. It threatens us. Heretics.

Attack the camp. Kill the humans. Bring them to us.

Nothing out of the ordinary.

She tried to keep her mind focused. But the human voices won out again. Her muscles contracted and her skull flared with pain.

Suddenly all the voices disappeared. She blinked, her blurred vision clearing to Ron standing above her.

"Kate, you with me?" he asked, gingerly touching her shoulder.

"Yeah... How long have I been..."

"A few hours."

"Felt like days."

"Leslie just finished up a chromatography experiment upstairs. Maybe it would be a good time for you two to swap."

Kate straightened in the chair. A few soldiers guarding the parking garage glanced at her, worry clear in their expression. She twisted to see Sammy at the computer behind her.

"Was it that bad?" Kate asked.

"You were screaming," Sammy said, twisting one of her dreadlocks. "You sure you're okay?"

Kate massaged her temples. "I need a break. Ron, you're right. Where's Leslie?"

"We just sent for her," Sammy said. She walked over and handed Kate a towel for the sweat.

"Thanks," Kate said. She felt a little embarrassed to

have her assistants treating her so gently, but she couldn't let pride get in their way.

"I can learn how to do this too, so it's not just Leslie and you," Ron said.

"We'll see."

Footsteps soon echoed down the stairs, and Leslie appeared.

"I'm ready to go," she said. "And I've got the last bits of data processing upstairs for you. Took me nearly the entire day to get it ready."

"Give me the rundown," Kate said.

"Figuring out what was in the grenade was relatively easy. It took me a few hours to run through the basic battery of biological agent assessments, but since we knew it was bacteria, that made it easier."

Kate braced herself. "It isn't a new variation of airborne VX-99, is it?"

"No, actually, it contained anthrax spores."

"Were they genetically modified?"

"Not according to the gene sequencing."

"There's something else this tells us," Kate said.

"What's that?" Ron asked.

"Anthrax isn't hard to grow or distribute, but before the war, existing strains in the United States were tightly guarded," she said. "Only a few national labs had access for testing and research purposes. Maybe that's another connection we can exploit."

"I can compile a list of all those laboratories and institutions," Ron said.

"This might be a long shot, but we already know that the person or people responsible for the New Gods had access to several DARPA technologies. The high concentrations of activity in those former research labs in

Denver and Seattle proved that."

"But those labs only housed parts of the research for the microelectric arrays and the neural programming technology for the webbing network."

"Exactly. And while Seattle turned out to be a site of Chimera research, there was no sign of the Prophet there. Based on the presence of anthrax in that grenade and all the crazy biological horrors like the bats, masterminds, network, and Chimeras, we need to be focusing on labs related to biodefense."

"We're looking for one sick former government biologist behind all this, aren't we?" Sammy said.

"I wouldn't be surprised. It was a rogue military officer who led to the initial VX-99 outbreak, and with the number of technologies the New Gods have used, it wouldn't surprise me to find out that some traitorous Department of Defense scientist or an entire research group is behind all this."

"But when we found out about Denver and Seattle, how would we have missed this place when we were tracking all that communication activity over the network?" Ron asked.

Sammy answered for Kate. "Firewalls, encrypted comms. Think basic cybersecurity, except adapted for a biological network. Whoever this Prophet is, he keeps proving himself smarter than we ever anticipated. If he was previously involved in national security, the guy would know to protect his digital and physical footprint."

"Sammy, I want you to dig a little deeper in the network with Leslie," Kate said. "See if you can find any dark corners of the network that might be protected by these firewalls. We need to redouble our search efforts."

"I'll get started now," Sammy said.

Kate turned to Leslie. "How about the biopsied Chimera tissues?"

"The last of the chromatography and PCR runs were just finishing when I came down. Should be ready for you in less than half-an-hour."

"Thank you," Kate said.

"Anything else you need from me now?"

"Tap into the network when you feel up to it."

"I'm ready."

Leslie eagerly took the seat where Kate had been as Ron prepared the webbing for her to integrate with. Once she was in the chair, Ron glanced at his wristwatch.

"She can probably withstand listening for a good four or five hours," Ron said. "I can join you up in the lab once we know Leslie's connection to the network is stable."

"Do it," Kate said.

She headed straight to the lab. A few of the chromatography machines were still humming and clicking as the pumps and injectors siphoned various samples through their lines.

Ron joined her a few minutes later, and they reviewed the data Leslie had told them about.

By then, the last of the chromatography runs had finished, which would give them some insight into the properties of the compounds they had identified in the Chimera's tissues.

"I want to cross-reference every active molecule and chemical compound we find in the biopsied tissues with a known list of pharmaceuticals and biological agents," Kate said. "If you find any matches, let me know."

"We're going to see if any suspicious compounds help us pinpoint a research group responsible for developing them, right?"

"You've got it," Kate said. She scrolled through the analytical results on the computer. "Any matches might tell us the original companies or institutions where these compounds were produced."

"I'm on it," Ron said.

They each worked at computers, side-by-side, poring over the results. It took several hours for the automated database search to return their queries. While Kate found matches for a few of the molecules, she discovered several with no known matches.

Ron came up with a similar list.

"Doesn't look like anything we've seen before," he said. "There's no way to tell where they came from."

Kate sighed. "I did find something interesting. See what you think."

"I'm all ears," Ron said, turning away from his computer.

Kate pointed to a pair of molecules on her screen. The long chain of lines and angles representing bonds between atoms was nearly indistinguishable between the two molecules at first glance. But Kate pointed to a smaller section toward the right end of the chain.

"The first molecule you see is one of the active components in VX-99," Kate said. "It confers many of the epigenetic changes that lead to the aggressive nature of the Variants."

"Following."

"In this second sample, the one we extracted from the Chimera, the last chain of molecules is different," Kate said. "It's impossible to say exactly what it does without extensive computational modeling and cellular studies."

"But you think that it could be enough to change the

molecule's function so it doesn't alter the neurological activity of the Variants?"

"It's all a theory, but bottom line, yes."

She could tell from Ron's expression that a light had gone off in his head.

"What you're telling me is that someone modified VX-99," he said. "This version turns people into actual super soldiers without destroying their intellect."

Kate didn't want to believe it, but it was hard to deny.

"This has to be someone who had access to the original VX-99 studies and samples," she said. "Someone with intimate government connections."

Kate tapped on the keyboard, clicking through to another molecule.

"There are a couple of compounds that look like they were adapted from other government projects. They have a sub-90% similarity match, but it's certainly enough to connect a few dots," she continued.

"Like what?"

"This one." Kate pointed to her screen. "It looks similar to an active compound DARPA was working on that can be used in cell targeting for drug delivery. It homes in on very specific cell types, which means that this mysterious VX-99 variant could act much faster on its target."

"VX-99 already turned people into monsters in days."

"Expediting targeting efficiency could decrease the dosage needed in a host while increasing the targeted signaling pathways."

"So a person would change in less than a couple days?"

"With the right conditions, the first changes would be nearly immediate."

"Good God," Ron said. He pushed away from his computer, slouching in his seat. "This is worse than a nightmare."

"There must be some more commonalities we can identify to find out who is responsible."

Ron swiveled his monitor back to face him. "I know you're good with the molecular data, but I'm more of a big picture researcher. We already have tons of data from your past research on what VX-99 does to a human to turn them into a Variant, including anatomical studies. But we don't have that kind of data for Chimeras."

"You're right. That could be just as helpful. Tell Jacobs we need a full workup on that Chimera they captured. MRI, CT, whatever they got. I want to know what that thing looks like under its skin."

Ron picked up their radio to make the call.

"No, better to keep this one quiet," Kate said. "Just in case anyone's listening who shouldn't be."

"Yes, of course." He started to head toward the door.

"Wait," she said.

Ron looked back.

"The last report we got back from Ghost said they have a Chimera in their custody, too. See if we can get the same data from the Canadians. The more, the better."

Ron disappeared into the hall to relay the message, and Kate continued working for another thirty minutes trying to fit the pieces of this scientific puzzle together. She was certain that the spider web of connections they were making would lead to a clue.

The radio on the lab bench crackled. "Doctor Lovato, are you there?"

It was Sammy. Her voice was tinged with worry.

Kate grabbed the radio. "What's going on?"

"We've got… we intercepted something. Leslie is headed in your direction right now."

A minute later, someone pounded on the door. Kate opened it to let Leslie in.

The woman's face was red. "We heard it! We finally heard it!"

"Heard what?"

Leslie took a deep breath. "They're in Las Vegas."

"Who? The collaborators? Another mastermind?"

"The Prophet. The New Gods, everything. They're headquartered in Las Vegas."

Kate nearly stumbled backward. "You're sure?"

Leslie nodded. "Sammy recorded the transmission. We're positive."

"This could be it," Kate said. "But you can't tell anyone. We cannot let this get out."

She hung up her lab coat and started to open the door.

"Go find Ron and tell him and Sammy to wait for me at the Variant tunnels."

"Where are you going?" Leslie asked.

"I need to tell Reed," she said. "And the president."

***

Another long day in Calgary had passed without incident. The sound of water dripping echoed through the warehouse far outside the city limits. Banks of sodium lights hung overhead, and pipes ran along the ceiling. Team Spearhead was taking their turn guarding the place, while Dohi and Ace watched Corrin.

But that was not why Fitz had trouble finding some shuteye.

"Can't get a lick of sleep?" Ace asked, his face ripe

with bruises and exhaustion.

Fitz sat up against a crate. "Impossible."

"Worried about an attack on Calgary?" Dohi asked.

Fitz gazed over at Corrin, who had somehow managed to nod off. The Chimera was in the corner of the warehouse, chained and shackled to a bolt in the concrete floor about twenty yards away from them. That was a result of the Canadians' orders when they had arrived, before the medics had taken General Kamer elsewhere into the outpost for medical treatment with Sergeant Prince. They had left Spearhead and Ghost to watch Corrin out here.

"Worried about him," Fitz said, gesturing toward the Chimera. "He got us out of Seattle and saved Kamer. I'm worried the Canadians are going to kill him."

Ace flicked a cockroach crawling toward him. "Yup, and it's a damn shame. I think the guy is being truthful with us, even if he is uglier than my ass."

"The Canadians are right to be suspicious," Dohi said, voice calm.

"What? You think he actually called the enemy in?" Ace asked, bushy gray brow raised.

"No. I just think there's something we're missing. I don't believe in coincidences."

"If you figure out how they tracked him—or us—I'm all ears," Fitz said.

"Maybe a GPS," Ace suggested.

"We didn't find anything on his clothes or on his body," Fitz said.

"They might've forced one of those devices down his throat or something," Ace said.

"No," Dohi said. "The only GPS trackers small enough to implant in a person or ingest have batteries that don't last more than a couple days at max, especially with the power required to transmit a signal from Banff to Seattle."

Ace opened his mouth to speak, but the sounds of footsteps clattering toward them interrupted him. Fitz scrambled to stand on his blades, and the other two followed suit. Corrin jolted awake.

The steps echoed in the wide space, until Neilson appeared with Toussaint and Daugherty. Behind them were another ten men, all military. A few gasped when they saw Corrin. Others looked terrified, and Fitz noticed several lift their rifles slightly, like they were ready to shoot Corrin down.

Fitz swallowed, was this it? Had the Canadians decided to come deal with Corrin and get rid of him?

Corrin's innocent, Fitz thought. *But will you die trying to protect him?*

"Master Sergeant Fitz," Neilson said politely. "We got orders from your science team in Houston. They want a full-body workup on Corrin. Medical image, biopsies, all of it."

"What for?" Fitz asked.

"Didn't say. These men have a truck waiting to transport Corrin in the loading bay. They need to take him to a medical center in the city but want to keep him out of sight. You want us to help with escort duty?"

Fitz looked at Corrin, then the men. "Yeah, that would be good."

He didn't trust the other Canadians, but his gut told him Neilson was a good man.

"Brass is anxious to get this thing out of here," Neilson said. He tossed the keys for Corrin's chains to Dohi. The Canadians had not even trusted the Americans to hold onto the keys, they were so worried about betrayal. "They're wondering how long it's going to be before these New Gods attack Calgary too, especially with the beast so close."

Dohi took the keys to Corrin.

"We've kept the guy locked down, under guard, and hidden since we got here," Fitz said. "He hasn't made a single call and hasn't once been out of our sight."

"I believe you," Neilson said. "But it would make people feel better to have hard proof that this Chimera didn't start the attack on Banff. And even more important, that he doesn't bring the New Gods here, too."

Dohi finished unlocking Corrin and helped the Chimera stand. Chains still shackled his wrists and ankles together.

"He helped us escape that attack," Fitz said.

"Yeah, but he's one of them, and all people know is the attack happened not long after that beast arrived at Banff."

"And what do you think?"

"I don't know what to think," Neilson said. "All I know is that I watched most of our people die in a matter of minutes. And now all we can do is watch the walls around Calgary for another attack that you and I both know is inevitable."

Fitz understood why the Canadians were nervous. Hell, he wasn't sure how the collaborators had found Banff, but Dohi was right. Somehow it had to be connected to Corrin.

"Where are we going?" Corrin asked, a slight tremor in his normal gravelly voice.

He sounded nervous.

"We're just doing some routine exams," Ace said. "Science team back home wants to know what makes you tick."

Corrin eyed the ten military men standing behind Team Spearhead. "You're not just leading me outside and putting me down like a rabid dog, are you?"

"Just medical stuff," Neilson said. "I promise."

Corrin nodded, but remained tense. "Fine. I'm used to being a medical experiment."

A minute later they were outside the warehouse next to the waiting truck. Ace helped Corrin inside, and Dohi and Fitz jumped up with them. The other ten soldiers piled in around them. Neilson patted the door and started to close it when Fitz reached out.

"Don't fuck us," Fitz said.

"We don't betray people," Neilson said. "You have my word, Master Sergeant."

Fitz kept his hand on the door for a moment, then relaxed and Neilson sealed the door.

The vehicle took off through the streets.

Fitz peered up through the window to see the Calgary Tower after they passed through the gate into the city. Once a tourist attraction, the structure now served as a military observation deck to oversee the base and its surroundings. He hoped the Canadians would see an attack long before it hit Calgary, but he couldn't help thinking that the tower could do nothing if the Variants decided to tunnel under the base's defenses.

The truck eased to a stop. Fitz readied his rifle again, still suspicious that the Canadians might try something. The door opened, and Neilson gave them a nod to hop out. Ace helped Corrin back out of the truck, while the soldiers formed a perimeter around them at a back entrance to the hospital.

Standing outside the door, a doctor in scrubs with a head shaved bald looked at them, his piercing green eyes never leaving Corrin. For a second, he said nothing, clearly in shock.

"Doc, you all right?" Ace said.

"Jesus," the doctor started, then blinked as if trying to dispel an illusion. "That thing... oh, God. I never imagined—"

"We going to do this or not?" Fitz asked.

"Ah, yes, of course," the doctor explained. "First up is the CT scan." He led them into the hospital, nervously glancing back at Corrin as they marched down the corridor, the soldiers flanking them. "We'll get a three-dimensional look at his skeletal system, along with the anatomical layout of his soft organs. It won't take very long, but..." The doctor studied Corrin. "Normally, I leave the patient in the machine alone. You don't want an operator exposed to excess radiation, but is that going to be a problem?"

"No," Corrin said with a slight growl, shuffling after them.

The doctor looked at Team Ghost as if he didn't believe the Chimera.

"It ain't going to be a problem." Ace tapped the side of his rifle for emphasis. "We'll be right outside, and he won't try anything, right?"

Corrin gave a sad nod.

The doctor took them into another room off the hall, and the Canadian soldiers waited outside. Inside were two imaging techs, a woman and man each wearing scrubs. Both took steps backward when they saw Corrin, shaking slightly.

"We're, uh, going to have to remove those shackles to do this," the doctor said.

Dohi followed the doctor's orders.

The doctor still watched Corrin suspiciously. But the Chimera didn't struggle when Dohi and the staff undid his wrist restraints and laid him on the scanning bed of the CT. Once Corrin was settled, they exited the room, joining Team Ghost behind the observation window.

Through the glass, Fitz watched the bed slide toward the huge donut-shaped CT machine. They waited for nearly fifteen minutes as Corrin's body traveled through the scanner.

"We're all done," the doctor said. "Quick and, uh, painless, right?"

Corrin gave the doctor an unamused look through the observation window. The doctor's two imaging techs entered the CT scan room and escorted Corrin back into the observation room with the rest of them. Ace and Dohi stood beside Corrin, ensuring he didn't move.

Images started to populate on the doctor's computer, processing in real-time.

"The next test is going to be a few biopsies," the doctor said. "We'll head down the hall to an exam room, and—"

"Wait," Corrin said. "I want to see what those assholes did to my body. Can I see?"

The doctor looked at Fitz for approval, and Fitz gave him a subtle nod.

"Sure, it, uh, won't take long. Just a couple more seconds, and the images will be done processing."

A black and white three-dimensional model of Corrin's body appeared on one of the monitors.

"That's it," the doctor said.

Corrin's eyes roved over the screen, his bottom lip trembling slightly.

Fitz scanned the skeletal structure. It didn't look too different from a normal human's, except that the ends of each finger and toe were long and pointed and most of the bones appeared thicker. He could see the shadows of the Chimera organs.

"I'm no doctor, but his organs look pretty similar to a human's," Ace said.

"That's right," the doctor said. "Beside the structural differences in his skeletal system, I don't see many differences." The doctor traced his finger along the image of Corrin. "Except here. That's odd."

Fitz noticed what the doctor was pointing at. A bright white speck.

"The contrast indicates this is about the same density as bone, but it is embedded in his muscle," the doctor said.

Fitz's stomach twisted. He looked at Dohi and Ace. "Could that be…?"

Their expressions told him they all had that same thought.

"I thought you said a battery wouldn't last," Ace said to Dohi.

Dohi stroked his goatee. "A battery wouldn't last. But then again, these people have made all kinds of strange biological weapons. Maybe…"

"It's my fault," Corrin grumbled. "Death follows me everywhere."

He looked down at his arm, and before anyone could stop him, he tore his left claw into his bicep. Skin peeled away to reveal glistening muscle.

The doctor stumbled out of the room with his techs.

Corrin dug into his flesh, howling in pain as he plucked out a metal capsule and pulled it from his flesh. Two small wires snapped off from where they had been attached to his muscle.

"Stop, Corrin!" Fitz reached out to the creature. His touch seemed to calm Corrin, who wept for the first time since they had captured him.

"I'm sorry," he mumbled. Saliva dripped off his fangs. "Just kill me… just get it…"

"I got a better idea," Fitz said.

Corrin glanced up with his golden eyes.

"If they're still tracking this thing, we can send it far from here. Send the New Gods on a wild goose chase and prevent an attack on Calgary," Fitz said. He took the bloody device, holding it like a hand grenade waiting to go off.

"Patch Corrin, up," Fitz said. "It's time we use him to our advantage."

Ace grinned and Dohi nodded.

"You good with that?" Fitz asked.

Corrin grunted. "If I get a chance at revenge, then I'm more than good with it."

— 10 —

On the way to Galveston, Beckham had learned that General Hernandez had arrived from Mexico. Just like Canada, they had sent only a few hundred troops instead of what they had initially promised.

Now he sat next to Rico and Horn at a dining table in an opulent room of the Moody Mansion, a once popular tourist attraction and museum. The neglected informational plaques hanging from the walls or posted on stands were covered in cobwebs.

"Think this place is haunted?" Horn asked.

"Maybe," Rico said. "You scared?"

"Nah, ghosts are afraid of me."

Rico raised a brow. "Maybe it's the BO, man. We do still have water at these outposts, you know?"

Footsteps echoed through the building before Horn could get off a retort. Three Secret Service agents entered, and Beckham rose instinctively, Rico and Horn doing the same.

Next came President Ringgold and General Souza.

"Thank you for making the trip back from Houston," Ringgold said as they saluted her. She motioned for them all to sit back down around the dining table, then checked her watch. "General Cornelius and the others should be here soon."

"Will General Hernandez or Vance be meeting with us?" Beckham asked.

"No," Ringgold said. "As far as they and everyone else on this island knows, this meeting isn't happening. There are too many people flooding into Galveston, and we don't want to risk the chance that any collaborators are among them. Loose lips, you know?"

A few more officers from Cornelius and Ringgold's armed forces filtered in before Cornelius arrived.

"That's everyone," Ringgold said, looking between them all. "We're gathered today with intel that can change the war."

Every exhausted face seemed to light up at the prospect.

"Until now, only a few of you were aware of the intel our science team recently recovered," she said. "Thanks to their work with the webbing network, they identified that the so-called Prophet and the heart of the New Gods operation is in Las Vegas."

"It is extremely important that you reveal this information to no one except those we've given prior clearance," Souza said. "Initially, when we got this intel, we considered sending an offensive with our new allies, but the risk of the collaborators finding out is too great."

So we're sending in a few fire-teams, Beckham thought. *Just like the past. A few good men and women to save us all.*

He wasn't sure it would be enough.

"If we don't hit the New Gods hard with our allies, then how are we going to stop this Prophet and all their forces?" he asked.

"We still plan on launching a counter-offensive on the New Gods, but our tactics rely more on surgical precision than brute force for this mission," Souza said. "We will distribute the other troops by priority to the outposts that need them the most."

The mood in the room seemed to shift as the officers waited to hear this new strategy. Beckham could tell none of this was what they had expected, especially after Ringgold had been promising more extensive offensive action against the New Gods.

"I know you're worried," Ringgold said. "And you have every right to be." She paused a second, as if bracing herself. "Last night we received word that our last outposts in eastern Florida were taken."

The room was silent for a long moment.

"This is no longer a war of superior technology or weapons or even numbers," Ringgold said. "We have to win by being smarter than our enemy with the forces we have left, and the people in this room are the best we have left. I'm going to let Cornelius and Souza fill you in on the details."

Souza leaned forward. "From our best estimates, Las Vegas is a cesspool of Variant activity. The city served no economic or military purpose to the Allied States during our reconsolidation, so we abandoned it and the Variants must have moved in."

Cornelius unrolled a map over the table. It was a satellite image showing the black and brown ruins of Las Vegas, dated from five years ago before they had lost contact with most of their reliable imaging satellites.

"Thank you," Souza said. He looked at the map and then pointed at a location northwest of where the once-famous hotels like the Bellagio, MGM Grand, and the Wynn had been. "The science team triangulated the signals. Most of them propagate from here, the University Medical Center."

He scanned the map and then tapped another location. "And while there aren't as many signals coming from here, the Palazzo is our second guess. We believe one of these locations is likely to house the Prophet."

"I take it he's not alone out there," Horn said.

"Intercepted communications over the network suggest the presence of at least four individual masterminds in the vicinity of Vegas," Souza said. "From past experience, we know the infrastructure and number of minions required to feed those beasts means we're likely looking at several hundred to a couple thousand Variants in the area."

"These reports lead us to believe the New Gods have spread through the city like a bad cancer," Cornelius said. "The science team also informs us the webbing network is unlikely to survive in the intense heat and sun exposure of the desert. That means it's highly likely the monsters have taken advantage of the vast network of empty tunnels, drainage pits, and water lines beneath the city, not to mention all the massive abandoned casinos and hotels. That will be where you'll probably find the highest density of webbing and monsters."

"From previous attacks on Variant hives, we know that bombing these types of nests can be ineffective at best and give us a false sense of security," Souza continued. "That's why we're relying on each of you to cut out this disease infecting Sin City at its roots, to ensure it never comes back."

"So no air support?" Horn asked.

"Air support will be limited," Cornelius said. "Not only are we limited by our diminishing stockpiles of ordnance, but the truth is our air superiority is ineffective at clearing out the vast, unknown networks of Variant tunnels underground. We can only truly cleanse this city of monsters by foot."

Souza nodded. "Our actions will be swift and fierce, catching the Variants unaware. In order to do that, we will come at the city in two main task forces of approximately a battalion size each. Task Force Alpha will be hitting Vegas from the north, roughly following what was Interstate 15. Task Force Bravo will come in from the southern approach on Interstate 15. Each battalion will split their forces, infiltrating the city both aboveground and through the storm drains and sewers. Company Cos will go over specific routes in more detail later.

"Team Ghost will lead the incursion into the UMC, which we believe is more likely to house the Prophet. The only Canadians that will know about this mission are the ones escorting Ghost from Calgary. Captain Beckham, you and Horn will head into the Palazzo."

Cornelius looked toward Beckham. "You will also be coordinating with TF Alpha and TF Bravo. Our goal is to distract the enemy with this larger force focusing on the main strip, drawing attention away from the special operations teams launching more covert attacks."

"We only get one shot at this," Souza said. "Once the enemy finds out we know they're in Vegas, they're liable to cut and run. So, we need to strike quickly, with both the task forces and special operations teams acting in parallel."

Beckham put a hand over his prosthetic, remembering the mission where he had lost so much of his body and soul. Without a doubt, this would be another one where good men died.

He glanced at Horn. The big man was scratching his beard, probably thinking the same thing. But like so many other times in the past, they had no choice but to serve and protect those they loved.

"This mission is going to be a success," Ringgold said. "We will cut off the head of this diseased snake, and the New Gods will wither and die."

"There's one more thing you all need to know," Souza said. "As the war has raged, it's always been our more experienced brothers and sisters putting themselves in harms' way. Unfortunately, that means many of them have been lost to the Variants. The two task forces will consist of many men and women who have very little experience outside of defending our walls."

Beckham thought of Timothy. He was one of the few recruits with actual experience outside the confines of their outposts. He had no doubt the young man would be sent away for this mission, but he held out hope that somehow Timothy would be safe.

"For now, I need all of you to make preparations to leave with your team," Ringgold said. "You are to report to mustering stations around Galveston in three hours for immediate departure. Like I said, we don't want to give the Variants any time to react or for any collaborators to send word back to the New Gods."

The room slowly emptied at Ringgold's dismissal, but she asked for Beckham and Horn to remain behind.

"The Allied States owes everything it has to you," she said. "I can't begin to tell you how frightened I am about the future, of losing you both, but this is it. If you can kill the Prophet, we can end this war."

"We won't let you down," Horn said.

"You never do," she replied.

Beckham simply nodded and left the room, more ready than ever before to fight the evil that had taken so much from them. It would be over soon, but before it was, he would have to kill a lot more monsters to keep the people he loved safe.

***

The heavy beat of the Black Hawk's rotors thrummed through Timothy's bones as he stared out the open side doors of the bird. Glimmering stars punctuated the night, and a full moon cast its glow over the desert landscape.

If he claimed he wasn't scared, that would be a lie.

But he was also ready for this battle, knowing he was part of something that could end up in history books.

Depending on who won, he thought.

He had known something was up when his team was ordered to return to Galveston from Houston, but it wasn't until he got his orders he realized how significant this mission really was.

Beneath them the world was a sea of black, barely visible. They had spent the past night and day on their way to the front lines, hopping between temporary encampments set up by scouts stretching from Houston to El Paso and then onwards to Vegas. His team, Recon Sigma, was assigned to Task Force Alpha, coming in from the north and clearing a route to their first objective, the Stratosphere Hotel.

While some of the other teams in the task force would take the storm drains and sewage tunnels underground, Timothy's team would be one of the few scouting out the enemy territory aboveground.

Once they converged on the Stratosphere Hotel, they would follow the strip south toward the Venetian Hotel and Casino.

Discreetness was key. If the New Gods got any

warning, the leadership would be gone before the Allied States' forces reached the city.

Timothy could feel the tendrils of exhaustion wrapping his insides, but the adrenaline of closing in on their target had kept him awake the whole time.

"Almost there," Ruckley said over the comm channel. She checked the glowing dials of her wristwatch and then pulled her sleeve back over the watch.

Wong checked his rifle, then nudged Boyd awake. "Hey, man, better get ready."

Boyd jolted awake. "Shit, we're nearing Sin City?"

Timothy nodded. "How the hell do you sleep over the sound of a helicopter?"

"It's a gift," Boyd said.

The other soldiers in the Black Hawk made final combat checks of their weapons as the chopper started its final descent. For a second, Timothy recalled those few minutes he had stolen with Tasha before leaving Galveston. He missed her and relished the moments they'd shared.

Reaching into his vest he pulled out something she had given him before he left—a bracelet of wooden beads. She had strung the beads over a piece of cloth cut from one of her shirts. It was meant to remind him she would be with him wherever he went, and she promised it would bring him good luck.

He slipped it over his wrist, hoping it would help him like she had said.

"Here we go," Ruckley said.

Timothy clicked down his night-vision goggles. The black-and-green world around him was filled with other choppers coming in low toward Vegas. Humvees, Strykers, and other vehicles that had been transported via

C-130s and other transport aircraft shadowed them on the ground.

He imagined how many Variants, Chimeras, and collaborators they would be striking down when they got to Vegas. Finally, he was a soldier fighting for his country, fighting to honor his dad's sacrifice.

The copilot turned back to them and shouted over the thrum of the engines. "ETA five minutes!"

"Ready, Private?" Boyd said, leaning toward Timothy.

"Hell, yeah."

He felt another flash of fear and wished he was back with Tasha for a moment. But as he looked around at the other men and women on the chopper, he realized this is where he belonged.

The chopper swooped in past hotels and casinos at the north side of the city. Many of the buildings were nothing but scaffolding and rubble. Timothy spotted a street covered in some kind of arched white roof, most of it bent and blackened. Next to it was a casino with only a few letters left on a sign that said "GOLDEN." Nothing about it looked golden now.

Another casino across the street had been nearly leveled, but its front wall still stood, announcing "FOUR QUEENS."

"Any sign of contacts?" Ruckley asked over her headset.

"Nothing yet! LZ is clear," reported the primary pilot.

The chopper dipped toward a street lined with abandoned rusty cars and mountains of trash. Some of the debris whipped around as they descended.

The wheels of the bird hit the street.

"Go, go, go," Ruckley said.

The soldiers jumped off the Black Hawk, ducking low

under the rotor wash. Timothy followed Boyd and Wong, Ruckley tailing them. A half-dozen other choppers disgorged men and women into the empty street. The soldiers spread out into their individual squads, forming a perimeter around those still unloading.

Once the last soldier had his boots on the ground, the choppers took off. Their engine noise dissipated as they vanished back into the night. The squads spread into the ruined city, taking their individual routes as they began the advance.

Ruckley signaled for Wong to take point, and Boyd took rearguard. They filtered past an old semi, its tires rotted and deflated. Timothy roved his gun barrel over their shadows, listening for any rasping growl, the clatter of claws, or clicking joints as they passed a couple of wedding chapels.

Ahead Timothy saw an enormous glass cone on a spindly tower, stretching far higher than the rest of the boulevard.

That must be the Stratosphere, he thought. *Our target.*

Timothy trained all his senses on their surroundings, looking for the predatorial eyes or snapping teeth of a monster. His skin crawled as he waited for one of them to shriek, announcing that the battle had begun in earnest.

All he heard was the soft pat of boots on the street and sidewalk, along with the distant engine noise from the vehicle convoys and choppers traveling elsewhere in Vegas. He looked toward the sky for a second. Additional troops would be parachuting into locations around the city, and he saw a few of their IR tags glowing in the night, signifying their successful descent.

Still, they saw no signs of the enemy.

The night's still young, Timothy thought. *And maybe the*

monsters are still all underground.

But he couldn't shake the feeling that the beasts had received warning of the assault. Maybe they were preparing a massive defensive effort. He pushed those thoughts away and followed Wong, who led Recon Sigma down the street ahead of the main forces.

Glass shards covered the sidewalk, and Timothy peered inside an old diner with moldy booths and chairs. Plates and tables were broken and scattered inside. Among the debris, he saw a pair of old skeletons that had been picked clean, claw and teeth marks covering the bones.

But no recent signs of monsters.

Somewhere far across the city they heard the rattle of gunfire. Then a few more bursts.

Ruckley held her fist up, and the team paused. Other soldiers sifting through the street and nearby buildings found cover.

Timothy scoped the street, looking for movement near a manhole cover and storm drain. Then he adjusted his aim over the windows of a nearby hotel.

Nothing there either.

The gunfire quieted, and the teams began advancing again.

Wong took them the final stretch toward the Stratosphere tower. Skeletal branches from dead trees and bushes rustled in the wind. A few nearby buildings had crumbled into oblivion, their façades torn apart by the bombing and fighting that had taken place here nearly a decade ago.

They passed rusted out Humvees. A few skeletons lay around them, the rags of their ACUs flapping over their limbs next to weapons in utter disrepair.

Since they hadn't run into enemy contacts, they were already ahead of schedule. Ruckley signaled for them to keep going, pointing toward the taller towers on the main strip. The closer they got, the more damage the structures had sustained.

Entire sides of buildings that were thirty, forty, or more stories tall were gone, revealing the guts of the former hotel rooms and restaurants inside. One hotel looked like some kind of circus tent, except half the tent's roof was missing. A creepy looking clown stood above a sign, pointing toward the hotel.

Teams were spread out between the buildings and even delving into the tunnels. By now he would have expected more than the few scattered gunshots they'd heard.

A voice called over their channels. "All teams be advised, this is TF Alpha Command. Recon Teams Delta and Lambda have found evidence of webbing network in drainage tunnels located near the main strip."

Wong navigated past a charcoaled transport truck, then past tables and benches scattered around a small restaurant advertising lobster rolls.

Then he froze.

Timothy swung his rifle around at the sound of rustling.

A shadow moved beyond a pile of rubble.

Recon Sigma advanced toward the chunks of concrete and pipes where Wong had spotted the movement. Ruckley signaled for Boyd and Wong to take one side as she and Timothy took another to flank their target.

As soon as Timothy crept past the broken concrete, a shrill cry erupted.

A creature with wormy lips shot toward him, claws

outstretched. He squeezed his trigger, sending a burst of rounds toward the monster. The shots missed, sparking into the concrete.

Jaw snapping, the beast slammed into Timothy's chest, catching his body armor. He fell backward, losing his grip on his rifle. His helmet smacked against the sidewalk, and his NVGs were knocked aside as the creature's mouth snapped for his face.

His hand caught the monster under its wrinkled neck, and he pushed up, muscles straining. Saliva sprayed over his face as the creature's teeth gnashed together. Gunfire cracked around him as the team took on a pack of the beasts.

He kept one hand on the neck of the Variant and reached toward his holster. Then he swung a fist hard into the face of the monster, connecting with a sickening crack. That did the trick. The creature reared back, and he reached back down and grabbed his father's pistol—the one Beckham had returned to him from Portland.

One trigger pull put a bullet through the enraged Variant's open mouth. A second took off half the jaw. The monster slumped over his chest.

He shoved it off, recovered his rifle, then put his NVGs back in place. Rushing over to Ruckley, he helped her finish off another starving beast. Then they turned their sights on the monsters after Boyd and Wong.

She pulled out her knife and stabbed the creature pinning Boyd down. Timothy sprinted to help Wong who was being slammed against the ground by a juvenile.

He strained to hold off the attacks, parrying with his rifle. Claws clanged against the weapon.

"Hold still, dammit," Timothy whispered. He had to aim for a weak spot where its arm met its shoulder.

Rounds lanced into the flesh, forcing it to turn. He put a burst into its face. The monster collapsed, letting out a long wheeze, and went still.

Timothy reached down and helped Wong up.

"Thanks," Wong said.

"They know we're here now," Ruckley said in a low voice. "Back into combat intervals."

Other gunshots far to their south sounded into the night as they spread out. Maybe TF Bravo squads, but no one in TF Alpha.

Timothy managed his breathing, his heart rate slowly returning to around normal. He made a goal of having it lower when they reached their first objective, the Stratosphere. More teams would rendezvous here as they prepared to take Vegas' main strip.

The team closed in a quick clip, moving fast. Timothy prayed the gunfire had gone unnoticed by the other monsters in the area, but he knew that was wishful thinking.

He scoped the Stratosphere as they approached.

Timothy saw something that looked out of place, like a gargoyle. At first, it was hard to tell if it was his mind playing tricks on him through the spotty NVGS.

He gestured for Ruckley's attention, then pointed up at the roof.

He flipped up his NVGs and used his scope to zoom in on a shape, twisted and malformed, like a Chimera or Variant, silhouetted against the stars.

It suddenly cranked back its head and let out a blood-curdling shriek.

Ruckley signaled for the team to find cover, but Timothy froze. The rest of the team ducked behind the rubble of a bombed-out restaurant, but he couldn't take his eyes of the rooftops.

Another creature appeared, howling. Then a third and a fourth. Soon they stood in lines like an army of screeching statues, their cries forming an unholy chorus.

They were coming from behind too, and Timothy slowly turned at a view that took his breath. Every rooftop along his sightlines was covered by the twisted silhouettes of monsters.

— 11 —

Fitz led Teams Ghost and Spearhead along with Corrin out from the belly of the DHC-5 Buffalo they had taken from Calgary. A lone Black Hawk was parked in the desert. Command had said the bird would be waiting for them. Beyond it, a good ten miles away, he saw tiny pinpricks of light pierce the black of night.

"They know we're here," Ace said. "We have to hurry."

Fitz picked up his pace. Getting to Vegas wasn't the only thing on his mind.

As he neared the chopper, the side door open. A shorter figure stepped out.

"Fitzie!" Rico called out.

Fitz ran over to her and wrapped her in his arms, savoring the feeling of relief that her embrace brought. While they were only apart for less than a week, it felt like a year with everything that had happened.

"It's so damn good to see you," he said, pulling away slightly.

"You, too," she said, leaning in for a quick kiss.

"Come on, guys, you're going to make me sick," Ace said.

Dohi cracked a half grin.

Fitz wished he had some alone time with her, even just five minutes. The look in Rico's eyes told him she must be thinking the same thing. That brief embrace was not enough.

But professionalism and the seriousness of this mission nixed that opportunity.

"Let's load up," Fitz said.

A crew chief passed headsets to Ghost and Spearhead. The reverberations of the Black Hawk's engines shook into Fitz's core as they took off, headed straight for downtown. Rico popped a piece of gum into her mouth.

As she chewed, she narrowed her eyes on Corrin. "So that's the Chimera? You sure we can trust him or it, or whatever you're calling this thing."

"Him," Ace said. "And yes, he saved our asses more than once."

"I'll take your word for it," she said.

"He's an asset," Fitz said.

Daugherty took a seat next to Ace. "He's also the reason Banff got attacked."

Rico shot Fitz a hard look.

"The New Gods implanted a GPS tracker in him using some of their weird tech," Fitz said.

"I assume it's gone," Rico said.

"Yeah, the Canadians sent some scouts out with it. Sent it far, far north into the mountains. It'll throw the New Gods off our trail and should save Calgary."

The chopper drew closer to the strip, and the team fell into silence, mentally preparing for action. Outside the open door, sparks of gunfire lit up the blanket of black canvassing the ruined city. Each flash was like a miniature lightning strike, illuminating the twisted ruins of what had once been Paris Las Vegas' Eiffel Tower or the cratered dirt where the Bellagio's fountains had long-since evaporated.

The crew chief guided the M240 back and forth, searching for a target, as the chopper soared over the apocalyptic landscape.

"Reaching LZ in two," said the primary pilot over the comm channel.

Fitz checked over his weapons again. Rico stopped chewing and took out a wad of gum. She tucked it under her helmet and gave Fitz a dimpled smile.

Fitz smiled back and then scanned the team.

Ace seemed to be mumbling to himself. The older man wasn't particularly religious as far as Fitz knew, but maybe after everything he had seen, he was warming to the idea. Dohi sat like a statue, calm and collected as usual. Next to Dohi, Corrin wore body armor the Canadians in Calgary had reluctantly given him. If he was nervous, he didn't show it.

Neilson remained stoic, but Toussaint had her eyes closed, her chest rising and falling in deep breaths as if she was trying to collect herself. Daugherty stared out the window, his hands pressed against the plexiglass, bottom lip shaking slightly.

Rico called over a private channel to Fitz. "You sure they're up for this?"

She nodded subtly toward Spearhead.

"They haven't been in the field as long as we have, but they're up for the task," he said.

Rico seemed to take his word for it. They both knew they needed the help with the loss of Lincoln and Mendez.

The chopper slowed and began its descent toward the University Medical Center.

This Prophet better still be here, Fitz thought.

After flipping down his NVGs, he saw the cubic

shapes of one building with a sign announcing "Trauma" and "Children's Hospital". The second building they had been briefed on had once been the UMC's burn center, but was reduced to piles of broken brick, twisted girders, and gravel.

"That's one less place to check out," Ace grumbled over the comms.

The pilot swooped in next to the Trauma and Children's Hospital units.

Their primary LZ, the hospital's helipad, was on top of a parking garage next to the building. But half the parking garage had collapsed, spilling concrete and rusted vehicles.

"Primary LZ is no good," one of the pilots reported. "Headed for our secondary."

The chopper banked toward the parking lot. Humvees, ambulances, military transports, and other vehicles were situated in mostly orderly rows around the asphalt. Between them was a wide space with the broken frames of tents and defunct air filtration units.

Fitz knew from their briefing this had once been a quarantine site during the beginning days of the first war.

The rotor wash from the descending chopper kicked up a few ragged chunks of tent fabric still clinging to the metal poles, and the wheels thudded onto the concrete. One of the crew chiefs waved them out while the other covered them with the M240.

"Radio silence," Fitz said.

They fanned out between scattered cots and crates of abandoned medical supplies, taking firing positions. Fitz's nerves sparked with electricity as the chopper lifted off, disappearing into the black of night. He searched the cars and vehicles parked around them, his eyes roving for a target.

As the thrum of the rotor blades disappeared with the bird, the echoing chatter of gunfire and low explosions from grenades boomed in the distance.

Fitz tuned into the public channels to hear frantic voices calling for reinforcements. Others requested medics. The fresh recruits that had joined the mission were having a hard time dealing with the sporadic skirmishes.

All the more reason for Ghost and Spearhead to find the Prophet quickly.

Fitz signaled to the others, gesturing to see if anyone had seen any contacts.

They shook their heads.

So far, nothing.

Fitz's stomach tightened. He had expected some kind of welcoming party, especially with the intrusion of the chopper. Had the science team been wrong about the Prophet's potential locations? Or had the New Gods' leadership already escaped?

He signaled for Dohi to take point, then for Toussaint and Daugherty to take rearguard. The others fell in beside him.

They filtered between the abandoned vehicles and quarantine supplies left in the parking lot, making their way toward the entrance to the UMC. The tall glass doors and windows leading into the atrium had long since been shattered. Crystalline glass pebbles crunched under Fitz's blades.

Dohi made it into the hospital's atrium first, taking shelter behind a column. He signaled that he still had no eyes on hostiles, but the others needed to join him.

Ace and Rico hurried behind Fitz, escorting Corrin for the Chimera's protection. Behind them came Spearhead.

When Fitz made it to Dohi, his NVGs adjusted to the low light inside. From instinct, he covered his nose with his wrist to mitigate the stench of death and sour fruit.

He pulled up his shemagh scarf to cover his face. Little good that did, but at least it made him feel like he was doing something.

Shouldering his rifle, he stepped into the vast two-story atrium. Long vines hung from the ceiling, pulsing and squirming. Webbing stretched along the walls as if it was the vascular system of some giant animal.

Vines snaked through skulls and ribcages of desiccated corpses that had long since drained of any living matter. Fitz scanned the escalators and stairs wrapped in webbing. This place was huge. It would take several hours to search the place from basement to top floor.

He turned back to Spearhead and the rest of Ghost. They would have to split up. It was the only way to find the Prophet before the battle being waged in the streets of Vegas cost the Allied States too much in lives and time.

Pointing to Spearhead, he gestured for them to start on the second floor, taking the stairs. Then for Ghost, he pointed to another stairwell at the back of the atrium. From the old building maps the science team had scrounged up, Fitz knew those stairwells would take them to the basement, where they would find the morgue, storage facilities, and research labs inside the hospital.

Neilson led Spearhead up the stairs. Their boots slurped on the webbing covering the floor.

Fitz followed Dohi toward the steps that would take them to the basement. He strained to listen for any growls or clicking joints. But all he heard was the drip of water and creaking in the walls between the distant sounds of the ongoing battle.

The team descended into the basement.

In the depths of the building, it was too dark even for their NVGs. No light penetrated the corridor, forcing Fitz to flip up his optics and turn on his barrel-mounted light. The others did the same. White beams of light pierced the cloak of black, revealing patches of webbing and the occasional knot of tendrils formed over a long-dead body.

Dohi halted, raising a fist, then signaled he had seen movement in a room to their left.

Fitz felt a tap on his shoulder. He turned to see Corrin, eyes glued straight ahead. Corrin pointed toward the room Dohi had indicated, then at his flared nostrils.

You can smell *them?* Fitz thought.

As if reading his thoughts, Corrin nodded urgently toward that door, his limbs trembling.

At Fitz's signal, Dohi went in low. Fitz followed, clearing Dohi's blind spots.

A growl exploded from the back of the room. Fitz raised his rifle, the light revealing two beasts with wormy gray lips, yellow eyes, and bony armor.

Juveniles.

He blasted their armor, rounds punching into the flesh of the first monster. The second leapt out of Fitz's aim, but Dohi unleashed a burst that took off a chunk of skull.

Clicking joints caught Fitz's attention, and he aimed toward the webbing-covered ceiling. A third beast they had missed before crawled like a spider over the webbing, dropping toward them.

It landed between Dohi and Fitz. Dohi went for his

hatchet, and Fitz slammed the stock of his rifle into the juvenile's jaw, cracking bone.

Corrin lunged in from behind, using his claws to slit the sliver of unprotected flesh between the armor plates of the juvenile. Blood pumped out and the creature collapsed, jerking.

"They have a weak spot there," he said.

"Damn," Ace said. "I'm really starting to like this... guy."

Fitz signaled to advance into the room.

Flashlight beams danced over the stainless-steel doors of body-sized drawers. Two huge metal slabs stained dark by blood were at the center of the space. Taut vines laced into the drawers, and Ace pulled one out to reveal a corpse that had fed those vines.

"Let's get the fuck out of this hellhole," he said.

Dohi was about to open the door leading out of the morgue when the comm channel crackled to life.

He signaled for Dohi to pause.

"Ghost One, Spearhead One," Neilson said, his words firing quick as an automatic rifle. "We got contacts! Need backup! Now!"

***

Azrael walked through the lines of two-meter tall banks of supercomputers covered in red vines at his Citadel. The air was sweltering and choking with humidity. This had been the birthplace of his communication network, back when he had relied on manmade computers.

He no longer needed most of them, although they had kept a few personal computers around for pedestrian tasks. The world of information technology he had created relied not on silicon computer chips, but rather engineered neurons, such as those in the behemoths that towered at the end of the two-story computational lab.

The bulbous mastermind pulled on red vines and let out long, rattling breaths, filling the air with a fetid odor.

Scions and human faithful alike moved about the space, using a few of the personal computers that Azrael still needed operating. Loyalists monitoring the communication network relayed updates on the battle in Vegas as well as their operations elsewhere.

He clasped his claws behind his back, soaking in the musty, bloody smell of the place. Along the walls, a few human prisoners writhed in nests of red. Their pained moans filled Azrael with great pleasure.

A human kneeled in front of him. "Prophet, I have news of the special operations teams."

"Speak."

The loyalist bowed his head. "Our guards captured a group of soldiers infiltrating the University Medical Center."

A jolt of shock shook through Azrael, but he refused to let it show. "Were they coming after *me*?"

"I believe so." There was fear in the human's voice.

"The humans listening in our network truly did track down those signals," Azrael said. "But that is exactly as we had expected." He placed a claw under the human loyalist's chin, forcing the man to look up at him. "Was this the infamous Team Ghost that our guards captured?"

The human shook his head. "No, Prophet. It was another group with the Canadian flag on their uniforms."

Azrael scratched at the scars along his jaw. "This is unexpected, but we may be able to use it to our advantage. Alert Elijah at once."

"Yes, Prophet."

Azrael lurked behind the other human loyalists and Scions monitoring battle reports.

"Prophet," said a Scion named Gabriel. "The heretics are still flooding the main strip."

Gabriel tapped on a monitor showing a map of Vegas.

"They are closing in on the Venetian. Should I execute the final orders for Operation Darkness?"

Azrael glanced at the monitor. Red blips showed where collaborators and Scions were reporting current enemy positions. He pictured the faces of those humans that had constantly stood in his way. Reed Beckham. Team Ghost. The infidels who refused to submit.

"Has anyone confirmed that Beckham and Team Ghost are here?" Azrael asked.

"Not yet, Prophet."

"Then we must wait."

"If we wait too long, the humans will—"

Azrael slashed out with his claws, drawing four scarlet lines down the side of Gabriel's face. To the Scion's credit, he didn't flinch.

"If you hold the faith, you *will* abide my words," Azrael said.

"Yes, Prophet," Gabriel said, eyes lowered. "It was foolish of me to speak like that."

One of the doors to the lab opened. Four Scions marched in with their cutlasses strapped over their backs. Between them limped a hulking form.

All the way from across the room, Azrael could smell the beast's festering wounds in his diseased flesh. It was the general, finally returned from Canada.

The Alpha stumbled toward him. One of his arms hung useless at his side.

"I am sorry to… interrupt, Prophet," the general said, dropping to his knees before Azrael.

His massive chest expanded and deflated in heaving gasps. Blood caked the rim of a bullet hole in his shattered elongated jaw.

Azrael looked at Gabriel, who was staring straight at him. "You have come at the perfect time. We are approaching victory in Vegas… and elsewhere."

"Yes, Prophet."

Azrael spun, holding his claws wide to the rest of the room. "Soon we will all taste victory! And even sweeter, we will feast on the flesh of our enemies."

A few monstrous howls rose, and human loyalists cheered.

"But only those who do not fail me will feast."

The general dared to look up at Azrael with eyes that sparkled with a hint of fear.

"Please, Prophet, I almost…" he began to say.

Azrael snapped his claws. Red vines from the floor and wall slithered around the general. They snaked into his nostrils, ear canals, and the bullet hole in his jaw, prompting the general to screech in agony. More vines wrapped around his wrists and legs, yanking him off the ground.

All the chatter in the operations center ceased, except for a few squawking radios. Even the mastermind was watching.

"You failed me once," Azrael said.

He gestured toward the mastermind. The vines stretched until the general's bones started to crack. The wounds he had sustained from his attack on Banff opened, fresh gouts of blood drizzling out.

Azrael snapped his claws together again. This time the

vines continued to stretch, and the general's roars shook through the room. A violent tearing sound ripped through the space as his limbs pulled free from their joints, bones and flesh torn apart by the gruesome contractions of the webbing.

The torso of the general dangled in the air, vines still holding him up by his head and neck. Rattling gasps escaped the creature as he let out agonized moans.

Azrael ignored the beast, facing his followers again. "We are close to destroying the Allied States. Do not let failure become a distraction. While the human armies are focused on Las Vegas, we will deliver a strike that will paralyze them forever."

The final breaths escaped the general's broken body, and the vines released him. His corpse slapped against the floor.

Azrael turned away from the dying creature. He had no more time to waste dealing with insolent fools.

He looked back at Gabriel and the others. "Bring me Beckham. Bring me Ghost. Bring me victory."

— 12 —

Dohi crouched at the entrance to a windowless second-floor corridor. They had traveled back up from the morgue through the hospital when Spearhead had called for backup.

The shrieks of Variants had sounded throughout the climb, but now the beasts had gone quiet. There was no sign of the Canadians. No streaks of blood. No bullet casings. Nothing to indicate where the team had gone.

Dohi was no longer sure going after them was a good idea.

The mission to find the Prophet far outweighed the lives of a single team, including even Team Ghost. But Fitz believed finding where the beasts had taken Spearhead would lead them to the Prophet.

For now, that was their game plan.

Sweat matted his ACUs and saturated his gloves as he gripped his rifle. The temperature in the hospital seemed to be rising.

Dohi clenched his jaw, holding his breath, waiting for orders.

"Should we try them on the comms?" Rico whispered.

Fitz shook his head.

Ace surveyed the area with his rifle, cutting through the darkness with his barrel-mounted tac light.

Corrin sniffed at the air. He leaned in close to Fitz,

then whispered, "Variants are close."

The air only got hotter as they made their way deeper into the hospital. Dohi blinked the sweat from his eyes. He came up on a corner and put his back against the wall, then snuck a glance around.

The coast was clear, and he shot a gesture to the team to relay the info.

Fitz signaled to continue.

Striding out with his rifle shouldered, Dohi finally saw the first tracks from Spearhead across the webbing covered floor.

Bodies hung from vines on the walls. Most were nothing but ragged corpses, a few pieces of leathery flesh hanging over tooth-marked bones. One man moaned, somehow alive despite his shriveled body.

Dohi shuddered, remembering his own experiences in the webbing. This man wouldn't survive being taken down from the vines, but Dohi couldn't just let him suffer.

There was only one thing to do.

He pulled out his hatchet, but then decided not to spill blood.

"Do you want me to end this?" Dohi whispered.

Sunken eyes focused on Dohi, full of relief more than fear. He gave Dohi a nod.

"I'm sorry," Dohi whispered. He held the man's gaze as he pinched his nose shut and pressed his hand over his mouth.

Dohi waited a few moments to make sure it was done. The other soldiers didn't say anything and continued past empty hospital rooms and gurneys left in the hall. A few windows allowed the team to flick off their tac lights and put on their NVGs.

Another dark three-way intersection waited for them at the end of the corridor.

This time Fitz motioned for Corrin to take point and listen. The Chimera exchanged places with Dohi who could already hear the soft squish of claws digging into webbing down the passage. The air reeked of rotten fruit.

Corrin sniffed at it, gesturing to confirm there were Variants nearby.

Leaning around the corner, Dohi saw the footsteps in the webbing led toward the end of the hall. Another set of stairs there provided access to the third floor.

In between his position and those stairs were six well-fed Variants. The beasts prowled along the webbing and pulled a few bodies from the tendrils.

Dohi focused on the faces of those human corpses, but their skin looked parched and curled off their bones. These people hadn't died recently.

Spearhead might still be alive, and if they had made it to that stairwell, that meant their last calls had been sent from at least one more floor above them.

After signaling to the rest of the group what he'd seen, Dohi looked down the hall without any monsters. An elevator shaft beckoned to him. One of its doors was jammed open by a gurney. He could see that behind those doors, there was no carriage.

Fitz signaled for Dohi to go up first and check things out, while the rest of the team waited here to avoid making extra noise.

Dohi snuck down the hall and slipped into the shaft. As quietly as he could, he climbed inside and started the ascent up to the next floor, hearing voices near the top.

Human voices.

He stopped near the bottom of the next open doors, listening.

It sounded like just two men, posted somewhere down the hallway.

Collaborators.

They were discussing the Canadians and how easy it was to capture them. Dohi's heart picked up a beat. The Canadians might still be alive.

"The Prophet is going to have fun with those heretics," one of the men said.

An idea bloomed in Dohi's mind, and he retreated down the shaft. By the time he got there, the Variants had moved on to sleep off their full bellies.

He explained what he had overheard to Fitz and the rest of the team.

"Let's send Corrin to talk to the collaborators," Dohi said. "See if we can find out where Spearhead is."

Fitz looked to Corrin.

"I'll do it," the Chimera said.

"Okay, go up the stairs," Fitz said. "We'll cover you from the elevator."

The team moved out. Dohi watched Corrin leave. In a few minutes, they would find out if the Chimera could truly be trusted.

By the time he got to the top of the elevator shaft, Corrin was already approaching the two collaborators at the nurses' station. One was a man with a black baseball cap, and the other had a matted beard.

The collaborators bowed their heads, shrinking back at Corrin's arrival.

"Sir, did Elijah send for us?" asked the man with the cap.

Dohi noted the name, guessing Elijah must be a Chimera leader.

"No, he sent me," Corrin said. "I need to see the prisoners. Take me to them."

The two collaborators exchanged a look.

"Take me to them," Corrin said, this time a little more fiercely.

The man with the beard looked up. Suddenly, the look of fear melted into one of skepticism.

"Where's your cutlass?" he asked.

The capped collaborator began to raise his rifle. "I've never seen you before."

Dohi raised his rifle out of the shaft.

"Elijah sent me," Corrin said. He growled.

"Prove it," said the man with the cap.

Both pointed their weapons at Corrin.

Dohi sighted up the guy with the cap and blew it off, along with part of his skull. Corrin lunged over the counter of the nurses' station and tackled the bearded man.

Glad we decided to let Corrin live, Dohi thought.

The team climbed out of the shaft and set up a perimeter while Corrin held the bearded man down, claws to his throat.

"Where's the Prophet?" Fitz asked. "And where are the prisoners?"

The collaborator shook in Corrin's arms. "If I tell you... if the Prophet..."

"The Prophet is the least of your concerns right now." Fitz stepped close to the collaborator. "You won't take another breath if you don't tell me where the prisoners and your Prophet are."

The collaborator raised a finger, pointing overhead.

"We… we took the prisoners upstairs. Up where the Scions went."

"Where upstairs?" Fitz asked.

"The lecture hall."

"If you're lying to us, this beast will rip out your throat," Fitz said. "Do you understand?"

The collaborator gulped, but nodded.

"The Prophet is with the prisoners?" Fitz asked.

"With our prisoners, yeah. That's right."

The man's eyes twitched, and he nodded a little too vigorously. But Dohi wasn't sure if he was lying. He had already pissed his pants out of fear, which made it difficult to tell.

Corrin yanked him up.

"Take us to them," Fitz said. "You scream, and you're dead."

Corrin started walking with the collaborator, holding the man by an arm.

When they reached the floor where the collaborator claimed the lecture hall was, Dohi took point again. The doors to the hall were wide open, and he snuck inside. True to the collaborator's word, he spotted Team Spearhead, but the Prophet wasn't here and the room was free of Variants.

All three of the Canadians were pasted on the walls above the seats facing a podium covered in webbing. Toussaint and Neilson were struggling against their restraints, vines covering their mouths. Blood dripped from Daugherty's nostrils. His head hung limp. Dohi noticed his chest was still.

He wasn't breathing.

Dohi waved the rest of the team in, and Fitz gave the order to Ace and Rico to set the prisoners free. They hacked away at the cocoons holding Spearhead in place, then gently lowered Toussaint and Neilson out first. The two fell to their knees, gasping for breath and retching.

Dohi checked on Daugherty, pressing two fingers to the man's neck. He held it there for a moment, hoping to detect a pulse, but his heart had stopped.

"Damn," he whispered. He looked to Fitz and shook his head.

Fitz snorted with anger.

"Where's the Prophet?" he asked their prisoner.

"I…"

Fitz grabbed him by the neck, and Corrin tightened his grip on his arm.

"Tell me or I'm going to make you wish the Variants had feasted on you," Fitz said. He kept his voice low, but the ferocity in it surprised Dohi. He rarely heard the master sergeant this angry.

Dohi's aim roved around the room, waiting for a pack of Variants to descend on them or more collaborators to spring from the doors at the back of the room.

"I don't know, he was here…" the man suddenly jerked away from Corrin and Fitz, running for the exit yelling, "Heretics!"

Corrin tackled the man and tore his throat out, but it was already too late. An undercurrent of electricity cut the air. It was as if the vines were suddenly coming alive, sending a pulsating tremor through the entire building.

***

Kate watched over Sammy's shoulder at the signals and words scrolling across the computer engineer's screen. They had spent the past couple days since Beckham and the others left in the parking garage of the hospital outside Houston, connected to the webbing in the nearby gaping tunnel.

"Woah, did you see that?" Sammy asked.

She pointed at a sudden spike in signaling activity.

"It's all coming from Vegas," Sammy said.

Kate thought of her husband and her friends on the mission. She almost couldn't bear the thought of them out there risking their lives, but she had to focus and play her part.

"Reed and the others should be at the sites where we think the Prophet is by now," she said.

"Yeah, seems like this influx of activity could be related."

"What can you tell so far?"

Sammy pointed at some of the words scrolling across the screen. "It seems like we're advancing faster than the Variants' expected."

"Maybe they weren't ready for us," Kate said. The unease in her stomach made her question whether she actually believed those words.

"There's something bad here, though," Sammy said. She pointed at another message. "Some collaborators are reporting they captured a special ops team."

Kate resisted the urge to cover her mouth.

"A Canadian team," Sammy said.

"Oh, God."

"You okay?"

Kate stepped away from Sammy's computer. "No... but I have to be. I will be."

She turned from the monitor. Leslie was still strapped into the network. She and Kate had been taking two-hour turns for the past six straight hours, trying to disrupt the

Variants' communications in Vegas by sending fake messages and commands. So far, they had managed to divert a couple of packs of Variants and groups of collaborators, sending them into the outskirts of the cities where no Allied States troops were.

The more wild goose chases they went on, the better.

"The Variants sound desperate," Sammy said. "They keep requesting reinforcements, and many have retreated out of the areas where our forces are pushing forward."

A few guards situated around the parking garage were looking their way, sharing expressions of relief to hear the direction the battle was going.

"I think they might actually be scared," Sammy said.

Kate hoped she was right.

Footsteps pounded down the stairs to the garage. Ron came running from the stairwell toward them, waving a notebook. "I found something!"

He was nearly out of breath when he slammed the notebook onto the table. On an open page were lists of names. Some were crossed out and others were connected by lines.

"I cross-referenced all the principal investigators of the biodefense and bioengineering related projects under DARPA's umbrella," he said.

"And you found a match to all the technologies we've uncovered?" Kate asked.

"Not exactly," Ron said. "There were a few labs that worked with the strain of anthrax we found in that grenade. But there was no overlap with them and the neural engineering groups."

Kate frowned. "Are you sure we aren't missing a government lab from that list?"

"Positive," Ron said. "Those labs in Seattle and

Denver were the only places the computer interface and microarray research was taking place."

"Damn. So how are they connected to DARPA biodefense research?"

"That's the thing. They aren't connected. Not really, anyway."

"So the anthrax samples were—"

Ron flipped to another page in his notebook. "The particular strain we found was a lab-created strain that I tracked all the way back to a Soviet Union program—Biopreparat."

"Wait, so this is some international plot now?" Sammy asked.

"No, no, no." Ron waved his hands. "Not even close. Lab records indicate this strain was stored at Fort Detrick in Maryland with USAMRIID. The only people with access to it were biodefense specialists in the government—and a few federal contractor groups."

"Which contractors?" Kate asked.

"All the usual suspects. Leidon, Blackwell, and BAH. But ignore those." He jabbed his index finger at a single name on the paper. "Here's the rub. This company, OrgoProct, was the only contractor I didn't recognize."

Kate narrowed her eyes, studying the name. It sounded vaguely familiar, but she couldn't figure out why. "Where did you find all this stuff?"

"A mixture of public records and old DARPA archives."

"What do we know about OrgoProct?"

Ron flipped to a page with a map. On it, he had circled various locations, including Seattle and Denver, that had names written next to them. "You remember Dr. Simon Wong from the University of Florida? Well, we already know he was involved in computer-neural interface research that took place in the California Bay area and Seattle."

He moved his finger to Denver. "There was another research group here led by Dr. Jennifer Yeatts. They specialized in communication networks, mostly digital, cybersecurity-type stuff."

Next he circled Portland, Oregon. "Dr. Bhushan Reddi had an academic group that focused on genetic engineering of viral agents here."

"Is that our guy?" Sammy asked.

"I can't say for certain, but I don't think so," Ron said. He continued, pointing to various locations around the former United States and listing names associated with projects investigating technologies that might've been related to the Chimeras, webbing network, masterminds, and more.

"All these people were doing DARPA-funded research?" Kate asked.

"Many, but not all."

"Then how are they connected?"

Ron had never looked so confident and self-assured. "It all goes back to OrgoProct. Each of these people served as a scientific adviser for the organization at one time or another."

Everything suddenly clicked together for Kate. "Good lord, if it wasn't someone in DARPA, if it wasn't some government scientist, their connection is through OrgoProct," she said.

"Exactly," Ron said. He rubbed his hands together. "This is what really tipped me off. Several of those unknown compounds we found in the Chimera's tissues were residuals from the gene delivery system of the modified VX-99 administered to the Chimera. I found an exact match from that same viral vector delivery system in OrgoProct's research reports that they submitted to the Department of Defense."

"And what was that delivery system supposed to be for?" Kate asked.

"It was supposed to deliver a set of genes targeting specific human cells," Ron said.

"Hold up," Sammy said. "What kind of genes are we talking about?"

"The genes were made to reverse the effects of VX-99 and X9H9."

"Oh, my God," Kate muttered. Then she recalled where she had heard of the company before. "I remember OrgoProct's reports years ago during the Great War. They were one of the many labs that tried to find a cure for X9H9 back when I was also searching for it. The government was enlisting every lab, every scientist they possibly could. But obviously OrgoProct didn't succeed, did they?"

"I don't think so," he said. "The last report was sent two days before you developed the bioweapon called VariantX9H9."

Kate winced at the name of the bioweapon, guilt eating at her for what she had created. It was meant to destroy the monsters that X9H9 had created. It worked, killing most. But it also had unintended consequences, turning those that survived into the Variants that plagued the world today.

All of that seemed like a lifetime ago, but now it was more relevant than ever.

"Can I see that last report?" Kate asked.

She took the paper from Ron, skimming through the

lengthy graphs and tables of data until she reached the final summary.

We're losing time. Most of our staff has succumbed to X9H9, including myself. I don't have the luxury to prepare for human trials, so instead I will try our cure on myself. I can already feel the fever settling in and the nausea. If this is the last transmission from us, you will know we failed. OrgoProct's efforts to reverse the genetic effects caused by X9H9 will have failed. The angel of death will have swept through the final survivors in Los Alamos National Labs.

I only wish we could have had more time.

-Charles Morgan, OrgoProct Chief Scientific Officer

"Los Alamos?" Kate asked.

Ron nodded. "Like many research companies, they were frequent users of Los Alamos National Laboratories. Much of their early research creating computational models of X9H9 and VX-99 took place there."

"I see," Kate said. "So this Charles Morgan? Is *he* our guy?"

"Sounds like he might've died after he administered his own drug, huh?" Sammy said.

Ron shrugged. "There's no way to confirm it."

"But if he was trying to reverse the genetic effects of X9H9 at the same time we deployed VariantX9H9 across the nation, what if there was some kind of genetic interference?" Kate asked. "What if our bioweapon negatively interacted with the effects of his?"

Ron nearly stumbled. "You're saying…"

Even Sammy followed their train of logic now. "Chimeras. His engineered drugs reversed some of the genetic changes as intended, but your VariantX9H9 made other changes."

"It's just a theory," Kate said. "It might be entirely wrong."

"But it fits, I think you might be onto something." Ron looked at the ceiling as if deep in thought. "Maybe I can run some simulations, see if this theory holds any merit."

"Okay," Kate said.

Ron started to head toward the stairs.

Something else bothered Kate. Thanks to Ron's list, they were able to explain the various hives of New God and mastermind activity they had discovered throughout the Allied States. But there was one city name that she hadn't heard.

"Ron, wait," she called out. "Was OrgoProct located in Vegas? Is that why there's so much Variant activity there?"

Ron looked at his notebook. "No, OrgoProct was in Santa Fe, close to Los Alamos."

"Were any of those research groups you mentioned in Vegas?"

"Not a single one."

"Then why are the New Gods there, especially if OrgoProct was in New Mexico?"

"I don't know," Ron said.

Kate wanted to be satisfied with the revelations he had uncovered, but the fact they had found no connections between the New Gods, Vegas, and any of these researchers and their respective research groups nagged at her.

They were missing something, and there was almost no time to find out what.

"We've got to tell Ringgold," Kate said. "I don't know if this Charles Morgan is our guy or if OrgoProct somehow became the epicenter of the New Gods in Los Alamos, but soldiers are dying in Las Vegas and if the Prophet isn't actually there, it's all for nothing."

— 13 —

Timothy crouched in the darkness. Gunfire sounded from nearly every direction. The flash of tracer fire coursed through the black night, and beasts howled and roared.

So far, the attacks had come in random intervals from packs of three or four.

Timothy glanced at the Wynn hotel though his NVGs. While the name was still visible, most of the front glass façade had shattered. Only sporadic panes of glass remained. Each of the dark rooms was a potential sniper position for collaborators or Scions.

Every step felt like it could be his last, his nerves tight from the potential of a sniper bullet.

While Wong was on point and Boyd watched their back on rearguard, Ruckley remained closer to him, watching the windows and rooftops.

Ahead he saw another hotel that had fallen into utter disrepair. The letters on the building's side said "SURE ISLAND".

Wong paused next to a military truck with deflated, rotten tires. Claw marks scarred the paint. He pointed to his eyes, then toward their right to what looked like the entrance to a mall nearly forty yards away.

Webbing stretched from the broken glass doors and windows, curling over the concrete. There was no mistaking the shadows moving within the structure. Pale creatures crawled over the tangled vines.

Ruckley pulled out her infrared binoculars and scanned the neighboring buildings. Then she gestured toward a sight that Timothy recognized from his briefings: The Grand Canal Shoppes at the Venetian.

That was their target.

Ruckley handed the binos to Timothy.

Another squad of soldiers was hunched down across the street. She exchanged hand signals with the other team lead.

Dozens of Variants crawled over the Grand Canal Shoppes. On the roof and in the darkened windows, he saw other moving shapes. It was difficult to tell if they were human or Chimera, but he could clearly see that they carried rifles.

"Looks like a hive," Timothy whispered. "Just like the science team said."

"We can't go straight at the building," Boyd said. "They'd cut us down before we got there."

"You got that right." Ruckley pointed to a panel of grating on the sidewalk that led to a storm drain. "That's why we're going underground."

Another rash of gunfire echoed somewhere to the south. Probably TF Bravo caught in another firefight.

Timothy felt the smooth wooden beads of his bracelet. He found strength in the simple touch as he watched Ruckley exchange more hand signals with the other squad leaders. The teams both got up and started to move into position to provide a distraction.

As soon as the first gunshot rang out and the other squads were pounding the Variants roaming around the Grand Canal Shoppes, Ruckley gave the order to advance.

Keeping low, Timothy hurried across the street, again bracing himself for incoming rounds and dodging between debris for shelter. He made it across the street a minute later with the rest of the team.

Boyd and Wong lifted the grate from the sidewalk, heaving it to the side. It let out a jarring scrape against the concrete, and Timothy crouched instinctively, scanning their surroundings with his rifle.

All the beasts and collaborators were too distracted by the incoming gunfire from the other squads to notice. The distraction was working.

Ruckley signaled Wong down first. Timothy followed, then came Boyd and Ruckley.

The stench of the place slammed into Timothy like he had run straight into a wall. He pulled a handkerchief over his nose and mouth. Goosebumps prickled across his skin.

Without any light deeper in the tunnel, they were forced to flip up their NVGs and turn on their tac lights. Slowly they navigated through the massive concrete tunnel. Webbing covered every surface, throbbing red in the pale wash of their flashlights.

Between the echoing fire aboveground, he listened for the scrape of claws down here, waiting for an ambush.

Keep moving Timothy, just keep moving.

Like his father had always told him, no matter what you did in life, you kept pushing forward.

He kept close to Ruckley, making their way past the rotting bodies of humans and animals stuck to the walls. Fissures in the concrete let through columns of shifting dirt and dust with each walloping boom of an exploding grenade above.

So far, it seemed the attack was working. The

monsters were focused on the main assault force. Teams like his, Recon Sigma, and the others could move into position within the Venetian and set explosives.

Then once Beckham and Horn or Team Ghost confirmed they had caught the Prophet, they would bring this whole damn hive down.

The storm drain dragged on. Another heavy thudding explosion caused a violent crack in the ceiling. Small chunks of concrete fell over their heads.

As the blast settled, Timothy heard a loud thump.

Wong held up a fist, and they all dropped into kneeling positions, lights aimed down the tunnel. Something huge burst into an intersection about fifty yards ahead, white flesh with massive limbs and batlike ears.

The beast turned their direction, letting out a shrill series of clicks, its ears twitching.

Timothy sucked in a breath at the sight of the monster.

It was an Alpha.

Ruckley gave the signal, and they opened fire.

The beast ducked into their gunfire, bullets riddling its flesh and sparking against the concrete around it. It barreled ahead on all fours, letting out a guttural roar.

Other hellish voices echoed behind the monster. Another five Variants galloped behind the brute, stringy muscles rippling beneath their skin.

As rounds lanced into the Alpha, it shuddered, absorbing the impacts and slowing.

Timothy heard another series of shrieks coming from behind.

He twisted, his flashlight illuminating the tunnel they had already traveled through. A group of ten juvenile

Variants with armored flesh chased after them.

"Ruckley, our six!" Timothy shouted.

She was probably doing the math like he was.

Those beasts were too close, too many of them. They couldn't sustain a firefight without solid cover. Especially not against the armored juveniles.

Ruckley grabbed a grenade from her vest, motioning for Timothy to do the same.

Beckham had taught him that a concussive blast in a confined place like this was risky. The force would be concentrated by the walls, tearing them apart if they threw the grenades too close to their positions.

If the blasts didn't destroy their organs, then it might bring the roof down on top of them.

From the front, the Alpha let out an angry yell, stumbling toward them, one of its legs limp. The other five creatures behind it rushed past. One fell in the gunfire. Another was shredded.

The ten juveniles were closing in from behind, too, jaws snapping, lips smacking together.

"Fire in the hole!" Ruckley said.

She threw her grenade like a major league pitcher. Timothy followed her lead.

The two grenades sailed toward the juveniles.

But the beasts were too fast. They surged past the grenades.

Timothy swung his rifle up, right when the first grenade detonated. The tunnel shook. Flames danced behind the monsters, swallowing part of the tunnel. Several juveniles were knocked off their feet. Then the second grenade exploded.

This time, the fissures in the ceiling spread with the expanding fire. More of the creatures stumbled. Timothy was knocked off his feet by the blast. He hit the ground hard, his ears ringing, head pounding.

Ruckley grimaced next to him, blinking away the pain.

More concrete chunks fell from the ceiling. Like an avalanche, the tunnel began collapsing behind them, swallowing the entrance they had come through with a monstrous roar.

Pieces rained from the ceiling on the dazed juveniles. They tried to stand and scramble away but falling concrete crushed their bodies.

The ceiling didn't stop collapsing after the beasts were swallowed in the rubble. The tide of destruction came toward Timothy and Ruckley.

"Move!" Ruckley yelled. She jumped to her feet and grabbed Timothy, pulling him into a run.

Boyd and Wong were in the process of changing their magazines while two injured Variants and the hobbled Alpha stumbled toward them.

Timothy tried to keep his rifle steady, but he was too shaky and didn't have a clear field of fire.

"Out of the way!" Ruckley shouted.

She stepped between Wong and Boyd and drained her magazine into the two beasts, then Boyd and Wong finished off the Alpha with bullets to its milky blind eyes.

The giant finally slumped forward, dead.

A cloud of gray dust and debris flooded around them as they rushed past the dead creatures.

Timothy tried to breath, but choked on the dust, coughing.

There was no going back the way they had come. There was only one direction to go now, just like his father had said.

Forward.

Covered in dust, Wong led them to a short ladder that took them to a loading dock for the Venetian.

A pair of Variants hunched near the entrance, on alert from the noise that had erupted from the tunnels. Ruckley and Timothy fired a few suppressed shots that killed the beasts, then hurried past the fresh corpses.

They followed the loading bay to the maintenance corridors that ran behind the shops and guest rooms. Wong took them through another door that opened into a wide space with a faux sky and false façades that made Timothy think he had stepped straight into Europe. Canals ran alongside the shops. The water had long since drained from them, and a pair of long gondolas lay sideways on the bottom.

Red webbing smothered everything, throbbing and squirming. More bodies hung from the walls and the ceiling, like a spider's web filled with fresh prey.

Ruckley pointed at Wong and Boyd. They prepared the fuses and detonation charges for a pair of C-4 explosives and set them into the corners of the wide atrium, then started to move to the next space.

Before they climbed a short bridge over the dried-out canal, a rumble shook through the hotel. They froze as another quake shook the walls.

A low explosion sounded in the distance.

Had one of the other teams detonated their explosives early? Or had Recon Sigma missed the mark and set their explosions late?

Ruckley looked between them frantically and broke radio silence. "Command, Recon Sigma One. We heard explosions. What's going on?"

"Recon Sigma, other units are reporting blasts from unknown sources."

Another explosion boomed through the walls, this one sounding closer to the Venetian. Cracks formed in the ceiling and chunks of plaster rained down.

Somewhere deeper in the hotel, another blast went off. This one was nearly deafening, and the whole building quivered as if it might fall.

Timothy stared at the empty corridors, realizing suddenly why the only resistance they had faced was outside.

"Guys, what are those drums doing down there?" Boyd asked. He shone his flashlight over a cluster of barrels with wires coming away from them.

"Those aren't ours," Wong said.

"Run!" Ruckley shouted. "Go!"

They were nearly at the loading dock when an explosion ripped through the hotel and shops, fire bursting through the doorways and windows. Ruckley and Wong disappeared behind a screen of falling rubble.

"Ruckley!" Timothy yelled.

He rushed back to the mound of broken wreckage, choking on the dust and smoke. Another fissure ripped across the ceiling, spilling debris and fire that blocked his path.

"This whole place is going to come down!" Boyd screamed.

He grabbed Timothy and pulled him away from a fragmented hunk of ceiling that crashed to the ground. Another rumble tore through the building. The wall to the loading dock collapsed, and Timothy stumbled through a billowing cloud of dust and ash.

Lowering his helmet, he pushed through the grit. Boyd was just ahead, almost to the open loading dock. Another wall crumbled, coming down with the ceiling, and burying them feet away from exit.

***

"Hostile down," Beckham said.

He lowered his rifle after dispatching a rogue Variant. It was one of the only creatures they had encountered so far. He was starting to worry Kate's team had been wrong about the Prophet being located in the Palazzo. The booms and explosions from nearby blasts that had rocked the building worried him even more. If they were on the wrong track, it could prove deadly.

A few teams had reported seeing explosives that did not belong to the Allied States, and command had warned all ground forces to keep an eye out for improvised explosive devices.

He had heard Recon Sigma, Timothy and Ruckley's team, calling command to request clarification on the explosions. Since then, they had been silent.

He hoped that was a good sign. That it meant they were still on target. But he could not help the worry filtering through his mind that maybe he was wrong.

Nonetheless, he continued to lead Horn through the Palazzo's casino.

Webbing stretched from the ceiling between the slot machines and card tables. They sifted through a lounge with dusty booths and toppled tables and chairs.

Webbing stretched from the ceiling between the slot machines and card tables. They sifted through a lounge with dusty booths and toppled tables and chairs.

A wave of explosions rocked through Vegas, small columns of dust falling from the ceiling. Their time to find the evil creature responsible for this madness was definitely running out, and his pulse thundered in his ears with each consecutive blast.

The radios came alive with the voices of frantic soldiers calling for help. Quakes shook the Palazzo.

Horn shifted around nervously. "That sounds close."

Another boom shook the tower. This time it sounded like it had come from the Venetian, where the Recon teams were supposed to lay explosives to bring down the Variant hives.

That was the second blast near Timothy's location.

"I'm breaking radio silence," Beckham said, no longer able to contain his worry. "Recon Sigma, Reaper One, do you copy?"

No answer.

"Recon Sigma, do you copy?"

Come on. Come on.

Still no answer.

They had to move.

"On me," Beckham said.

He took them back through the casino, smashing over the organic webbing. They raced toward the lobby just as another rumble tore through the building. Marble columns fell on either side of them, slamming into the floor.

"This way!" Beckham said, taking them out of the Palazzo and through the shops in front.

They raced between the stores, the whole complex quaking. Dark smoke clogged the corridors. Pieces of the ornate façades fell away in miniature rockslides. They were nearing the exit when cracks fissured through the ceiling and part of it came down in front of them. Pipes and support beams swung dangerously, just a foot or two from their faces.

Beckham navigated around the deadly obstacles. He struggled to breathe, the smoke filling his lungs as they advanced into another smoke and dust-filled atrium. A few columns surrounding an ivory statue toppled. Glass rained down from a dome in the roof, slashing at their ACUs and armor.

One large piece shattered on Horn's helmet, but he barely flinched.

As Beckham ran, he thought of Timothy, praying the young man was out of the Venetian. But something had definitely gone wrong. The detonations weren't supposed to happen for another hour and with Recon Sigma not responding, his mind filled with dark possibilities.

Had Timothy been trapped inside, buried under the rubble?

Beckham felt a chill trace his spine at the thought. He shouldered his rifle through a cloud of smoke, cautious of any ambushing Variants. He thought he heard the sound of clicking joints, but it could have been the structure coming down in all the chaotic clamor.

Finally, he saw the exit doors and rushed out onto a landing where he paused to stare in horror.

Up and down the strip, casinos were caught in rolling oily clouds of smoke and ash illuminated by ravenous flames. The biting air stung his eyes and lungs, harkening back Operation Liberty, back in those last days of the first war when he had run through New York's streets as the entire city imploded, caught in a massive bombing run.

Only this time, it wasn't his side doing the bombing.

Illuminated by the roaring flames devouring the city, the silhouettes of monstrous shapes flitted between the smoke clouds descending on scattered soldiers fleeing the destruction. TF Alpha was surrounded and attacked by

Chimeras, collaborators, and Variants.

Other soldiers took cover behind burned out cars and trucks or slabs of concrete, only to be overwhelmed by gunfire or an Alpha erupting from a manhole, leading a pack of Variants.

Beckham desperately looked for a way he could turn the tide of this battle. But despite their experience in the field, he and Horn were just two retired operators. They were not equipped for this onslaught.

"Contacts on our ten!" Horn said.

He unloaded a hailstorm of lead, ripping into three charging beasts. Geysers of blood sprayed from where rounds tore into their bodies.

The monsters tumbled over their own dead limbs.

"Don't fuck with the mountain!" Horn bellowed. He fired another burst at a pack, cutting all three down before they could get too close.

Beckham searched for a way out, but something held him in position. He had made a promise to Timothy, and now that it was clear the Prophet had laid an ambush, all that mattered to him was finding the young man and getting him out of here.

He wouldn't leave Timothy behind a second time.

"Recon Sigma, please respond!" Beckham said.

Another explosion erupted behind them, heat rolled over them, searing Beckham's skin. He urged them forward, heading south along the strip. The Palazzo trembled, large portions of the walls giving away, glass bursting from the windows. The entire tower fell into itself, letting out a grating protest of screeching metal and tumbling concrete.

Huge clouds of debris puffed into the air, mixing with pillars of flame and black smoke.

Beckham took to the sidewalk, ducking with Horn behind a wall as a wave of dust and grit surged over them. The tsunami of powdery air covered them, grit pelting them. Spikes of pain stabbed all over his exposed flesh. Despite holding his breath, Beckham still got some of it into his lungs, prompting a guttural cough.

A voice crackled over the main channel.

"All teams, be advised, air support and evac en route to extraction points. ETA fifteen mikes."

Horn looked at Beckham for orders, coughing deeply.

"I'm not going to that extraction point now," Beckham said, eyes watering from the smoke. "I've got to find Timothy. You can go if you want."

"You think I want to leave without that guy? Hell, no. Let's go get him!"

Horn led the way toward the Venetian where Timothy's team would have set their charges. Beckham struggled to breathe as he moved, his battered muscles screaming for oxygen that wouldn't make it to them. But the thought of finding Recon Sigma fueled him with energy.

"You okay?" Horn asked. He had stopped to let Beckham catch up.

"Don't stop moving," Beckham said.

Horn checked him with a quick flick of his eyes, then pushed onward, navigating the piles of scree toward what was left of the loading dock of the Venetian. An iron girder had smashed a semi-truck. Part of a wall had flattened another truck.

Dead Variants littered the ground, and others were crushed in the remains of broken crates and fractured concrete.

Beckham spotted an arm reaching out of a pile. The

gloved hand told him it wasn't a monster.

Horn and Beckham rushed over to the buried soldier. They heaved off the crates to reveal a torso and a head, badly burned. The face was nearly unrecognizable, charred and bleeding. His nametape read Wong.

"Hey, brother, are you with me?" Horn asked.

"Help…"

"We're getting you help." He hated lying, but he could tell the wounded soldier wasn't long for this world.

Horn suddenly got up and ran over to a bundle of pipes.

A death rattle escaped the lips of the man Beckham was with. Beckham had seen this before. Sometimes soldiers hung on just long enough to not die alone. He closed the guy's eyes, saying a brief prayer in his head, and hurried over to Horn.

He was already lifting pipes off Ruckley, tossing them like they were nothing but sticks. As he uncovered her, Beckham saw the extent of her injuries. Half the sleeve on her right arm was torn, her arm burned and blistered. Her left sleeve had been burned off too. The stitches from her injuries along her bicep had been torn open again, puckering to reveal the glistening red beneath.

"Ruckley," Horn said, strapping his machine gun over his back. He started to lift her. "We're going to get you out of here."

Beckham kept his rifle trained toward the street. "Contacts back across the street."

The cacophony of gunfire and flames nearly drowned out his voice.

He put a hand on Horn's shoulder. "We need to get out of here."

"We're not leaving her here. She's still alive."

Horn cradled Ruckley in his arms. She groaned, eyes fluttering open.

"Master Sergeant," she muttered.

"Where's the rest of your team?" Beckham asked.

Ruckley winced. "I… I don't know."

— 14 —

"Everything's falling apart," Ringgold whispered as she looked over the report from the science team.

She wanted to throw her coffee mug against the wall of the war room deep in Galveston's former Harbor House Hotel. Instead, she took a breath, trying to keep control while everything was spiraling away from her.

Once again, the New Gods had overwhelmed their forces in a matter of hours.

And like before, she was left wondering how.

She hoped someone on her team, anyone, could tell her something helpful. But so far General Cornelius, General Souza, and Lieutenant Festa didn't know anything more than she did.

Her team wasn't doing much better at keeping their emotions in check than she was. Festa and Souza both wore grimaces on their face like they had knives twisting into their sides.

"Someone, anyone, give me a sitrep," she said. "What in the hell is going on?"

"Our teams are being routed and pushed back from the strip," Souza said. "They're taking heavy losses."

"Then get them out of there now!" Ringgold said in a voice just shy of a shout.

"We're trying to execute selective evacuation protocols," Cornelius said.

"Everywhere we try to ID an LZ, it turns hot in

seconds," Souza added. "Primary and secondary LZs are occupied by hostiles. There are no clear evac sites."

"Then *make* some," Ringgold said, losing her patience. "We need to help these people. Can we reroute them somewhere we *can* secure?"

"We're working on that, ma'am," Cornelius said, face growing red with frustration.

He joined some of the officers huddled around the computers at the side of the room. They pored over the maps and monitors displayed in front of them, voices rising frantically.

Another team of communications officers manned computers coordinating the movements of the two task forces through the streets of Las Vegas. A fifty-five-inch monitor on one wall showed a map of the city, along with red blips to indicate where the ground forces had spotted hostiles. Green blips designated the locations of Allied States troops.

Too many of those green blips representing individual divisions and squads had already been crossed out as reports of confirmed KIAs filtered in. She watched another rash of green blips get crossed out, and an almost palpable pain struck through her gut.

"I'm getting confirmation that the explosions the teams are reporting aren't from our demo crews," Souza said. "The bombs going off were planted well before our teams got there."

"What... but..." Ringgold began to say.

"This was a trap," Cornelius said dryly. "They set enough explosives to bring down the whole damn city. They knew we were coming."

"How?" Ringgold asked. "How are they ahead of us every single damn time!?"

No one had an answer and avoided her gaze.

Ringgold looked back down at the message Kate had sent her hours earlier. The doctor had reported a Santa Fe-based company operating out of Los Alamos National Laboratory called OrgoProct. Their science division was led by Charles Morgan, which seemed to link all the strange technologies of the New Gods. The evidence was circumstantial at best, but the story seemed to make more sense as Ringgold thought about it.

The most startling revelation was that the New Gods had no known ties to Las Vegas.

Was this a New Gods' stronghold? Was it even an actual base?

Maybe it wasn't. Maybe this was all a façade.

One thing was certain, the Prophet was more intelligent than any Alpha she had faced in the past decade. She was going to have to think well outside of the box to beat the evil abomination.

"Have we found any of their leadership?" Ringgold asked.

"No," Souza replied. "However, Team Ghost is still within the UMC where they reported strong resistance. That kind of resistance might indicate New Gods leaders are nearby."

"So there's still hope," Ringgold said, clinging to any remote chance they might yet succeed with their initial objective. But that ephemeral hope was fading with every KIA reported on the monitor. "Have we heard anything from Ghost recently?"

"Not since they went radio silent."

"Almost all other units, even those on the retreat, are still engaged in skirmishes," Cornelius said, returning to the table.

He clicked a button on his keyboard, and the main monitor in the room shifted to the view from a helmet-mounted camera on a TF Bravo squad leader.

The rattle of gunfire sizzled over the speakers. Flames erupted over the parapets of the Excalibur hotel. A few of the towers on the castle had crumbled.

"Hostiles at our twelve and three!" a voice yelled over the speakers.

More flashes of tracer fire cut through the black of night. Ghoulish screams filled the comm as monsters swarmed from the flames, hurdling over the debris and ripping into the soldiers.

Ringgold turned away at the sound of tearing flesh and anguished yells.

"This is what the evac sites look like," Cornelius said, voice weak.

Cornelius switched to a feed from a helicopter. A door gunner manned an M-249 as the chopper swooped low over the fires spreading through the Vegas streets. The gunner raked machine gunfire over a pack of Variants, riddling their diseased flesh with bullets.

Despite the gunner's best efforts, a pack of the beasts broke into the lines of soldiers on the ground.

Ringgold's stomach clenched, her mouth going dry. Any hope she had had that Team Ghost might still find the Prophet was overshadowed by the massacre unfolding on the Vegas strip.

The New Gods had set this deception perfectly, luring her people into their clutches like a trapdoor spider. But what was their goal? To slaughter her forces or was something else going on?

She looked around the room at the exhausted faces, scrambling to organize a battle that seemed to have already been lost. Grainy images of the Variants played across many of the screens, along with a few videos of collaborators. The maps of enemy units showed several collaborator units and plenty of Variants.

But no Chimeras.

That sent another wave of chills through her.

"How many Chimeras have been reported?" Ringgold asked.

"I'm not sure," Souza said. "But not many. Maybe a few dozen. Initial reports of Chimeras turned out to be mostly collaborators."

Ringgold looked at the ceiling, considering the implications, mind racing. "If this really were brains of the New God's operations, we would have seen more of them, don't you think?"

"Yes, I thought so too, but it's possible they are all protecting the Prophet," Souza said.

"Or they are preparing to launch an assault while we've got all our focus on Vegas," Festa suggested.

"Send warnings to every remaining outpost immediately," Ringgold said. "Every able-bodied man and woman should already be on the wall, but they need to know how serious this is. They must be prepared for anything. An attack tonight could be worse than anything we faced before."

"Yes, Madam President," Festa said.

He began making calls to the twelve outposts scattered between Houston and Key Largo, the last of the Florida outposts. A few of Cornelius' comms officers came over to him, pointing at a map they laid on the table.

"We now have alternate evacuation routes set up for the two task forces," Cornelius said. "They'll be headed north out of the city, where parts of Las Vegas Boulevard are still intact."

He used the map on the monitor to discuss the routes with Ringgold for a few minutes before Festa returned to the table. His face was awash in pallor.

"What's wrong?" Ringgold asked. "Are there problems with the outposts?"

"Worse, Madam President," he replied. "We just got a transmission from the First Fleet in Puerto Rico. Scouts have reported seeing vessels of all kinds and sizes headed toward them, like some kind of scrapped together navy."

Ringgold didn't need to ask who those vessels belonged to. "Put me in touch with Vice President Lemke now."

Festa tried the encrypted line to Lemke, but no one answered.

Come on, Dan. Tell me what's going on.

The line continued to ring.

"I'm getting a new signal from the USS *George Johnson*," Festa said. He patched the line in.

"Command, this is Captain Harmon of the George Johnson," the voice said. "The Variants—they just—they swam under us before we could spot them. Then they started climbing up the sides of our ships. They're overrunning the *George Johnson*. We can't hold them back for much longer."

Festa spoke to the captain while Ringgold went to Souza, who was still trying to contact the vice president at Central Command.

"How could they have known about Puerto Rico?" Ringgold asked. She lowered her head in despair, trying to make sense of what was happening.

A few minutes later, the line with Captain Harmon had severed. They couldn't reconnect.

The room fell into silence for several grueling moments.

"All this time we thought the science team was listening in on them," Souza said. "Maybe they were the ones listening in on us."

Ringgold looked at the two generals, feeling sick. "The Prophet got us to focus all our attention on Vegas, one big honey trap, while they swept through from the east."

Cornelius shook his head. "I... I never saw this coming either, Madam President."

"Is there anything we can do to help Central Command?" she replied.

"Nothing we send will arrive in time," Cornelius said. "We don't have the supply chains. Most of our surviving air units are focused on evacuating Las Vegas, and the few naval units stationed in Galveston couldn't make it until at least a day after the enemy arrived."

"We need to put everything we have into protecting what little assets we have left," Souza said. He paused, appearing as if he didn't like what he was about to say next. "Let's hope the vice president can hold Central Command, because I'm afraid Puerto Rico is on their own, Madam President."

***

Azrael crouched in the open door of the MH-65 Dolphin. The chopper had been recently acquired after one of their successful conquests on the east coast of Florida, yet another benefit of their dominance over the Allied States.

After dealing with the general, he had left Los Alamos almost immediately to personally join another mission crucial to crippling the Allied States.

He had not originally planned to go, but he could no longer rely on Scions or Alphas like the general to get things done for him. And this mission was too important to fail.

Fortunately, by the time his flight from the Citadel had gotten him to the transfer point for this chopper, the battle over San Juan, Puerto Rico was almost won. He had arrived just in time to join in the final destruction.

The former Coast Guard chopper took him and six of his best hunters over the remains of the ancient walls of San Juan, built during the Spanish-American War. Fires bloomed through the darkness and tracer rounds pierced the night across the city.

His forces had prioritized destroying their comms so the Allied States had almost no warning of the destruction taking place down here.

The Allied States military still stubbornly held a few strongholds, but their navy was crushed and soon he would unleash the beasts standing with him in the belly of the helo. These six represented one of his new death squads, hunters whose minds and bodies had been tuned for one thing: eliminating the most tenacious heretics.

In the port, smoke fingered away from a burning helicopter on the deck of the USS *George Johnson*. Azrael had never met the former Vice President that the Zumwalt Class destroyer had been christened after, but he was going to meet Vice President Dan Lemke very soon,

A pair of cruisers and a frigate were tilted at odd angles, smoke rising from their superstructures from the surprise attack hours earlier. They were half-sunk just off the piers near Old San Juan where cruise ships once docked.

The remaining ships represented the majority of the once dominant Allied States naval forces. A decade ago, an enemy helicopter would have been shot down before the pilots even saw the ships, but Azrael would be close enough to piss on them in a few moments.

He watched as more of his forces skittered up the hull of the warships from the smaller yachts and motorboats pulled up alongside them. Each of the smaller vessels had been filled with a mixture of Variants and Scions.

His faithful creatures now stalked the upper decks of the destroyer and the nearby escort ships, hunting down the scattered crew members. They had been preceded by seaborne Variants with gills and webbed claws and feet who had swum underwater, then overwhelmed the crews in a surprise assault.

A voice crackled over his headset. "Prophet, our forces are cleaning up the last survivors of the First Fleet crew."

It was one of his faithful Scions.

"Very good," Azrael said. "Have you located Vice President Lemke?"

"There's no sign of him aboard the ships."

"Alert all forces to focus their hunts. He cannot be allowed to escape."

The chopper circled low over an aircraft carrier with a top deck puckered by ruptured metal. A single team of sailors held the bridge and fired at the deck where Variants advanced, using piles of debris for cover.

A few bullets pinged off the chopper, and the pilots pulled away.

Azrael took one last look as the chopper left them behind. Another explosion burst from inside the carrier, and it too began to list, no doubt taking on water. It was just a matter of time before Azrael's forces took the final heretics.

The voice of another Scion commander broke over the comms. "Prophet, we believe we've identified the vice president's position."

"Where?"

"He was spotted in Punta del Morro. We believe there might be another sub positioned at that location."

"Take me there," Azrael said to the collaborator human pilot. He changed his headset channel to the Naval Commander. "The heretics are trying to escape with a sub at Punta Del Morro. Find it and destroy it."

He turned to the six Scions in the helicopter.

Before they had been chosen, they had come from different walks of life. They had risen above their frail human pasts, cut up and put back together to become something far greater.

Azrael looked at the Scions in turn. "You are the best of my hunters, and tonight you get a chance to carry out your most important mission yet—find the heretic Dan Lemke."

"We carry the faith," the six death squad members replied.

"The first of you to find him will be rewarded with as much flesh as you can eat," he said. "Whatever human prisoner you desire will be yours."

The chopper descended over an overgrown grass field in front of the Castillo San Felipe de Morro. Layers of castle-like walls rose above choppy waves, bulwarked by towers between the gates. Azrael leapt out first, wielding his saw-toothed cutlass. The other six followed, each carrying a rifle, their swords strapped over their back.

As the chopper lifted off again, the thrum of the

engines faded against the cacophony of the ongoing battle.

Azrael surveyed the open lawn behind them leading to Old San Juan. Human corpses lay strewn over the grass. Thrall Variants tore into them, devouring the corpses. Other prisoners were shackled by collaborators deployed to capture as many humans as they could. Those prisoners were taken to the Santa Maria Cemetery overlooking the sea to await their transport back to the Citadel. They were destined to become labor or food for his growing army.

One of the Scions near Azrael pointed a crooked, clawed finger to the gate leading into the castle. "I smell humans. Alive. They went that way."

"Find them!" Azrael yelled.

The six soldiers rushed through the gate and entered a cramped courtyard filled with doorways under white arches. Azrael narrowed his eyes, studying each of the entries.

"That way," the lead Scion said.

The beast led them into a dark corridor. Stone steps took them down into another tunnel. Azrael sniffed the air. He could smell the stink of humans, their pungent body odor and sweat.

They could not have gotten far.

Darkness filled the tunnel, far too black for a human to see, but Azrael and his augmented soldiers used their enhanced sight to scan for prey as they delved deeper under the castle, north toward where the point met the sea. If Lemke made it to those waters and into his sub, Azrael would fail.

He hadn't come all the way to Puerto Rico while his forces fought the heretics in Vegas just to let one of the most powerful human beings left in the world slip so easily between his claws.

"We're getting close!" one of the Scions said. "I can smell it!"

Sniffing the air, Azrael too detected the scent of flesh and fear.

Though their eyesight was preternaturally strong, even they couldn't see as the final traces of surface light vanished in the tunnels. The death squad turned on the tactical lights fixed to the barrels of their rifles. Beams of white light probed the darkness, cutting through the black to reveal mold-covered stones and rubble.

They took a corner, raw adrenaline filling Azrael. He grinned imagining the fear that must be striking through Lemke at this moment. It had been too long since he had taken part in a hunt like this, and he had to hold in a primordial howl.

They came to another intersection, taking a sharp left, still following the scent trail. Between the sound of their claws on the stone, Azrael heard something else. The clatter of boots and shoes on concrete.

"They're just ahead," he growled.

The death squad charged, sprinting through the darkness, their lights bobbing.

Muzzle flashes lit up the passage, followed instantly by the sharp crack of gunfire.

One of the Scions yelled out in agony, her body crumpling. The other five took cover and returned fire, allowing two of the soldiers to advance.

More flashes of gunfire illuminated the tunnel in strobing blasts, and another Scion went down. Azrael sighted up targets and fired at them in turn.

Human cries sounded from the men caught in the hail

of his bullets. Another Scion crumpled from a bullet to the head, leaving only two of his soldiers.

The smell of blood in the air was too strong, awakening the primal animal within Azrael.

"On me!" Azrael screamed.

The remaining two Scions let loose a salvo that lanced into a pair of soldiers. The rest of the group of heretics disappeared around another bend in the tunnel, and Azrael barreled after them with his Scions.

Starlight bled into the next section of the tunnel. They had reached the end under the fortress, and a salty seaborne breeze swept through the corridor. Three human soldiers waited with their rifles shouldered.

Azrael slid under the gunfire, but one of his loyal comrades was not quick enough. The beast was cut down in a spray of bullets.

He fired from the ground while the final Scion lay down covering fire. All three of the human soldiers slumped over, dead or dying.

The screams of agony were enough to fuel Azrael and the remaining Scion. He leaped over the soldiers, letting his final soldier finish them off with a cutlass.

Azrael ran out into the weeds and grass of a pathway overlooking the Caribbean.

Three men in ACUs ran, covering a man who had to be the vice president. The final Scion joined Azrael as they stalked the human prey toward a concrete platform.

Amid the choppy water crashing against the black rocks past the pathway, Azrael noticed a Zodiac bobbing. Three men waited in the rigid-hulled inflatable boat. Beyond the craft, a submarine had pierced the surface of the deeper waters.

"Do not hit the heretic," Azrael said. He raised his

rifle next to the final Scion and lined up the sights. Two of the soldiers collapsed under the well-aimed shots, but return fire from the Zodiac forced Azrael to roll away.

He got up and charged ahead, aiming toward the third soldier. His surviving Scion covered him, providing suppressing fire against the men in the Zodiac.

Unstrapping his cutlass, Azrael flanked Lemke and the final soldier, catching them off guard and stabbing the guard through the guts. The man slumped against Azrael, gurgles coming from his mouth.

Azrael used the man as a human shield as he strode toward the vice president.

"No, no, no!" Lemke said, still running for the boat.

Gunfire from the remaining Scion tore into the Zodiac, killing two of the three men. Azrael withdrew his cutlass and pushed the still breathing man to the ground. Slotted eyes on the heretic, Azrael bolted forward.

When he was just within reach, Azrael lunged toward him, snagging his claws through the back of Lemke's shirt. A scream rang out as Azrael pulled the vice president to the dirt.

Several final gunshots rang out before the last Scion ran over.

"All hostiles eliminated," he growled.

No longer masked by the sounds of gunfire, Azrael heard the churning engines of his fleet converging on the submarine still waiting for Lemke.

He yanked the vice president to his face, drawing him close, eye to eye.

There was certainly fear in the man's gaze, but there was also an undeniable anger.

"You won't win," Lemke said, wincing.

"Oh, I have already won, "Azrael snarled. "You are

just too naïve to see it. This is the end of the Allied States and the end of you."

— 15 —

Dohi searched the patient rooms and offices on the fifth floor of the University Medical Center of Southern Nevada for some sign of the Prophet. He picked through the tangles of webbing lining a hallway as they made their way toward the administrative offices.

Distant booms from the main strip still sounded like thunder, and the UMC shook slightly with each impact. It sounded like the other teams were getting pounded out there, especially from the constant chatter over the comms.

Dohi had turned off the public channels to concentrate on his own team, Spearhead was in bad shape. Neilson could hardly stand and Toussaint had a swollen face, one of her eyes sealed shut by swelling.

Fitz stayed close beside Dohi with Corrin, while Rico and Ace watched their six.

No one dared speak. Too many monsters stalked the corridors, searching for them.

Sporadic shouts called up the stairwells. Howls and shrieks blasted through the elevator shafts. The collaborators and Variants were searching the building for them, and Dohi knew it wouldn't be long before they caught up.

He just hoped they found the Prophet first, assuming the beast was even still here.

Every passing minute that seemed to be less likely.

But *something* was ahead. The webbing grew denser, clogging the halls. Dohi could almost feel the network pulsating. He hacked away at clumps of webbing blocking the passage with his hatchet. Fitz used a knife to saw through strands.

We have to be getting close.

Working together, they pushed through to an area with expansive windows that had once overlooked the surrounding medical center. Now those windows were mostly blotted with viny growths.

The stench of death grew stronger, bringing with it the telltale odor of rotten fruit.

His NVGs picked up what little light sifted through the windows, revealing a space choked in vines. Cubical walls and desks had been toppled, making space for dozens of cocoons where bodies rotted, their nutrients shuttled away by the vines snaking through the corpses.

Dohi breathed though his mouth, trying not to suck in the fetid odor, and continued past.

A flash of movement burst through a corridor ahead. He raised his fist, and counted at least five Variants, hunched. Most of them were feeding, but a few scanned the darkness for prey.

He signaled to the rest of Ghost. Fitz directed Ace and Rico to flank the Variants on the right side while he and Dohi took the left. Team Spearhead stayed behind with Corrin.

Dohi tried to mask the sounds of their approach but it was nearly impossible with the slurp of his steps. Their only saving grace was another rash of explosions in the distance and the overpowering odor of the dead and dying masking their own smells.

He held his hatchet at the ready, and Fitz gripped his Ka-Bar. The Variants stood in front of another set of wooden doors which were cracked slightly open.

If something was in there, maybe the Prophet, Dohi didn't want to give any warning that they were outside.

He peeled back more vines until he was just a few feet from his first target Variant. The beast gnawed at a bone. Another two were focused on a cocooned body, pulling out stringy lengths of flesh and chewing them.

Fitz counted down with his fingers.

Three.

Dohi inhaled sharply, cocking back his hatchet. With his other hand, he pulled out his knife.

Two.

He took a step forward and aimed at the spine of the first Variant.

One.

Dohi lunged, swinging the hatchet. It cleaved into the creature's diseased flesh and cut into bone with a sharp crack. Fitz attacked the second, catching it from behind and sawing his knife straight through the cartilage and flesh at its throat.

Ace and Rico engaged two others, leaving a final abomination that twisted toward Dohi with an open mouth, ready to let loose a shriek.

Dohi threw his knife into the black hole, breaking teeth as it plunged into the throat. The monster shuddered, then fell backward.

The others circled around the open doors, their targets down. Dohi wiggled his hatchet free and then retrieved his knife.

Fitz signaled for Team Spearhead and Corrin to join them. Toussaint and Neilson were in no shape to perform

NICHOLAS SANSBURY SMITH & ANTHONY J. MELCHIORRI

room-clearing maneuvers, but they kept close behind.

Dohi prepared to enter what he hoped would be the lair of the Prophet. All the dense webbings led to this spot. If someone or something was controlling the operations in Vegas, it would be orchestrating the monsters from this place.

He raised his rifle, heart climbing into his throat with anticipation.

A nod from Fitz and Dohi slipped into a vast room, zeroing in on movement at the opposite end. Past the stringy columns of webbing, shapes rushed their position, letting out growls and snarls. Behind them was a much larger creature, hunched to fit into the room, its flesh hanging in folds like the surface of a brain.

A mastermind.

But was this mastermind the Prophet?

Either way, it wasn't alone. A group of Variants crawled around the room.

Fitz gave the order to open fire.

Dohi sighted up a Variant on the webbing, the others following his lead. Bullets lanced into the beasts, dropping them from the ceiling and walls.

In only a few seconds, several were bleeding out on the ground. Another group of four careened from a side door. More suppressed gunfire echoed in the room. Two monsters crashed forward against the webbing, dead. One of the survivors slammed against Rico, knocking her on her back.

"No!" Fitz charged the monster and grabbed its shoulders, trying to tear it off Rico.

The other Variant shouldered into Ace, knocking him flat on his back.

Dohi couldn't get a clear shot without risking hitting

Ace. Instead he tackled the monster, freeing Ace.

The creature hissed and snapped at him, teeth coming inches from his face. Dohi pushed the head back, but it was stronger than he was and inched toward him with jagged, yellow teeth.

A bulky shape lunged overhead.

Ace.

He wrenched the Variant's head back, twisting it violently until a sickening pop echoed in the room. Ace gasped for breath, letting the monster drop, then offered a hand to help Dohi up.

Ten feet away, Rico and Fitz had recovered and approached the mastermind.

Only now, Dohi had time to see what kind of room they were in. Chairs were scattered throughout the space and a long table lay on its side. What used to be glass walls appeared to have shattered, letting the vines spill out from a neighboring corridor. Behind the mastermind were more sweeping views of the city covered in fire and smoke.

The beast was nearly twice as tall as any of the operators, but it seemed to cower at their approach. Using claws, it tugged on the tendrils of the network, undoubtedly sending messages for help.

"Ain't no one coming to help you, sweetheart," Ace said.

"This looks like the heart of the comms network," Dohi said. "But unless that thing is the Prophet, I don't see anything else."

"This hunk of meat is the Prophet?" Rico asked.

Corrin squinted from where he stood near the entrance of the room, tugging on a few of the red vines. "No, this is just a normal mastermind." He held the vine.

"It's scared of us. That's why it's sending all these messages."

"You sure?" Fitz asked.

"Yes, the Prophet is not one of these organic computers," Corrin said.

"Fine," Fitz said. "Kill it."

The group opened fire on the beast, aiming for its head. Bullets plunged into the flesh, drawing blood wherever they pierced. The monster writhed, pulling hard on the vines, backing away from the gunfire. One of its eyes popped, viscous fluid leaking out, and the monster let out a pained roar. It fell backward, arms still flailing, and broke the windows behind it.

Beaten back by gunfire, the mastermind plummeted out, snapping vines. A moment later, Dohi heard a sickening smack against concrete.

"Let's move," Fitz said. He pointed toward the corridor they hadn't yet explored to their right.

Did the Prophet go that way before they had arrived? Were the other New Gods leaders waiting for them?

Before they moved, voices filled the first corridor where they had come from. Spearhead hobbled into the room, shutting the door behind them quietly.

Neilson signaled that they had seen more contacts.

Those voices grew louder, permeating under the door. There was no mistaking their rasping, crackly words. Chimeras were on their way. Dohi tensed, aiming his rifle at the door, waiting for them to burst through.

But the beasts went quiet.

Corrin sniffed at the air. "I smell something sharp. Like gun powder, except…"

"TNT," Dohi said in a low voice. "They're setting explosives."

"Just like the rest of the city," Fitz said. "We have to get out of here."

They ran down the new corridor to their right.

A few lone Variants lurched at them from the shadows. They dispatched them quickly, then ran into a stairwell. Dohi looked down the winding stairs from the fifth floor. Monsters had reached the second floor and were climbing quickly. A few let out hunting cries when they saw Dohi.

He ducked back into the hall. "We can't get down that way."

A low explosion boomed behind them. Wood splintered, the doors to the conference room breaking. Smoke billowed down the corridor.

Fitz signaled for the team to take firing positions.

As soon as the first dark shadow moved within the smoke, Ghost and Spearhead unleashed a fusillade of gunfire.

But unlike the Variants before, this time their enemy fired back. Bullets punched into the walls and webbing around them. The team scrambled for cover, but there was nothing but knots of webbing and a few gurneys to hide behind.

"Keep low!" Dohi shouted.

From the smoke, collaborators emerged wielding rifles and pistols. The first few went down in a barrage of fire from Rico and Fitz. But then came the real threat, a group of Chimeras in armor, gripping machine guns and wielding saw-toothed swords.

Their golden eyes practically glowed in the low light environment, and they moved like professional soldiers, advancing on Teams Ghost and Spearhead.

The beasts outnumbered them three-to-one.

They couldn't stay here. Running down the stairs back to the ground floor would be suicide too, which left one option.

"On me!" Dohi yelled. He fired a burst of suppressing fire and then ran for the stairs, bullets searing past him.

Fitz switched on the comm. "Command, this is Ghost One, we need immediate evac! Surrounded at the UMC!"

There was no immediate response and with the distant explosions, Dohi began to wonder if anyone was out there to answer.

"Command, this is Ghost One, do you copy?" Fitz tried again.

A familiar voice surged over the channel.

"Ghost One, this is Reaper One, report your position, over."

"Beckham," Dohi whispered. If anyone could save their asses, it was the former lead of Team Ghost.

***

A thud rang out from an impact against the locked door on the rooftop, rattling the crates and debris Team Ghost had stacked against it.

"Get ready," Fitz said.

The team had already taken firing positions behind the ducts and rusted air-conditioning units around the rooftop. Rico was next to Fitz behind a unit near the cornice lining the perimeter of the roof.

"Stay close to me," he said to her.

Corrin sheltered beside Ace and Dohi. Neilson propped up his rifle on a ventilation shaft, aiming at the doorway with Toussaint crouched nearby.

The roars of the beasts surrounding the building nearly

drowned out the gunfire cracking through Vegas. Thuds continued on the door, each one knocking more of the stacked crates away.

"At least I got to see you one last time, Fitzie," Rico said. "If I'm going to die, I want it to be next to you."

"We're not going to die," Fitz vowed.

Shrieks of monsters from all sides of the buildings made it hard to believe his own words.

"Reaper One, Ghost One," Fitz called over the radio. "Is our evac en route?"

"Copy that, Ghost One," Beckham answered. The line crackled with static, interspersed by gunfire. "I'm trying to locate all members of Recon Sigma, but I called in a special favor. Hold tight."

Fitz didn't have time to guess what the favor was going to be. A pair of creatures clambered over the edge of the roof, their mouths opening to let out howls. Their muscles flexed as they leapt, and their tongues whipped over their wormy lips.

"Conserve your ammo, and watch your firing zones," Fitz called out. The rooftop was wide, but the close proximity of the soldiers made firing extremely dangerous.

He switched to single shots and didn't fire until he had a clear target. The first shot thunked into the closest creature's muscled chest, knocking it off balance. The monster crashed next to the other beast that Rico dispatched with a head shot.

"Contacts!" Neilson yelled.

All around the roof, the Variants crawled over the railings. Gunfire lashed out from the two teams, taking down the first wave easily. Corrin hunched, growling, waiting to join the fight with his claws.

As a second wave emerged, he stood and let out a roar.

Fitz fired at the blurs of diseased flesh.

Each second turned into its own hellish eternity, and he resisted the urge to avert his gaze and check the smoke-clotted sky for a helo.

The door to the roof access stairwell finally exploded open. Fitz turned toward it as four Chimeras rushed out, slinging fire. Bullets punched into the air conditioning unit, forcing him down close to Rico, their faces nearly touching, eyes locked.

"Stay down," he said.

He switched to automatic fire, knowing it would take more than a single well-placed round to kill these creatures. Holding in a breath, he popped up and fired a burst straight into the face of the lead Chimera.

Another was hit by a blast that crippled its legs.

Even as the two surviving beasts found cover, five more rushed out. Four ducked behind shelter immediately. The last one stood in the doorway, firing as rounds punched into its armor and flesh.

Fitz only got a glimpse, but he could tell the Chimera was larger than the others and wore a tattered cape along with the front of a human skull as a mask.

Could he be the Prophet?

Rico fired from around the air conditioner while Fitz reloaded. The beast zeroed in on them, returning fire.

Ace and Dohi continued to attack the monsters crawling over the edge of the buildings, while Toussaint and Neilson provided suppressing fire to allow Fitz to select his shots. He was easily the best marksman. It was on him to take the leader down.

The Chimeras pushed forward, their gunfire and

growls growing closer. They outnumbered Spearhead and Ghost, and the ever-present threat of the Thrall Variants climbing the walls closed in.

Fitz needed to make a move soon or they weren't making it off this roof alive.

"Rico, cover me!" he said.

"Wait…" she began to say.

Fitz bolted toward a vent stack closer to the Chimeras.

From his vantage point, the flanks of two of the beasts were visible. Corrin suddenly ran out to meet them, screaming, "ELIJAH!"

He slammed a fist into the skull mask, shattering it. The blow knocked Elijah to the ground. Fitz used the opportunity to put a burst of bullets into the face of another distracted Chimera.

Another Chimera turned and sprayed the vent stack he had moved behind with rounds. Fitz hunched down, bullets crashing against his position. Rico remained flat against the roof.

More Variants dragged themselves over the railings, snarling with rage and hunger. Neilson and Toussaint killed a swathe of them, but the monsters kept coming. They appeared to be thinner than those inside the building, clearly desperate for a fresh meal.

The Chimeras were just as determined. Fitz got up to see two of them had taken down Corrin while their hulking leader advanced with a saw-toothed cutlass in hand. Heading right for Rico

"JENI!" Fitz yelled.

She turned with her rifle, bringing it up to deflect the blow meant for her head. The impact sent her sprawling backward. Her helmet thudded against the roof.

Time seemed to slow as Fitz tried to find a shot.

Gunfire slammed his position, one round slashing his cheek it was so close. He tried to get up again, but more bullets streaked by.

"Dohi, Ace!" he bellowed, straining to be heard over the gunfire.

The pair reacted immediately, providing cover fire for Fitz. When the Chimeras recoiled from the concerted fire, Fitz rushed the leader that Corrin had called Elijah. The grotesque half-man swung toward Rico with his cutlass, knocking her rifle from her grip.

Fitz slammed into the massive creature from behind. A blow like that would be enough to knock the air out of a normal man and take him down.

Not this abomination.

Elijah dropped his cutlass and wrapped his arms around Fitz. Injuries from his torture in Seattle reignited, bruises and lacerations burning with agony. His teeth ground together, and he tried to kick at the Chimera as he lifted him off the ground, bringing them face to face.

Only part of the skull mask remained, but the rest of the scarred face was visible. Fetid breath puffed as Elijah began to crush Fitz's ribs. Rico started to push herself up, but the creature slapped her down with its free arm.

She fell back, blood gushing from her nostrils.

Fitz reached for his blade, but his arms were trapped.

"I got other plans for you, Fitzpatrick," the creature said in a crackly voice.

Elijah suddenly slammed Fitz to the ground. A sharp pain swam up from his spine into the back of his skull, and his vision went blurry, blackness threating to overwhelm his vision.

"I've been waiting for this moment," Elijah said. "The Prophet will reward me handsomely for your corpse."

"Elijah!" another scratchy voice said.

Fitz blinked, seeing a second Chimera, but this wasn't an enemy.

Corrin strode over, blood gushing from multiple wounds.

The half-man stood to face the Chimera, wielding the cutlass Elijah had dropped.

"So you're the traitorous heretic?" Elijah said.

"This is not the path to your so-called salvation," Corrin said. "You can still join us and end this evil."

"Fool!"

Elijah let out a roar and stormed toward Corrin while Fitz scrambled over to shield Rico. By the time he got to her, Corrin was swiping at Elijah with the cutlass. Elijah blocked each blow with his claws.

Across the roof, Dohi, Neilson, and Toussaint had finished off the other Chimeras and were fighting the last of the Variants.

"I'm okay," Rico said. "Help the others."

He got up with his rifle, trying to get a clear shot on Elijah, but the creature had picked up Corrin, squeezing him and forcing the smaller Chimera to drop the cutlass. He swung Corrin toward the edge of the rooftop.

Fitz put a burst into Elijah's back, knocking him forward. Corrin slammed into the railing, and then fell over the side.

"No!" Ace shouted. He let out an angry yell as he used the butt of his rifle to slam Elijah in his back.

A throbbing pain still beat at Fitz's head, but he forced himself to stand. He pulled out his knife and stumbled over to help Ace. He lunged at Elijah with the blade. The creature knocked Fitz back with a swipe of his arm and scooped up his cutlass.

Ace pulled out a pistol and fired at Elijah, but the bullets hardly phased the beast. It brought the cutlass down on his wrists, severing them both in a single slice.

"No!" Fitz yelled. The creature hit him again, knocking him backwards.

Ace staggered, looking down at Fitz while blood pumped out of both wrists. They locked eyes as Elijah swung the cutlass again, straight at Ace's neck. This time it didn't cut all the way through, leaving Ace's head hanging partly from his neck.

Elijah let out a roar that masked Fitz's own scream.

Using his claws, he cut through the gristle, and held Ace's severed head up, his voice rising into a war cry.

Fitz reached for his knife as Elijah strode toward him.

"You're next, Fitzpatrick!" he shouted.

A flash of motion came from the railing. Corrin had climbed over. He lowered his shoulders like a linebacker ready to blitz and slammed into Elijah so hard that the Chimera went airborne, still holding Ace's head.

Elijah hit the ground and turned. Fitz got up and Rico did too, firing her rifle. Elijah erupted in a frustrated screech and then bolted away into the stairwell leading from the roof.

Dohi ran over with his hatchet and blade in hand, and Corrin scooped up the dropped cutlass.

"On me!" Fitz shouted. The survivors all closed around him, preparing their weapons for the next wave. They could already hear them coming up the sides of the building.

Fitz held up his pistol in one hand and his knife in the other, trembling from the shock of losing Ace. Dohi was looking around, still unaware of what had happened to the older operator.

"Where is—" he started to yell.

The chainsaw roar of an M-249 cut him off. A Black Hawk rose over the rooftop, a crew chief manning the machine gun and firing into the climbing monsters. The rotor blades washed away the oily clouds of smoke rising around the building.

Once it had completed a full flight around their perimeter, the crew chief stopped firing and the chopper swooped in close to the roof, the side door open.

"Get in!" Fitz said.

Rico put an arm over his shoulder, and he helped her toward the bird. Once they were all inside, he stared at the bloodstained roof where the headless body of Ace lay sprawled.

"I'm so sorry," Fitz choked out.

Climbing monsters continued to ascend faster toward the rooftop, driven by the scent of spilled blood.

The crew chief passed out headsets to them, and Fitz turned his on.

"You okay, Jeni?" Fitz asked.

A wet sheen covered her eyes. "Ace… he's…"

Dohi looked over. "What happened to Ace?"

Fitz bowed his head, unable to talk.

Toussaint checked over her rifle, and Neilson peeled off some red vines still clinging to his ACU that he'd never gotten the chance to remove.

Dohi slammed a fist into the bulkhead.

"I promise we will kill Elijah," Corrin said through clenched fangs.

"That beast wasn't the Prophet, was he?" Fitz managed his voice still shaking.

"No," Corrin said. "He's one of the members of the Prophet's Council… but he's not the Prophet."

The primary pilot's voice crackled over their headsets. "Master Sergeant Fitz, I'm Liam Tremblay, an old friend of Beckham's."

"Thanks for risking your neck for us," Fitz said. He tried to hold himself together for whatever came next. The name, Tremblay, sparked a distant memory. "You're the one who flew Beckham down to Colorado."

"That's right," Liam said. "Beckham told me you all could use my help. I'm just sorry I couldn't make it here sooner."

Fitz wiped his forehead with the back of his hand. It came away with a mixture of sweat and blood. "Where are we headed?"

"To Beckham's location."

"Where is he?"

"The Venetian."

Fitz looked out from the window in the side door to see pillars of massive flames ravaging the city. Black pillars of smoke blocked out the stars.

Amid it all, Fitz spotted the main strip, illuminated by flames and gunfire.

They had just escaped one hell, and now they were headed straight into another, missing another member of Team Ghost.

— 16 —

Smoke poured around Beckham and seeped into his lungs. The shemagh scarf he had used to cover his nose and mouth hardly helped. He coughed with each struggling breath, searching through the ember-filled atmosphere with his rifle pressed against his shoulder. His night-vision goggles were worthless in the screen of black and gray, and he had resorted to using his barrel-mounted light.

With his M249 SAW strapped over his back, Horn carried Ruckley in his arms. She cried out in pain as he navigated the rubble, but she still managed to hold her pistol with her good arm, too stubborn to keep it holstered.

The crack of gunfire burst through the roar of the flames devouring the destroyed hotels and casinos along the Las Vegas strip. Howls shrieked through the darkness like angry banshees, and the public channels on the radios were filled with desperate calls.

"Taking fire!"

"Recon Bravo, Eagle Four, we need to leave now. Hostiles—"

More static, more voices lost to explosions and the cacophony of the ongoing battle.

Beckham knew they didn't have much time before the last of the helos took off. He could only hope that

Tremblay would hold out and still be able to give them a ride.

By all counts, the mission had failed, but there was one objective Beckham would not give up on. One reason he had not yet run to one of the evacuation sites transmitted to them by Command.

I can't leave Timothy.

They stopped at an intersection. Somewhere past the smoke, he heard the clatter of claws against asphalt.

Beckham looked over his shoulder, stifling a cough. His lungs were burning, and he had to duck low, gasping for what little oxygen remained in the scorching air.

Horn was hunched low, still holding Ruckley. Sweat carved through the ash on his face.

The crack of gunfire sounded to their left. Could that be Timothy?

A sudden growl cut through the air to their right, and Beckham dropped low. Horn reached for his sidearm, gently lowering Ruckley in case he needed to fight.

They remained frozen as the smacking and pop of Variant lips sounded from behind the dark fog. Claws scratched over concrete as a pack of beasts sprinted past.

The only benefit of the burning city was that the smoke and fire masked scents.

Horn tugged on Beckham's sleeve, gesturing toward Ruckley.

"We have to get her out of here," Horn said. "She's not doing so hot."

She wasn't going to last much longer in the smoke. And truth be told, neither would the two operators.

"We can't leave Timothy," Beckham replied.

He had made a promise. And if he left Timothy behind, he knew that choice would haunt him like a terrible cancer eating at his mind, sending it to the dark places he had worked so hard to get past with the help of Kate and friends like Big Horn.

Now he needed to be that friend to Timothy.

"You go with Ruckley and get to an evac site," Beckham said. "I'll keep searching."

"Hell no," Ruckley said. "I ain't leaving the kid either."

Horn smirked. "I'll do whatever she says, boss."

Wasting no time, Beckham pushed onward through the rubble of the Venetian.

Horn picked Ruckley up and followed through a cloud of smoke. On the other side, forms of construction equipment appeared like monstrous creatures. Small cranes and aerial work platforms were tangled in a jumbled mess outside a loading bay with semi-trucks and trailers. Part of the concrete ceiling of the bay had collapsed and crushed two of the trucks.

Beckham took the long way around the docking bay. Congealed or not, the fuel inside those trucks could act as a bomb if the fire got too close.

He had nearly passed the loading dock completely when he heard the pop of gunfire from inside, followed by an angry shriek. He narrowed his eyes, trying to make out movement deeper within the bay. Everything was covered in a layer of gray smoke and shadows.

"I'm going in," he said to Horn. "Keep watch with Ruckley."

"Careful, brother." Horn set Ruckley down and shouldered his M249.

Beckham advanced, eyes flitting from the ceiling to the shadows of the bay. Fires burned throughout the place, chewing through debris.

A sudden groan and crack sounded overhead. He

dodged as chunks of the ceiling gave way, spilling rubble. Some of it hit his prosthetic hand, the embers melting the plastic where they touched, and sizzling through his ACU.

He hurried forward, listening for Variants. Any hope of smelling their putrid stench was masked by the odor of melting plastic and fuel.

Another cough tore through Beckham, this time making him double over. He tried to catch his breath, knowing the noise could also get him killed.

A second hole in the ceiling formed, spilling more burning detritus.

He lunged to the side, scraping his flesh-and-blood arm across the concrete floor. Concrete and pipes crashed to the ground behind him, cratering the floor.

Then he heard the tap of claws. He braced himself, swinging his rifle up, ready for an attack.

But the beasts those claws belonged to weren't headed toward him. They were going deeper into the smoke-filled dock.

Straight after prey, he guessed.

More gunfire burst in the space, echoing.

The tormented shrieks of injured Variants followed.

Beckham rushed forward. Behind him another semi-truck went up in flames, fire swelling toward the ceiling. Heat washed over him.

He heard voices ahead.

Human voices.

Beckham's heart leapt, pulse racing.

"Timothy!" he yelled. The sheer effort caused another coughing fit to wrack his lungs, but he pushed forward against the pain and heat.

"Help! We're in here!" someone shouted.

The ceiling had caved in, but Beckham could see movement behind a few chunks of marred concrete. A few scattered, bleeding Variant bodies lay nearby, some of them burned so badly they couldn't move.

"Horn, I found Timothy," Beckham said over the radio. He scrambled over the piles of scree on all fours like one of the monsters.

"Hell yes, that's great news, but you better get your asses out here before the place goes up in flames!"

"Copy," Beckham said. He hunched and directed his tac light into the cavity beneath the debris, illuminating an ash-covered face.

Relief flooded Beckham, temporarily assuaging his burning lungs.

"Timothy, are you okay?" he asked.

"Yes, but I'm trapped."

Beckham roved the light to reveal a few pipes had pinned his legs. Behind him another man had an arm and shoulder trapped under a block of concrete. A grimace painted his face, blood dripping from lacerations in his scalp.

"Boyd needs our help, too," Timothy said.

"Hang on!"

Beckham used one of the pipes as a lever to push a pair of smaller concrete slabs away. They toppled away from the debris and cracked against the floor.

Behind him another explosion burst. The heat seared over his back, and the odor of burning fuel grew stronger over the smoky air.

He used the pipe to lever up another concrete chunk from Timothy's leg and a few of the other pipes trapping Timothy rolled away. The young soldier pulled his foot free with a pained grunt. Beckham held out a hand, helping Timothy stand.

Another crash of falling concrete sounded nearby.

"Let's help Boyd," Timothy said.

He limped to his downed teammate. The man looked like he was barely clinging to consciousness, no doubt enduring endless waves of pain. Together, Beckham and Timothy tugged at the concrete holding Boyd in place. The man yelled in pain when they lifted it off his arm, and he reeled on the ground from the pain.

Timothy lugged the bigger soldier off the ground, wrapping Boyd's good arm around his shoulder.

"Hold on, brother," Timothy said. "We're getting you out of here."

They hobbled back through the smoke and growling flames. Halfway to the exit, a blinding flash of light cut through the smoke, followed by a concussive wave that threw Beckham forward. Pieces of metal and concrete shrapnel tore through the air. His helmet thudded against the concrete, the side of his face scraping on the ground.

His ears rang from the blast, and the taste of blood filled his mouth. He pushed himself up, rising to a knee. Timothy was already helping Boyd back up to his feet.

Beckham lurched forward, dizzy from the blast. His ribs ached, head pounding, ears ringing. He pushed forward until he reached Timothy, and together they stumbled toward the exit.

More of the ceiling and roof gave way behind them, clouds of dust rolling after them like an avalanche, fanning the flames and plumes of smoke.

"Go, go, go!" Beckham tried to say. He couldn't even hear his own voice, but he saw their exit ahead.

Horn was waving at them, and Ruckley had managed to get back on her feet. The sight filled Beckham with the energy he needed to guide Timothy and Boyd out of the blazing bay.

The world still sounded muddled when they made it out into the street. Beckham thought he heard voices on the comms. Horn was yelling something, but he couldn't make that out either.

A wave of smoke and dust blasted out of the loading bay, forcing the team down. Beckham coughed, trying to block Timothy with his own body as grit pelted them.

When the dust settled, he saw Horn pointing at something on their six. Beckham turned, looking past the dumpster Ruckley was hiding behind.

Dark silhouettes moved amid the smoke and dust.

At first, Beckham couldn't tell if they were enemies or soldiers.

His hearing started to return, the persistent ringing beginning to die down. He knelt behind the cover of a burned-out forklift, Horn steadying his machine gun nearby.

A high-pitched clicking and shrieking dispelled any notion that these might be allies.

Hot wind blew through the street, clearing the smoke momentarily.

An Alpha strode toward them, its batlike ears twitching. Fire cast its body in shadows that highlighted the bulging muscles beneath its gray flesh. Behind it came a pack of juveniles and Variants.

Timothy leveled his pistol at the beast.

Beckham tried to bring up his rifle, but the weight was almost too much to keep steady. He turned to look for an exit route, but there was nowhere to run.

"On me!" Horn said.

He stepped in front of the group, his M249 centered

on the pack of misshapen, diseased, beasts.

"You want some of this, you motherfuckers?" he shouted. "Come and get it!"

***

From the helicopter, the flash of gunfire below looked like lightning cutting through dark storm clouds. Dohi leaned out the side door as Tremblay brought the Black Hawk toward Krueger Drive, on the south side of the Venetian.

For a while, they had been unable to reach Beckham, Timothy, or Ruckley. Dohi had worried it might be too late to save them and after Ace's death, he could not deal with another devastating loss.

When Horn had finally answered on the comms, Dohi had let out a breath of relief.

The rotor wash of the chopper kicked up the pillars of smoke, dispelling the dark clouds enough for Dohi to see the Alpha and its monstrous brethren rushing toward a small group of soldiers pinned up against a burning loading dock.

The creatures had fanned out, some taking to nearby walls, others darting for cover.

"Take us down between the Variants and Beckham!" Fitz yelled over the comm.

"Too much debris near Beckham," Tremblay called back. "But I've got a patch of street fifty yards to their east that should work. We can still block the Alpha from Beckham that way."

"Do it," Fitz replied. "Ghost, Spearhead, form a perimeter and cover Beckham and the bird as they get the injured aboard."

The crew chief on the door-mounted gun began to spray rounds into any creature that made the mistake of leaving cover.

Rounds suddenly pelted the helo, forcing the pilot to bank hard to the right.

"We got hostiles across the street!" yelled the primary pilot.

More bullets rattled against the side of the chopper. A round caught the crew chief in the chin, taking off part of it. He slumped, falling out of the chopper to the road below.

"Get us down!" Fitz shouted.

The chopper lowered to the ground as more rounds slammed into the helo, some punching through the metal.

Dohi spotted one of the Chimeras. The half-man hid behind a slab of asphalt. He aimed at the creature as they approached the ground.

The wheels hit the street, putting the bird between where Beckham was toward their west, closer to the main strip, and the Alpha and Chimeras charging in from the east.

The first Chimera's head popped up, and Dohi pulled the trigger. A burst of rounds took the top of the skull off.

That's for Ace, you asshole.

The second Scion went down from a headshot from Fitz.

"Let's move!" he screamed.

Dohi hopped out with Rico, Fitz, and Corrin. They fanned out to make a perimeter as Neilson and Toussaint laid down covering fire, one of them jumping to the M240.

"We got more coming from the west!" Horn called

NICHOLAS SANSBURY SMITH & ANTHONY J. MELCHIORRI

over the comms.

Dohi turned to see that beyond the helo, well past Beckham's position, beasts flooded in from the main strip, forcing Beckham and Horn to open fire while Timothy ran toward the helicopter with Ruckley in his arms. Another man from Recon Sigma limped after them.

They were still a good thirty, forty yards away.

The Alpha and its brethren barreled toward the chopper from the east, racing toward the bird. At this pace, they would be there before Timothy made it with the injured soldier and Ruckley, even with Beckham and Horn trying to hold off the second pack of twisted creatures.

The Alpha pushed past a few of the dead monsters, smashing them as it ran over their bodies. A few bullets caught the monster, tearing through its muscle. But it didn't let the rounds stop it.

"Use the M240!" Dohi yelled into the comm.

Toussaint turned the weapon on the beast. A few rounds lanced out from the machine gun, but the weapon jammed.

Dohi cursed and aimed for the head of the Alpha. It ducked away, vanishing in a cloud of drifting smoke. He let his rifle fall on its strap, whipping out his hatchet in one hand and his knife in the other.

Images of Ace's beheaded body smacking against the rooftop flashed through his mind. He let out a primal war cry to match the Alpha's.

Corrin followed, gripping his cutlass in both clawed hands. A Variant burst through the smoke, and he took off its head with a swift stroke like he was swinging for a homerun.

Dohi sliced at another thrall that burst from the

smoke, maw snapping at his blade. He hit it in the skull with the back end of his hatchet, cracking open its head like an egg.

The Alpha kept to the barrier of smoke. It fell to all fours, waiting to strike.

As Corrin distracted the smaller Variants, Dohi ran at the Alpha with his blades up over his head. The creature burst out to meet him, striking at his chest. He dodged the attack and cleaved a patch of thick muscle from the beast's shoulder. The Alpha swung again, hitting Dohi in the chest and knocking him back.

Gunfire slashed out around them, piercing the flanks of the other Variants.

The Alpha reared back, rising to its full height like a grizzly bear. Dohi dodged under another series of blows, striking out with his weapons, cutting at the barreled leg muscles.

Smoke stung his nostrils, making his eyes water. He blinked past it, desperate to keep his focus on the gigantic abomination. Every other sound seeming to fade away except for the growls and roars of the Alpha.

Thoughts of Ace, Lincoln, Mendez, and all the lives torn apart by the monsters fueled him.

Attack after attack, he dodged, then parried and counterstriked.

Dohi hunched beneath slicing claws, and lashed out at the beast's ankle, cutting deep into the tendon. The monster crumpled to one knee, letting out a cry of agony.

Its milky white eyes flitted up, as if it was trying to see as its batlike ears crinkled. Another series of clicks escaped its mouth as he prepared for the finishing blow.

But as he brought his hatchet up, the monster surged forward, slamming into his body. He flew backward, crashing violently into a charcoaled car.

Pain throbbed through his body, but he ignored it, propelled by the mental pain of his lost brothers and sisters. He moved as the creature got up on both legs again, grunting in agony.

It sliced at him, but he was much faster this time. He bolted away, and then circled, lashing out with his knife and hatchet to cut the creature across its side and back.

Spinning toward him, he seized on the perfect opportunity, jabbing his knife into an eye. The orb popped so loud he could hear it over the gunfire. He brought the hatchet down with all his strength on the skull, splitting the bone.

The monster reeled backward, collapsing, but still struggling. Dohi tugged the hatchet and knife out, then struck out again and again. Hot blood sprayed over his face. The creature groaned, and its limbs finally stopped twitching.

Voices called his name, but he ignored them. He continued to carve the beast until he felt a hand grab his shoulder. He held up his blood-soaked blades, ready to strike the Chimera that had stopped his attack.

"Come on!" Corrin said, voice crackling. "We need to leave!"

Dohi looked up to see the Blackhawk was finally loaded up. He and Corrin ran back to the bird.

Corrin had laid waste to several of the thralls with his cutlass, and the other soldiers had taken down the rest of the pack with bullets. Dozens of gray corpses lay in the street and in the loading bay area.

Another wave of hungry Variants rushed down the street, chasing Dohi and Corrin back toward the helicopter. As soon as they were inside, it lifted, but several of the beasts were close enough to leap into the air, claws extended.

Another pack had charged in from the east, and three jumped into the opposite open door of the chopper before Beckham could get it closed.

One of them lunged at the injured man from Recon Sigma. Timothy aimed his pistol at the beast, shooting it until the monster tumbled backward, falling back. Dohi threw his hatchet, hitting one of them in the chest. The third pounced on Ruckley.

"Hell no!" Horn rumbled.

He grabbed the creature by the back of the neck and yanked it off, then slammed its head into the deck, over and over until it caved in. He tossed the limp body out of the chopper.

Fitz closed the side door, sealing out the shrieks and sporadic gunfire as the helo rose past the swirling smoke.

Dohi sucked in breath after breath. He finally crashed on the blood-soaked deck. Across from him, Horn leaned down to check Ruckley while Rico and Fitz tended to the other man on Recon Sigma, whose nametape read Boyd.

Corrin wiped his cutlass over his pant leg, eyes locked on Dohi. "Are you okay?"

Dohi nodded, trying to speak, his throat scratching, still raw from the smoke.

"I'm sorry about Ace. He stuck his neck out for me, even when no one else trusted me," Corrin continued. "I won't forget him."

"None of us will," Dohi said.

— 17 —

Azrael looked out over his land. The sun peaked over the mountainous horizon, red and orange light bleeding across the sky. It had been a full day since the victories in Las Vegas and Puerto Rico. Much of his fleet was escorting the ships they had captured there, preparing for their next battle as they headed west into the Gulf of Mexico.

The collaborators he had acquired over the years with adequate knowledge of operating the vessels were supplemented by those new prisoners they had enslaved and forced into service through the promise of brutal torture to them and their families.

He had only recently flown back to his lab on one of the civilian model planes they had commandeered from the forces they had defeated on the island, and he was anxious for the next step of his plan.

But before he could proceed, he waited for the return of Elijah and the rest of his forces from Las Vegas. They had spent the previous day ensuring there were no lingering survivors and taking multitudes of prisoners who Azrael hoped would fuel the New Gods in their final campaign.

Soon the entire Allied States would be nothing but smoldering ashes.

Ringgold would bow to his power when he gave her one final choice: join them or die.

He leaned against the railing on the terrace of a building that served as his communication center. From his perch, he had a clear view of the mountains and all the roads leading up to his base.

This was where his empire had begun.

To the casual observer, the facilities and warehouses around him appeared no different than they had during the first war. Like the human loyalist base Mount Katahdin in Maine, he ensured that everything was carefully camouflaged, keeping the important facilities out of sight and surveillance for as long as possible.

So far, it had worked. The heretics may have infiltrated smaller satellite bases around his kingdom, but they hadn't found this stronghold.

This holy place was where he had first worked to help the United States, back when he thought he was developing a cure like Dr. Kate Lovato for the X9H9 virus plaguing the country.

But fate had other plans.

Azrael had unwittingly fulfilled the true mission behind the VX-99 program. The Scions were the perfect predator and soldier.

He had started a new world order, rising from the ashes of humanity's self-destruction.

The fiery orange and red sunrise of dawn melted away to clear blue skies. Black specks appeared over the western horizon, growing larger.

Azrael drew in a deep breath of warm air. These were the first of his faithful legions returning from Las Vegas.

He took the stairs down from the terrace and strode between the spread of white and tan buildings stretching between parking lots. Voices called out from Scions commanding groups of chained human prisoners as they lugged crates full of ammunition and fuel into a warehouse.

These were the slaves healthy enough to be of service to the New Gods, but stubborn enough that they would not serve loyally. They would be put to use until their bodies gave out, and then they would be plastered in the webbing network permanently, nutrition flowing from their meat to feed the growing network of masterminds and other godly creations.

Among the slaves were a few Scions—or members of the Fallen, as Azrael liked to call them.

Those were creatures that had shown disloyalty. He had given them the gift of joining the ranks of the New Gods, and they had squandered it. They were the flawed part of his creation. Soon the new batches would be completely indoctrinated.

Anger flashed through his augmented body as he observed the Fallen hoisting crates into the back of a truck.

"Quicker!" the Scion said.

A female Scion with long wiry hair draping over her bony shoulders snarled at him. "Screw you, monster."

The faithful Scion struck the female Fallen with an electric cattle prod.

"Kill this small-minded beast if she disobeys you again," Azrael said.

"Yes, Prophet," the Scion said.

He struck out at the Fallen with the cattle prod again. The Fallen writhed in pain but didn't let it stop her from snarling at Azrael.

"We chose you, and yet you spurn us." Azrael placed a foot on her sternum, pressing down so she struggled to breathe. "You have been gifted so much. Why do you waste it? Why do you cling to your silly notions of humanity?"

He leaned in toward her, baring his fangs.

"Your side has already lost."

With that, he slashed at her face, leaving crimson tears in her flesh, then kicked her away.

Satisfied, Azrael turned and continued toward an expansive parking lot.

The buzz of the cattle prod and an anguished cry sounded from behind him again. He relished in the female's pain.

Guards stood sentry at the parking lot. They bowed at Azrael's approach, then turned back toward the surrounding terrain for any threats. A squadron of helicopters drew close. Among them were a few civilian models, in addition to a Black Hawk and a Little Bird.

The Black Hawk hit the ground first, and the side door slid open. Human loyalists readied the camouflage netting and tents to conceal the choppers as a group of Scions poured out. Blood covered their clothes and stained the cutlasses strapped over their backs. They strode toward Azrael, pride evident in each marching footstep, but they kept their eyes low out of respect for him.

He stood there watching, his cloak flapping behind him in the wind. He could smell the scent of death lingering over the loyal Scions as they knelt on the pavement.

The final Scion left the troop hold of the Black Hawk. He carried something roughly the size of a soccer ball wrapped up in an olive shemagh scarf mottled with dark stains.

"Elijah," Azrael said as the Scion approached.

"We've returned to serve, Prophet," Elijah said,

dropping to one knee, his tattered cape falling over his battered body.

"Rise."

Elijah stood, the object still cradled under his left arm. Bandages covered his limbs and several spots on his torso. Dried blood had soaked through them.

He kept his head bowed, blood dripping past the broken human-skull mask he wore. "I brought something back for you, master."

"Show me."

Elijah let the shemagh scarf fall, then gripped a human head. The long white and gray beard was tangled and matted in dried blood.

"Who's this?" Azrael asked.

"A member of Team Ghost," Elijah dropped the head, then fell to his knees again. "Prophet, I failed you. This is not one of the men you requested. I lost many of my soldiers to a sacrilegious Fallen Scion that was with Team Ghost and—"

"Quiet," Azrael said calmly. He reached toward Elijah, placing his claws under the soft flesh of his chin. "Look at me."

Elijah glanced up with golden eyes. "Prophet, I beg your forgiveness. Give me an honorable death and cleanse me of my failure."

Azrael stood and stepped away from Elijah, considering his fate. He appreciated the loyalty of the Scion and the fact he had actually killed one of the elusive members of Team Ghost. Not to mention the trap was a success.

"You brought back something the others before you could not," he said. "This will strike fear in their numbers to see yet another of their heroes dead."

"I will kill those that remain, master. I swear it."

Azrael motioned for him to stand. "You have proven yourself faithful."

Elijah rose as Scions and human loyalists began to lead military prisoners away from the birds. The fresh meat shuffled along, together with ropes.

"Very good," Azrael said, unable to stop from grinning. "One of these wretched beings is bound to tell us where we can find Ringgold. There are only so many outposts left in the Allied States after all."

"That was what I had hoped, too," Elijah said.

Azrael gestured to Elijah, then the rest of the Scions assembled before him. "Go treat your wounds, then begin the interrogations."

He locked eyes with Elijah again. "Then once we have the intel we need, you'll have your chance at redemption. Team Ghost will be yours."

***

President Ringgold sat next to Chief of Staff Soprano in the EOC at the Harbor House Hotel in Galveston. Generals Cornelius and Souza, along with General Vance and Colonel Stilwell from Canada and General Hernandez from Mexico, were seated around the conference table. Comms officers surveyed the computers lining one of the walls.

The Las Vegas mission had been an abject failure, and they had been reorganizing their defenses since the survivors had returned. But their failure had not been limited to Sin City.

"We still haven't heard anything from Lemke, have we?" Ringgold asked.

"Nothing," Souza said. "The last transmission we received from Puerto Rico was when the USS *George Johnson* reported being overrun by Variants. Since then, it's been silent."

"They could have repositioned to another island," Souza suggested. "They're probably maintaining radio silence to prevent the New Gods from finding them."

"Lemke's a smart man," Ringgold said, trying to reassure herself as much as the others. "He'll have found a way to survive."

Cornelius nodded. "I hope so."

"How about Los Alamos?" Ringgold asked. She had kept the science team's report about OrgoProct and Charles Morgan close at hand, wondering if they had been right. That maybe the New Gods were based in New Mexico instead of Nevada after all.

"You can see the latest images we took of Los Alamos," Souza said, showing the National Laboratory. "We haven't seen any signs of activity there. It looks just as it did when it fell during the Great War."

Ringgold withheld the curses begging to be let out. "Then where in the hell is this Prophet? How are these monsters spying on us and we can't even figure out where they're keeping all their forces?"

No one had answers.

"Madam President," one of the younger comms officers said, his voice excited. "I'm getting an incoming transmission. It seems to be coming from a computer that belongs to the Centcom facilities."

"From Puerto Rico?" Ringgold asked.

"I'm not sure," he said. "It's on our encrypted lines with the right machine ID, but I can't geolocate the signal."

"Put it through."

The comms officer accepted the transmission. "It's... it's a video."

"Let's see," Ringgold said.

The video replaced the views from the flyover. It showed an auditorium with red webbing stretched over the seating. Two hulking masterminds were positioned on either side of the stage. Between them was what looked to be a throne made of red organic webbing.

"What in the hell is this?" Ringgold asked.

"I don't know," the comms officer said. "But I do know this is a recording. That's all I can say for sure."

A figure strode to the center of the stage wearing a dark cloak. His fingers ended in hooked claws, and his face was a patchwork of scars. His nostrils were little more than slits above his wormy lips and pointed teeth.

When his golden eyes locked onto the camera, a chill snaked down Ringgold's spine. She could almost sense the creature's intelligence seeping through the image on the screen.

"That's... a Chimera," General Vance said.

The beast sat on his throne, clawed fingers clenching into the red vines of its armrest.

"This message is for President Jan Ringgold," the Chimera said in a gravelly voice. "I am Prophet Azrael, the leader of the New Gods you have failed to defeat."

Ringgold stared at her mortal enemy. Evil radiated from the eyes of the monstrosity. He was responsible for so much death and devastation.

"Las Vegas was not your only loss last night," Azrael continued. "Your foolish attempts to establish a foothold in Puerto Rico were an absolute disgrace. We took the island from your pitiful forces in a matter of hours. I want to show you just how easy that was for us."

The video went black, before coming back online to a view of the streets of Old San Juan. Once colorful buildings with colonial architecture were pocked with bullet holes. The camera followed a group of collaborators who were advancing through the streets trailing a pack of Thrall Variants.

Sporadic gunfire sounded in the distance. The monsters surged forward, pouncing through windows and doorways. Some pulled human soldiers out of buildings, tearing the poor souls apart or dragging them away.

The camera view shifted to another angle. Three helicopters soared above the collaborators, spitting gunfire into the Thrall Variants. Suddenly light flared from neighboring buildings.

LAW rockets punched into the choppers. They exploded and spun out of control, slamming into buildings and the street.

The video showed other equally horrifying scenes.

More small seacraft drawing close to the San Juan port, unloading monsters and collaborators that overwhelmed the Allied States vessels docked there. Variants with webbed hands and feet emerged from the waves, scaling the sides of Allied States naval vessels.

Ringgold had prayed that Vice President Lemke and the First Fleet had somehow survived. That maybe Souza was right, and they were hiding out now, biding their time. But the silence from Puerto Rico had inspired all manner of nightmarish thoughts.

This video showed those thoughts were accurate.

After what seemed like an agonizing eternity, the video switched back to Azrael.

This time, a line of Scions stood on the stage with him.

One Scion with a broken human skull as a mask held a hostage who wore a black cloth hood tied over his head.

"The weapons your government created started this, and I will finish it," Azrael said.

With a snap of his clawed hands, the Chimera with the macabre mask tore off the hood from the hostage's head.

Ringgold gasped at the sight of her vice president.

"Son of a bitch," Cornelius said, balling his fists.

Bruised and beaten, Lemke stood on the stage next to the Chimera. His hands were tied together by a rope and another cloth was pressed into his mouth as a gag. Blood dripped from cuts along the side of his face.

Azrael stood from his throne and strode to Lemke's side. He used one claw to slowly peel away the flesh along one of his arms.

Lemke yelled in agony, his cries distorted by the cloth in his mouth. The Chimera guarding him held him upright, preventing him from backing away as Azrael flayed the man alive.

Ringgold wanted to look away, but she couldn't bring herself to do so. Part of her kept hoping that Team Ghost would show up and save him.

This was no old action movie, though. There was no saving him from these abominations.

Azrael turned toward the camera.

"I am pleased for you to witness the pain I can inflict. This is just a glimpse at what is to come," he said. "All because you have arrogantly tried to dethrone me. You heretics must learn. We will not hesitate to punish each and every one of your insolent followers."

He tore the gag from Lemke's mouth.

"Don't give in to this filthy bastard!" Lemke said.

Azrael used a claw to cut off one of his ears, then

threw the piece of flesh and cartilage into the air, catching it with his teeth and eating it.

Ringgold looked away, tears streaming down her cheeks.

The vice president let out a long wail, and she turned back, eyes narrowed, to see his intestines slopping out onto the stage.

The Chimera behind Lemke let the vice president collapse to the floor. Azrael pressed his boot against Lemke's neck, preventing him from breathing.

"You have tried and failed to stand against me," Azrael said. "And still, I am willing to show you some mercy. Abdicate, release your tyrannical hold on your country. Then I will consider some of your people to be among my chosen, to be elevated as Scions."

Azrael took his foot off Lemke. The vice president gasped for breath. A nearby Chimera handed him a cutlass.

"Or if you do not submit, then understand that we will destroy you and what's left of your country." Azrael aimed the cutlass at the vice president.

"No," Lemke said, voice rasping. "Don't submit!"

Azrael swung the cutlass down, separating his head from his body.

"You have three days to decide," Azrael said.

The video ended.

General Souza bowed his head.

Ringgold shivered, unable to contain the emotion boiling inside her. Soprano put a hand on her back.

"I'm sorry," he said. "I'm so sorry."

"This isn't your fault," Souza said.

Ringgold shook away the shock, wiped at her tears, and looked at the team.

"What do we do now?" she asked. "Should I..."

She didn't want to bring herself to say it, but she was no longer sure about their future.

"Do we surrender?" Vance asked, completing the question she was afraid to voice aloud.

"No, hell no," Cornelius said. "If we do, that son of a bitch will kill every one of us and enslave our families."

"Slavery is worse than death," Soprano said.

"After Puerto Rico, Vegas, your entire country, you think we can actually win at any point in the future?" asked General Vance. "That *thing* is too powerful now."

"What choice do we have?" Souza said.

"He gave us a choice," Vance replied.

Hernandez snapped out of his shock and slammed his fist on the table. "I would die before I become a creature like him. You ask my people, and they will tell you the same!"

All eyes turned toward Ringgold. She fought to control herself and push the images of Lemke's horrific death from her mind.

There was only one way forward. Giving in to the New Gods, as Lemke had said in that video, was not an option.

"You should not have to ask me." She stifled the sobs threatening to overtake her. "I spent a few years in New Hampshire. You know the motto."

"Live free or die," Cornelius said. "I'm with you, Madam President."

"In three days, I will defend Galveston by myself if that's what it takes," Ringgold said, speaking as clearly as she could, stymieing the tide of grief building inside her. "If any of you want to submit to him, know that you've made yourself our enemy. Otherwise, in three days, we'll stand right here on this soil and fight.

One by one, the others nodded in agreement.

"Notify Commander Jacobs immediately to recall all operations from Houston, consolidating them here in Galveston," Ringgold said. "We need everything we've got in one location. That includes ensuring every single person who can lift a gun. Everyone must help to defend this base. No exceptions."

"We'll get the message out," General Souza said.

"That includes me," Ringgold said. "It's been a long time since I've fired a weapon, but General Cornelius, I was hoping you could give me a refresher."

"Absolutely, Madam President," he replied.

"Good," Ringgold said.

"I'll begin preparing our forces," Cornelius said.

Hernandez started to stand. "I will request reinforcements immediately. We cannot sit idly by while one of our closest military and economic partners is destroyed by this beast and his monsters."

"Thank you," Ringgold said. She looked to General Vance. "Are you ready to send those thousand troops your country initially promised, too?"

"Please understand that it's out of my control, but I think this latest video will serve to change a lot of minds up north."

"Thank you," Ringgold said. "For those doubting we can win, remember this. Our enemy believes they are Gods, but they bleed and feel pain. And they'll soon learn they're mortal like the rest of us."

— 18 —

Kate wrinkled her nose at the smell of rot and death wafting around her when she entered the parking garage beneath the hospital outside of Outpost Houston.

Banks of lights illuminated the tunnel plastered with red webbing. Commander Jacobs had doubled the number of men down here since President Ringgold had sent word that an attack on Galveston was imminent.

Kate didn't feel any better with the increased troops. The video from Azrael's throne room continued to haunt her. This monster had single-handedly brought the Allied States to its knees, and his forces only seemed to grow stronger by the day.

At least she wouldn't be stuck in this hellhole for much longer. As the president withdrew their defenses from Houston, she had requested the science team return as soon as possible with them.

The team would have to abandon their efforts outside the tunnel and figure out a new way to help the war efforts.

All in the matter of three days.

Kate wasn't sure how they could accomplish anything of scientific merit in that short amount of time.

A cry of pain distracted her from her thoughts and Kate turned away from the tunnel. Leslie jerked in the chair near the tunnel where she was tapped into the network, her eyes closed.

Ron and Sammy stood nearby, watching the computer.

"Anything useful before we pack up to leave?" Kate asked Sammy.

Sammy squinted at the monitor, scanning the spikes of communication signals she had intercepted. "Everything is gibberish."

"They knew the whole time we were listening, and they used it against us," Kate said. "We missed the scouts they sent all around the country. We missed the attacks on Puerto Rico, and we still don't know for certain if the Prophet is Charles Morgan and if he is at Los Alamos. But we do know they are coming after us again, only because they told us."

Ron lowered his head and rubbed his eyes.

She could tell the researcher was exhausted and scared. She didn't blame him. Fear was a constant companion in all their lives. Part of her just wanted to give up and spend the last few days with her family.

But so long as they still lived and she had a chance of saving them, she could not give up.

"Sammy, is there any hope you can follow their communication signals again?" Kate asked.

"They've re-encrypted everything."

"How long would it take for you to decode?"

"Days, maybe a week. Maybe longer, even with the software we've got."

"We don't have a week. We've got three days."

"I know, but..." Sammy slapped the desk.

"It's okay." Kate put a hand on the young woman. "Just breath. We can figure something out if we work together."

Leslie cried out again, drawing stares from several soldiers.

"Should I disconnect her?" Ron asked.

"Not yet," Kate said. "I need to know more about this new encryption before we head back to Galveston. What's the issue?"

Sammy took in a deep breath, exhaled, and stepped back to the computer.

"They're using what I can best describe as a kind of rolling code. Or something similar. Every time I think I'm remotely close to figuring out how they're encrypting their signals, everything changes," she explained. "Suddenly the frequencies and data they were sending are all altered, so I can't track down what anything means anymore."

"You're saying it's impossible to figure out what they're saying?" Kate asked.

"Impossible? No, it can be hacked. But not in three days."

Kate considered it. Understanding the Variant communication signals once again might give them some leverage. If they were lucky, maybe Sammy could figure it out earlier than she estimated. They might be able to get a read on how many beasts were headed their way.

But she did not want to rely on luck. Not with the future of the Allied States at risk.

"You're positive you can't solve it in three days?" Kate asked.

"Positive as a proton." Sammy said, cracking a quick grin. "Okay, probably not as funny given the circumstances. Basically, we're screwed."

"I don't know about that," Kate said, starting to pace behind the computer station. "There must be something else we can do."

"I'm telling you, there's not a damn thing I can do to

decrypt these messages any faster. It's like creating a vaccine for a virus in a week instead of a year."

"I understand…" Kate said. She stepped away to think.

Sammy was right that they wouldn't be decoding messages anytime soon, and the New Gods had seemingly weaponized the organic network against the Allied States. But that did not mean there weren't other options to use the network against them.

Perhaps there was something they could do to disrupt the upcoming attack—and better yet, prevent the New Gods from ever using the webbing again.

"Sammy, Ron, pull Leslie out of there," Kate said. "I've got an idea."

A few moments later Leslie was detached from the microarray connections and webbing. She rubbed the back of her neck where the webbing had been removed, wincing.

"You okay?" Kate asked.

"Yes, I think so," Leslie replied.

"Good. Everyone, gather around." Kate waited for her team before starting in on her idea. "Unless anyone has an idea, I think trying to intercept messages from the webbing network is a waste of time. Ringgold wants us back in Galveston."

"So everything we've done… it's been for nothing?" Leslie asked.

"No," Kate said. "We stopped plenty of attacks when we first figured this out. We bought time for outposts that were able to evacuate, and most importantly, we found intel that helped us identify our enemy."

"True," Sammy said. "And with all our work behind-the-scenes, I was able to run some image analysis programs. I can say with an eighty percent certainty that Prophet Azrael in the video was Charles Morgan. Everything he said matches exactly what Ron guessed."

"Eighty percent certainty isn't good enough," Kate said. "But if we're assuming we know who this guy is, thanks to that video, we have a better sense of our enemy. It seems like a man who might think he was wronged by our government, by our science. And who feels like he is truly delivering the future of mankind to us in the form of the Chimeras."

"Basically, a huge fucking asshole," Sammy said.

"I won't argue with you about that," Kate said. "But we know he's intelligent. He understands a variety of technologies and isn't afraid to use them to his own benefit."

"He's an evil, arrogant bastard," Leslie said.

"Perhaps we can harness his arrogance," Kate said. "Science is only good with the proper checks and balances. I always found that my best results came when I was working with people smarter than me, unafraid to tell me when I was wrong or when we should consider different experiments."

"This guy is working with a bunch of monsters," Ron said. "I wonder how many brains they've got behind their operations."

"I have a feeling he doesn't like when people tell him he's wrong," Kate said. "But he's not surrounded by idiots. We can't forget about the masterminds and the Chimeras, plus everyone connected to the network and those that helped build it."

"I wish we could just burn it all down," Sammy said.

"That's exactly what we're going to do." Kate looked at the webbing around the tunnel. "We don't need the army. That throne, that entire room, was covered in organic webs. I would be willing to bet that even the webbing around Houston shares enough connections for those webs to transmit signals directly into that throne of his, whether it's in Los Alamos or somewhere entirely different."

"But we can't listen to anything coming from that throne room, though," Ron said.

"I don't plan on listening to it anymore. I want to destroy it. Like killing a weed by destroying its roots, I want to poison the whole network."

"With what?" Sammy asked. "I could maybe come up with a computer virus that scrambles their signals or something, but that'll still take days and will only work on those physical computers attached to their network."

"We're not talking about computer work anymore," Kate said. "A mentor once told me that to destroy a monster, I would have to create one. And we're going to do that again."

"You want to develop a new bioweapon?" Ron said, bottom lip shaking.

"Not exactly," Kate said. "The development work has already been done for us. We still have the concentrated weaponized anthrax from that grenade, right?"

"Yes," Leslie said. "More than enough to kill a quarter of the outpost here if we released it."

"Good. We can move our operations safely back to Galveston, and culture more of the anthrax bacteria."

"More? We're talking about a weaponized pathogen! You want to use it against the New Gods?" Leslie asked.

"Yes."

"That's insane," Ron said. "If we deployed it and the wind blows wrong, it could infect our people. I know it's not contagious, it won't spread once it infects people, but it will still kill so many."

"We won't be aerosolizing it," Kate said. "I want to grow as much as we can in the next two days. The *anthracis* bacteria that causes anthrax is extremely easy to culture and divides rapidly. It won't take long. Then I want to aliquot boluses of the bacteria into syringes."

"Inject the anthrax?" Ron asked.

"I get it," Sammy said. "Instead of a digital computer virus, we're going to use a biological one."

"You got it," Kate said. "Only it's not a virus. It's a bacterium. We can selectively inject it into various webbing network sites our scouts and other outposts have uncovered. Those vines will die off as the bacteria spreads, and even better, they'll actually serve as living bioreactors for the anthrax bacteria, allowing the bacteria to spread up and down the network, slowly killing every connected piece of webbing."

"It's like we're setting an unstoppable forest fire," Leslie said.

"And if we spread out the injections, we can avoid any dead ends and ensure they can't prevent its spread before it's too late for them," Kate said.

"Why not just bomb the network or physically burn it for that matter?" Ron asked.

"We have no idea how widespread the network really is," Kate said. "And we already know bombing is ineffective from the tactical nuclear weapons we previously deployed. While the tunnels help conceal the webbing network from the air, they don't do anything to shield them from microscopic bacteria traveling through the cells inside the webbing. Any other questions?"

Sammy raised her hand. "Are you going to teach me to

help culture the bacteria, too? I need to do something helpful."

"You got it," Kate said.

"By infecting the network, don't we also risk killing off everything attached to it, including every human and animal prisoner."

"I'm afraid this is the only way," Kate said. "Whether we win or lose the battle for Galveston, the bacteria will keep fighting, routing out any surviving masterminds, beasts or hives attached to the webbing."

Kate stared at the tunnel, picturing the bacteria spreading like a wildfire with grim satisfaction. "It will be our last gift to the New Gods."

***

Fitz basked in the warm sun at Seawolf Park on Pelican Island, an island situated across the water at the northern edge of Galveston. The USS *Seawolf*, a submarine from World War II, along with a destroyer escort, the USS *Stewart* were drydocked there. Both had served as an open-air museum before the Great War of Extinction.

Today the site had transformed to allow for a memorial service for all the lives lost in the battle for Las Vegas. Men and women in uniform lined up, facing President Ringgold at a podium.

As the wind whipped at her hair and pantsuit, soldiers stood around a few caskets sitting in a series of small wooden rowboats in the grass near Ringgold. Each casket had an Allied States flag draped over it.

"Today we say goodbye to those who made the ultimate sacrifice," Ringgold said. "Today we carry their memories and spirits into the crucial days ahead. Know that they are watching over us and fighting beside us, as determined as any of us to preserve the freedoms we have so valiantly fought for."

President Ringgold saluted when the soldiers positioned near the small boats moved them toward the concrete pier surrounding the park. Another group of soldiers removed the flags from the caskets and began folding them.

Fitz watched in reverence as they finished folding the flags, retreating as others placed the boats with their casket cargo into the Gulf, setting each on fire, then pushing them to sea.

A bugler played "Taps" as the boats drifted out in flames. What remained of the caskets and the few bodies they had brought back from Vegas would find their final resting place at the bottom of the Gulf of Mexico.

He felt tears forming over his eyes as he maintained his salute. He sensed the same despair in Rico and Dohi who were next to him. How many times had they stood side by side to say goodbye to their brothers and sisters?

They were all that remained of Team Ghost. He regretted that they had not even been able to bring Ace back to give the man the burial he deserved. The older man should not have even had to fight this war. He had been past retirement age for a special ops group like Ghost, but Ace had never shied from a fight or the calling to protect the country and people he loved.

The bugler finished, and Fitz let out a sigh. Most of the people who had come to pay their respects dispersed.

President Ringgold lingered for a moment, watching the fingers of smoke streaming away from the boats before following her cadre of Secret Service agents to a

Jeep. It drove away, accelerating back to the EOC to continue planning the outposts' defenses.

Fitz, Rico, and Dohi joined up with Beckham, Horn, and Timothy, all of whom were moving back to downtown Galveston, following the rest of the mourners.

They walked in silence. Fitz found Rico's hand as they walked, squeezing it gently. Her touch brought him a swell of reassurance, even at this dark hour.

"We've lost so many," she said. "Mendez, Lincoln, and now Ace. It's never going to be the same, no matter what happens next."

Of course there were also all of their comrades who had died in the first war, people like Tanaka, Jensen, Riley, Meg, Garcia... Fitz used to find strength in remembering them, but now it just made his heart ache.

Beckham looked out at the Gulf of Mexico. "I've watched too many brothers and sisters give their lives for this country. Every time, it hurt worse than the Variant acid that took my leg and arm."

"That's why we must win," Dohi said. "So their sacrifices weren't for nothing."

"You bet your sweet ass we'll win," Horn said, clapping the tracker's shoulder with a big hand.

"We better hurry then," Fitz said. "We're running out of time and ammunition."

"I don't need bullets," Dohi said. "My hatchet and knife are sharp enough."

"Guess we'll be making some homemade bombs and sharpening some swords," Horn said. "Just like when I was a teenager, except I can't get arrested for it."

They all laughed for a moment.

"Better than bullets and bombs, we have each other," Beckham said. "We're back together again. And we're still breathing, which means we still have a shot."

Beckham put an arm around Timothy.

"So what's the plan?" Rico asked. "I mean, the brass has to be planning something together better than pipe bombs made by Horn."

She gave Horn a side glance like he was nuts.

"Even if the science team is right, that the Prophet is actually in Los Alamos, we don't have the manpower right now to launch another major offensive," Beckham said. "Truth is, we're better off defending this place, where we already have our heels firmly planted."

"But you know how the old saying goes," Fitz said. "The best defense…"

"Another mission like Vegas will mean there isn't anything left for our defense. I'm working with Commander Jacobs to coordinate a strong defense strategy, though."

"Have you consulted with Corrin?" Dohi said.

"The Chimera?" Horn asked.

"Yeah," Dohi said. "He might be one of our best advantages. He knows the New Gods intimately, and has the predatory senses of the enemy. He can tell you how to conceal our men or find blind spots in our defenses we might not have realized."

"Corrin has proven to be extremely reliable, and he really does want to do whatever he can to help," Fitz said.

"So you really trust him?" Horn said.

"Yes," Fitz and Dohi said simultaneously.

"He didn't screw us in Vegas," Rico said.

"Yeah, but morale matters," Beckham said. "What will people think if we drag out a Chimera to consult on our defenses?"

"It doesn't matter what they think," Fitz said. "Corrin

could be a godsend. Take advantage of him while we've got time."

"Fitzie's right," Rico said. "The guy helped save my life, and I think he had a soft spot for Ace. He's just as pissed as we are. Give him a chance to help. You won't regret it."

"I'll consider it," Beckham said.

"When people see Corrin walking around with a hero like you, they'll have to trust him," Fitz said. He knew Beckham didn't like being called a hero, but that was the truth. His name had spread quickly through the country after the Great War, and he had become somewhat of a living legend.

Now that they were in the face of imminent destruction, Fitz wanted Beckham to know it was no time to be humble.

"I'll see what I can do," Beckham said. "I don't want people any more scared than they already are. We can't look desperate by bringing Corrin out to help us."

Rico let out a sad laugh. "Truth is, we *are* desperate."

"Amen, sister," Horn said. "For now, I'm going to check on my girls, then to the hospital to see Ruckley. Want to make sure the docs are treating her right."

"I'm supposed to grab some food with Tasha," Timothy said. Then he looked up at Horn sheepishly. "If that's okay with you."

"Long as you keep your paws to yourself," Horn said with a raised red eyebrow.

"Big Horn, I've got a meeting with Jacobs in the afternoon," Beckham said. "He's organizing all the new defenses and troops that we recalled from Houston. But I'll meet you in the hospital after I check in on Javier."

The group split up, with Dohi heading to check on

Corrin who they had left under guard. For the first time in what seemed like forever, Rico and Fitz were alone.

It felt strange, but good at the same time.

They continued walking along a sidewalk neighboring the port. Men and women were moving precious crates of ammunition to resupply points along the walls. Watchtowers and machine gun nests were bolstered with camouflaged netting that not only concealed their positions but helped protect somewhat against any possible bat attacks.

In only a few hours, Fitz and Rico would be back in meetings, trying to come up with a game plan on how Team Ghost could best help defend the last true strongholds of the Allied States.

Unlike Beckham and Horn, they didn't have any family to see in the meantime.

All they had were each other.

"I missed you, Jeni," Fitz said. "I was worried sick about you when I was stuck in Canada."

"Me too, but we're together now."

"And it's going to stay that way." Fitz stopped, took her hands in his own, and faced her. "No matter what happens, I'm never leaving your side again. We're in this thing until the end."

"Until the end," Rico agreed.

Fitz pulled her into an embrace, kissing her in the middle of the street. He relished the warm touch of her lips on his, memorizing every feeling, every sensation flooding him. He did not know how many more opportunities like this they might have left.

All he knew was he had to enjoy what they did have. Just the two of them, strolling together accompanied by a salty breeze and a promise that maybe, just maybe, if they survived this, there would be more of these moments.

Fitz held her close, her head pressed against his chest. "We're going to make it through all of this together. I promise."

— 19 —

Azrael entered what was once the world's most advanced and powerful linear accelerator, a monumental achievement in the field of particle physics. It was now the world's largest collection of heretics and traitors.

Elijah walked beside him, fresh scars and wounds healing nicely. Puckered flesh from bullet holes were covered in reddened scabs and black stitches. Despite injuries that would debilitate, if not kill, a normal human, Elijah walked with a powerful gait.

"You appear strong, but how do you feel?" Azrael asked.

"Ready to fight again," Elijah said, head bowed. "I hold the faith. Pain does not matter."

They paused just inside the linear accelerator where the loyal old doctor, Murphy, waited for them. He bowed, his hunched back making it seem almost painful. "Prophet, I am ready to show you our newest creation."

"Good, take us."

Murphy turned, talking as they walked. "I would like to show you his strength in comparison to some of the Scions we've made previously. I hope you will be pleased."

Murphy took them past a bevy of long metal tubes and wires, all covered in snaking red vines. Moans and anguished cries filled the concrete passage. A pungent mix of body odor, blood, and human waste hung on the humid air.

He ignored the hands grasping at him for help. Cocooned human slaves hung along the walls and ceilings. With their success in Las Vegas, the New Gods had nearly doubled the number of heretics serving their purgatory here.

"How many of these will join the chosen?" Azrael asked.

"We have enough VX-102 to administer to approximately three hundred immediately," the old doctor said. "Many of them would be physically ready by the time we invade Galveston."

"Physically, but not mentally," Azrael clarified, stabbing a claw toward the fierce soldier.

He paused by a man with veins bulging over his naked muscles. A crew cut crested his bloodied head. He directed hard eyes full of rage at Azrael. He was one of the recent arrivals. No doubt an experienced and well-trained soldier.

The man screamed against the glue covering his mouth, his muscles straining and eyes bulging. The webbing snaking from his nostrils and mouth prevented him from uttering anything more than a guttural cough.

Elijah bared his teeth, snarling at the man, who glared back as if he wanted to fight.

"I like this one," Azrael said. "He will serve me well. Start with him."

"Yes, Prophet," Murphy said. "It takes longer to break down the mind than the body, and this one will be a good test."

"You have continued to exceed my expectations, even in your frail body."

"I have worked with our Scions and masterminds to ensure the proper amount of physical duress is applied, along with the constant deluge of promises of a better future for themselves and humanity if they choose to hold the faith," the doctor said. "I find this combination of physical discomfort and psychological assurances alters their mindset quickest."

"Excellent."

He strode past more new prisoners, clawed hands laced together behind his cape. These soldiers were all wonderful specimens to carry out the physical labor required to expand the New Gods' empire.

Normal humans were not the only creatures imprisoned here.

"The sight of these *animals* makes me sick," Elijah said, spitting on the floor.

All along these walls were the mutated bodies of Fallen Scions. These were the rebellious ones, the ones that the mental reprogramming regimen hadn't quite worked on.

"None of these beasts have complied with even intense levels of reprogramming," Murphy said. "They retain a defiant nature that I have not been able to break."

"A shame," Azrael said. "We wasted precious VX-102 on their pathetic bodies."

"Still they may serve some good, Prophet," Elijah said.

"Certainly," Azrael said. "They make for even better physical laborers than the humans. They're stronger, faster. We have ways of controlling them, even if they shirk the mental leashes we try to fasten around their minds."

"Yes, of course, Prophet," Elijah said. "I merely suggest that they may also make good practice prey for

257

NICHOLAS SANSBURY SMITH & ANTHONY J. MELCHIORRI

our elite Scions. Human prisoners are too easy for us to hunt and dispatch. These ones may help us to better train our Scion forces in the days ahead."

Azrael raised a clawed hand, and Elijah flinched. Instead of delivering a punishing blow, Azrael merely clapped the Scion's shoulder. "That's an excellent idea. This is one of the many reasons I gave you the general's position. A beast like the general or any other Alpha Variant can only really think about their primal needs, killing and eating. But you, my blessed creation, are so much more than that."

"Thank you, Prophet. I live to serve."

The sudden sounds of screams and tearing flesh rose over the chorus of pained groans.

"What's going on?" Azrael asked. "Have you lost control of these beasts?"

Murphy wringed his knobby hands together. "No, no, Prophet. I swear it."

Azrael picked up his pace past the rows of the Fallen Scions and human heretics. His eyes locked onto a single Scion standing in the middle of the pathway. Blood dripped down his flesh. Around his feet were the disemboweled corpses of three other Scions.

Elijah stepped defensively in front of Azrael. To Azrael's surprise, Murphy hurried ahead, reaching the Scion whose back was turned to them.

"Stop!" Murphy said.

The Scion slapped the doctor to the side.

Azrael growled and pushed Elijah out of the way. He strode out to meet this Scion. The beast stood almost a foot taller than him, and thick muscles swelled under blood-soaked flesh. Healing surgical scars traced up and down naked flesh. Fangs protruded from his wormy lips.

"Do you know who I am?" Azrael shouted in a crackling voice.

Elijah hurried over to stand next to him.

"Recognize your master!" Azrael screamed.

He grabbed the Scion around his meaty throat. The Scion resisted at first, but as soon as he locked eyes, the warrior stopped struggling.

All aggression immediately evaporated, and Azrael loosened his grip.

The Scion dropped to one knee. "Prophet, I am sorry."

Murphy stood and plucked sticky red vines off his white coat.

"Who is this?" Azrael asked.

"My latest creation," Murphy replied. "The one we recovered from Mount Katahdin."

"What is your name?" Azrael asked.

Elijah snarled again at the other Scion, still ready to strike.

"I have no name yet, Prophet," said the Scion.

"What *was* your name?" Azrael asked.

"Nick," the Scion said. "But that was another lifetime, before I was chosen."

"Nick," Azrael said. He disliked the plebian way it clicked off his tongue. Such an uninspired name for a chosen Scion with this power. "Why have you killed these Fallen?"

"Prophet, I told him to wait for us," Murphy said. "I told him—"

"Silence. I did not ask you."

The Scion gestured toward empty spaces along the wall where the Fallen Scions had been cocooned. "They were speaking blasphemy."

"What do you mean?"

"I was watching the prisoners as Murphy asked, but they spoke ill of your name."

"What did they say?"

"I cannot repeat such heretical sayings."

"You will, and you will do it now," Azrael said. "Unless you are one of the Fallen."

The Scion from Katahdin shook. Not from fright, as far as Azrael could tell, but rage.

"They said that you would lead us all right to our deaths," the Scion once called Nick said. "That the bitch Ringgold would have us all killed, and you were an idiot to believe you could defeat them."

Azrael laughed. "That's what they believed?"

The Scion nodded.

"You heard nothing but the blathering of mindless idiots," Azrael said. He turned to the doctor. "Who were they?"

"These prisoners were former soldiers, guards from outposts in Florida."

"They watched the fall of their outpost, they were chosen, given this treatment, and they still had hope of victory?" Azrael asked. "These heathens are better off dead."

He walked down the passage, eyeing the shredded flesh of the Fallen Scions, their white bone protruding from red muscle and congealed blood.

"You did all this by yourself?" Azrael asked.

"I did."

"He's one of my best creations," Murphy said. "I had hoped he would restrain himself enough that you could see this display of power in person. We can prepare another batch of prisoners, if you'd like."

Azrael looked at the remains of the Fallen Scions this beast had destroyed. "That won't be necessary. I'm assigning him to my personal team."

Elijah seemed to rear back slightly. Perhaps he was jealous or worried this new warrior would steal honor from him.

That was good. Healthy competition among his ranks drove their strength and power.

Azrael looked back to the new Scion. "Tell me who you were when you were a human."

"I was a father, a protector. A husband until..."

"This family? Where are they?"

The Scion shook again, golden eyes bulging from his head. His nostrils flared. "The man known as Beckham took them from me. He and a human traitor, a boy named Timothy, attacked my home. They called in an air strike that slaughtered all the innocent men, women, and children the New Gods so graciously sheltered in Mount Katahdin."

"Ah, Beckham. I know him well, but this Timothy, he's new to me." Azrael stepped closer. "You want vengeance. You want retribution for what they did to you."

"Yes, Prophet."

"I understand. Look at me, Scion."

Their golden eyes met.

"Forget your name. Remember your thirst for revenge. You are Abaddon, the destroyer of heretics."

"Thank you, Prophet."

"Now let us find some prisoners to feast on," Azrael said.

Elijah and Abaddon marched with him back toward the human prisoners. Their eyes hungrily examined each writhing heretic.

"Soon you will be feasting on the flesh of your enemies, and tasting the sweet blood pumping through their veins," Azrael said. "Team Ghost, Kate Lovato, Jan Ringgold, and the most infamous heretic, Reed Beckham, will be our final victory."

***

Kate wiped the sweat off her forehead with the back of her hand. She had just finished unloading the last box of laboratory supplies from the transport truck into their new lab in the Galveston hospital.

Moving the laboratory from Houston to Galveston had taken her, Sammy, Leslie, and Ron the better part of the morning, but she knew it was necessary. The Allied States simply couldn't afford to keep defending Houston and Galveston. They had to consolidate their forces, and that included the science team.

Leslie motioned to the boxes in the laboratory. "Kate, why don't you go see your family for lunch. We can take care of unloading everything and finishing the anthrax bacteria cultures."

"I can help," Kate said.

"I remember the last time I saw my daughter," Ron said, voice choking up. "And my God, it wasn't enough. That was eight years ago, and if I could go back, I would give anything to spend one extra day with her instead of spending so much time in the lab."

"Kate, my whole family is in this lab right now," Sammy said. "You all are the only ones I got left. And frankly, I've spent enough time with you three." She gave Kate a grin. "But you have other people to see. Other people who need you, even if it's only for a moment."

Kate got the message. Her team was right. There was no way any of them could know what might happen tomorrow, but she could control what happened now.

"Thanks, I hope you all know how much you mean to me," Kate said. "I'll be back soon as I can."

"Don't hurry too much," Sammy said, giving her a wink.

Kate left the hospital and melted into the throngs of civilians and soldiers flooding through the streets of Galveston, finding new temporary shelters or carrying out orders to bolster the island's already formidable defenses.

She hoped that all this extra effort was enough, because every single person she cared about in this world was on this little patch of Texas.

In front of the apartment building where her family was sheltered, she saw Beckham was already outside with Javier at a table. Beside him was Horn and Jenny. Spark and Ginger were playing tug-of-war with a branch.

Kate almost broke at the sight of what would have been a normal day back at their former home on Peak's Island. She halted to watch them from afar for a few seconds, remembering those days when safety was not an illusion.

She took a mental snapshot of the scene to save for what would come tomorrow. When the enemies were barreling down on the walls and the horror of monsters returned, she would have this image to inspire her and keep her fighting.

"Kate," Beckham said. He stood and waved her over. "What are you doing here?"

"Turns out my team could handle things on their own for a bit," she replied.

Javier ran over and hugged her. "Second time in one day. This is great, I've got something to show you."

"Oh yeah?" Kate looked at Beckham suspiciously.

"I was just telling Dad that I've been practicing some boxing moves Connor taught me," Javier said. "I'm ready to fight some Variants."

Kate pulled him close against her side with one arm. Normally she would have scolded him, but today he needed confidence and she had to admit it was good he was learning to defend himself.

She waved at Connor, the Secret Service agent that had been protecting Javier and the girls. He was watching over them all now and gave a friendly wave back.

"Where's Tasha?" Kate asked.

Jenny gave her a playful smile. "She's with Timothy."

"They went for a walk together," Horn said. "Told 'em to stay within view of other humans."

"And you think they're going to listen to that?" Kate asked with a laugh. "Big Horn, I imagine you still remember when you were a teenager."

"God damn…" his words trailed off.

"Give them this time together," Beckham said. "They deserve it as much as anyone else."

"He's right," Kate said. "I'm just glad we're all still together. For better or worse, we're all one big family now."

"We're just missing Fitz and Rico," Beckham said.

"They're off on a 'walk', too," Horn said, using his fingers to indicate quotation marks in the air.

"Days like this I really wish Mom was here," Jenny said. "I can hardly remember her now."

"Oh, honey," Kate said. She went to the younger girl and gave her a hug.

Horn sulked. He rarely spoke of Sheila anymore, but Kate could tell the big guy was thinking of her now.

"When this is all over, are we going to move back to Maine?" Javier asked.

Beckham and Kate exchanged a glance. Even if they were victorious, returning to Maine was probably not an option.

"What about a nice house along the Gulf, somewhere we can enjoy the beach almost every day instead of just in the summer?" Beckham asked. "I kind of like it here."

"The beaches in Mexico are better," Horn said. "But I can't speak Spanish worth shit except to order a *cerveza*. So Texas will have to do."

"Gingers like you don't do well in the sun," Kate said with a slight smile.

"I'll make sure he wears sunscreen," Jenny said.

That earned a few laughs from the group.

"Really, I like it here and so do the dogs," Jenny said. "Tasha seems to like it too, when Timothy is around."

"Oh, we're not letting that young man stray too far ever again," Beckham said.

"No, we aren't," Horn agreed. "I'm keeping my eye on him. For more than one reason."

Kate spotted two more figures walking toward them. "Speaking of lovebirds…"

Fitz and Rico waved as they crossed the streets and joined the group at the tables.

"Please, help yourselves," Beckham said.

Jenny held out a plate of cut apples.

"Thanks," Fitz said. "Sure is a nice day."

"You always liked the calm before the storm," Rico said. She gave him a playful elbow in the ribs. "But don't lie, you're just happy 'cause you're with me again, aren't you, Fitzie?"

Horn laughed. "You know, I'm pretty sure the guy used to hate it when you called him that."

"Oh, he still does," Rico said. "But he's learned to deal with it."

"Because deep down he actually likes it?" Kate asked.

"Nah, that isn't it," Fitz said. "I just realized Rico's too damn stubborn to ever stop doing something I dislike, and I use up all my energy fighting monsters to fight her on it."

"It only took him eight years to learn that," Rico said with a laugh.

"At least he figured it out," Beckham said.

"Hey, where's Dohi?" Javier asked. "I wanted to show him some of my new moves."

The young boy kicked the air and chopped it with his hands.

"Nice," Fitz said. "But I'm afraid Dohi's looking after someone right now."

Kate had a feeling it was the captured Chimera Corrin.

Ginger and Spark grew tired of the tug of war and trotted over to Jenny and Javier. Spark dropped the stick on the ground and Javier picked up the slobbery toy.

"Gross, guys," Jenny said.

Javier threw the stick and the dogs rushed after it, barking. Jenny laughed and ran after Spark and Ginger. They bounded over the grass, stumbling over each other in a desperate attempt to get at it first.

Kate relished those moments. The conversation, playing with the dogs, and just being with those she loved more than anything had been something she had missed desperately. It was just the break she needed from work, and a good reminder of why they were fighting so hard.

Part of her felt like she should be working, but now she was enjoying the moment with no idea if there was a future where she could enjoy time like this again with her family and friends. Besides, they had prepared as much as they could, and the kids needed something to look forward to. Some hope to cling to when all else appeared dire.

— 20 —

An hour after lunch with the family, Beckham sat in a seat next to Horn in the cramped Galveston hospital room where Ruckley was being treated.

"Damn, you look like the female version of Rocky Balboa after a debut with Variants," Horn muttered.

"And you smell like a garbage can," Ruckley said, her voice coming out in nearly a croak. She cleared her throat. "I keep having nightmares about ugly monsters, then I wake and see something even worse."

She looked at Beckham. "Not you, Captain."

Horn laughed. "Us ugly people got to stick together, that's why I came to see your mug."

"You do smell," Beckham admitted.

"You kidding?" Horn asked. "I showered. The girls made me do it, too. They said I was stinking up the whole shelter."

Ruckley smiled, but it turned to a grimace.

"How are you feeling?" Beckham asked. "The doctors told us you'd been struggling when you first got back."

"Exhausted now, but I've dealt with worse. I'll get out of this bed soon. I'm not going to let you guys go back out there without me."

"Don't push yourself too hard," Beckham said.

Ruckley gave him a glance that flitted from his prosthetics to his face. He knew what she was thinking, but she respected him enough not to say anything.

He held up his partially melted prosthetic hand with his other hand defensively. "All right, just don't do anything I wouldn't do." Then he felt the smile fade, and he leaned in toward the hospital bed. "In seriousness, I also came to thank you."

"For what?"

"You helped keep Timothy safe," Beckham said.

"And he helped keep me safe."

"He's a good kid."

Ruckley nodded. "He's a man now, don't forget that."

"You're right," Beckham said.

"Damn straight," Horn added, grinning. "Anyone who goes into battle as many times as Timothy has is a real man, and a brave one at that." His smile faded, and he patted the handrail alongside the bed. "You know, you scared the shit out of me. And that's not an easy thing to do."

"What do you mean?" Ruckley asked.

"We've lost too many good people," Horn said.

Beckham heard an unusual slight crack in Horn's voice.

"I was worried you were going to be one of 'em, and frankly..." he looked at Beckham, his freckled face turning a bright red.

Realization set in, and Beckham held back a smile.

My god, Big Horn actually likes a woman, he thought.

Horn had never even laid eyes on the opposite sex over the past eight years since he lost his wife during the fall of Fort Bragg, but Beckham had always encouraged him to find love again.

That was the last thing he had expected to happen in the thick of the new war.

"I was worried you weren't going to make it," Horn said after the long pause.

"Don't worry, bub," Ruckley said. "It's going to take more than a crumbling casino to kill me."

"I'm just glad to see you back to your old self," Beckham said. He started to stand, checking his watch. "I've got to talk to Commander Jacobs and Corrin. Big Horn, buddy, why don't you stay here?"

Horn shrugged.

"Yeah, keep me company," Ruckley said. "Long as you don't get too close."

"I really smell *that* bad?"

"Yeah," Beckham said with a grin. "Yeah, you do."

"Hey, Captain," Ruckley said.

Beckham paused and turned toward her.

"I promise, even if the doctors don't like it, I'm getting out of this bed to join the fight before they come," she said. "I can't sit here while people die for me out there."

Beckham opened his mouth to speak, but Ruckley cut him off.

"Don't try to convince me otherwise. I'd rather die in the battlefield defending this country than in a damn hospital bed."

With that, Beckham left the hospital and headed back out toward the street. Crowds of civilians walked in large clumps as soldiers ushered them to shelters. Many were new arrivals, people who had fled the fallen outposts, somehow managing to make it here with their lives.

Beckham couldn't help thinking how many people were still out there in this country, fighting for survival like Ruckley and Timothy had. They deserved help just as much as anyone inside these walls.

He shook the thoughts aside as he entered a former

history museum that now served as Jacobs' headquarters on Galveston. Stairs took him down to a floor filled with what had once been expensive jewelry ranging from near prehistoric times to the modern era. Beyond the glitter of the jewels and gold was another room guarded by six men.

Commander Jacobs stood outside of it talking to Dohi.

Corrin stood behind them, his hands shackled.

"You don't need to put this guy in cuffs," Dohi said. "He's not an animal."

"We're taking a big risk parading him around already," Jacobs replied. "I trust you, but I trust those shackles more."

"If Ace were here…" Dohi's voice trailed off as Beckham approached.

The burn scars across Jacobs' face glistened in the intense overhead lights.

"Captain Beckham, we're just about to begin our test," he said.

Beckham glanced at Corrin. The Chimera was quiet, but he wore a scowl.

"Maybe Dohi's right," Beckham said. "The shackles might be too much."

"If we want this charade to seem real to the Chimera we have locked in here, we've got to treat him like the other beast," Jacobs said.

He indicated the door to the vault. Where the museum curators had once stored valuable artwork and historical artifacts, Jacobs' men now kept the Chimera prisoner that Beckham had captured outside of Houston.

The plan was simple. They would lock Corrin in the cell with the other beast, and Corrin would hopefully get them some much needed intel.

"Remember, we need confirmation of where the Prophet is, any verification that the science team is right about Los Alamos," Beckham said to Corrin. "If there's any intel we can get about that site or the New Gods' forces, it might be helpful to our cause."

Corrin nodded.

"You backstab us, I will drive my own knife straight into your skull," Jacobs said.

"And I would welcome it," Corrin replied.

"Just get this over with," Dohi said.

Jacobs glared at the Chimera. "Team Ghost speaks highly of you. I still can't decide if they're crazy, but I hope you prove them right." Then he gestured at the guards. "Take him away."

The six guards grabbed Corrin roughly. He struggled against their grip, thrashing, as soon as one unlocked the prison cell.

Jacobs beckoned Beckham and Dohi to a computer monitor set up nearby. The view on the monitor showed the concealed CCTV camera inside the cell where their prisoner Chimera was already chained to a wall.

The guards secured Corrin and his shackles next to the prisoner. One kicked Corrin's gut for good measure, and Corrin wheezed.

Beckham didn't like it, and neither did Dohi, but he knew it would help sell the lie to the other Chimera that Corrin was loyal to the New Gods.

The guards left and locked the door. For a few minutes, Corrin huffed, catching his breath. The other Chimera stared at him.

"Heretics," Corrin hissed, his voice crackling over the computer's speakers.

"Vile creatures," the other Chimera agreed. "How did they catch you?"

"A scouting party."

"The Prophet sent others?"

"Yes, after your team went silent," Corrin said. "He sent us to find out what happened. Evidently like you, we failed."

The other Chimera let out a low roar. "These heretics will pay."

"The Prophet knows that we're here, and he knows that the president is here. He'll help us seek revenge."

"The Allied States president is here?" the Chimera said, all but confirming to Beckham that this was a recent revelation to the New Gods.

"Yes."

Even through the computer monitor, Beckham could see the enemy Chimera salivating.

"When I break from these chains, I will slaughter the filthy heretics," he said, snarling.

"We must first find a way to break the chains, but we would be wise to be careful."

"Yes."

"I overheard them talking about the Prophet and Los Alamos. They know more than we thought. Perhaps it's best for us to find a way to free ourselves, then take the head of the president back with us on our own."

The enemy prisoner tilted its own misshapen, scarred head.

This was their chance to find the true location of the New Gods, and if Corrin had blown it, then they would gain nothing from this Chimera.

"Los Alamos?" the Chimera said quietly.

Corrin nodded.

"You're right. If we can kill her and return to the Prophet with such good news, we will be rewarded with all the flesh we can eat."

Jacobs looked at Beckham. "Maybe this Chimera of yours isn't so bad after all."

"Elijah told me if I returned to him with the head of any member of Team Ghost or the generals here, I would be made a member of the Council," Corrin said, reciting a lie he had prepared before.

"Elijah said that to *you*?" The Chimera sounded eager. "He made me similar promises. I was supposed to try and bring my trophies back alive."

"Alive? Why?" Corrin asked.

"To serve us. And if they don't do it willingly, they can join the ranks of the slaves and the Fallen."

At Commander Jacobs' command, one of the guards rapped on the cell door. "Shut your mouths before I crush your faces in!"

The theatrics seemed to help convince the Chimera he was talking to a fellow prisoner.

"The Prophet wants Reed Beckham and his family more than any of the others," the enemy whispered.

Beckham froze.

"That son of a fucking bitch," he whispered.

"I do not know what the Prophet wants with them, but it should be beautiful," the Chimera said, nostrils flaring.

The conversation continued until Beckham and Dohi were satisfied. Now he had questions. He nodded, and Jacobs ordered the guards to intervene. Two of them opened the cell door and one slammed the stock of his rifle against the enemy Chimera's mouth. The other kicked Corrin back.

A group of four more soldiers in riot gear rushed in to restrain him and make it look even more realistic.

"You're going to your own separate cell, you piece of shit!" one of them yelled. "After I beat the hell out of you."

The cell door slammed shut behind them, and the guards let go of Corrin. The Chimera joined Jacobs and Beckham, wiping blood from his fresh wounds.

"How did I do?" Corrin asked.

"Well done," Beckham said. "But I have a question. What exactly are these Fallen?"

"I'm one of the Fallen," Corrin said. "Scions—Chimeras—who haven't been brainwashed into their cult. We're the ones who they treat like slaves after they've turned us into these disgusting monsters."

"And there are a hundred in Los Alamos?" Dohi asked.

"Sounds like it," Corrin said. "I can't confirm, because I was never at Los Alamos."

"That Chimera said there were hundreds of human prisoners, too," Jacobs said.

"I'm not surprised. We had plenty of prisoners in Seattle. Most eventually became food."

Beckham tried not to picture his family, but he couldn't help but imagine them as slaves. They had to do something to help those people, and maybe...

"What are you thinking, Captain?" Jacobs said.

"Nothing good, but this is giving me an idea. Something that could give us an advantage if we get the right people to carry it out."

"Like us?" Dohi asked. "Ghost?"

"Like Team Ghost," Beckham said. He turned to their Chimera ally. "And Corrin."

***

Ringgold watched the sun rise over the Gulf of Mexico with Chief of Staff Soprano walking beside her. The view might have been partially blocked by the tall watchtowers overlooking the beach, and the rolls of razor wire gracing the tops of walls and fences, but she tried to find beauty in the hues of orange and red bleeding over the horizon.

This might be her last sunrise as the president of the Allied States. It might be the last sunrise over what remained of the free people of the Allied States.

Tomorrow morning was the deadline for her to submit to Azrael and his Land of the New Gods. Today would be filled with preparations for that fateful moment, when the forces of that monster descended on her to try and take what little they had left.

A group of Secret Service agents shadowed her as she and Soprano walked down the street. She headed toward a pier that had been built along the shore. A half-dozen sailing ships and yachts were docked there. Some had already launched to sea, fleeing from the upcoming battle, but more had showed up to help the fight.

Seeing other citizens answer the call to action filled her with confidence.

Two of the agents walked ahead onto the pier, then ducked into a forty-foot yacht. Once a luxury vessel, the military had since requisitioned it to transport troops and refugees. It had most recently found its way here from the Florida Keys, after transporting nearly fifty people to Galveston.

"All clear, ma'am," one of the agents said as he returned to the top deck. "They're all waiting for you below."

One of the agents helped Ringgold up onto the vessel as gentle waves rocked it. Soprano followed. They then went down into the belly of the seacraft where a long wooden table was surrounded by a few chairs bolted to the deck on one half and a plush booth bench on the other.

At the table were General Cornelius, General Souza, LNO Festa, Captain Beckham, Master Sergeant Fitzpatrick, and Doctor Kate Lovato.

She drew strength from having these people join her in this boat today. They were advisers and confidantes, each adept and skilled in their vocations. But they were also her friends, the closest thing she had to family left in this world.

They stood as she descended the last steps toward them.

"Thank you all for being here this morning," she said. "Please, have a seat."

Soprano wedged his way into the cramped space to stand behind her.

"No matter what happens tomorrow, you have stood beside me through the worst times in American history, and I thank you from the bottom of my heart," she said. "We've adapted and overcome challenges no one ever dreamed this country would face. And tomorrow might just be the strongest test yet... But I didn't call you here to spout a bunch of inspirational platitudes."

She looked at everyone in turn, again soaking in the confidence she drew from their presence.

"You all have been actively involved in the defenses of the base, and while I trust our allies from Canada and Mexico to help in that matter, what we have to discuss here must stay classified," she continued. "A few of you have presented ideas that may improve our odds tomorrow. I want to explore these opportunities and see how we can support them. Dr. Lovato, please give us an update on your mission."

"Madam President, my team has isolated the strain of anthrax bacteria from the grenade the Chimera scouts brought to Outpost Houston," Kate said. "We produced enough to seed the Variant network with the bacteria. It's not a complex bioweapon, but it's effective. With it, if we choose our locations carefully, we estimate that we can infect over ninety percent of the Variant network and any masterminds or other beasts attached to it."

"I take it that infection won't completely destroy the network in time to stop tomorrow's attack," Ringgold said.

"I'm afraid not. However, if our teams deploy the weapon in time, they can destroy small parts of the network as the bacteria continues to breed and kill the webbing."

"Will that help us?" Cornelius asked.

"It will at least cut off the front-line forces from communicating with their base during the battle," Kate said. "The destruction will likely continue well after tomorrow, too."

"That sounds promising," Souza said. "How many teams would you need to carry out this task?"

"Sammy was able to provide projections for us." Kate unfurled a map over the table, pointing to locations around the Houston area and beyond. "Even if we stick close to base, we estimate that we can achieve ninety percent coverage via bacterial spread if we attack these fifteen targets."

"Fifteen teams?" Festa asked. "That's a lot of

manpower we won't have on our walls. Can we use less?"

"I don't think so," Kate said. "But we can use small teams. Maybe three people at most. Just enough to ensure that at least half the teams inject their samples so we can succeed. Using fifteen small teams will ensure that even if one team is eliminated, we still have the other fourteen target locations in play."

"Fifteen separate teams will also get the job done much faster than a handful of teams trying to travel between multiple targets," Souza said.

"Exactly," Kate said. "That means they can return to the walls as soon as they're done, well before the attack commences. I know it will be dangerous out there tonight. With the New Gods preparing for a dawn attack, we don't know what our teams will face. But we've got to do this if we have any hopes of destroying their network."

"Can we launch the injections earlier?" Souza asked.

"My lab techs are packaging the bacteria and spores now into syringes that these teams can inject into the webbing sites we've identified. They'll be ready to go by tonight, so we can launch these missions before the attack on Galveston commences. That still gives our teams time to return to base."

"Also, from what Kate tells me, this network may reach all the way out to Los Alamos, where they suspect the Prophet may be," Beckham said. "Thanks to Corrin, we confirmed that the Prophet's headquarters is there. This could very well kill him."

"I don't see why we don't just bomb them," Souza said. "We have some bunker busters left."

"We have, at best, circumstantial evidence from the science team and the word from a single Chimera," Cornelius said. "You want to expend what little ordnance we have left on Los Alamos?"

"If it will kill the Prophet, yes," Souza said.

"We don't know that it will," Cornelius said. "Los Alamos is an enormous facility. It's going to take more than a few bunker busters to completely wipe it out, and if we miss, he escapes."

"As much as I trust Dr. Lovato, our flyover of Los Alamos revealed nothing," Festa said. "This might very well be a setup like Las Vegas. The Chimera scout could just as easily have been told to give false information after his capture."

"This Prophet is not a dumb strategist," Cornelius said. "I do think he could conceal his location if he chose. So I'm not convinced Los Alamos *doesn't* contain a New Gods' facility. But even if it does, what if this Prophet isn't actually in Los Alamos when we bomb it? We can't be sure he's there right now, and we have no way of knowing his current location."

"That's true, as much as I hate to admit it," Kate said. "Since we can't listen in on the network, there is no way to track him. If we bomb Los Alamos at the wrong time, when he's away from the base, then we'll lose him completely."

"Not to mention the New Gods claim to have control of the First Fleet," Cornelius said. "He might be on the First Fleet for all we know. Either way, they've now got more formidable firepower and we might very well need every last bit of airborne support and ordnance we have to fight against our own naval vessels."

Ringgold felt sick at the thought, but she knew Cornelius was right.

"There's one other thing that we haven't even discussed," she said. "According to the intel from the prisoner Chimera, there are hundreds of *our* people imprisoned there, and I'm not going to kill them on a hunch that the Prophet is there."

Souza seemed to consider that. "Given the conversation, I suppose these bombs would be more impactful if the New Gods forced our hand and we needed to use them on the First Fleet."

"Agreed," Cornelius said. "Let's focus on using our remaining ordnance to defend Galveston first. Then if we survive this battle, we can inventory what we have left and see if we can deploy it in an offensive move. But none of that really matters if we can't defend this island."

"You're absolutely right," Ringgold said. "Priority number one is keeping Galveston alive."

"Madam President, I have an idea on how we can destroy Los Alamos without diverting too much of our defenses," Beckham said.

"What's that?" Ringgold asked.

"I'm recommending Ghost launch an attack on Los Alamos while the New Gods have their attention turned toward us. They won't see it coming."

"We already decided we can't send an attack like last time," Souza said. "There's no way we can afford to send our best team to what could be a slaughter. We would need an army."

"We have one," Beckham said.

Ringgold stared at the Captain for a moment. "Explain, Reed."

"As President Ringgold mentioned, we know there are hundreds of human prisoners in Los Alamos, many of which I'd guess by now are probably soldiers captured in Las Vegas."

"No surprise," Souza said. "They'll be feeding on

them, I'm sure."

"Yes, but they also use many for hard labor," Beckham said. "Just like how the collaborators try to convert humans to work for them, the New Gods have been culling our people for converts. They also perform experiments on them and turn them into Chimeras, which takes time."

"Like Corrin," Fitz confirmed. "He was once a free man, but was held against his will when they turned him into a Chimera."

"Exactly like Corrin," Beckham said. He turned toward Fitz. "You've seen Corrin in action. You trust him, right?"

"At this point, yes, I can say without hesitation, we can trust him."

"There might be a hundred more Chimeras like Corrin, who don't want to be a part of the New Gods, waiting in Los Alamos," Beckham said. "They're dry tinder, waiting for a spark."

"If they're half as angry and loyal as Corrin is, then that'll be more than enough," Fitz said.

"That's why I'm recommending sending Ghost with Corrin into Los Alamos," Beckham said. "Start an insurrection. The New Gods will have to fight us here in Texas while at the same time trying to put down an internal rebellion, all while anthrax is spreading through their networks."

Ringgold's thoughts turned toward her deceased friend and vice president, the final moments of his life playing across her mind.

"Anything we can do to send these evil abominations back into the pits of hell sounds good to me," she said. "We must cause as much damage as possible with what few resources we have over the next twenty-four hours if humanity has any hope of survival."

"We're all about inflicting damage," Fitz said with a half-smile.

"And Dr. Lovato, if I understand correctly, even if we lose the battle for Galveston, your bioweapon will continue to attack them," Ringgold said.

"That's right," Kate said.

"We owe it to our allies in other countries to do this," Ringgold said. "Even if we can't stop the New Gods, perhaps this weapon will. We'll rid the world of the monsters here that the United States inadvertently seeded the planet with. Then there will still be hope for humanity. And should we survive, we can resume talks of more aggressive offensive actions against a crippled enemy. Anyone opposed to this?"

Everyone shook their heads.

"Good," Ringgold said. "As soon as we're done here, General Cornelius and Captain Beckham, I'd like you to identify teams capable of delivering these anthrax doses to the Variant network."

"Yes, Madam President," they both replied.

"Look, I understand these strategies give us a chance, but they pull away much needed forces to protect the people here, innocent people," Souza said. "I'm also concerned the New Gods might be planning to use biological weapons like anthrax since they had it on their Chimeras before. What's to say they don't also have more weapons like that they plan to use against us?"

"You're absolutely right," Ringgold said. "General Cornelius, do you still have your stock of gas masks available?"

"Yes," Cornelius said. "I'll distribute them among our

troops. We'll requisition everything else we can to help protect our men and women on the walls."

"We can help the hospital and combat medics prepare standard issue chemical and biological warfare medications from the pharmacies," Kate said.

"I can dig into our warehouses, too," Cornelius said. "We inherited a great deal of the CDC's Strategic National Stockpile years ago that might come in handy."

"Good," Ringgold said. "Lastly, I've confirmed both Canada and Mexico will finally send the reinforcements they originally promised after their respective generals shared the video of Lemke's death from the New Gods."

"When will they arrive?" Kate asked.

"A few planes will arrive in the middle of the night." She paused. "Unfortunately, they're just as low on vehicles, fuel, and ammunition as us. Most of their troops aren't estimated to make it until approximately 0800 hours tomorrow."

"That might be too late," Fitz said.

"We must hold out as long as possible for their arrival. It's up to all of you to make that happen. Any more questions?"

The group remained silent.

Ringgold stood. "Good. We all have work to do. Let's go make what's left of our country and those who have made the ultimate sacrifice proud."

— 21 —

"So it begins," Horn said.

Timothy sat in the passenger seat of the Humvee that Master Sergeant Horn drove using a pair of NVGs to navigate the wreckage outside of Outpost Houston. They were on their way to a northwest suburb. Their mission was to deploy the anthrax-containing syringe on one of the Alpha holes identified by a recon team.

"You get some time with your girls and the dogs?" Timothy asked.

"Yeah, but never enough," Horn said. "How was that walk? You stayed out in public, right?"

Before Timothy answered, Horn spoke again.

"I was watching, so I'll know if you're lying to me."

Timothy felt his face warm and fingered the bracelet Tasha had given him as he considered his response. He wasn't sure how to answer that one without getting a dressing down if Horn was telling the truth.

But he had a feeling Horn wasn't here to bust his balls. The guy was probably here because Beckham had sent him to watch out for him.

They weren't alone, thankfully, not that Boyd could do much to help if Horn did want to kick Timothy in the ass.

The injured solider sat in the back of the SUV. He wore a cast from the hairline fractures in his wrist, and Timothy knew the man was in a lot of pain, but Boyd had insisted that he come along.

The three of them made up one of the fifteen teams that were assigned to inject the anthrax bacteria the science team had prepared.

"No answer?" Horn said. "Probably for the best. It's good that I like you."

"I'm thankful for that, Master Sergeant."

"Call me Horn, Big Horn, but not Master Sergeant, sir, or future dad-in-law." He directed his NVGs at Timothy.

Dad-in-law?

Timothy was at a loss for words again, but then Horn gave him a big shit-eating grin.

"I'm fucking with you, man," Horn said. Then his face grew serious again. "Except for the dad-in-law part. Don't be getting any big ideas too soon."

"Okay." Timothy gripped his rifle, trying to pay attention to the road too, since Horn seemed to be more interested in chitchat.

"Don't tell him I told you, but Beckham wanted to be here too," Horn said. "Unfortunately, he got stuck on wall duty."

"Good for morale," Boyd said. "Hell, even before I met the guy, I heard stories."

"Was I in them?" Horn asked.

"The big ginger oaf who could squeeze the life out of a Variant?" Boyd asked. "Of course, brother. Team Ghost was—and is—a legend."

"'Big ginger oaf' better mean the motherfucking, ass-kicking mountain machine," Horn said.

"Right, that's exactly what I meant," Boyd said.

Timothy chuckled and watched the highway. It was devoid of life, filled with vehicles left to rot on the cracked asphalt.

All the good humor they had shared quickly

evaporated as they drew closer to their target. In the green hue of his optics, Timothy spotted desiccated skeletal forms lying against the side of the highway.

"Stay frosty," Horn said.

He took an offramp and guided the Humvee down a road framed with large trees and overgrown weeds. He had to slow the vehicle as they thumped over debris in the street.

Ahead, vacant apartment buildings loomed against the star-studded sky. Images of the slaughter in Vegas flashed through Timothy's mind. The broken windows and rotting balconies would be perfect places for collaborators or Chimeras to set an ambush.

He steeled himself, studying their surroundings for any sign of motion.

The fear creeping into him now could not hold him back from their mission. Kate had told him that what they were doing could change the tide of the battle when the New Gods launched their attack.

They had to succeed at all costs.

Horn drove past the apartments to a tree-filled neighborhood full of houses. Then he braked to a stop.

"We're almost there, and we're going to hoof it the rest of the way," he said. "Once we're out, it's radio silence and quiet. You got that, boys?"

"Yes, Master…" Timothy said. "I mean, Horn."

"Got it," Boyd said.

"And Boyd, you got the anthrax, right?" Horn asked.

Boyd patted his pack. "Ready to inject a little pain into that shit."

"Good. Let's roll."

They jumped out of the Humvee, and Horn took point with his M249.

Wind howled over the tall grass. Leaves rustled everywhere Timothy directed his suppressed M4A1. He sniffed the air, trying to detect a hint of the rotten fruit odor from a Variant.

So far, there was nothing. No howls, no claws tapping on the asphalt, no growls.

If he remembered correctly, they just needed to head northwest to a small colony that had been set up in a Houston suburb called The Woodlands. The community had a few nearby parks along with an old golf course that had been turned into a farming operation.

Horn took them toward the remnants of a fence that had once surrounded the safe-zone. Most of the wooden panels and stakes had been torn apart, broken by attacking Variants.

Timothy followed, stepping over a segment of the fallen fence, trying not to cause any noise. His boots landed in mud on the other side with a soft squelch, and he froze, waiting for a reaction.

Horn kept moving between thickets of trees and weeds that rose to shoulder height. The thought of a Variant rocketing toward him beneath the cover of the foliage circled his mind.

He tried to ignore it.

All he could do was keep his senses honed like he had been trained.

Beyond the fallen fence and mud was the golf course that had been turned into a farm. Dense weeds covered it as neglected crops rotted away. Stalks of corn wilted, leaning or folded over. Insects had chewed through much of what hadn't already died.

Timothy listened for popping joints over the rustle of the vegetation in the breeze.

Horn signaled the path was clear, then took them between the rows of bad produce. A clubhouse loomed at the other end of the field.

Razor wire still topped the roof, along with a couple of empty machine gun nests. The tunnel was supposed to be on the other side of the structure.

Already Timothy could smell the webbing. At least, he hoped it was just the webbing. The odor of decay and death drifted on the breeze as they approached.

They walked cautiously in combat intervals. Horn was the first to get there. He checked the windows, then flashed a signal to move around the building.

Timothy walked at a hunch, following the wall of the clubhouse to a parking lot with six abandoned cars and trucks. Even with his NVGs, he could pick up the glint of moonlight reflecting off the hundreds of bullet casings scattered over the lot.

A major battle had gone down here, and Timothy wondered if any of the two-hundred colonists had survived.

Horn skirted between the vehicles, using them as cover. He waved for Timothy but motioned for Boyd to stay.

Timothy followed, keeping closer now as they approached the rancid odor drifting from the hole. The stench grew so intense it made his eyes water. He fought through it until he reached the lip of the hole.

A glance down revealed the same disgusting sight of red webbing crawling over the walls like tentacles from some earthen kraken. Despite the smell, no creatures emerged from the darkness.

Horn looked back toward the clubhouse and waved for Boyd.

But Boyd was nowhere in sight.

"Where the hell is he?" Horn muttered.

Timothy searched for their comrade, but didn't see him now either. His heart thumped wildly. Not only was he injured, but Boyd carried the anthrax that was crucial to their mission.

Horn motioned for Timothy and they started to backtrack toward the clubhouse, keeping low.

They were losing time so long as Boyd was missing. They needed to hurry and deploy the anthrax, then make it back to the Humvee so they could return in time to help defend Galveston by sunrise.

A sudden pop of gunfire shattered the eerie quiet.

Timothy flinched at a throaty yell. *Boyd.*

A Variant answered with a piercing howl that sounded like it was no more than a few hundred yards away.

Timothy tightened his grip on his rifle and searched for the target amid the tall vegetation, his jaw clenched. As he and Horn advanced, Timothy realized he didn't feel a single hint of fear.

Just anger.

He was so damn sick and tired of the beasts killing his friends. It was his turn to bring fear to the enemy.

***

The drone of the modified Beechcraft King Air 90 filled the spartan cabin as the craft passed over New Mexico.

Despite the cramped confines of the small aircraft, it felt empty to Fitz. Lincoln, Ace, and Mendez were gone, as were so many other former members of Team Ghost.

Fitz couldn't help but think of Apollo, too. He would have done anything to have the dog with him now. But at least he had Rico and Dohi. Plus, the newest and strangest addition to their team, Corrin, who was shaping up to be their biggest asset.

He felt a twinge of guilt for not being back at Galveston, defending the island with his friends Beckham, Horn, Kate, and Timothy. The troops at Galveston were as prepared as they could be, but Fitz feared they wouldn't be able to stop the imminent assault.

If the science team and the intel that Corrin had squeezed from their imprisoned Chimera was right, then all hope lay on Team Ghost and taking out the Prophet.

The success of this mission would be like a knife jab into the side of the New Gods, finally killing their leader and liberating hundreds of prisoners in one fell swoop.

He had no illusions that this mission alone would end the war, though. The New Gods were likely already positioning themselves around Texas, and the First Fleet was on a collision course with the Texas beachside base, carrying an army of the abominations.

Even if their mission in Los Alamos ended in victory, would he still have a country to return home to?

All it takes is all you got. Fitz looked at the others, noting their determined expressions. *And we still got a lot.*

A voice came over the speakers in the cabin. "Five minutes until drop."

It was Liam Tremblay, the brave Canadian who was one of the few civilians willing to fly out over enemy territory. Fitz felt a little better having the man that Beckham had personally recommended for their HALO drop into Los Alamos.

"This is it, Ghost," Fitz said to the others, talking loudly to be heard over the hum of the engine noise.

Dohi looked up from sharpening his knife.

"Tonight, we jump into what could be the most important mission of our lives," Fitz said. "And I couldn't be prouder to do it with you."

Rico smiled and Dohi nodded, but Corrin simply looked at the deck.

"I'm talking to you too, Corrin," Fitz said. "Never thought we'd have a Chimera on our team. But you saved our asses in Seattle, came through for us in Vegas, and you're our key to success on this mission."

"You're one of us now," Dohi said.

Rico smiled, but Fitz could tell it was forced. She hadn't seen what Corrin was capable of yet. Soon she would be a believer.

"I will do anything to destroy the people who took everything from me," Corrin said in a raspy voice. "I'm with you, my friends. Thank you for placing your faith in me."

Dohi held up his knife. "Tonight the Prophet will take his last breath, right before I take his head."

Rico glanced briefly at Fitz. Over the past few days, they had talked about how Dohi was acting differently. Losing Ace had hit him hard, and he still hadn't mentally recovered from his captivity in the webbing.

All of them had been through a lot.

Hell and back, and now to hell once more.

"Two minutes," Tremblay reported. "Good luck. I'll be praying for you all."

Dohi stood with Corrin. The Chimera strapped himself into the tandem-diving harness with Dohi, then they waddled to the hatch where a lone crew chief waited. Rico and Fitz strode after them, side by side.

The crew chief gave a thumbs-up, then opened the hatch. Wind tore into them as it filled the cabin. Fitz flipped down his night vision goggles.

A green light blinked above the hatch.

"Godspeed, Ghost!" the crew chief yelled.

Dohi jumped out with Corrin, disappearing into the void.

Rico went next. Fitz positioned his blades at the edge, his heavy pack filled with extra water and nutrition for the prisoners weighing him down. At the crew chief's instruction, he threw himself out. For a moment there was nothing but pure weightlessness, then gravity took hold and he flipped head over blades.

Wind tugged at his ACU, pulling and pushing on his body. He fought his way into a stable falling position with his eyes angled toward the ground and his arms and blades spread outward. Unlike the other team members, he was top heavy thanks to his prosthetics. Without the minute control of flesh-and-blood legs, it made controlling his dive slightly more difficult as he relied more on his arms to navigate the cloudless sky.

He watched both of the infrared tags below him and followed their descent.

The team directed themselves to a clearing in the trees just north of the main cluster of buildings on the Los Alamos campus. He rotated his wrist enough to check his altimeter, waiting for the last possible moment to deploy his chute.

Counting down the seconds, he kept his eyes on the others, all swooping into their final positions.

The ground was now only two-thousand feet below them.

Wait. Wait.

Fifteen-hundred feet.

He spread his arms wider to slow his descent.

Then, one thousand.

Fitz released the pilot chute. A rapid whipping sound followed as the main parachute deployed. The harness tugged against his body as his chute bloomed outward and immediately slowed his descent. He grabbed his toggles and drifted the rest of the way down into the grassy clearing, performing a two-stage flare and then running out the momentum as soon as his blades hit the dirt.

He slowed to a halt, removed his harness, and secured the chute by stuffing it haphazardly back into the deployment bag. Dohi and Rico were finishing up the same thing. They deposited the bags next to tree trunks while Corrin crouched and sniffed the air.

Fitz gave the signal to advance, and Dohi moved up to point position with Corrin. The two expert hunters started the trek through the trees.

Dohi guided them through the trees and then held up a fist. Fitz listened for the sounds of animals or other creatures but heard nothing. If the New Gods were really here, they had likely devoured every living thing in the area.

But Dohi... no Corrin, had heard something.

The Chimera sniffed the air and slowly scanned the forest.

A distant howl rang through the trees.

Fitz and Rico crouched, surveying the green forested scenery for hostiles. He couldn't tell if the howl was one of the creatures simply on the hunt or if they had been detected.

Another howl answered the first.

Fitz counted the passing seconds, waiting for the smack of sucker lips or the crunch of claws over the pine needles and rock. With the thermal vision, at least they had a better chance of spotting any camouflaged beasts lurking in the dark.

Corrin turned back to Dohi and nodded, then continued prowling through the woods.

The distant rustling of the wind and creaking of branches followed them all the way to the northern edge of the National Laboratory campus. Corrin and Dohi perched behind bushes to observe the area. Fitz used a tree for cover, looking out over the pale shapes of the buildings, warehouses, and parking garages looming over the expansive campus.

From their mission briefing, they had selected several of the larger buildings that were suspected sites for prisoners, and Corrin was pointing right at one of them.

That meant something had piqued his olfactory senses. He made another hand gesture, indicating he detected Variants.

Through a screen of bushes and trees, they could see the edge of a street. Dohi made a path through the foliage and found shelter in the woods adjacent to the roadway. Directly across from them was a tall building with large glass windows and a shorter white building with huge steel doors but no windows. A parking garage was another hundred yards down the street.

Fitz flipped up his NVGs and fished out his binos. A few human guards stood around the entrance to the parking garage, and a group of six Scions marched past them on patrol. They were protecting at least two dozen vehicles, from a handful of military Humvees to pickup trucks with mounted machine guns.

Further down the road were transport trucks, parked under camouflage netting to conceal them from the air.

Shapes moved around beside them. Human or Chimera, he couldn't quite tell from this distance.

Dohi motioned for everyone to get down.

Getting down on his belly, Fitz heard why a few seconds later.

The growl of a helicopter coming to life echoed through the night, followed by the whoosh of rotor blades. Moments later, a Black Hawk rose from between the buildings before accelerating toward the east.

Two civilian AW109s and an AS350 AStar joined it, racing away into the night.

Corrin slowly got up to look at a warehouse across the street he had pointed at earlier.

"The smell is coming from there," he whispered.

Fitz nodded and prepared to give the advance signal when another rumbling engine sounded. A semi-truck trundled down the street, headlights illuminating the edges of the road.

The team went prone again.

Once it was clear, Fitz gestured to Dohi. The tracker rushed across the street toward the warehouse. He pressed himself against the wall of the facility, following it to a door. Then he looked into a window and turned and motioned for the team to follow.

Fitz and the others joined him, and Dohi opened the door. Fitz moved his finger to the trigger in anticipation of guards.

But they met no resistance as the team entered a vast, empty room reeking of something rancid—something worse even than the gruesome underground hives and web-covered tunnels.

Cages were stacked in columns nearly fifteen-feet high. All appeared empty, though red webbing stretched between them winding between the thin bars.

Fitz roved his rifle back and forth, looking for signs of life. Nothing moved except for the slowly pulsating tendrils of webbing.

Most of the enclosures were no taller or wider than three feet. They appeared much too small for people to fit comfortably inside.

Then again, the New Gods didn't care about their prisoners' comforts.

Dohi pointed at the floor of one of the cages. It was covered in what looked like soil, except that it had a pungent, acidic odor.

"Guano," Dohi whispered.

"Gross," Rico said quietly. She covered her nose with her sleeve.

Fitz looked around in a mixture of awe and fear.

All these cages, the hundreds of them in this otherwise empty warehouse, were once filled with bats. Mutated creatures like the ones that had plagued the outposts of the Allied States. The odor of the guano indicated the bats had been here recently.

"Jesus," Fitz whispered. He knew exactly where these bats were heading.

"Should we warn Galveston?" Dohi asked, sensing his thoughts.

Fitz wasn't sure. Doing so could jeopardize their mission. If the New Gods intercepted radio activity in Los Alamos, their attempt to incite a covert insurrection would be over before it even began.

For that reason, he shook his head. "They're ready. They can handle the bats."

Dohi nodded and started to lead them out of the warehouse back into the cold night on the eastern side of the building. Outside, he crouched behind a line of bushes near a street heading north. Across the way were other buildings and laboratories.

Using his NVGs, Fitz spotted three patrols of soldiers, at least a dozen Scions. Engines rumbled somewhere else in the base. Somehow, Ghost had to get around all of them, identify the prison, recruit their army, and do it all before dawn.

He looked at his watch. They were already behind schedule.

The clock was ticking, and they couldn't afford to waste any more time. Neither could their friends, family, and countrymen counting on them back in Galveston.

— 22 —

Beckham strode along a steel-panel-bulwarked wall on the west side of the secured island coast. From his vantage point, he could see the sliding gate of the island's outer walls leading to the old Interstate 45 bridge connecting Galveston to the rest of Texas. The defensive forces had loaded the bridge with explosives earlier to stop a potential attack from that direction.

They would sacrifice the bridge should things get bad, cutting off their only route to the mainland.

But they wouldn't need it anyways. There was no escape plan. All they could do was fight to the last breath, just like the soldiers at the Alamo.

He shook away the thought.

This would be different than the Alamo. Beckham had faith because they had something the soldiers at the Alamo did not: Team Ghost and Kate's science team.

Stars studded the blanket of darkness above them, but they were being swallowed by fast-moving clouds. A bank of fog rolled toward them from the east.

"I smell rain," Sergeant Ruckley said, walking beside him.

She walked with a bad limp, as if each step was sending a pain through her body. This is what it had come down to, using injured soldiers, some only able to walk because of pain meds.

They needed every person and every gun on the walls.

They paused near the open entrance into the top level of a guard tower that looked like a pillbox built into the wall. It had reinforced walls and small windows offering shooting lanes over the side of the island. Commander Jacobs was inside speaking to a few soldiers standing next to an M249 on a tripod.

The engineers and soldiers had also positioned three automated Phalanx CIWS turrets adapted to cut down any aerial threats around the island. The closest was located at the *Ocean Star* Offshore Drilling Rig museum just off the pier near the Harbor House Hotel. Another was near the hospital at the northern side of the base, and the third was south of their position, closer to the airfield.

Commander Jacobs finished giving orders and joined Ruckley and Beckham outside the entrance to the tower. "Everything's set. We're just waiting on the first groups to return from injecting the anthrax."

Beckham looked back toward the bridge. "No one's made it back yet?"

"I received word from the first few teams that they'll be back soon. Recon Charlie reported seeing a few Variants out there. Most of the other groups have remained radio silent."

"Any word from Recon Sigma?" Beckham asked, referring to Horn and Timothy's team.

"Nothing yet," Jacobs said.

"I'm sure they're doing fine," Ruckley said.

Beckham had wanted to go with, but he trusted Horn and he was needed here to help with the final defenses.

"Recon Sigma went to one of the farthest sets of tunnels northwest of Houston," Jacobs said. "I wouldn't expect them back any time soon."

"And we still got a long time before dawn," Ruckley said. "Trust me, I've been up and down the northeast with Timothy. Driving through Houston and injecting a bit of anthrax is nothing that young man can't handle."

"I know you're right," Beckham said. "How about news on the First Fleet?"

"We haven't spotted them yet, but this cloud cover isn't helping. Seems like a storm is rolling in. They can't hide from us forever, though. Our final aircraft are on standby to send them to the bottom of the Gulf."

"Good," Beckham said.

His thoughts turned toward the men, women, and children who were too young, old, or sick to defend the base. Those who could carry a rifle were scattered on the wall with more experienced soldiers or helping to guard the civilian shelters. Even Horn's oldest, Tasha, had been given a pistol, in case things turned especially ugly.

"Do we need to make another loop to ensure all civilians are at their designated shelters?" Beckham asked.

"It's already done," Jacobs said.

Beckham nodded. He thought of Kate and her team, set up at the former University of Texas Medical Branch Hospital. They were some of the best protected people on the island, along with the engineers running the SDS equipment.

"Any reports of seismic activity?" Beckham asked.

"Nothing to indicate any tunneling Variants yet," Jacobs said. "We're keeping a close eye on everything."

One of the soldiers in the bunker near them called for Commander Jacobs.

"Excuse me," Jacobs said.

Beckham turned back toward the west where Houston lay beyond the increasingly cloudy horizon, wondering where the New Gods would start their attack.

Wherever they did attack, he was confident his people had prepared the best they could with the resources they had.

Jacobs returned a few minutes later.

"Just got word the first three teams reporting successful anthrax injections into the network are less than five minutes from the bridge," Jacobs said.

Beckham checked his watch. "Good. We've got another five hours before dawn."

"Still plenty of time for Horn, Timothy, and Boyd," Ruckley said.

"More than enough," Jacobs agreed.

Beckham nodded and started to speak. "We can—"

Suddenly, the buzz saw whine of the modified Phalanx CIWS turrets erupted from the *Ocean Star* Offshore Drilling Rig just off the pier. Fifty rounds per second exploded from the weapon in a series of bursts from its rapidly rotating barrels.

"What the hell are we firing at?" Jacobs shouted.

"The CIWS detected something," an officer replied.

"Rockets? Missiles?" Jacobs asked.

Another burst of fire spat from the Phalanx, modified rounds piercing the black of the night. A series of smaller explosions glowed red and orange amid the low-hanging clouds.

"Bats!" Beckham shouted.

From the northern most point of the base and the southern, the other two Phalanx CIWS systems roared to life.

"All spotlights on!" Jacobs said. "Scramble anti-air units! Shoot anything that flies!"

The lights speared into the dense clouds, sparking

around the base, and air-raid sirens wailed to announce the beginning of the battle for the survival of the Allied States.

Two of the soldiers in the barricaded tower handed out shotguns filled with all the buckshot, birdshot, and other munitions they had scraped together for just this purpose. Beckham strapped his rifle over his back and took one of the shotguns.

"Get down," he said to Ruckley.

She ducked near a wall with a pistol. The weapon was all but useless against the small bats.

Raising the shotgun, Beckham waited for the explosive-laden little devils. The horror they were capable of made his heartbeat accelerate in anticipation. Each grotesque, genetically modified bat carried only a small amount of explosives, but the rain of hundreds or more of those suicidal monsters over any outpost or base was devastating.

The radar-guided point-defense system guided the firing barrels toward unseen targets masked by the clouds. More explosions rolled through the sky, followed by miniature rumbles of thunder.

The fog slowly covering the base made it damn near impossible to get a good visual on any potential targets. Beckham roved his shotgun wherever the Phalanx aimed, waiting for the first of the mutated beasts to descend like miniature demons from hell.

A couple of soldiers got antsy and fired.

"Hold your fucking fire until you have a target!" he yelled over the noise. "Ammo doesn't grow on trees!"

"I thought we had until morning!" Ruckley shouted. She held the pistol in a shaky hand and aimed it at the sky. "This is way earlier than the Prophet said they would attack!"

"Did you really trust that beast?" Beckham yelled back.

More booms rocked through the sky. Beckham could smell the odor of burned flesh and explosives.

The first of the CIWSs suddenly stopped firing. The second followed soon after, and less than a minute later, the third went silent. The sirens continued to blare but Beckham could hear conversations over the noise.

"Is that it?" a soldier in the tower called. "Did we stop them?"

"I think so!" another said.

Jacobs had his hand pressed against his ear, listening to his radio. "Negative! The Phalanxes are out of ammunition! The bats are still coming!"

A small silhouette flickered underneath the clouds, caught in a spotlight.

Beckham twisted, adjusting his aim, and fired. His shotgun kicked back against his shoulder, and the bat disappeared in a spreading fan of flames that illuminated the clouds. The small explosion revealed an entire flock of bats.

More booms of shotguns rang out in a deafening chorus. Each shot cut through the beasts, setting off chain reactions of explosions as the bats flocked together.

All Beckham could do was aim, fire, pump in new shells, and repeat. He blinked past the sweat trickling over his face. The smell of burning flesh growing stronger and closer.

Heat washed over the guard tower platform, as the bats advanced their relentless attack.

The first explosion rocked one of the buildings behind the walls. A scream filled the night, followed by a radio transmission calling for medics.

Other explosions ripped through buildings, former hotels and restaurants and offices bursting into flames from the blasts.

Firefighters scrambled throughout the base, desperately trying to put out the spreading infernos.

Nearby, a cloud of bats rocked into a section of the western wall. A chain of blasts kicked up clouds of smoke and fire. Razor wire, soldiers, and weapons disappeared in a blinding flash.

Beckham tried to keep his aim on the bats above his position, but each resonating blast stoked the images of Javier and Kate and Tasha and Jenny in his mind.

He tried to turn off the tide of emotions and become the machine he had once been in battle, but never had that been more difficult. Adrenaline pumped through his vessels, his mind shutting out the chaos. He focused on the descending monsters as the fight to stop the beasts grew more desperate.

The shells he had had in his pockets, bandolier, and tac vest were now gone. He reached into an ammo box placed near his position, grabbing the few remaining shells, then pumping them into his shotgun.

The spotlights continued to probe the clouds, shotgun blasts and explosions echoing over Galveston. He expended the final shells and switched to his M4A1.

The weapon was nowhere near as suitable for taking down flitting airborne targets like the shotgun, but he had no choice.

As soon as he brought it up the explosions faded away, until there was only the emergency sirens and screams of the injured and dying.

A light rain started to fall, but it wasn't enough to put

out the raging flames.

Beckham checked the tall form of the hospital toward the northeast silhouetted in the fog, relieved to see no flames were leaping from it. At least for now, the science team was safe.

Ruckley cautiously lowered her pistol. "That was just a warning, wasn't it? Just to show us they still hold all the cards."

"Yeah," Beckham said with a grunt.

He maintained his aim on the clouds as rain splashed over his face. It would be just like the New Gods to send a follow-up attack when they had let their guard down and were helping the injured after that slaughter.

The New Gods soon proved he was right.

A few more bats fluttered from the clouds and the soldiers opened fire.

This time there were no explosions. The dead bats spiraled to the ground. One landed just outside the wall.

"Captain, look!" Ruckley said.

A cloud of what appeared to be white smoke spread from the dead bat.

"Gas, gas, gas!" Beckham shouted. "Masks, now!"

He pulled on his own mask and strapped it over his face. Jacobs passed on the warning to the wall garrison, activating a new alarm that shrieked over the base.

Soldiers on the wall and in the tower near Beckham fixed their masks into place. But for those who had been injured in the explosive attack, there would be no escaping the poison spewing from this new round of bats. The second wave of beasts had landed throughout the base, tendrils of white smoke spewing out from the small canisters attached to their bodies.

As flames continued to chew through the surrounding

buildings, poisonous gas filled the night air. The attack was quickly becoming deadlier than he had feared.

At this rate, he wondered if they would even survive until dawn to meet the real monsters.

***

Dohi ducked behind a parked semi-truck. A group of Chimeras marched down the street with cutlasses strapped over their backs and rifles cradled over their chests.

Corrin knelt beside him, and just a few yards back, Rico and Fitz were positioned behind a Jeep just behind the truck's trailer. They had scoured another building large enough to serve as a prison. All they had found was pulsating webbing and rotting corpses.

For all Dohi knew, that cavern of death could have been the former prison they were looking for. As their mission wore on, he worried the army they had sought to raise might not exist. Searching building by building had only deepened those fears.

Ghost needed a shortcut, a quicker way to find the prison, if it did still exist. Dohi ducked at the sound of more footsteps headed their direction.

"Humans," Corrin whispered.

Dohi risked a glimpse around the tires, seeing the Chimera was right. All four collaborators walked casually down the street.

Our ticket to the prison, he thought.

As the collaborators drew closer, Dohi whispered a plan to Corrin. The Chimera listened intently, nodding, then crouched near the front of the truck, ready to intercept the collaborators.

Dohi remained hunched behind the tires, peering around the rig. Fitz and Rico had disappeared behind the Jeep.

Before the men passed in front of the semi-truck, Corrin strode out in front of them feigning the confidence of a New Gods Scion.

"What are you doing?" he said with a growl. "Did you not listen to your orders? You're supposed to be helping me with prisoners."

"But—" one of the collaborators began, looking at the others in confusion.

Corrin snarled and cut the man off. "Say another word and it will be your last." He turned and began walking behind the rig. "Follow me or you'll be the next strung up on the webs."

The four men did as instructed. As they trailed the Chimera, Rico and Fitz sprinted around the other side of the truck to ambush them from behind.

Corrin stopped and looked at Dohi, giving him a slight nod.

At that signal, Dohi lunged from his hiding spot with his hatchet in one hand and knife in the other. The hatchet crunched heavily into the lead collaborator's skull.

Corrin drew his cutlass. The blade sliced through the air in a violent swoop, the gruesome weapon lopping off the head of another collaborator.

The other two turned to run, but Rico and Fitz cut them off with their weapons leveled straight at them as Dohi retrieved his hatchet.

"Make a noise and you're both dead," Rico said.

The collaborators both halted and held up their hands. Dohi relieved them of their weapons and Corrin aimed his cutlass toward the men.

"I'm only going to ask you this once," Fitz said. "Tell us where the prisoners are."

Neither answered.

"First of you to tell me gets to live," Fitz said.

"The linear accelerator!" one blurted.

The other collaborator tried to run, but made it only three steps before Dohi's hatchet hit the man in the back of his head.

Dohi walked over and yanked it out with a wet squelch, eying the final collaborator. The captive man stared in horror. He was young, maybe in his twenties, with a long beard and floppy ears like an Alpha Variant's.

"Let's go," Fitz said. "Bring him."

"If you lied to us, your death won't be nearly as quick and easy as your pal's," Rico said. She bound his wrist with plastic ties while Fitz took his shemagh scarf off and fastened it around their prisoner's mouth as a gag.

Dohi knew exactly where the linear accelerator was and took point, leading the group back into the shadows of the base. Every few minutes they paused to hide from hostiles, progressing slowly toward their target destination. Their trek took them to the outskirts of the laboratories, where the forest once again bordered the streets.

The cover of the trees allowed them to advance without having to stop for patrolling guards, and they reached the northernmost entry to the linear accelerator facility.

A group of four Chimeras stood guard outside the entry, cradling rifles.

Even from where Ghost hid behind rocks and trees across the street from the accelerator facility, Dohi could smell the overwhelming odor of humans forced to live together in close confines.

Fitz gave the order to take the Chimeras down.

Suppressed rounds tore into the fleshy parts of their body unprotected by body armor. Three dropped immediately, but one survived the gunfire and lifted his rifle to fire.

Dohi finished the beast with a shot to the face that cracked through the night.

The team bolted toward the corpses with Corrin handling their prisoner.

It turned out the man wasn't lying.

As soon as they cleared the entry, Dohi flipped up his NVGs to a ghastly scene.

Sickly yellow lights hung overhead, illuminating red webbing that covered the lengths of wires and pipes stretching further than he could see. Everywhere he looked, he saw bodies cocooned in those webs.

He scanned the vast space for guards. Seeing none, he started to check the closest prisoners.

While some looked like little more than sacks of flesh and bones, many appeared stronger. That was good to see.

The team had brought a few extra bottles of water and nutrition, limited by the weight they could safely dive with, but it wasn't enough. Not even close.

Mouths that weren't clogged with red vines called out for help.

Dohi went to the closest one. It was a woman who looked to be in her twenties wearing a soiled ACU. He cut away the vines holding her in place and then caught her when she sagged forward.

"Hold on," he said. "I've got you."

He helped her down to the ground.

"Water," she muttered.

Dohi reached to his side and grabbed his bottle, bringing it to her lips.

"Not so fast," he said. "Easy."

She looked familiar to him, but he couldn't quite place her.

"It's going to be okay," he said. "We're going to get you out of here."

"You... you're here to save us?"

"Yes," Dohi said. "What's your name?"

"Corporal Esparza..." She glared over his shoulder at the collaborator.

As soon as Dohi had freed her, he grabbed the man by his beard.

"Wait, no, you said..." the collaborator started.

Dohi pulled him to the ground and stomped on the side of his face, knocking him out. He looked over at Corrin. "Sling this bastard up in one of those cocoons."

"With pleasure," Corrin said.

While the Chimera dealt with the collaborator, the rest of the Team worked on freeing the others. As the group of liberated human prisoners grew, those strong enough started to help. Ghost shared the extra provisions and water they had brought, helping to rejuvenate the prisoners even just a little.

"What's your plan?" Esparza asked.

Fitz handed her a rifle they had taken from a Chimera. "We fight, and you help us."

The woman wiped blood and dirt from her face and smiled. But Dohi noticed some of the freed prisoners looking at Corrin skeptically.

"What the fuck is this beast doing with you?" asked one of the men.

311

"He's with us," Fitz said.

"You trust this... thing?"

"He's the reason we found you all," Rico said.

"You all owe him your life," Fitz said.

Esparza turned to the others. "This is Team Ghost. You've heard the stories. You know what they've done. If they trust this Chimera, we should too."

A few of the released prisoners grunted their agreement. The man who had initially voiced his concern over Corrin gave a reluctant nod.

"Keep working," Fitz said. "We need all the help we can get."

"Are we getting reinforcements?" one of the prisoners asked.

"You're looking at them," Dohi said. "Everyone else is fighting for survival in Galveston. There's barely anything else left of the Allied States except that island and us tonight."

"Jesus Christ," another prisoner said. "Do we have more guns than the ones you brought?"

"We're going to have to get more," Rico said.

Corrin pointed down the corridor. "There are more weapons in here."

"An armory?" Fitz asked.

"No, beasts like me," Corrin said.

"Dohi, go with Corrin to release them," Fitz said. "Rico and I will organize the others."

Dohi and Corrin hurried toward the other end of the accelerator. He searched down his scope again to ensure no guards had entered the facility yet.

They stopped when they reached the section where the Fallen Chimeras were secured against the walls. Their scarred bodies were wrapped in even more glue and vines than the normal humans.

The golden eyes of the first prisoner watched. A patch of glue adhered to his sucker lips prevented him from talking.

As soon as Dohi pried off the strip with his knife, the Chimera screamed in his face, forcing Dohi back.

"Quiet," he said.

"Just kill me!" the creature wailed. "I won't work for you any longer!"

Corrin jumped over to help. "It's okay. We're friends. We've come to free you."

The Chimera glared at him, then back at Dohi. For a moment, Dohi worried he was going to have to kill the beast.

The Chimera's face remained in a snarl, saliva dripping from his teeth. Other Chimeras covered in webbing watched, their golden eyes studying Corrin and Dohi.

"We're here to free you." Dohi turned to speak to all of them. "We need your help to fight back against the New Gods."

He faced the first Chimera again.

"Join us," Corrin said. "We might not win against the New Gods, but we will die fighting as free..."

"Men," Dohi said.

The creature held his gaze and nodded.

Dohi finished cutting him down, and Corrin started on the others, using his claws to tear through the tendrils imprisoning them. Ten minutes later, a growing group of freed beasts had started to cut down the rest of the Fallen Chimeras. Some spoke in low growling voices, musing about their newfound chance at revenge.

Dohi counted twenty-five freed Chimeras when the doors to the other end of the linear accelerator opened.

All of them turned to a group of six collaborators who rushed in with weapons. The collaborators stopped in their tracks when they saw the freed horde.

"You want revenge?" Corrin said. "Now's your chance!"

The group rushed toward the collaborators. None of the men even bothered to fire. They turned and ran, their terrified screams echoing throughout the facility. Dohi aimed his rifle and shot their legs one by one.

The Chimeras caught up to the collaborators writhing in agony on the ground, tearing into their flesh. Blood splashed across the floor as the beasts got their first taste of revenge.

With the other freed prisoners behind them, Fitz and Rico caught up to Dohi. The three of them picked up the collaborators' weapons and began handing them out. Rifles. Pistols. Knives. And even a machete.

"You have your army, Master Sergeant," Corrin said to Fitz. "Now put us to use."

Sirens wailed over the constant patter of rain. But above the clamor, Kate heard the faint voices of those injured in the bat attacks screaming throughout the hospital. She was a few floors below, in the hospital's former clinical laboratory, but their cries carried through the vents.

While most of the patients were receiving intensive medical care, including the use of respirators and ventilators to keep them stable, those who were most ill wouldn't ever recover without the right antidote. That was something she and her team could help with. In an isolated portion of the lab, Leslie and Ron had already prepared reagents for assays to analyze samples from the gas attack.

Kate was in the main section of the lab with Sammy to monitor the remote computer stations left connected to the webbing in Houston. Although they couldn't decrypt the signals flowing through the network, they could monitor the total volume of signal activity.

On the other side of the lab, engineers monitored reports from the seismic detection sensors installed around Houston and Galveston.

Kate supervised it all, going from station to station. She was back with Sammy when the door burst open. A combat medic entered, sweat dripping down her face. Her ACU was covered in blood and ash. She carried a tray filled with small plastic vials.

Ron emerged from the isolated section of the laboratory when he saw her.

"Dr. Lovato, we've got the first set of blood samples," the medic said. "We've already used Mark 1 NAAKs on all the patients, but the docs want to be sure we're doing the right thing."

Kate handed the tray to Ron. He rushed them back into the isolated section of the lab where they had prepared the standard point-of-care blood analysis assays to detect potential toxins.

"Those nerve agent-antidote kits have 2-PAM chloride, diazepam, and atropine, right?" she asked.

"Yes, Doctor," the medic answered.

"So long as this is just a normal nerve agent, we should be in the clear."

"But if it isn't…" the combat medic shifted nervously. "How long does this take?"

"Just a few minutes," Kate said. "These tests were developed well before the Great War in response to potential nerve agent attacks in the Persian Gulf War. They're designed to be quick."

"Good. The doctors want answers now. At least fifty patients we brought here are in serious condition."

"What do the symptoms look like?"

"Nausea, vomiting. A large portion of the patients reported intense pain in their muscles, and many are having trouble controlling their limbs."

Those were all symptoms of a nerve agent. Kate wanted to scream. The evil of the Prophet and his army was unmatched by any of the creatures or men she had faced in the past.

"All we can do now is watch for new symptoms until we get definitive answers," she said.

Ron emerged from the isolated portion of the laboratory after another few minutes. "I've got the results from the first blood samples."

He handed her a printed-out page.

Kate skimmed the report. "We can confirm organophosphate poisoning in all these samples. Definitely a nerve agent." She scrolled through the report. "We're looking at soman."

"Soman, got it," the medic said. "The 2-PAM chloride and atropine will knock it out then."

"Good," Kate said. "We'll continue looking at the blood samples to make sure there's not something else in there that we missed."

"Thank you, Doctor," the medic said, hurrying out of the lab.

"Good luck." Kate was glad to have helped, but she knew the death and misery had just started. Soon they would be dealing with the injuries from gunfire and claws that she had seen far too many times.

As if in answer, a thunderous boom shook the hospital. She braced herself, waiting for an explosion.

One of the computers chirped, indicating a seismic disturbance.

"Just thunder," said the engineer monitoring the screen. "The storm is messing with our equipment, but that's all it is."

Kate exhaled. "Ron, I want you and Leslie to continue processing the blood samples. Just because we found soman in the first few doesn't mean that's the only thing the New Gods were using. Check for other biological agents or weaponized pathogens."

"You got it," Ron said, then returned to the isolated portion of the lab.

Kate moved to the section of the lab where the team of engineers were monitoring seismic disturbances.

"Have you picked up anything unusual?" Kate asked.

"No, Dr. Lovato," the engineer replied. "The only seismic activity we detected was from the explosions hammering the ground around Galveston. After that, it's been quiet except for this storm."

So far, it seemed the New Gods hadn't been tunneling into the ground anywhere near Houston or Galveston.

Cries sounded from the hallway, and Kate looked up just as another gurney was pushed past by two paramedics. A patient on it writhed in pain, covered in blood and blackened skin.

Kate's thoughts rushed back to the shelter where Javier, Tasha, and Jenny were. She had checked in with Connor twice now, and he had reported they had been safe from the blasts and the gas. That knowledge did nothing to assuage the dark feelings hanging over her mind like the storm over Galveston.

She went to Sammy's station, trying to keep focused. "How many teams have delivered their anthrax samples?"

"So far, six," Sammy said. "I'm seeing a slight reduction in network signals. You think it's working?"

"We won't know for sure unless we can kill off more of the webbing. The infection isn't instantaneous, so it's no surprise that it's taking a while." Kate looked at the computer. "Can you quantify the damage we've done to the network?"

"Keep in mind, the situation is evolving, but as the bacteria propagates, so too does the signal attenuation. I'm noticing a drop off in the overall number of signals at about five percent right now."

"That's not much at all."

"No, it isn't," Sammy said.

"We only have a couple hours until dawn and the New Gods show," Kate said.

The color drained from Sammy's face. Kate had a feeling she knew what Sammy was thinking.

"If at least a few more of those teams don't get their injections into the webbing soon, it's not going to make much of a difference for us, is it?" Kate asked.

"Correct," Sammy said coldly.

Kate clenched her jaw out of anger. She had truly thought their work would have a more substantial impact tonight, but it seemed their efforts might not really affect the network until after the fighting was over.

Sammy looked like she was about to say something, but the radio next to her computer buzzed to life.

"Doctor Lovato, this is Commander Jacobs. We're confirming Recon Omega is reporting another successful injection. They're now returning home."

"Good," Kate replied. "Can I have a sitrep on the other teams?"

"Recon Tango and Recon Oscar are confirmed KIA. November and Kilo are MIA, but last transmissions indicate probable KIA. We lost contact with Recon Delta and Echo. Sigma is still out there, but ran into hostiles. They've been radio silent since."

Kate clenched her jaw again at the mention of Sigma. That was Horn and Timothy's team.

She shook away her fear and decided the only thing she could do right now was believe they were still alive. She couldn't bear the thought of losing them both.

"That's not enough," Sammy whispered. "It won't cause a collapse if we don't get at least another bolus injected."

Kate stared at the map of the planned injection sites on the monitor. The dot representing Recon Sigma's target glowed red.

"There's still hope," Kate said. "If Sigma is out there, they'll come through."

"Yeah, maybe," Sammy said, sounding dejected.

"Horn and Timothy know what they're doing. They have to survive. We've just got to trust them."

She said it as much to convince herself as Sammy.

Another chirping computer pulled Kate's attention away from Sammy's computer, and she rushed over to the engineering team.

"Is it the thunder again?" she asked.

Stepping between two of the engineers, she watched spikes of seismic activity scrolling across the screen.

"No," one of the engineers replied. "This is happening across the northwest side of Houston. If I'm reading this right, we've got at least five separate groups of Variants traveling through the tunnels and making new ones."

"Inform command," Kate said.

The engineer nodded to another man who picked up the radio.

Kate looked at a map of Houston and Galveston that showed the epicenters of the detected seismic activity. One of these points was moving close to the Woodlands, toward the northwest of Houston right where Timothy and Horn were supposed to be.

The second wave of the New Gods' attack was coming, and they were right in the path.

* * *

"Recon Sigma, this is Command," a communications

officer said over Timothy's radio. "Seismic activity confirmed near your position. Variants headed your way, ETA ten mikes."

"Sigma One, copy," Horn replied.

"Be advised, you're the last team in the field. We're all counting on you."

"Copy," Horn said.

Timothy caught his gaze.

"You heard 'em, it's up to us," Horn said. "And we're not going to disappoint."

Rain fell over them in waves as they continued to follow the trail of clawed footprints in the mud. Blood covering the smashed grass showed where the beasts had dragged Boyd away. The sheer amount told Timothy that his friend was no longer alive. But hopefully he still had the anthrax they needed to inject in the webbing.

Timothy thought he felt the ground rumble slightly beneath his feet. He hoped it was just his mind playing tricks on him and command was right about them having a full ten minutes.

He gripped his rifle in his soaked gloves and angled the barrel down the path. It led them into a neighborhood and over the front yards of two houses.

Thunder rumbled overhead, lightning cutting through the sky.

They passed through another line of trees, following the trail through a yard of overgrown grass. Horn motioned for them to get down at the sound of squawking and scratching claws on the adjacent street. Timothy ducked low in the cover of the overgrown grass. He crept through the grass with Horn to get a better look.

Next to a rusted-out pickup truck nearly a hundred

yards down the street, Timothy could make out three twisted shapes headed north. They were dragging a large body behind them.

"They still have Boyd with them," Timothy said. He brought his rifle up just as the beasts started to disappear behind a minivan. "Can't get a clear shot now."

"We got to take them out before they get wherever they're headed," Horn replied.

He signaled to the backyard of the house. They ran hard to cut off the Variants. After passing by rotting decks and rusted swing sets, they raced back to the front yard of another house.

They took up firing positions between two cars parked side-by-side on a driveway, and Timothy flipped up his NVGs to peer down his scope.

The three creatures skittered toward them, still a couple hundred yards from the south. They had plenty of time to set an ambush.

As Timothy centered his sights on the first Variant, he noticed a collar around its neck.

"You were right," he said to Horn. "Someone's controlling these Thralls. As soon as we open fire, whoever's in charge of them is going to come after us."

Horn readied his M249, setting up its bipod on the hood of one car, aiming north. "I'll deal with the collaborators or whoever the hell else might be here if they show up. You take the beasts down."

"You're sure?"

"We got no other choice, kid."

Timothy aimed at the diseased flesh of the lead monster dragging Boyd. A hot anger rushed through him, and he squeezed the trigger.

Rounds punched through the chest of the monster,

and the grotesque mutant collapsed to the wet asphalt next to Boyd.

The other two creatures let out furious roars and got down on all fours. Timothy lined up his sights and held in a breath as they barreled toward him.

He squeezed a burst off into one of the beasts, rounds lancing into its barreled chest and limbs. Blood sprayed from the devastating wounds as it tumbled over itself, skidding across the asphalt.

Before he could adjust his aim for the third monster, gunfire north of their position exploded behind him. He had been right. The assholes controlling the Variants weren't far. Rounds pinged against the car where Horn had propped up his M249.

The heavy thump of the machine gun was nearly deafening, drowning out the shrieks of the monster galloping toward Timothy.

His world narrowed down the scope of his rifle. He took another breath and squeezed the trigger. The bullet found the target, but the creature still kept coming.

"What the fuck," Timothy said.

He centered his aim again with the Variant only a few yards away. The burst finally knocked it off course, and it slid across the ground.

Timothy put a final round into the head, just to be sure. Then he turned to look in the direction Horn was firing.

Two collaborators ducked behind cars, trying to get close. When they made a move, Timothy took one of them down, and the second man dove for cover.

A spray of rounds from the M249 cut down another enemy rushing down the street for a new position.

Timothy roved his scope over the body to see it was a human collaborator.

Scouts, probably.

Thoughts of his father, of his captivity in Mount Katahdin, and of the destruction of his former home in Maine flooded his mind.

He wanted to tear apart every last one of these evil men, but the wooden beads of the bracelet Tasha had given him bumped against his wrist, reminding him he had more to live for than revenge.

Even if he and Horn were better shots, the collaborators might already be sending people to surround them. The two of them couldn't hold out forever. Most importantly, they had a bigger mission at stake.

"Cover me, and I'll get the anthrax," Timothy said.

Horn gave him a nod before unleashing a hail of bullets. Return fire speared into the cars as Timothy sprinted away. More bullets seared through the air past him. A couple sparked against the wet asphalt. He slid next to Boyd and hid behind the first Variant he had killed as rounds thumped into both corpses.

Timothy reached over and searched Boyd's pockets for the syringe of anthrax. Boyd's throat was torn open, and his eyes were locked open in a look of horror.

"I'm sorry," Timothy said.

More bullets slammed into the Variant and Boyd, forcing Timothy to draw his hand back. He waited a moment then tried a new pocket and found the plastic syringe.

"Got it!" Timothy yelled.

He stashed it in his vest and drew himself up into a low firing position, providing cover fire for Horn. The big man raked the M249 back and forth, then took off running.

Shouts from the collaborators carried over the rain as Timothy retreated to the backyard of the closest house. Horn was huffing and puffing, but managed to keep running toward the golf course bordering the backyards. They didn't slow until they found cover in a tree line, and even then, they pushed themselves forward, never completely stopping until they reached the edge of the webbing-covered tunnel.

Water ran over the sides and down into it, turning it into a muddy mess.

"I'll cover you," Horn heaved. He aimed back the way they had come.

The ground seemed to rumble, but this wasn't thunder. The monsters in the tunnel were close.

With the anthrax in one hand, Timothy dropped to his belly, still gasping to catch his breath. He lay flat and stretched to reach one of the tendrils within the tunnel. With a jab, he got the needle into the throbbing red vine and depressed the plunger.

A howl erupted from deeper inside the tunnel. The stench of rotten fruits filled his lungs. His body shook as the walls trembled more fiercely. The click of joints and growls of bloodthirsty monsters echoed toward him.

"Hurry up," Horn said.

Timothy backed out and began to stand, but Horn yanked him down in the cover of the tall grass.

"We got more company," Horn said. "Collaborators caught up to us."

"Can't stay here. The Variants aren't far behind."

"I fucking hate running," Horn said. He stood, ready to move. "Don't leave me behind, kid. I still haven't given you permission to date my daughter."

Timothy almost laughed but a burst of gunfire made him flinch.

Another terrifying tremor rumbled the ground, the shaking more violent. Another spot of grass twenty yards to their west pushed upward.

A familiar, terrifying clicking shriek sounded from the newly formed hole as Timothy took off running with Horn. They both watched the ground burst upward in a geyser of wet soil and long grass. An Alpha pulled itself out, and Variants poured out after it.

"Faster!" Horn yelled.

Timothy had never run harder in his life. He pushed himself to his physical limit, his lungs burning with the effort. Horn was starting to fall behind. Timothy eased up and took a moment to look at their pursuers.

Monsters galloped over the wet ground, tearing through the grass, and gunfire flashed from the golf course.

"KEEP RUNNING!" Horn yelled.

Timothy took off again.

Images of Tasha flashed through his mind. She was waiting for him back in Galveston. If he didn't make it back, he wouldn't see her again. He wouldn't be able to help her from the incoming army of monsters descending on their base.

And if he didn't save her dad, they would both be screwed.

He skidded to a stop and aimed to take out the closest Variants, buying the big man some extra time.

The creatures bolted into the fire, not even trying to avoid the bullets.

Horn stopped to send a burst of rounds into the

enemy's ranks, taking down two of the lead beasts, but the Alpha never stopped.

"Come on!" Horn yelled.

They reached the street where they had left the Humvee, and Timothy spotted the truck. By the time they made it there, the Alpha was halfway down the street with a pack of Variants flocking around it.

Horn opened the driver's door as Timothy dove into the back seat. He didn't even have time to shut the door before Horn pushed down on the pedal. The vehicle lurched forward, but then jolted to a stop.

Timothy looked back to see the Alpha had grabbed the back bumper, water sluicing over its diseased flesh.

"Come on, baby!" Horn said.

The Humvee growled, tires squealing. Timothy pulled out his pistol and fired at the back windshield. Glass burst outward, and bullets punched into the meaty flesh. The Alpha held on until a couple rounds smashed through its snout.

The vehicle tore away, ripping out of the Alpha's claws. The beast ran after them with the entourage of smaller monsters and the collaborators, bullets slamming against the back of the Humvee.

Horn navigated out of the neighborhood and onto the highway, leaving their pursuers behind, never letting up on the gas.

"Jesus Christ in Heaven," Horn said. "We clear?"

"I think so," Timothy said, still gasping. "So... does this mean I got your permission to date Tasha?"

"We'll see," Horn said.

Water fell in sheets over the windshield, the wipers swishing back and forth. Horn dodged past a wrecked vehicle, and Timothy climbed into the front passenger seat.

Horn picked up his radio. "Command, Recon Sigma One. We got the anthrax injected. Headed back to base now."

"Copy that," the comms officer replied. "Good work, Recon Sigma One. What's your ETA?"

"Fifty minutes if we press it."

"Better hurry up or you will be cut off," the comms officer said.

"Copy," Horn said. He slammed the radio down.

"Cut off?" Timothy asked.

"The bridge," Horn said. "They're going to blow it."

"If they do, we're stuck on this side of the bay with all those monsters."

"My girls are on that island, Temper. You sure as shit know I am not letting us stay on this side of the bay while those beasts try to take Galveston."

Timothy checked to make sure his belt was secure.

"Yeah, better hold onto your ass, kid, because tonight, this mountain is a fucking volcano, and I'll fly this fucking Humvee if I have to," Horn said.

— 24 —

Ringgold stood on the ten-yard-wide watchtower platform atop the roof of the Harbor House Hotel in Galveston. Beside her stood Cornelius, Souza, and Soprano.

She had insisted on being outside the confines of her bunker to stand side-by-side with the troops sworn to protect this country.

As a concession, Festa was inside the hotel, coordinating with a team of military officers and the representatives from Canada and Mexico. Festa would serve as the designated survivor, taking control of the defenses in a secure underground headquarters should something happen to Ringgold.

In the middle of the platform, two armed communications officers had laptops and radios set up on a table behind a steel enclosure. Three snipers were situated in nearby watchtowers and two-person teams manned M240s set up behind sandbags on the catwalks above the steel walls.

A reinforced steel roof protected them from the light drizzle of rain. The fog had mostly lifted, and the storm was retreating, providing sightlines to both the I-45 bridge and the Gulf of Mexico. They had lost radar in the bat attack, rendering them otherwise blind. To watch for the First Fleet, Souza had deployed two 25-foot Coast Guard Response Boats.

For the first time in her career serving her country, she carried an M4A1. She had spent every spare minute training with the weapon.

She was not the only one holding a weapon like this in combat for the first time.

Their defenses were filled with individuals who had been drafted days ago. Refugees and even the injured stood on the walls. Soprano was armed with a shotgun that he carried awkwardly. Ringgold wondered if he was more of a threat with it, than without.

"The Variants are closing in," Cornelius reported. "ETA forty-five minutes."

"How far is Recon Sigma?" Ringgold asked.

"They're expected to arrive around the same time."

"That's cutting it too close."

"We'll have to blow the bridge before the monsters arrive, whether they're here or not."

Ringgold could not imagine giving an order that would condemn some of her closest friends to almost certain death, but decisions like this were part of the burden she faced as president.

"Delay blowing the bridge as long as possible," she said. "But I would like—"

"Madam President, I'm sorry to interrupt," Souza said. "I just heard from Festa. The First Fleet was reported just under twenty klicks out by one of our Response Boats."

Ringgold let her rifle fall on its strap and picked up her binoculars. She looked toward the east. Sheets of rain blocked any chance of seeing the distant fleet emerge over the horizon.

"How many ships?" she asked.

"Without radar, hard to say, but the scout reported seeing the USS *George Johnson* and three other First Fleet ships. They were preparing to launch dozens of smaller boats filled with collaborators, Variants, and Chimeras."

"They're preparing for a full-on beach invasion," Cornelius said.

"Begin our aerial attack," Ringgold said.

The general relayed the order, and moments later, the first few jets took off from the runway to their south. Other planes followed, military and slower civilian craft flying off with what little ordnance they had left.

A distant flash of lightning cut through the sky. The minutes ticked by as the planes flew through the clearing storm toward the enemy fleet.

The increasingly heavy thrum of her pulse sounded like war drums in her ears at the thought of what they would soon face. The USS *George Johnson* had been equipped with the best anti-aircraft weaponry the Allied States had left. She could only hope that the New Gods did not know how to operate such advanced equipment.

Unfortunately, she had also witnessed what had happened when the Allied States underestimated their enemy. Even if a fraction of their forces knew how to use the weapons, the ships could prove devastating to their forces.

"Our squadrons are almost in position," Souza said.

A few moments later, one of the pilots came over the radio. "Command, Eagle One. Approaching targets."

Ringgold could almost picture the ships cutting through the dark waves that the pilot must be seeing.

"Commencing bombing," said Eagle One. "We are—"

The line suddenly went dead.

Souza stepped closer to the radio operator. "The hell just happened?"

The operator shook his head. "I think they were shot, sir."

Distant flashes of light strobed through the gray clouds over the horizon, like more lightning strikes behind the clouds. But there were far too many blasts for it to be from the storm.

"We're going down!" another voice cried over the channel.

"Command, we're taking heavy fire!"

"Engine failure! They hit—"

"I can't hold out!"

"All systems are failing! Target is still—"

More explosions bloomed across the gray horizon. Frantic voices filled the lines.

Souza picked up the radio. "All pilots, this is Command. Concentrate all weapons on the USS *General Johnson*. You can't let it get through."

"Command, Eagle Three," a pilot said. "We've lost contact with a third of our units."

Souza turned away from the radio, his jaw clenched, fingers curled into a fist. "Damn it!"

"It would've been even worse if these monsters really knew how to use that weaponry," Cornelius said. "All our aircraft and our base would be gone. We're lucky they must not have half the expertise our Navy did."

"Bombing still underway," Eagle Three reported. "We're hitting it with everything we've got."

The rumble of the explosions barreled into Galveston like an unstoppable chorus of thunder.

"Command, Eagle Six," another pilot. "All ordnance deployed. Returning for reload."

"Eagle Six, can you confirm that all enemy anti-aircraft weapons were eliminated?" Souza asked.

"Affirmative, all weaponry on the *George Johnson* is disabled! It's spitting fire, sir. She's not going to be floating much longer."

Cornelius raised a fist, and Souza exhaled. Ringgold nodded at both of them, but the victory was short lived. Eagle Six reported two cruisers still had active anti-aircraft weapons.

Ringgold watched the first of the surviving aircraft returning to Galveston. Comm chatter painted a grim picture of the damage to their beleaguered air force.

She turned back to Soprano.

"Go confirm with Hernandez and Vance to see if there is anything the Mexican and Canadians can do to make their troops move faster," she said.

"Yes, Madam President," Soprano replied.

"New Gods land units are now twenty minutes to the bridge according to seismic activity," Cornelius said.

"Sigma?" she asked.

"Still en route, just ahead of them."

Ringgold raised her binos back to the Gulf Coast. Planes were taking off into the screen of rain and clouds again.

The first dark silhouettes of the First Fleet appeared over the choppy waters.

She zoomed in, and while she couldn't make out all the details, the looming shape of the USS *George Johnson* was evident. Half its superstructure vented flames. The massive ship steamed ahead straight toward Galveston, but was listing precariously to its portside.

Two cruisers barreled alongside it. Fingers of smoke rose from each vessel, and most of their decks seemed enveloped in fire. Munitions exploded as the flames spread, shooting geysers of spreading debris into the air.

The smaller crafts that Eagle Six and the Coast Guard Response Boats had spotted were churning alongside the bigger ships, struggling to maintain speed in the violent waves.

"Unless the New Gods brought their own munitions, we know what was on those last ships for the anti-aircraft weapons," Souza said. "They can't have much left now, especially after all that damage."

"I hope you're right, because we're sitting ducks," Ringgold said.

Tracer fire spit into the sky from the cruisers. She watched in horror as the rounds tore into the lead aircrafts. A couple of the pilots managed to avoid the incoming fire, rolling away or diving underneath, but they disappeared in billows of white smoke and fire when missiles struck them.

Only a few made it through with a combination of expert maneuvering and sheer luck.

Blasts from the decks of the cruisers as the aircraft dropped their payloads. Part of the decks gave way, flames roaring out like enormous demons from the underworld. Crews on both ships started lowering lifeboats and another wave of smaller craft over the side. Some even jumped straight into the roiling waters.

The guns on the USS *George Johnson* remained quiet, but she could still see the shapes of surviving enemy soldiers on the decks.

Another wave of explosions rolled over the cruisers.

"Command, Eagle Six," a pilot reported. "We scored direct hits on the escort cruisers. Coming in now to finish off any survivors on the *George Johnson*."

Another explosion rolled over the superstructure of the destroyer. Flames erupted from holes torn into the bent metal, but the ship continued to carve slowly through the water.

That ship might be going down, but the battle wasn't over.

Sirens wailed over the base once more. Soldiers raced for their battle stations along the walls, and spotlights raked the waters, illuminating the incoming boats.

Ringgold could do nothing but watch them draw closer.

A loud grating sound scraped over Galveston as the sinking *George Johnson* ground into the sand and rock offshore. Momentum carried it forward, kicking up waves, its ruptured keel slicing into the shallows until finally it lurched sideways, beached nearly four hundred yards from the Galveston beach.

The two burning and dying cruisers made it slightly further before they too succumbed to the same fate. Smaller motorboats and yachts chugged past them, advancing over the rolling waves, and crashed into sand banks.

From each of those smaller vessels, men and monsters jumped over the sides. Ringgold tried to keep track of the dozens upon dozens of creatures pouring off the boats and through the shallows.

Tracer fire lanced from the walls. Low thuds resonated over the beach from grenades and mines. Geysers of sand, fire, and shredded body parts spewed into the air.

A few helicopters they had on reserve made passes over the beach, spitting gunfire and launching rockets into the enemies stampeding over the sand.

Collaborators returned fire with their own rockets. One streaked into a Black Hawk, erupting in a flash of light. The pilots managed to put the damaged bird down on the beach, but a pack of Variants were on them before they could escape the wreckage.

"We've got more incoming," Cornelius said, pointing at the *George Johnson*.

While flames danced from the superstructure, a stream of smaller shapes flung themselves over the side into the water. Others raced down the ladders tracing the hull, leaping into rigid-hulled inflatable boats, lifeboats, and some of the other small craft nearby.

"There must be hundreds of creatures and collaborators on that ship," Cornelius said.

Ringgold roved her binos over the enemy soldiers, spotting squads of heavily armed Chimeras with their cutlasses.

"Madam President, seismic activity indicates the rest of the New Gods' land forces are poised to cross the bridge in less than two minutes," the comms officer said. "Recon Sigma is on the bridge now."

She turned her binos back to the bay. A lone Humvee raced across the long bridge. Only about five-hundred yards behind them, the first rush of monsters followed, galloping across the asphalt.

"Blow the bridges as soon as Sigma is across," she said.

A moment later, explosions ripped down the bridge, red and orange balls of fire devouring the pillars holding it above the bay. Concrete gave way, falling in chunks, and almost as if in slow motion, the bridge began to collapse. Variants flailed as they plummeted with the debris.

Soprano rushed back up the stairs to the platform, chest heaving.

"You have good news?" Ringgold asked.

Souza and Cornelius both looked at Soprano.

"I'm sorry," he said. "The Canadian and Mexican forces are still hours from arrival. We're on our own for now."

Ringgold felt her stomach churn. The enemy had arrived by sea, air, and land. She had done everything she could to prepare, but still it felt like it was not enough. The only thing left to do was fight.

Raising her rifle to her shoulder, she readied herself for battle.

***

Gunfire cracked across Los Alamos.

Keeping low, Fitz advanced up a narrow street between two laboratory buildings, headed north with Team Ghost and a small army of Chimeras and humans. It had been hell fighting through the streets and doing their best to stay concealed from the few guards left around the base.

But they had unexpected help keeping the guards occupied.

While most of the prisoners had followed them, a few distrusting Chimeras and scared human prisoners had run off. Those fleeing prisoners were enough to draw many of the remaining enemy guards away. That distraction had helped Ghost, but it was a terrible choice for the prisoners.

Screams rang out, some of them human as the monsters found them.

"Should've stayed with us," Fitz said.

"They chose their own deaths," Dohi said.

Fitz tried to understand the callous words. This was

NICHOLAS SANSBURY SMITH & ANTHONY J. MELCHIORRI

not the Dohi he knew—the Dohi who would do anything to save another person. But Fitz understood how trauma and PTSD could turn a good heart black.

That kind of trauma could not be dealt with now. Instead he focused back on the mission and took shelter behind a truck to sneak a glimpse at an intersection to the east. A friendly Chimera had confirmed that just a few blocks in that direction was the command center for the New Gods.

Fitz surveyed the building. Camouflage netting covered two machine gun nests and maybe a little over ten Chimeras perched along the roof. Collaborators were entrenched behind sandbags and aiming out of windows.

Prowling Thrall Variants screeched and howled in the street. The smell of blood and sound of battle had them riled up. The only thing holding them back were the collars around their necks.

Fitz turned to his team, telling them what he had seen.

"We've got the numbers," Dohi said. "Nearly thirty Fallen Chimeras still with us, and thirty human prisoners strong enough to fight."

"But less than half have firearms," Rico said.

Corrin clicked his claws together. "But *we* have weapons."

"Still, it's suicide running headlong into that command building," Rico said.

Fitz listened between a few more distant gunshots and the rattle of machine guns.

"If we don't do something quickly, they'll finish off the last of the fleeing prisoners, then find us," Fitz said. "The only reason we're still alive is because they sent damn near everything they had to Galveston."

All they needed to do was get to the Prophet,

assuming he was even here. The command building was so close, but trying to sneak in with this army would not work.

Fitz signaled to the Chimera that had told them about the command center. The filthy half-man hunched down, reeking of body odor and festering wounds.

"The front western entrance to this place is well-guarded," Fitz said. "What's our best alternative?"

"There's a couple of secured doors on the north and south sides," the Chimera replied.

"Those machine guns will cut us down before we can get close enough to get inside," Rico said.

"What about tunnels?" Fitz asked. "The throne room was covered in webbing. We know the network goes inside."

The Chimera looked uncertain. "I don't know."

"I do," Esparza said. She was the first prisoner Dohi had released and was the strongest of the freed humans. "They forced me down there a few days ago to find soldiers who could join their ranks."

"Do you think you could get us to that tunnel?" Fitz asked.

Esparza nodded.

"We can't fit everyone through like that," Dohi said. "I've seen what happens to people in there. A little bit of panic, and they'll run wild, get us all killed."

"Let me lead the Chimeras," Corrin said. "We can divide the forces. Humans with firearms can take the southern side of the building, and I will take my team to scale the walls on the north. That should give you enough distraction to sneak underground."

Fitz was quiet for a moment, listening to the distant sounds of collaborators and Chimeras rounding up the other prisoners. He hated for so many to sacrifice their lives, but Corrin was right.

This was the most effective way to get inside.

"Let's do it," Fitz said. He signaled to another human prisoner who had been a ranking officer before being captured in Vegas and told him to lead the humans. They divided up their ragtag army and relayed their plans.

Fitz looked at Corrin one last time as the Chimera readied his forces. "Thank you, Corrin. You've done more than we ever could've asked."

"It's time to make the Prophet pay," Corrin said. "Good luck, Master Sergeant Fitzpatrick, and to the rest of you."

Dohi reached out toward him. Corrin didn't seem to know what to do at first, but then he clenched Dohi's hand carefully in his own.

"Good luck, brother," Dohi said.

Corrin held his grip for a moment, then nodded and led his troops away.

At the same time, the human prisoners swarmed from their positions, cutting across the street and filtering between the other buildings. Those with weapons provided covering fire, allowing the army of liberated prisoners to spread out in combat intervals.

The Thrall monsters raced toward the human forces, and the machine guns behind them churned with the throat growl of automatic fire.

"Let's move," Fitz said.

Esparza took them back down the street, then cut across a block east toward an open road with three large holes. Red tendrils of webbing grew out of them. She pointed toward one, and they climbed inside a tunnel that reeked of carrion.

Dohi took point, leading them through the darkened tunnels with his NVGs. They advanced at a run, and the sounds of battle outside grew muffled the deeper they went. Fitz's blades squished into the webbing and crunched over bones. They passed by dead humans and animals pasted on the walls.

Esparza directed them through a few intersections until they reached a hole leading to the surface.

"This is it," she whispered.

Fitz approached cautiously. Thick stalks of red webbing stretched upward. Sickly yellow light glowed from above. The smell here was worse than anywhere else in the tunnels.

A few rumbling growls filtered in from the room above. Those were sounds Fitz was all too familiar with.

Masterminds.

From the floor of the tunnel, he could look straight up toward a ceiling covered in a spiderweb of red. This was definitely the auditorium they had seen on the video.

The sounds of the battle raged outside, reminding him of the sacrifices made so they could get here. They had to hurry. The lives of all those outside in Los Alamos and even those in Galveston depended on it.

He signaled for Esparza to back up, then beckoned Rico and Dohi. They all pulled M67 grenades from their tac vests and handed them to Dohi. He lobbed them up one by one through the hole into the throne room.

A few surprised raspy voices cried out, followed by three violent blasts. Chunks of webbing rained down into the tunnel.

"Go!" Fitz yelled.

Dohi took to the webbing and climbed up it with Esparza and Rico swinging themselves up after. Fitz was the last one up, entering the area between the stage and the seating. Smoke and the scent of burned flesh drifted through the air. Pieces of severed webbing squirmed across the floor.

Fitz searched through the dissipating smoke for targets. As it cleared, he spotted the two giant masterminds on the stage, bleeding from shrapnel wounds in the folds of their pink flesh. He turned to scan the seating area, seeing a few dead Chimeras sprawled around smoking sites where the chairs and webbing had been blown to scrap.

Other beasts closer to the back rows of webbing-covered chairs were recovering from the blasts. Two situated at the entrance of the room were already moving into firing positions.

Fitz signaled for Dohi to flank them from the auditorium's north side while Rico and Esparza dropped down behind the seats. He popped up and shot one of the advancing Chimeras through its grotesque face.

Then all hell broke loose, gunfire punching into the seats.

Fitz ducked down and flattened his body. Using his elbows, he army-crawled to a new spot as bullets punched through the plastic seats behind him.

Webbing and broken bits of the chairs sprayed over his body. Esparza got up to fire from an adjacent row, giving Rico and Fitz time to find another position.

As soon as they were clear, Fitz gave Rico a nod. They rose to sight up their next targets, but the return gunfire had already stopped. A cry of agony roared across the enclosed space, and a final Chimera thumped to the ground near the entrance.

"Clear!" Dohi called.

Dohi stood over the last Chimera with blood dripping off his hatchet and knife. The team all turned to the stage where the two masterminds yanked on the webbing to call in reinforcements.

"Prophet isn't here," Dohi said.

"Come on, we have to move," Fitz said.

Dohi led toward the doors, but they burst open before he could reach them. Four juveniles with collars around their necks lunged inside, growling and snapping.

One barreled toward Dohi. He stumbled backward and fell, giving Fitz and the rest of the team clear firing lanes.

"Covering fire!" Fitz shouted.

They unleashed a torrent of rounds into the armored skin of the beasts as the creatures bounded toward Dohi. Fitz aimed for their faces, seeking out their weakest spots. A well-placed shot to an eye killed the lead creature, tripping the others. Two of the remaining three went down in the gunfire, but the survivor pounced on Dohi.

He jammed his knife right through the chin of the beast and deep into its skull.

Fitz aimed at the entrance, spotting shapes in the darkness.

Three or four muzzle flashes suddenly lit up the open doorway.

"Down!" he screamed.

Bullets plunged into the chairs and webbing around Team Ghost. A round slammed into Esparza's shoulder, and she fell backward, crumpling against a chair.

She pressed a hand against the wound. Blood gushed between her fingers.

More rounds hammered their position. Fitz couldn't see their assailants or Dohi, but he could hear them.

Another four juveniles rushed in screeching, and Dohi screamed back a blood-curdling war cry.

Rico crawled past a few destroyed seats to another position. A monster suddenly leapt over the seats in front of her.

"Jeni!" Fitz yelled.

She swiveled onto her back, bringing her rifle up to parry the snapping teeth of the creature. Fitz tried to aim, but another juvenile swiped at him from the seats he was behind.

The creature grabbed him by his collar and yanked him up, ripping his rifle strap with its claws and tossing him to the aisle. He hit the ground hard but drew his holstered M9 with just enough time to fire at the beast as it lunged for him. Bullets smashed into its armor but didn't kill the wretched thing. It grabbed his prosthetic blades and pulled him closer, right into biting distance as he fired into the armor of its neck and face.

"STOP!" came a gravelly voice.

The bleeding juvenile loosened its grip, whimpering and backing off.

Fitz turned his gun on a Chimera with a ragged cloak striding down the aisle holding a cutlass. A broken skull covered his face.

Elijah.

The abomination that had killed Ace.

"Put your weapons down or you all die," Elijah said. "This is your one chance!"

Fitz swallowed his anger and took a stolen moment to assess the situation while he kept his pistol trained on the skull mask. He couldn't see Dohi, but Esparza was down. Rico was in the grip of a juvenile and six Chimeras marched beside Elijah. They split up, advancing down the sides of the throne room.

"Put down your weapons or your little Rico dies," Elijah said. "The Prophet has chosen you. There is no need for you to waste your lives heedlessly."

The beast looked away from Fitz to Esparza. "But not you, heretic."

At the snap of his claws, a juvenile leapt over a seat and ripped into her.

"NO!" Rico shouted.

Fitz kept his gun aimed at Elijah as the monster tore Esparza apart, the sickening sounds of teeth on bone cutting through the air.

"Rico's next if you don't submit," Elijah said.

"Don't do it, Fitzie!" Rico yelled.

Saliva from the juvenile dripped onto her face.

Fitz was about to lower his gun when Dohi leapt over the seats. With his hatchet and knife in hand, he ran for Elijah, screaming at the top of his lungs.

A Chimera tried to stop him, but Dohi whirled and sliced open the throat of the monster and then slammed his hatchet into the face of a second Chimera. With only his knife left, he jumped onto a seat and then launched himself into the air toward Elijah.

The Chimera was caught off guard, and Dohi slammed into him, knocking him down. He brought the blade to Elijah's throat but did not kill him.

"BACK OFF!" Dohi yelled to the other Chimeras.

The beasts throughout the room gave each other confused looks.

"Do it, or he dies!" Dohi shouted.

"If you kill me, your friends die," Elijah growled. "I would readily give my life for the Prophet. But there is only one way out of this for you. Team Ghost joins the

New Gods or the New Gods feast on your flesh."

"I'd rather die than join," Rico said.

"Fitz," Dohi said. "Tell me what to do."

Even if Dohi killed Elijah, they would all die in this throne room—and the Prophet would still be out there.

"You're outnumbered, and your pathetic forces are on the verge of complete defeat," Elijah said. "I am giving you the only way you make it out of here alive. Join us. Join the Prophet."

"Where's the Prophet?" Fitz asked, trying to buy time.

"In Galveston, leading our forces to victory." Elijah chuckled under his mask despite the blade pressed against his throat. "It's over for your beloved country."

Dohi looked over his shoulder at Fitz, shock painted across his expression. Elijah took advantage of the mistake, grabbing him and tossing him aside. He rose to his feet with a cutlass in hand and angled it down at Dohi.

"You weak, pathetic traitors," Elijah said. "You should have surrendered when you had the chance."

The resounding thuds of explosives and the constant roar of gunfire filled the air. Beckham had his shemagh scarf pulled up over his nose, but there was no keeping out the biting odor of smoke.

Soaked from the sheeting rain, he and Ruckley were still on the catwalk stretching along the ten-foot-high, steel-panel wall surrounding the inner core of the base. Command and the hospital facilities were tucked away behind these walls, as was much of downtown Galveston.

From the catwalk, they could see the bay and the bridge four miles to the southwest.

Behind them, a platform led to a tower where Commander Jacobs was posted with his officers. It offered one of the best vantages on the island and was well protected by reinforced layers of wall topped with razor wire.

Minutes ago, they had all watched Timothy and Horn arrive in their Humvee, just before the soldiers guarding the bridge had blown it. Beckham had received radio confirmation that his friends had made it through the first sliding steel-and-razor-wire gate where the Gulf freeway met Galveston Island.

Those outer walls and gates had taken too much damage in the bat attack to be defensible, so the soldiers assigned there had fallen back. They were now positioned on a second set of barricaded steel-panel gates with two watchtowers about a mile to the southwest connected to the same inner core walls that Beckham and Ruckley were on.

From what Beckham could tell, the second position was about to get hit hard.

He lifted his binoculars to scan the choppy water of the bay. The pale flesh of Variants broke the surface of the opaque waters as the beasts swam toward the shore.

And it wasn't just monsters headed their direction.

Two Black Hawks descended to the other side of the bay to pick up stranded collaborators. Once they pulled back into the sky, they raced over the water toward where Horn and Timothy had taken refuge.

"We've got incoming birds," Beckham said through the tower door to Jacobs. "Do we have anything down there left to take them out?"

Commander Jacobs stepped out and shook his head. "The aerial-defenses were either destroyed or expended during the bat attack."

"Shit," Ruckley muttered.

"If they breach that, the Variants coming in from the west will flood downtown and command," Jacobs said.

"Then we need to stop those choppers," Beckham said. "Permission to take the M72 LAW rocket launchers and a Humvee."

Jacobs thought on it a moment, but then nodded. "Take out those birds, but be careful, Captain."

Beckham started down a set of stairs with the weapons as Ruckley hobbled after him. He lost sight of the choppers when he reached the street under the wall. They loaded up into the Humvee and took off, Beckham navigating around a few stubborn fires and craters from the bat attacks.

After driving with the pedal pressed against the floor, the inner gate with its two watchtowers came into view beyond a screen of smoke. He estimated he was only a quarter mile from the inner gate when he saw the two choppers that had been racing across the bay again.

This time, they had made it over where Horn and Timothy were supposed to be.

Muzzle fire flashed from the birds as door gunners swept their machine guns over the walls and the two watchtowers beside the gate.

With each passing second, the gout of gunfire over the defensive positions grew thicker, and Beckham feared soon it would be too late for Horn and Timothy.

He couldn't lose them. Not now. Not after all they had been through.

You're not going to lose them. You're going to save *them.*

"See if you can get Horn on the radio," Beckham said to Ruckley. "Tell him to meet us at the bottom of the gate and look for our Humvee."

"On it," Ruckley said.

While she tried to contact Horn, tracer fire pounded the first helicopter. The pilot banked hard to strafe the machine gun nest. The turning bird gave Beckham a clear view into the troop hold that was filled with Chimeras.

The beasts positioned in the open troop hold joined in with the door gunner to rain hell on the troops stationed in the towers and along the catwalks lining the walls inside the gate. As both choppers began to lower over the gate, the Chimeras pulled out their cutlasses, to prepare for hand-to-hand combat on the walls.

Beckham drove faster, but then slammed on the brakes around the next corner. The Humvee squealed to a stop behind the wreckage of an overturned semi-trailer.

"Out!" he shouted.

Ruckley opened the passenger side, and he jumped out and opened the back door to retrieve the launchers. As he grabbed one and threw the other over his back, Chimeras leapt from the two choppers, landing in the ranks of soldiers while swinging their swords. The crack of gunfire echoed over the cries of soldiers clashing with the Chimeras.

"Horn!" Beckham shouted. "Timothy!"

He scanned the soldiers now engaged in hand-to-hand combat across the walls and towers, but didn't see either of his friends.

"Look out!" Ruckley said.

One of the Black Hawks suddenly swooped low, forcing them to take cover behind the Humvee as the door gunner let loose a spray of fire. Bullets cracked against the hood and windshield, peppering the side of their vehicle.

Beckham hunched down with Ruckley until the torrent was over.

The bird flew away and strafed the wall again, tracer fire lancing out in a violent spray. Rounds punched into soldiers fleeing for cover. Dead bodies tumbled back off the catwalks and smacked against the ground with sickening thuds.

The other Black Hawk was turning now too, coming back in for a second attack.

"Fuck, we have to hurry," Beckham said. "We need a distraction."

"I'll do it," Ruckley said. "You take them out."

"How?"

"I'll drive, you fire," she said.

Ruckley got into the driver's seat and fired up the

engine. It groaned but turned over and she drove away.

Beckham pulled out the arming pin of the LAW rocket launcher, extended the weapon, and shouldered it. One of the choppers took Ruckley's bait and turned away from the wall, giving chase. He lost sight of her and focused on the bird.

Beckham aimed, leading the cockpit, then squeezed the trigger bar. The rocket blazed from the tube. For a fleeting second, he feared he had missed, but the shriek of tearing metal sounded, followed by a low explosion. The rocket had punched right into the top of the troop hold.

With the screech of protesting metal, the bird plummeted sideways before bursting into a fireball against the pavement.

The second Black Hawk began to turn, but instead of going after Ruckley, it started toward his location.

"Oh, shit," Beckham said.

He ducked for cover behind the overturned trailer.

Bullets pounded the sides, piercing the thin metal. He waited for the right moment before bolting away for the wreckage of a pickup truck with flames sputtering from under its hood.

Beckham had hoped the smoke would obscure the pilot's vision, but the door gunner continued to pound his new location. Glass rained down on him as he flattened his body to the pavement and crawled under the back bumper.

The front wheels both exploded.

He had to move or he was going to die, pinned under a burning truck.

As he prepared to make his move, the bark of a second machine gun joined the fight. He clenched up, anticipating the fire, but the bullets weren't intended for him. He slid out from the truck and watched as the door gunner tumbled out the troop hold.

The pilot pulled away, giving Beckham a perfect shot.

"Got ya, motherfucker," he said, drawing himself up into a kneel and firing.

The rocket speared into the tail and sheared it off. The helicopter spun, tossing Chimeras out from the hold. Some survived the fall and tried to crawl away, but a Humvee swerved around a corner and slammed into them.

Ruckley gave a thumbs-up sign out the window.

"Reed!" a deep voice yelled.

Beckham turned back to the other truck, his heart flipping when he saw it was Horn and Timothy. Singe marks and ash covered their ACUs, but they appeared uninjured.

"We have to help reinforce this gate!" Horn said.

"Ruckley, keep the Humvee ready for us!" Beckham said.

He followed Horn and Timothy back toward the semi-trailer where they had a clear view of the fighting on the catwalks and watchtowers. At least ten Thrall Variants had climbed the walls from the other side of the gate and were leaping onto the catwalks to join in the skirmish, fighting beside the remaining Chimeras.

Most of the soldiers defending the gate appeared too young or too old to be fighting. As he ran, Beckham saw a boy no older than fourteen standing next to a guy with a white beard who had to be pushing seventy. The man held up a rifle to block a cutlass. The strike knocked him to his back on the catwalk. He shielded his face with a hand, and the Chimera cocked back his blade for the killing blow.

Before Beckham could unsling his rifle, a burst of gunfire erased the creature's face.

"Nice shot!" Horn said.

Timothy adjusted his aim and then took out a Variant prowling toward a young soldier.

Half the Variants were at the top of the walls, mixing in with the Allied soldiers on the platforms.

"Watch your zone of fire!" Beckham shouted. He shouldered his rifle and went to work, sending bullets tearing through a few beasts still climbing over the lips of the walls. Three of the Chimeras dropped to their knees and aimed toward Beckham in response to the incoming fire. Before they got off a round, Horn's M249 slung a fusillade of fire into their augmented bodies.

Timothy helped Beckham pick off the rest of the monsters one-by-one.

Their efforts were enough to regain control over the gate, and the surviving soldiers finished off the last few Chimeras.

Horn jogged over to Beckham, and they shared a brief hug. After pulling away, Beckham pulled Timothy into a hug too.

"Good timing, Captain," Timothy said.

"Good shooting."

The sounds of distant explosions and gunfire reminded him this was just one battle of many.

"Hold your positions and keep fighting!" Beckham yelled to the surviving soldiers along the wall. "This victory proves we can win!"

Beckham led the way back to the Humvee.

"Good to see your mug," Horn said to Ruckley.

NICHOLAS SANSBURY SMITH & ANTHONY J. MELCHIORRI

"You smell like always," she replied. "But yeah, good to see you."

Timothy chuckled as they jumped into the vehicle and started to drive back toward the command post. As Ruckley steered around the wreckage of a Black Hawk, the radio crackled with a chilling report.

"Breach on the seaborne wall! Reinforce immediately!"

"Fuck, we need to move," Beckham said.

"We've got hostile choppers on the hospital now, too!" another voice stated. "Requesting immediate assistance!"

Beckham tried calling back on the radio, dialing it in to reach Kate, but there was no answer.

"No, no, no," Beckham said, slamming his fists on the Humvee's dash.

Horn put a hand on his shoulder.

"Ruckley, take us there now," Beckham said.

"You got it, Captain."

The Humvee sped down the debris-littered road. Beckham reloaded his rifle and tried to remain calm, but he struggled to contain his breathing.

"It's going to be okay," Timothy said. "We'll save her."

Beckham nodded, praying his young friend was right.

***

Azrael leaned out of the passenger seat of the MH-6 Little Bird helicopter, taking in the scent of burned flesh and death. Corpses littered the streets. Blood flowed freely.

It was a shame. Many of these humans could have joined the New Gods. But their ignorant and selfish leader had sacrificed them all in a futile attempt to preserve this pathetic country. Jan Ringgold was probably cowering deep underground, stubbornly hiding while she used her people as a shield of meat.

He would find her, and she would pay for this foolishness.

But first he was headed to Doctor Kate Lovato and her team. He had used the remote sensors his Scions had found in the Houston tunnels to track them down. It was a bit premature to be coming in this far to grab the scientist, but Azrael didn't want to give her a chance to escape. Besides, other choppers were depositing collaborators and Variants around the island, and more of his forces flooded in from the breached walls on the eastern shore.

Twenty Scions from his death squads were already waiting on the hospital rooftop. They had made quick work of the few guards there.

The Little Bird touched down in the middle of the human corpses. Azrael strode out, the rotor wash kicking up his black cloak.

One of his Scions that had waited for his arrival knelt before him. "Prophet, we are ready."

"Rise, Abaddon," Azrael said.

The Scion stood again, facing him with golden eyes peering out behind a black mask.

"I want Kate and her team alive, but kill everyone else," Azrael said. "Have all our ground forces in the area secure the exits."

"Yes, Prophet," Abaddon said.

Abaddon turned and led the death squads into the building, rushing down the stairs. From pre-war schematics of the hospital, Azrael knew the clinical laboratory was on the second floor. That would be the most logical place for the science team to have set up their labs.

As Azrael followed his warriors into the building, he heard the cries of the injured. These helpless, weak humans would serve no purpose other than to feed his army.

He wasn't sure why anyone would want to protect these breathing corpses, but a group of soldiers had set up a barricade of patient examination beds just inside the hall on the third floor.

"Kill them," Azrael said.

A group of four Scions led by Abaddon scaled the wall, their claws finding purchase just like their Variant brothers. They maneuvered above the barricade and dropped behind the beds.

Agonized screams and the ripping of flesh echoed through the hallway. When those last dying moans grew silent, the four Scions emerged. Blood dripped from their maws and talons.

Azrael continued the trek down the hallway to a doorway that would take them to the second floor. As he passed patients, some of his forces peeled off to kill and feed. Azrael had given these humans all a chance to submit, a chance to accept his mercy. But Ringgold had refused, so he and his talented hunters showed them no quarter.

Some humans tried to crawl or scramble away, one of them running in front of Azrael. He reached out and grabbed the young man by his throat, lifting him up and crushing his windpipe. Then he tossed the limp body away.

His forces dominated any stubborn heretics foolish

enough to fight them in the enclosed space, lashing out with their rifles and cutlasses when the skirmishes devolved into hand-to-hand combat. They churned through the facility like a wildfire devouring dry fields of grass.

A final group of soldiers had constructed another barricade in front of what looked to be the clinical laboratory. Abaddon waved his cutlass toward them, and the Scions charged. Bullets cut into their ranks, dropping a few, but the meat of the Scion ranks crashed into the barricade.

Patient beds tumbled. Chairs splintered and broke. Human soldiers fell back, screaming as the Scions pounced on them.

Azrael strode past them as his loyal followers ripped their flesh. His stomach growled hungrily as blood spilled over the floor, but his desire to find the infamous Kate Lovato exceeded his appetite.

He was close now.

As he stepped into the doorway, he spotted a group of scientists huddling in the back of the lab.

Azrael motioned for his soldiers. Together, they broke through the windows with their swords and rifles.

The Scions flooded in and surrounded the group. One of them was standing. To no surprise, it was exactly the person he had come here to see.

"Doctor Kate Lovato," he said. "I've waited a long time to meet you."

"And I, you, Doctor Charles Morgan," she said.

"That name is no longer mine. Call me Azrael."

"I'll call you a monster, because that's what you are." She spat at him, hitting him in the face. One of his Scions grabbed her by an arm, his claws cutting through her white coat and drawing blood. She let out a surprised cry of pain.

Azrael roared and swung his cutlass right across the neck of the soldier. The Scion let go of Kate, pressing his fingers against the flap of bleeding flesh.

"I told you, no harm comes to her!" Azrael shouted.

The creature writhed as blood poured around his claws, and Abaddon dragged the disobedient soldier away.

"You don't have to do this," Kate said. "I know you were once a scientist who wanted to help humanity."

"I am helping," Azrael replied. "I offered mankind a way to evolve."

"This isn't evolution. It's madness."

"Ironic, considering you're responsible for what you see before you." Azrael gestured toward his Scions. "It was your bioweapon that altered my cure. It created the Scions and the Variants. And now you are trying to fight us, to make us extinct. Why do our lives not matter?"

"Because you're trying to destroy all of us," Kate said. "You preach about saving humanity, but you're destroying it, Doctor Morgan."

"That is not my name!" In a fit of anger, he shoved her.

Her head hit the wall with a heavy thud, and she collapsed. A woman with dreadlocks yelled out in surprise, bending to help.

"It's okay, Sammy," Kate said to the other woman.

To Azrael's surprise, Kate pushed herself back to her feet unaided.

"I'm trying to elevate humanity," Azrael growled.

Kate rubbed the back of her head. "You cannot elevate humanity by turning us all into monsters or enslaving us."

"I gave you a choice. All of you."

"A choice of slavery or death, like you gave them?" She indicated the Scions with a wave of her hand. "How many of your people are sacrificing their lives needlessly to satisfy some grudge you've carried for over a decade?"

She turned to his Scions, appealing to them. "This Prophet of yours is nothing but a fraud. He's using you because he's angry about what happened to him, not because he's ushering in some great future."

A couple of the soldiers looked at Azrael, almost as if they were uncertain who to believe. The others growled at Kate.

"Ignore the heretic," Azrael said as calmly as he could. She was no longer worth his time. He lunged forward and grabbed Sammy this time. "You care about this woman, don't you?"

Kate said nothing.

Azrael picked Sammy up by the neck. She kicked her legs and pulled at his fingers, her mouth opening, trying to suck down air that she couldn't breathe.

"Tell me where President Ringgold is," Azrael said.

Kate held up a hand. "Please, let her go."

Azrael tightened his grip, watching his victim turn pale.

"Tell me, or I will crush her windpipe," he said.

Kate looked conflicted, her eyes flicking between him and Sammy.

"All I want is to talk directly to your president," Azrael said. "If you don't tell me, I will slaughter every living soul until I meet her. You'll be helping your people by telling me exactly where to go."

Sammy gasped for air, blinking.

"Tell me where the president is hiding now!" he yelled.

Gunfire cut him off, the sound ringing out from the hallway. He heard the screams of humans, Chimeras, and Variants, another battle raging in the hospital.

"Tell me!" he roared.

Sammy's eyes were bulging now.

"Let her go!" a man yelled.

"Ron, stop!" Kate said.

Ron rushed Azrael, his hand outstretched for Sammy. Before he could even touch her, Abaddon's cutlass came down, separating the man's head from his torso.

"RON!" another woman in a white coat yelled.

Sammy's movements became weaker and slower.

"Is no one going to tell me?" he asked.

The other woman in the white coat finally broke, tears streaming down her face. "They're at the Harbor House Hotel! Please, let her go!"

Azrael tossed Sammy at the woman.

More gunfire erupted down the hall, closer now.

"Someone's broken through our lines outside," one of the Scions said, his voice crackling. "Our loyalists said it looks like Reed Beckham was with them."

Azrael snarled.

While he yearned to wait here and face Captain Reed Beckham, Master Sergeant Fitzpatrick, and all those other foolish traitors to make them pay for the pain they had caused, there was one other person more important to him.

President Jan Ringgold.

"Secure these prisoners," Azrael said to his soldiers. They tied the science team up in cables and ropes from their packs.

"Stay here with one death squad," Azrael said to

Abaddon. "If I have learned anything about Beckham, it's that he would fight through hell to see his pathetic wife. Take Reed, Ghost, or anyone else who shows up here alive if possible. If they cannot be taken alive, then destroy them."

"Yes, Prophet," Abaddon replied.

Azrael turned to leave but hesitated.

"Do not fail me," he said.

His gaze moved to Kate.

"I'll see you soon, Doctor," he said.

— 26 —

Gunfire echoed through the hall. Timothy had not stopped firing and running through the hospital since they had taken out a squad of Chimeras guarding one of the entrances.

He pushed through a second-floor corridor filled with dead beasts. Beckham and Horn were far ahead, firing and taking down guards while Timothy helped Ruckley limp through the destruction.

All around them, disemboweled patients littered the hallways, some of them missing limbs.

His mind raced, wondering how the civilians were faring as the enemy tore through Galveston. Were Tasha, Jenny, Javier and the dogs safe?

Horn and Beckham had to be worried sick, but they weren't showing it. Both men were machines, killing with calculated precision and moving past the macabre scenes without flinching.

All Timothy could do was take things one at a time. Advance to this corner, clear a hallway. Each time, his vision narrowed to the corridor and enemies before him. That mentality had gotten them through the hostile forces so far.

They reached another section of hallway choked with the bodies of soldiers, patients, and hospital staff who had given their lives. The smell of death and cordite hung heavy in the air as the team advanced.

"Almost there," Beckham said. "Just one more turn on our left."

Ruckley hobbled after him, carrying her M9.

They slowed when they approached the next corner. Beckham had told them the lab doors were situated at a T-intersection. Horn peered around the edge, then motioned that he had seen two hostiles.

Timothy's heart sank. Had they already killed the science team?

He looked toward Beckham, but the experienced operator's face was hard as steel. Beckham appeared to be considering their next moves. He motioned for Horn and Timothy to go down another hallway and loop back around so they could come at the lab from a different side, flanking the sentries. Beckham and Ruckley would stay behind, taking the sentries head on, keeping their attention while Horn and Timothy took them out.

Timothy nodded and ran down another set of halls. More bodies lined the corridors, and he tried not to let his eyes linger on all those who had lost their lives down here.

Focus, Timothy thought again. He remembered what Horn had told him before. Tomorrow they would mourn the dead; today they would fight to save the living.

He and Horn made it all the way around to the other side of the laboratory wing. They could see the sides of the two sentry Chimeras facing straight down the hallway where Ruckley and Beckham were.

Broken glass covered the hallway.

Timothy kept his rifle shouldered and took cover behind a sideways chair, providing him just enough shelter to stay out of sight. The Chimeras began to sniff the air, their nostrils pointed up.

Beckham and Ruckley opened fire and both creatures dove for cover, right into Timothy and Horn's sights. They blasted the armored beasts, killing them instantly.

"Let's go," Horn said.

Timothy leapt over the busted chair and followed Horn. They jumped through the broken windows into the lab and then ducked behind the cover of the massive lab benches.

Beckham and Ruckley continued firing toward the lab entrance from the hall. Timothy leaned around a bench, seeing a pair of Chimeras standing over the scientists and engineers who had been working here.

Timothy shifted to another position to see how many other Chimeras were in the room. As he did, a beast in a black mask leapt over the lab bench, knocking aside computers and plastic vials. He landed hard on top of Horn and slammed his head into the ground.

Timothy leveled his rifle, but the half-man dodged past the burst of gunfire as it scrambled on all fours, slamming his shoulder into Timothy's face.

The impact knocked Timothy back, his vision blurring. He felt clawed fingers tighten around his neck and blinked to see golden eyes staring at him.

"Never thought I would see you again," the creature growled. The crackling voice sounded vaguely familiar.

The beast picked Timothy up and slammed him against a lab bench. Panicked cries rang out from the scientists and engineers.

Timothy tried to pull his knife, but the Chimera grabbed his hand, pinning him on his back to the bench.

Horn was still struggling to stand, his head rolling on his shoulder. Other Chimeras were firing into the hallway, keeping Beckham and Ruckley back.

The Chimera leaned closer.

"Do you not recognize me?" he snarled.

He pulled back his mask. His graying flesh was covered in scars and his nose was barely existent, but if Timothy squinted through his blurred vision, he could almost see the man, the collaborator, that this Chimera had once been.

"How about now?" the Chimera asked.

Timothy tried to talk, but he was too stunned.

"I am Abaddon," the Chimera said. He pushed down on Timothy's sternum. "But before I was chosen, I was called Nick."

Timothy felt something pop in his chest. His vision went hazy, and his heart raced.

"You destroyed my family," Nick said. "Now I'm going to make you suffer agony like you've never known."

The gunfire in the hall continued in deafening bursts. Horn was starting to push himself upright, but the big operator looked dizzy, like he had suffered a traumatic concussion.

"Do you know how that feels?" Nick asked, leaning down toward Timothy. He spit in his face. "Losing everything?!"

Timothy struggled to breathe, but he managed a nod.

He pictured his father's body on Peak's Island and the faces of Donna and Bo, before they had died in the bat attack in Portland. He imagined his mother and the rest of his family who had been killed in the first war.

Nick had suffered his own share of misery, too. Now he was crazy, driven insane by the death of those he had loved. The true embodiment of evil. A twisted Chimera, fighting and killing for the New Gods.

Timothy felt the wooden beads of Tasha's bracelet against his wrist. He still had something left to fight for.

"Do you know what it feels like?!" Nick roared again, demanding an answer.

Timothy stretched one hand toward his hip, toward the holster there, fighting against the pain coursing through his nerves. He tore his pistol out and pushed it against Nick's stomach. He pulled the trigger once, twice, three times.

The Chimera staggered backward.

Timothy got up and fired again, but Nick still managed to pull his cutlass from his back and started to swing it down. A hand grabbed the Chimera's wrist.

"Don't fuck with the mountain's future son in-law," Horn said.

Before the beast could turn toward Horn, Timothy leveled the gun into Nick's face and pulled the trigger.

He crumpled to the ground, right in front of Horn. The big man ducked down to pick up a rifle. Three remaining Chimeras were distracted and firing down the hallway, holding back Beckham and Ruckley.

Horn took them down in three bursts.

"That's what I'm talking about!" Horn shouted. He wobbled, uneven on his feet.

"Clear!" Timothy called out. He leaned on a lab bench, trying to catch his breath. Every gasp felt like someone was twisting a knife in his side. Blood dribbled down his face as he finally limped toward the scientists and engineers.

Kate was kneeling beside one of her injured scientists. Her eyes were wet with tears. Another researcher was already dead, beheaded by the abominations.

"You okay, Kate?" Horn asked.

Timothy bent down next to her.

She nodded and rose as Beckham rushed into the lab. They met each other in a deep embrace while Timothy moved to stand sentry with Ruckley.

"Jesus, you all right, Temper?" she asked.

"My ribs…" He grimaced in pain.

"You guys did good," Ruckley said to Horn.

"Wasn't me," Horn said. "It was all Temper."

Beckham and Kate parted. She glanced down at the headless corpse and closed her eyes.

"We need to get the rest of you to safety," Beckham said.

"There's no time," Kate said. "The Prophet was here. He's headed for President Ringgold now. You've got to stop him."

"I will." Beckham looked at Horn. "Ruckley and Timothy, you stay with them."

"I can help," Timothy said.

"No, you can't," Kate said. "I'm sorry, Timothy, but you might have a broken rib or worse after that. You push yourself, you'll die."

"She's right," Beckham said. "Timothy, protect the science team. Big Horn, you okay?"

"Got a concussion probably, but it's not my first. Had plenty in my football days. I can manage, boss."

Beckham measured up Horn with an uncertain look, but Timothy knew that like Ruckley, Horn was going to fight whether he could or not.

"Ruckley, take the science team to shelter in the basement of the hospital," Beckham said. "There's a storage facility near the morgue you can lock down and hide in until this is over." He clasped a hand over

Timothy's shoulder. "You did good. Made me and your dad proud."

"I did what I had to," Timothy said. "Now go kill that bastard for me and my dad."

***

Dohi awoke on the stage in the throne room, blinking until his vision cleared. He felt the warm grasp of webbing tendrils over his chest, holding him in place.

On either side of the stage were the masterminds. Both of them moved lethargically from their injuries. At the front of the stage, Rico and Fitz were pinned down by webbing and guarded by a pair of Chimeras.

Crunching and ripping came from the seats bordering the stage where three juveniles feasted on Esparza's remains.

"Ah, you're awake," came a voice.

Elijah jumped onto the stage, striding over while holding a cutlass.

Dohi fought against his constraints, anger warming his entire body.

"Bring in Murphy," Elijah said.

Rico and Fitz squirmed as a side door opened and three collaborators in rubber aprons pushed out a surgical cart. An old doctor with a bent back followed them onto the stage, shuffling along.

The chatter of gunfire reverberated in from outside the building, and the four Chimeras guarding the throne room shifted about, almost as if they were nervous, keeping their weapons aimed at the entrance.

"Call off your dying dogs, Fitzpatrick," Elijah said. He bent down and poked a hole in the glue over Fitz's mouth with a claw so he could talk. "Tell the heretics outside that this battle is over, or we will transform her right now, right in front of you." He angled his sword toward Rico. "Right, Murphy?"

"Without painkillers of any kind," the doctor said.

Rico thrashed, her voice muffled by the glue over her mouth.

Elijah snapped his claws. One of the damaged masterminds lifted a tremoring hand to pull on the red webbing. A few vines dangled from the ceiling, descending toward Rico and shedding damaged pieces from the attack.

The intact pulsating red tendrils wrapped around Rico's wrists and legs. Then they pulled her up, snapping her free of the other restraints and yanking her into an X-shape. Thinner strands snaked into her nostrils.

Dohi could almost feel the sensation himself. Dark memories of his time in the tunnels returned. He knew the pain and horror. He remembered the voices that would now be calling into her head from other humans imprisoned in the organic network as she became integrated with the webbing.

"Call off your forces," Elijah said.

Fitz remained silent, clearly trying to buy time.

"You heretics are hopeless," Elijah said. He nodded at Murphy.

The doctor bent down to examine the tools on his surgical cart. He opened one of the stainless-steel boxes. Dohi had just enough of a view to see a roping chunk of intestine on ice.

The three juveniles that had devoured Esparza began to prowl around the stage, their yellow eyes sizing up Rico and Fitz hungrily.

"The first step is integrating Variant organs into her body," Murphy said.

"And it is an extraordinarily painful operation," Elijah added.

Fitz glared at the beast, then over at Dohi.

Stay strong. All it takes is all you got, brother.

Murphy examined the surgical blade he had selected, rotating it in the dim light of the throne room. He brought it close to Rico. She writhed in the grip of the vines, but in response, the webbing stretched more tautly.

"No!" Fitz shouted.

Dohi pushed against his restraints, trying to free a hand. If he could get one free, maybe...

A Chimera strode over and put a cutlass to his belly.

"Move again, and I gut you, heretic," he grumbled.

A rash of gunfire exploded somewhere outside the throne room. This time, it sounded like it might have even come from inside the command building. The Chimera lowered his cutlass and turned his back to Dohi.

The doctor looked up from his cart of tools. Four Chimeras moved toward the entrance to the throne room.

At that moment, Dohi braced his feet against the wall and summoned all of the strength in his legs, pushing against the webbing covering his chest. His nerves screamed as he strained muscles already bruised from his injuries.

But thoughts of what the beasts had done to Ace and Lincoln and Mendez fueled him.

Vines ripped away, and he lunged forward with an animalistic war cry, ramming hard into the Chimera. Dohi grabbed a sheathed knife on the back of the soldier's belt.

More gunshots came from the hallway, followed by

cursing screams.

Dohi drowned it all out.

His world shrunk to his target as he pulled the knife and rammed it into the side of the creature's neck. He punched another hole into his throat, then a third.

The Chimera slumped, gushing blood, and Dohi picked up the cutlass.

He held the blades out and shouted, "Come and get it!"

The Chimera guarding Fitz strode over, swinging his own blade. Dohi jumped back from the slicing blade. The beast swung again, and Dohi ducked lower, the air above his head whooshing past. He struck out with his cutlass, splitting the creature's belly open, and then closed in to stab his knife into its neck.

The vines around Rico coiled tighter like a boa constrictor around prey, and Dohi could see the color draining from her face as he searched for the next hostile.

Elijah stood beside the doctor Murphy and his three cronies. They all watched, saying nothing. The juveniles prowled toward him, waiting to strike, and two other Chimeras aimed rifles at him.

"What now?" Elijah asked.

"I'll kill you all," Dohi said. He stood his ground, chest heaving, fresh blood dripping off his blades.

"Like your bearded friend tried?" Elijah laughed. "You have the heart of a warrior, but your faith is misplaced. You won't leave this room alive."

Dohi looked over at Fitz who was squirming on the ground. Rico stared down at them both, face pale and eyes bulging.

Elijah pointed at the masterminds, and webbing snaked from the floor, wrapping around Dohi. He hacked through the climbing tendrils and jumped away, but the juveniles easily cornered him.

This was it. Nowhere to run.

Soon he would see Ace, Mendez, and Lincoln again.

Reunited as brothers in death.

He raised the blades and screamed again, charging at the juveniles.

The creatures hesitated, seeming confused. They twisted, growling and looking at the doorway.

At the entrance were four more Chimeras. At first, Dohi thought they were more enemies.

But he recognized one.

Corrin.

He and his companions had killed the remaining Chimera guards near the entrance. Corrin stormed the room while unleashing a hail of bullets, his team of three Chimeras following him.

The guards near Elijah returned fire and dove for cover as the juveniles bounded away from Dohi, launching themselves toward their new targets. Two of Corrin's allies went down, and Elijah jumped off the stage to avoid the onslaught of incoming rounds.

Dohi wasted no time rushing straight for Rico.

Murphy shrieked and tried to cower behind her, but Dohi swung the cutlass into his bent back, slicing it open. The three assistants had already fled.

Rico looked down at Dohi as he hacked the vines holding her in place. She collapsed to the stage in a heap of limbs. The vines around her chest wriggled and loosened.

"Fitz," she moaned before her eyes fluttered closed.

Dohi scrambled over to free his other friend while his enemies were distracted. A few slices was all it took. Fitz broke through the rest of his restraints.

He crawled over the stage toward Rico, and Dohi took off for the remaining Chimera fighting with Elijah. Corrin's last ally went down in a blaze of fire, but at least the juveniles were all dead now.

Dohi leapt off the stage and stabbed his knife into the head of a Chimera firing next to Elijah. The other beast turned his aim toward Dohi as he crashed to the ground.

With a swift strike, Dohi speared his cutlass into the Chimera's guts, then pulled down, spilling ropy intestines. He withdrew the blade and stood to face Elijah. The big Chimera was now holding two swords.

Corrin advanced down the aisle, snarling.

"It's over," he said.

"Not for me, you heretics!" Elijah screamed.

Dohi climbed over broken seats and joined Corrin in the aisle, approaching Elijah with their swords cocked back.

"For Ace," Dohi said.

Corrin nodded.

The two soldiers swung their blades toward Elijah. He met their blades with his own in a shrieking crash of metal on metal, sparks flying. The impact of the metal-on-metal sent both Dohi and Corrin stumbling backward.

Dohi fought through the pain of his injuries, standing unsteadily. Corrin looked to be in equally bad shape, blood streaming from a bullet wound to the shoulder and another to his arm.

On the stage, Fitz was giving Rico mouth-to-mouth resuscitation. She had been in worse shape than Dohi thought.

"There's no way you get out of here alive," Corrin said.

"Perhaps not," Elijah said. He paced in the narrow aisle, stalking and sizing Corrin and Dohi up like a lion examining its prey. "But I will take you with me."

Howling, he lunged toward them, swinging his blades. Dohi parried the attack, nearly losing his grip on the sword from the tremendous force of Elijah's strike. Corrin swung, but Elijah dodged out of the way and then struck back, splitting part of Corrin's chest to reveal muscle and the white of his ribs.

"NO!" Dohi screamed.

He tried to thrust his blade into Elijah, but Elijah struck out with his other weapon. This time Dohi was too slow to deflect the blow. The blade cut into his thigh. He went down hard a few feet from Corrin.

Elijah stabbed Corrin through the chest, skewering him with a crunch. The smaller Chimera struggled, grasping at the blade with his claws, trying desperately to keep Elijah from pushing it deeper.

Grunting, Dohi forced himself upright with his blade in hand.

He swung the cutlass one last time, summoning every bit of power he had left in his battered body. Elijah tried to avoid it, but he had been too intent on killing Corrin.

The blade cut into the broken skull mask covering his face. Blood and flesh flew away with the shattered bone.

Elijah let go of the blade in Corrin's chest, turning toward Dohi as he swung again with all his might. The blade cut into his neck, tearing through the flesh and cleaving bone until his head hung to the side by a few bits of stringy muscle.

Dohi kicked him backward into the broken seats. The Chimera tumbled over the side, his head snapping free and rolling away.

"Corrin," Dohi said.

He crouched next to his friend, gasping for air.

"You did it," Corrin croaked.

"*We* did it, brother," Dohi said. He eyed the sword sticking through Corrin's chest, trying to determine how best to remove it.

"It's okay," Corrin said, no doubt seeing the realization in Dohi's eyes. "I'm ready for death."

"No, you're not going to die. I won't lose another brother."

"I died a long time ago, my friend. Fighting with you and Ghost was a great honor…"

Corrin blinked. "Don't forget me, friend."

"I won't ever."

His eyes locked with Dohi as his chest went still.

"Corrin," Dohi said. "Corrin…"

He put a finger to his neck but there was no pulse. With a deep sigh, Dohi gently closed his friend's eyelids, then pushed himself up.

Dohi staggered, his injured leg threatened to give out. Blood soiled his pants from the deep wound. He used the cutlass as a crutch to walk back to the stage where Fitz was still holding Rico in his arms.

"Corrin?" he asked.

"Gone," Dohi said. "Is Rico okay?"

"She's in shock, but she's breathing. We have to get her out of here."

"I'll finish the masterminds," Dohi said. He picked up a rifle and aimed at the beasts, but as soon as he brought up the weapon his vision blurred. He stumbled, then fell to one knee.

"Dohi!" Fitz shouted.

Dohi collapsed to his back, eyes on the web-covered

ceiling. Fitz scrambled over.

"Dohi, stay with me," Fitz said.

He tried his best, but his vision went dark, and in his mind's eye, Dohi saw Ace, Lincoln, Mendez, Corrin, and the spirits of all the warriors lost over the years.

I knew I would see you again, brothers.

"Madam President, I have good news and bad news," Souza said.

"Good news, first," Ringgold replied.

"We just got word from Ghost. Los Alamos is now under our control." He put down the radio, but he didn't smile. "Unfortunately, the Prophet was not there... he's here in Galveston."

"What?" She tightened the strap of her rifle, then felt the bulge under her jacket where her M9 was tucked into her waistband for reassurance.

The command staff on the balcony of the watchtower platform all looked over, and the three Secret Service agents on the platform shot Ringgold nervous glances.

"Doctor Lovato was taken hostage by him, but the Prophet fled when Captain Beckham arrived," Souza said. "Captain Beckham is now hunting the Prophet with Master Sergeant Horn."

"Beckham will take him down," Ringgold said, ready to breathe a sigh of relief.

"I hope so," Souza said. "Doctor Lovato warned us that the Prophet is coming for you."

"Good thing we have two of our best soldiers hunting him," Ringgold replied. She looked out over the watchtower platform at the Harbor House Hotel. The rain had stopped. All the enemy choppers had been taken out, but there were still thousands of enemy forces out there.

Columns of oily smoke snaked into the air across the base. Constant gunfire and the thuds of explosions resonated from every direction between screams of pain and shrieks from hunting beasts.

Cornelius walked over with his M4A1 cradled over his chest. "We're getting reports of more breaches along the eastern and western walls."

He looked out over the eastern part of the base. "Don't worry, Madam President. We will hold them."

Soprano rushed over with another handheld radio. "I'm hearing that Variants are invading some of the civilian shelters on the southern part of downtown."

Ringgold felt a wave of sickness. "Is there anything we can send to help them?"

Cornelius looked out over the raging fires and flashes of gunfire to the west. "We can pull a few teams away from the walls."

"Make it happen," Ringgold said.

Cornelius nodded at one of his men.

Another explosion bloomed just a block away to their south. Flames roared up the side of a former hotel. The tongues of fire illuminated nearly twenty Variants and juveniles galloping down the street. A massive Alpha heaved the charcoaled husk of a car toward a group of soldiers behind a barricade of sandbags.

"Take them out!" Cornelius said.

A gunner on the platform directed his M240 and fired into the ranks of the monsters. Blasts from the sniper rifles followed. The Alpha lumbered toward the sandbags, rounds punching into its muscular frame.

"Jesus," Cornelius yelled. "Give me that."

He reached out for a sniper rifle and took it from the soldier. Slinging his M4A1 over his back, Cornelius then shouldered the long rifle, aimed, and pulled the trigger.

The top of the Alpha's head flew off, and the beast dropped in front of the sandbags. Cornelius handed the gun back to the soldier and walked back over Ringgold.

"Nice shot," she said.

Cornelius unslung his rifle, and Souza shouldered his weapon as more creatures advanced on the streets outside the hotel.

"Madam President, you should shelter inside," Soprano said.

Her Secret Service agents moved toward her, ready to escort her down the stairs into the hotel.

"No," she replied, raising her rifle. "I'm ready to fight."

Cornelius raised a brow. "I sort of regret running against Lemke and your party now. God rest his soul, but you know what I mean."

Ringgold nodded. "I'm sure he gladly would have run with you on the ticket."

The shriek of Variants silenced them.

"Oh, Jesus," Soprano said. He crossed his chest and then pumped his shotgun.

"Get ready!" Cornelius yelled.

Gunfire from collaborators on another rooftop pinged off the walls. The agents surrounded Ringgold, bringing their rifles up as she aimed her barrel, recalling the lessons Cornelius had taught her over the past few days. She kept the sights on the center mass of her target and fired.

Each squeeze of the trigger was deliberate and careful, the stock of her rifle kicking back slightly against her shoulder. A collaborator dropped from one of her rounds.

She paused for a moment from the shock of taking a human life. The Variants were one thing but...

No, these men are also monsters.

The sound of gunfire and screams snapped her back to reality. The beasts were coming from all directions now, storming through Galveston. She aimed at the Variants, trying to hit them, but they moved so damn fast.

A jammed round forced her to lower her rifle and clear the chamber. By the time she shouldered her rifle again, some of the fighting on the streets had turned into hand-to-hand combat.

The Chimeras and Variants lunged at the men and women clinging to survival, tearing at their flesh with claws and teeth.

Again and again, she squeezed the trigger.

The crack of gunfire sounded all around her, answering the howls of the beasts threatening to overwhelm them from below.

An hour of the fighting raged until corpses littered the street. Puddles on the asphalt turned red with blood.

Seeing all of the pale corpses of the monsters filled Ringgold with hope that they could hold out for the arrival of the Mexican and Canadian reinforcements.

A strange moment of silence passed over the watchtower as she reloaded. Sporadic gunshots echoed, but they seemed more spread out and further away.

"Anyone got eyes?" Cornelius called.

"We're getting reports of movement to the north!" Souza called from the enclosed area with the comms officers.

"I see them!" one of the snipers called out from the

north wall. "A whole—"

Before he finished his sentence, half his face was blown away by an incoming round. His body fell backward. Cornelius took the position and opened fire.

"On me!" he shouted.

Souza and a group of three soldiers moved over to help. Ringgold strained for a look at the targets, her Secret Service agents following her. Between the columns of smoke, she saw Chimeras running toward the hotel.

One of those monsters wore a black cloak that she recognized from the horrific video of when Lemke had been butchered. A phalanx of Chimeras ran close to protect the huge beast.

Variants and juveniles swarmed onto the street from neighboring buildings.

Gunfire suddenly pounded the platform. Ringgold went down on her stomach, the Secret Service agents crowding her. She watched as Cornelius jerked back from a round to the shoulder. He regained his balance and kept firing.

A pair of the machine gunners and the three snipers on the other walls rushed to help thwart the incoming attack.

One of her Secret Service agents tried to help Ringgold back to her feet when a bullet lanced through his throat. Blood sprayed on her as he collapsed on top of her body.

"Get her out of here!" Cornelius yelled.

Soprano grabbed Ringgold, and with the help of the two surviving agents, pulled her out from under the dead man. She watched in horror as a set of claws reached up and grabbed a sniper at the wall, pulling him over the side.

Soprano started to pull her away from the north side as Chimeras climbed over the platform and tore into the soldiers there. One of the beasts struck Souza in the face with a cutlass, severing his jaw. He reached up, but then fell to the platform, his dead eyes on Ringgold.

"No," she choked.

Cutlasses hacked into the soldiers, separating limbs and heads. Cornelius and three of his men rushed to stop the advancing monsters.

"Let me go!" she yelled at Soprano.

He loosened his grip, and she raised her rifle, her two remaining agents aiming their own weapons. They both went down suddenly, from sniper rounds.

Rage flowed through her as she ducked down and changed her magazine, struggling to click it into the rifle.

"Madam President, watch out!" Soprano called.

She looked up as a Chimera climbed the wall and dropped onto the platform. Soprano stepped in front of her and fired the shotgun into the super soldier. It jerked backward and growled at Soprano who pumped the weapon.

"Oh fuck," he said.

He turned to look at Ringgold as the Chimera thrust his cutlass through his chest, skewering him before yanking the blade out.

Soprano dropped in front of her, whispering his final words. "I'm sorry."

The Chimera started toward her, blood gushing from the shotgun blast to his side. He raised his cutlass when a bullet burst through his eye.

Cornelius ran across the platform, lowering his pistol. He grabbed Ringgold and started to pull her away, but five Chimeras had cornered them, three on one side and two on the other.

She came together with her back against the general.

"This is it," Cornelius said. "Make each bullet count."

He raised his pistol and Ringgold aimed her rifle, fighting the sheer terror and shock gripping her body. Two of the Chimeras fell under their fire, but the other three made it through. One slammed into Cornelius and locked his claws into the general's arm, squeezing and forcing him to drop the pistol. A headbutt to the face from the creature knocked Cornelius unconscious.

Another creature yanked her rifle away and then angled a cutlass at her.

"We have the heretics!" screamed the half-man guarding Cornelius.

Another monstrous shape climbed over the side of the wall.

Azrael.

He heaved himself onto the platform, then surveyed the carnage. With a snort, he pulled his cutlass from over his back. He stalked toward Ringgold, black cape fluttered behind him.

The three Chimeras parted, letting him approach. Cornelius was still limp on the ground, unconscious.

"It's over," Azrael said. "You have lost, Jan Ringgold."

"It's not over," she managed to reply.

Azrael narrowed his golden eyes, the point of his cutlass touching her neck. "After all this time, you still don't understand." He gestured out over Galveston with his claws. "You have killed your people by failing to submit and join the New Gods."

"Death is better than slavery," she replied.

Ringgold held his gaze and inched her hand toward the pistol tucked under her jacket.

"We took Los Alamos," she said, trying to buy time. "We freed your prisoners, and they've joined us."

Azrael prodded his cutlass under her chin, forcing her head up. "I'm not worried about a group of dying, weak heretics. We will take Los Alamos back after we finish taking Galveston."

"Maybe, but you won't be there to see it."

At first, Azrael looked confused.

She whipped out her M9 and aimed it straight into his gut. A pull of the trigger put a round into his flesh, making him jerk back. His eyes widened slightly as she fired two more shots. Both bullets, making him recoil. Before she could fire a fourth shot, a cutlass came down on her hand from one of the Chimeras.

She tried to pull the trigger again, but her finger wouldn't work.

A glance down and she saw her severed hand laying on the floor of the platform next to the pistol.

Blood pumped out of her wrist, and the pain set in, electricity cutting through her nerves. She let out a scream as the pain pierced her shock.

Azrael grabbed her by the throat and lifted her off the ground.

"The Allied States is mine," he roared.

***

Beckham lunged over another dead Variant in the stairwell inside the Harbor House Hotel leading up to the watchtower platform. Horn followed him, wobbling slightly as he took the steps two-at-a-time, the effects of the concussion getting to him.

The advance here had been difficult. He and Horn had

traveled through abandoned and burning buildings, avoiding as many of the enemy forces as they could. Twice they had to stop and engage Chimeras, but they had made it here.

Now came the hard part.

Leading the way, Beckham snuck up the last few steps toward the platform above the hotel. He paused on a landing and pointed up with his prosthetic hand, gesturing to Horn when he heard a voice.

"We will never surrender…"

Beckham wasn't surprised that it was President Ringgold.

He glanced back at Horn who nodded back. They advanced slowly, their weapons at the ready. As they reached the top of the stairs, Beckham spotted both Ringgold and Cornelius on the platform against one of the four-foot-high walls.

Three Chimeras loomed over them, two with cutlasses drawn, and a fourth, larger beast stood between them. It had to be the Prophet, Azrael.

The abomination of science and nature angled his sword at the president, but then slowly turned, sniffing the air. His golden eyes landed on Beckham.

"Reed Beckham, is that actually you in the flesh? Ah, I can smell your fear."

Two Chimera guards walked over to the top of the stairs wielding their cutlasses while the third Chimera drew up its rifle and fired.

"Down!" Beckham screamed. He slammed into Horn, knocking him down the stairs as bullets slammed into their former position. By the time they got up, the two Chimeras had rushed down the steps to the landing.

One of the creatures pounced on Horn, knocking him

down the stairs while the second beast swung the cutlass at Beckham. He countered the blow with his rifle, deflecting the blade.

The Chimera pushed hard and pinned him to the landing. Beckham swiveled enough to get the monster off his chest, leaving a slight opening for the creature to chomp down at his neck. The Chimera took the bait, and Beckham whipped up his arm to block the attack. The creature bit into it, tearing at his limb.

But Beckham felt no pain.

The monster had attacked his prosthetic and did not yet seem to realize his fatal mistake.

With his good hand, Beckham reached for his Ka-Bar and stabbed it into the side of the beast's exposed neck, unleashing a torrent of crimson.

The creature clawed at his own neck to try and staunch the bleeding, his mouth opening and closing in desperation, as if begging for his life.

Beckham shoved it off, then scrambled to grab the Chimera's cutlass.

"Boss, look out!" Horn said, still wrestling with the other soldier on the stairs below. Gunfire lanced into the landing, and Beckham grabbed the dying Chimera to use him as a shield from the Chimera with the rifle that had nearly killed him and Horn before.

The beast was at the top of the stairs now, firing down. As soon as it stopped to reload, Beckham pulled out a pistol from the holster of the dead Chimera he was using as a shield and aimed, firing into the face of the sniper. The monster toppled down the stairs and landed on top of Beckham and the other creature.

Beckham fell back under the weight of the dead Chimeras, his head hitting the landing hard. As he squirmed to get free, a figure emerged on the platform above.

"I've waited too long for this," Azrael said. "Get up and face me!"

"Boss, no!" Horn called out.

His voice sounded distant, but Beckham could see him on the landing below.

Horn had managed to get out from under the Chimera. He smashed the beast's skull against the brick wall of the stairwell. Over and over, he bashed the head, the monster spasming with each blow.

Azrael walked down the stairs, a blood-soaked cutlass in hand. "I was going to give you one last chance to join the New Gods, but now I'm just going to gut you and your ugly friend and drape your intestines over the walls."

Howls and shrieks of approaching Variants sounded over the grisly voice of their master.

Beckham tried to free himself, but the weight of the two creatures was too much to lift at the awkward angle he had fallen. He still held the pistol, but he couldn't raise it enough to shoot Azrael where he stood.

The Prophet moved slowly down the stairs, gripping his stomach with one hand and limping. Blood drooled out of multiple gunshot wounds.

If the brute kept coming closer, then soon he would be within Beckham's aim. He prepared to fire the pistol, hoping Azrael hadn't seen it.

Azrael reached down and heaved the smaller Chimeras off Beckham, then stomped on his wrist before he could pull the trigger. His fingers splayed from the impact and the pistol clattered down the steps.

Beckham cried out in agony, unable to hold in the scream.

"BOSS!" Horn shouted.

Variants pounded up the stairs toward him as he got up, weaponless except for his fists.

"Horn," Beckham choked.

"Look at me!" Azrael shouted.

Beckham met the soulless gaze of the monster and prepared to meet his fate. He had held onto hope that he could save Galveston and his family, but how could they win against such evil?

Azrael suddenly looked down the stairs as the Variants bounded up the stairs.

"I want you to watch," Azrael growled.

Four Thrall Variants jumped to the landing where Horn waited with his fists raised. The creatures shrieked, sucker lips smacking, ready to feed.

"Fuck you!" Horn yelled. He punched one of them in the face, breaking the jaw with a crack. Then he picked up a second and tossed it down the stairs. The other two beasts jumped onto him, sinking claws into his flesh.

"HORN!" Beckham yelled.

The Variants slammed Horn into the railing along the wall, before they all tumbled backward down the stairs out of Beckham's sight. He heard the bodies tumbling and smacking against the wall and stairs with sickening thumps.

Images of Horn's girls and then his own family flashed through his eyes.

All the people he loved. Those who still lived. Those he had lost.

Thousands of lives depended on the outcome of this battle.

He could not let them down. He could not let his country down.

Beckham felt the cold blade of a cutlass tracing up his vest to his chin.

"I'm going to eat your heart first," Azrael said. "And I will make your wife and son watch."

Beckham swung his prosthetic hand at the blade, but Azrael countered it with a blow that cleaved off the prosthetic and the straps holding it to the remnants of his flesh-and-blood arm.

Then he brought the cutlass above his head and let out a deafening howl.

Three loud gunshots rang out from above.

For a moment, Azrael looked at Beckham, confusion and shock in his gaze. Beckham detected something else there. Something primal. A human emotion beneath the face of the monster.

Fear.

Azrael's mouth gaped open, and he dropped the cutlass.

When he fell to the side, Beckham saw Ringgold looking down at him with a pistol in her remaining hand. She dropped the weapon and grabbed the stump where her other hand had been.

Heavy footsteps pounded behind Beckham, and he turned, ready to face yet another attacker.

Instead, he saw a familiar face.

"Boss," Horn gasped. He towered over Beckham, bruised, bloody, and bulging muscles throbbing. A true mountain of a man.

He reached down to help Beckham to his feet. Holding on to each other, the Delta Operators and best friends made their way up the stairs to their president.

She had sat next to Cornelius again, resting her back against a wall.

The grizzled general had his eyes closed. At first, Beckham feared the man was dead, but when he felt the general's neck, he detected a weak pulse pressing up against his finger.

He turned to Ringgold next. "Thank you. You saved my life."

"Just paying you back for all the times you saved mine," she said with a weak smile.

Beckham used his knife to cut strips off the shredded sleeve over his missing prosthetic, wincing in the pain from his injured wrist. He used the strips as a tourniquet to stop her bleeding, but she had already lost so much. It covered her shirt and pants.

"You're going to be okay," he said.

She could hardly nod. "Is it over?"

Beckham wanted to tell her yes, but gunfire still rang out between the screams of people and the howls of beasts.

Horn picked up an M4 and checked the magazine, then slammed it home.

"Boss, we've got more incoming," he said. "We better get the president and general out of here."

"No," Ringgold said. "You go. Save your families."

"I'm not leaving you," Beckham said.

A sudden clash of footsteps sounded from the stairwell at the center of the platform leading up from the hotel. Three collaborators emerged, covered in blood and ash. Before they could so much as aim their rifles, Horn mowed them down with an M4.

"We have to move," Beckham said. "Come on, we're getting you—"

Ringgold wrapped her fingers around his injured wrist. Then he saw the blood coming out from under her jacket and realized why there was so much.

She had a second wound, a bullet to the abdomen.

"I'm sorry," she said.

"No, Madam…"

"Reed, I'm not going to make it," she said, her voice sounding weaker than before. "And if we do win this fight, I need you to promise me you'll keep fighting."

"I'll never stop."

He reached out to press his hand against her stomach to staunch the bleeding.

"It's too late for me." She shook her head. "Let me die with dignity."

Slowly, he pulled his hand away.

"Reed, I need you to promise me," she said.

"Anything. Just tell me what."

"Run for president. Preserve our… democracy. Protect this country." She coughed. "The country and the *world* are going to need you."

Beckham hesitated, but he couldn't deny his president her dying wish.

"I will," he said. "You have my word."

A slight smile passed across her face, and a final sigh rushed out of her nose.

"Godspeed, Madam President," he whispered. He blinked away the tears and bent down to kiss her on the forehead.

Scattered gunshots rang out, drawing closer.

Horn looked away from the wall toward Ringgold. "Is she…?"

"She's gone," Beckham said.

For a moment, Horn was quiet and bowed his head. "I'm sorry, but there's not time to mourn. We have to get to the shelters."

Beckham nodded. "Help me with the general."

Horn bent down and slowly lifted Cornelius, preparing to hoist him into a fireman's carry despite his injuries. The general's eyes opened slowly, roving across the platform, and Horn helped him lean against the wall instead of picking him up.

"No," Cornelius muttered, Horn offering him his shoulder. "Is she…"

"She's gone, sir," Horn said. "Let me help you. We have to move."

Horn and Beckham bent down, but Cornelius pushed himself up on his own.

"What about Command?" Cornelius asked. "Is Festa still alive?"

"I'm not sure," Horn said.

Cornelius picked up a rifle, wincing in pain from the wound in his shoulder.

"You good?" Beckham asked.

"I'll make it," he said.

They both looked at Ringgold one last time before proceeding to the stairs and heading down.

As they made it to the lobby of the hotel, Variants looked up from their meals between the scattered desks and snarled. Horn took one out with his rifle, and then fired bursts at the others, sending the thin beasts sprawling in pools of their own blood.

Beckham held an M9, but his wrist hurt so bad, he wasn't sure he could pull the trigger. Feeling helpless, he stumbled along toward the street. Cornelius limped along slowly, struggling to keep his own weapon up.

Despite the beating Horn had taken, the injuries didn't seem to slow the big man down.

He took point, firing calculated shots in the Thrall

Variants they encountered on the street. Gunfire exploded in waves across Galveston, and Beckham feared, even if they made it to shelter, it wouldn't be long before the beasts found them again, finishing the job the Prophet had started.

After eliminating another pack of monsters, Beckham finally saw the concrete bunker with its thick steel doors where their kids were hiding. Corpses of humans and monsters lay all around it, but the doors still appeared secured, locked from the inside. They approached cautiously, walking through smoke drifting away from a burning truck.

A distant rumble sounded, forcing them to stop and crouch behind the truck. As the noise grew louder, they turned to the east. Black dots flew across the sky, getting larger as they approached.

"Are they ours?" Cornelius asked.

Horn scoped the sky, and then lowered the weapon with a smile. "Must be the reinforcements our allies promised. Just in time to clean this place up."

Beckham kept moving to the shelter as the aircraft closed in on Galveston.

The noise of their engines enveloped the island, and parachutes bloomed in long lines behind them, troops descending toward this now sacred patch of Texas.

Beckham tapped on the steel door with the pistol in his injured hand. "Captain Reed Beckham, open up!"

The door clicked, unlocked, and opened a hair. Connor, the Secret Service agent, assigned to protect his family, looked out.

"Oh, thank God," Connor said, opening the door. "Kate just radioed in asking where you were."

"She's okay?" Beckham asked.

Connor nodded, locking the door to the shelter behind them. "Safe as of ten minutes ago."

He let Cornelius wrap an arm around his shoulder, then guided him to a seat near the entry. Muffled gunfire and shrieks exploded above them, and the lights to the shelter sizzled on and off over the frightened faces.

"Dad!" shouted a young voice.

Beckham and Horn both rushed over to greet their kids. Javier hugged Beckham, and Tasha and Jenny both embraced their father. A few booms rumbled through the shelter full of civilians, and Beckham tightened his arms around his son.

"Dad, you're hurt," Jenny said.

"I'll be okay. Are you girls fine?"

Tasha loosened her grip. "Timothy is okay, right?"

"I think so," Horn said. "He's with Kate."

A radio positioned near the shelter's door came to life. "Lieutenant Festa calling all shelters. General Vance and Hernandez of the Canadian and Mexican militaries have confirmed the arrival of their reinforcements. They are helping our troops retake the streets. I repeat, we are retaking Galveston! The enemy is falling back!"

"I guess this might not be the Alamo after all," Horn said. "We're actually going to win this thing."

Beckham wanted to smile, but not everyone had gotten the ending they deserved.

"Where's the president?" Connor asked.

"She died protecting the country she loved," Beckham said. "And in the end, she saved us all."

— Epilogue —

Fitz wandered down the beach with Rico by his side. His blades sank into the yellow sand with each step, forcing him to walk slowly. That worked better for Rico anyway.

Bruises covered her skin, and she walked with a limp from the vines that had nearly torn her apart.

They strolled along the parts of the beach that met Galveston. The debris had mostly been cleared, allowing them to get close to the sun-glinted waves rolling in from the Gulf.

"Warm sunlight, seagulls, sand," Rico said. "I could get used to this, Fitzie."

"Yeah... me too."

They sat and stared for a while, taking in the view before wandering back toward the city to meet their friends. Horn and Ruckley were already at a picnic table with Beckham and Kate. Sammy was there too, standing next to Dohi who sat in a wheelchair. A brace surrounded his bandaged leg. He had been at the brink of death when a few Chimeras and freed prisoners helped Fitz administer first aid to him in Los Alamos, stabilizing him enough to get him back to Galveston

Everyone looked in rough shape.

Timothy had a swollen and scratched face, but Fitz wouldn't have been able to tell that he had a bruised rib if he hadn't already known. The young soldier was sitting by

Tasha at the adjacent table, both smiling like kids in a candy shop.

Javier and Jenny tossed sticks toward the waves for Ginger and Spark. The dogs raced after the sticks, kicking up rooster tails of sand.

"Five days of cleanup," Rico said. "And five days of…"

She let the words trail off. Fitz knew what she wanted to say.

Funerals and memorials.

The troops from Canada and Mexico had assisted with cleaning up Galveston and helping take care of both the injured and the dead after clearing the city of the final beasts. But there was still too much work and mourning to be done before the Allied States could even begin to discuss the next stages of restoration.

Fitz squeezed Rico's hand.

They had a long road ahead of them, but he was eternally grateful to be alive with his friends.

"Damn, I was just about to eat your food," Horn said, as they approached the table. "Just kidding. Kind of. But seriously, this shit is delicious."

He took a bite of a burrito, chewing with his mouth open.

Ruckley shook her head. "You smell, you have no manners, and you curse a lot. Did anybody every tell you that you're kind of an ogre?"

"Exactly your type," Timothy said.

Ruckley gave him a glare.

"Hey, it's obvious you two are perfect for each other," Timothy said.

Tasha and Jenny both chuckled, which told Fitz they must be warming up to the idea of their dad getting back out there.

Fitz clapped the big guy on the shoulder and then helped Rico lower herself to the table.

"You going to offer me some?" Fitz asked.

Horn reached out and started piling pieces of roast chicken onto a plate. Then he passed it to Fitz and Rico.

"Don't judge," Horn said. "I'm just preparing for the winter."

"Funny, because I thought Texas winters weren't that harsh," Tasha said.

Horn stopped eating a half-picked-off wing and looked toward Beckham. "I really can't catch a break with them." Then he glanced at Javier. "Kid, are you like this with your parents?"

"No way," Javier said.

"Because you're a young, respecting gentleman," Horn said.

"They aren't as big as you either," Javier replied.

Horn dropped the half-eaten wing on his plate and wagged his head.

Beckham laughed.

"Javier, apologize," Kate said.

"I'm sorry you're big around the middle," Javier said with a shrug.

"Not quite what I had in mind," Kate said.

Horn let out a contagious laugh that got everyone to join in. Everyone, except for Dohi. Fitz noticed the man's smile lasted for only a brief second.

"I'll be right back," Fitz said to Rico. He stood and went over to Dohi.

"How are you doing, brother?" Fitz asked.

Dohi simply nodded.

"It'll get better," Fitz said. "Everything will. We just

have to trust in our future."

Dohi gave another slight nod, but he didn't appear convinced. A dark shadow seemed to hang over him that Fitz knew would not go away anytime soon. Not after everything Dohi had witnessed and survived. The best he could do was offer his friendship to Dohi and support him through the nightmares that would haunt him.

"We're here for you, brother, and that will never change," Fitz said.

Dohi smiled this time, a bit longer than the last grin. Fitz got behind his chair and pushed him up to the table next to Rico, who handed over a plate of food.

"Thanks," Dohi said.

Javier leaned over the table, looking at Fitz.

"Mr. Fitz, do you think you'll keep being a soldier?" he asked.

Fitz hesitated a moment, Rico watching him.

"You know, I think I'm getting too old for this stuff," he said.

"Well, I'd be happy to take over Team Ghost if you ever step down," Timothy said.

"Maybe someday, kid," Horn said. "But not anytime soon. You got something to live for."

Tasha smiled as Horn winked at her.

"I want to be a soldier, too," Javier said.

Kate sighed. "How about starting out by helping me in the lab? I've still got work to do, and you might like it."

"I can teach you how to do some cool stuff with computers, too," Sammy added.

"Sounds boring," Javier said.

"Computers are cool," Fitz said, winking at Kate. "Maybe it's time I learn some of that computer stuff for retirement."

"You say that now, but look how retirement worked out for us," Beckham said. "You never really retire from this job, no matter what the paperwork says, and sometimes boring is good, son."

Javier shrugged.

"Want to look like me, kid?" Ruckley said, lifting her bandaged arms slightly. "Stick to the labs. Your body will thank you."

"Yeah, you definitely don't want to look like this lady," Horn said.

"You're such a…"

Ruckley let her words slide, and Horn grinned.

"You know, if my arm wasn't in a sling, I would elbow you right in the ribs, you smelly oaf," she said.

"You're right. I've been rude. How about I make it up to you?"

"What did you have in mind?"

"How about dinner tomorrow?" Horn asked.

Ruckley raised a brow, like she wasn't sure what to think. "You serious?"

"Is that a yes then?"

"If you shower, sure."

"God, first Timothy and Tasha, now you guys," Jenny said. "So gross."

She feigned a disgusted expression, then picked up a stick and walked away with the dogs.

More laughter spilled from the group.

Fitz returned to Rico. She leaned her head against his shoulder as they watched Jenny play with the dogs.

After everything they had gone through, he finally felt a sense of peace. And he vowed he would do everything in his power to ensure that it would last. If that meant staying a soldier, then so be it, he would never stop fighting for his friends, family, and flag.

***

Beckham drove to the port of Galveston with Kate and Cornelius.

A month had passed since they had defeated the New Gods in Galveston. While the island was on the path to recovery, there were still plenty of signs of battle. Craters pocked the streets, and rubble still lay in piles where buildings had burned and collapsed.

But repairs were already underway on other buildings like the Harbor House Hotel which remained the new command center for the Allied States.

Beckham looked toward the port while he drove around the potholes and cracks in the road. He slowed as they passed a four-foot high wall made of bricks recovered from many of the destroyed buildings. Each brick was inscribed with a name representing someone who had died in Galveston.

In time, they would replace that memorial with a more permanent one. As the Allied States spread back into reclaimed territories more memorials would be constructed, lest the nascent nation ever forget the sacrifices their people had made.

Kate broke the silence. "I got good news about the Fallen Chimeras we rescued. Most have been moved to the colony in Houston. Our doctors have been able to take care of their unique medical needs."

"That is good news," Cornelius said.

"Especially since there hasn't been any attacks or violence from or against the Chimera refugees as we first feared," Kate said.

Beckham looked at the bricks they passed. Somewhere in that wall was one with Corrin's name. The Chimera would be proud to hear that report.

"It's a good start," Beckham said. "The Chimeras deserve a new shot at life."

"And I'm also happy to report that Sammy has confirmed over ninety percent of the network is dead due to anthrax," Kate said. "We haven't detected any signals passing through the network since the defeat of Los Alamos, too. Whatever monsters that are left out there won't be able to reorganize or reunite through any webbing communications."

"I've heard rumblings from some of the Fallen Chimeras that they would be willing to assist in our hunts to root out any of those remaining enemy forces," Cornelius said. "Their senses—as Corrin showed—would be enormously valuable to our recon groups."

"I agree," Beckham said. "We can start training them with our next class of recruits. It will be imperative in taking back our territories and rescuing stranded people out there."

Beckham thought about what was left. It wasn't much. Only a few outposts in Alabama and the Panhandle of Florida had been confirmed as safe for resettlement. Once they started moving refugees they would need to focus on revitalizing agriculture and industry, but it would be a long process. For the next six months, managing their existing supplies would be the key to survival. That and working with their allies.

As they neared the port, Beckham spotted a massive cruiser docked along the pier that the United Kingdom had promised months ago. An entire contingent of

European workers had arrived with the supplies.

Next to the British Naval Cruiser was the sole surviving ship in the First Fleet they had been able to restore with the help of their allies over the past month. It was a five-hundred foot-long Arleigh Burke class destroyer that had managed to survive the battle with minor structural damage.

A large crowd had gathered in front of the ship, soldiers and civilians spread over the street.

"Big turnout," Kate said.

"That ship gives us all something to rally around," Cornelius said.

Beckham parked and they all got out, starting toward a temporary platform built around the bow of the ship. A group of six Marines stood stiffly around the platform.

"Ringgold would be very proud of what we've accomplished together, Captain," Cornelius said.

"I can't thank you enough, General," Beckham replied. "You have helped save our country."

"You knew her better than perhaps any of us left on this island today. I imagine she would be looking forward to what you accomplish next."

"What *we* will accomplish next," Beckham said.

Cornelius nodded.

"Perhaps there's a better strategy for us to work together, on the same presidential ticket," Beckham said.

"Are you asking me to run with you?"

"I suppose now is as good as time as any," Beckham said.

"I'd be proud to be your vice president."

Beckham was slightly taken back. He figured Cornelius would want the top slot.

"Don't act surprised," he said. "I know it's what Jan

would have wanted."

Beckham reached out and Cornelius met his hand, sealing the deal with a shake.

"I look forward to working with you to restore our country," Cornelius said.

"We will bring it back from the brink, General," Beckham said.

"I look forward to where the country's headed with you two working together," Kate said.

"Fortunately, we have some of the greatest scientific minds in the world on our side, too," Beckham said. "That'll be equally important to our future."

"You can say that again," Cornelius said. "We wouldn't be here today without you, Doctor."

Kate smiled and then looked to Beckham. "You ready for this?"

"Yes." He gripped her hand and they started toward the crowd and the ship.

Beckham was relieved to have her blessing to run, and even more relieved to have Cornelius running with him. What they needed right now was to support one another and work together, despite any differences they might have.

As they approached the crowd, Beckham spotted his friends and family already here.

Horn was with Javier and the girls, Fitz, Rico, Dohi, Timothy, Ruckley, and all the others. A month ago, they had all gathered in mourning and remembrance as they buried loved ones, but today was a brief reprieve from their sorrow.

Perhaps one glimmer of light in a time marred by darkness.

Beckham walked up a few steps to the platform and

then took to the podium. Kate joined him, standing by his side.

He looked at the city in the distance, seeing the ongoing restoration efforts and thinking of all the lives lost there. Next, he surveyed the survivors who had gathered here.

"Today, I am honored to stand before you as a soldier for this great nation," he said, his voice echoing over the speakers set to either side of the crowd. "Many gave their lives so we could be free, and while we have a mountain of work ahead, we have something more important that President Jan Ringgold taught me about."

He paused, scanning the faces of his friends and family.

"We have hope. Even at the bleakest moments of her presidency, even when others cowered in fear, she carried the torch of hope for us, blazing a pathway for us to follow into a future filled with opportunity," he said. "To the very end of her life, she carried that hope. I am only here today because she took us this far. Now, it's up to each and every one of us to take our turn carrying that torch."

Kate picked up an old bottle of champagne that had previously been set beside the podium. She handed it to Beckham.

"That's why, on this day, I'm proud to christen the newest ship that we reintroduce back into the Allied States Navy, the USS *Jan Ringgold*." He moved from the podium and toward the ship, breaking the champagne battle against its hull.

Applause broke out over the crowd.

Beckham stepped back to admire the ship. It was a patchwork of repairs, and while it likely would never be restored to the same strength and functionality, it was a symbol of their country.

Damaged, but striving to recover, like all the survivors.

Beckham knew that with diligence, hard work, and with the people in this country who had gotten them this far, there was hope that he would never let die so long as he lived. And if they were lucky, they would pass that on for generations to come. Generations who would not only survive in this great country, but thrive.

A new society would be built from the ashes of the inferno that had enveloped the country.

From this Dark Age, the Allied States would emerge again, and Captain Reed Beckham was ready to lead the charge with his wife, family, and friends.

–End of Book 4–

I hope you enjoyed *Extinction Cycle Season 2: Dark Ages*! Writing the Extinction Cycle has been an honor and a highlight of my career. Sharing the adventures, trials, and tribulations of Team Ghost, Doctor Kate Lovato, and all of the heroes in these stories is something I will never forget. I want to thank each and every one of you loyal readers for following along over the course of this series. If you'd like to continue the story and see a sequel at some point, please leave a short and honest review letting me know. This is the best way for me to gauge whether readers want more books. Thank you so much for reading and thanks to Doctor Anthony J. Melchiorri for helping me bring this story to life!

Sincerely,
Nicholas Sansbury Smith
Greatwaveink@gmail.com

Want more Extinction Cycle now?

Visit Nicholassansburysmith.com and try one of the spin-off series by AJ Sikes, Adrian Smith, or Walt Browning.

About the Authors

Nicholas Sansbury Smith is the New York Times and USA Today bestselling author of the Hell Divers series. His other work includes the Extinction Cycle series, the Trackers series, and the Orbs series. He worked for Iowa Homeland Security and Emergency Management in disaster planning and mitigation before switching careers to focus on his one true passion—writing. When he isn't writing or daydreaming about the apocalypse, he enjoys running, biking, spending time with his family, and traveling the world. He is an Ironman triathlete and lives in Iowa with his wife, their dogs, and a house full of books.

Anthony J Melchiorri is a scientist with a PhD in bioengineering. Originally from the Midwest, he now lives in Texas. By day, he develops cellular therapies and 3D-printable artificial organs. By night, he writes apocalyptic, medical, and science-fiction thrillers that blend real-world research with other-worldly possibility, including works like *The Tide* and *Eternal Frontier*. When he isn't in the lab or at the keyboard, he spends his time running, reading, hiking, and traveling in search of new story ideas.

Printed in Great Britain
by Amazon